THIS BLEEDING CITY

Alex Preston

faber and faber

First published in 2010
by Faber and Faber Limited
Bloomsbury House
74–77 Great Russell Street
London WC1B 3DA
This paperback edition first published in 2011

Typeset by RefineCatch Ltd, Bungay, Suffolk
Printed in the UK by CPI Bookmarque, Croydon

A CIP record for this book
is available from the British Library

ISBN 978–0–571–25171–1

2 4 6 8 10 9 7 5 3 1

Alex Preston lives in London with his wife and two children. He was born in 1979. He studied English at Hertford College, Oxford as well as Birbeck College, University of London and is currently completing his Phd at UCL. He writes a fortnightly column on finance for the *New Statesman* magazine. He was previously a trader in the City of London. *This Bleeding City* is his first novel.

Praise for *This Bleeding City*:

'Preston has an undoubted storyteller's instinct; *This Bleeding City* is consistently engaging.' Patrick Neate, *Guardian*

'Written by a real insider . . . [this fact] gives it a rare golden ticket quality.' *Dazed and Confused*

'If one more person recommends Alex Preston's This Bleeding City to me I'll start to sniff a Senate-style conspiracy.' Mariella Frostrup, *Psychologies*

'Gripping.' *Literary Review*

'A moving and powerful debut - the best fictitional evocation of the despair of materialism so far.' Oliver James, author of *Affluenza*

'Fascinating . . . [Preston] should be applauded for bringing to life a world that is generally only written about in terms of catastrophic but dry figures in news stories.' *Spectator*

'Preston's evocation of the panic and false rationalizations that engulf those in the middle of a plummeting market is convincing.' *TLS*

'Preston writes beautifully . . . Compelling.' *Metro*

'A timely story about what happens to love in the morality-free zone of the Square Mile.' *Elle*

'Striking   rough his
pages . . .   *it*

'Preston makes the economics accessible, twinning material excess with extravagant prose.' *Daily Mail*

'The novel's love stories take several wrenching twists, drawling the reader into genuinely moving moments.' *Irish Examiner*

'Undeniably magnetic . . . Preston is a gifted writer . . . Intensely gripping.' *City AM*

'It is in the undoing of the City and the ravages of the first major crash in years that Preston shines.' *New Statesman*

'Stark, poetic debut novel . . . A timely book.' *Monocle*

I never properly understood how the financial system collapsed until I read this compelling work.' *GQ.com*

'One of the most moving books I have read . . . This Bleeding City stands out from other credit crunch books.' *Daily Gloss*

'10 Must-Reads This Summer: Gripping and moving from the very first page.' *Business Standard (India)*

'The book wipes clear a steamy window into a small, panicked investment bank as all the tickers in London City turn red.' *Sunday Business Post*

'Spot -on in his characterisation of a generation barred from self-fulfilment by its own materialism, as well as being an addictive read.' *Bookmunch*

'An excellent debut novel . . . goes far beyond the confines of the thriller genre, emerging as a work of complex, well-drawn characters and real emotional power.' *Waterstone's Books Quarterly*

'This is a debut novel of promise, edgy and tense, sealing up a specific moment in our capital's history up perfectly in a time capsule.' *Booktrust*

'Striking emotions and sharp observations about hopeless lives horribly skewed towards blatant materialism.' *Outlook India*

To Ary

PROLOGUE

At the End of the City

I remember shouts far off across the trading floor, the humming of computers and the ringing of telephones. I remember streamers of sunlight that blazed into the room. I remember all of this. I remember the photo of you and Luka that sat in its silver frame on my desk. Then, shuddering, I remember the moment when a beam of light shimmered at the edge of the photo frame and I realised I'd left him in the car, and fear raced up my arms and into my chest.

Scattering research papers behind me, I ran towards the door and out to the elevators, jamming the button thumb-white hard. One lift went up, then another. I made for the stairs, taking the steps down five, seven at a time, then through the doors and outside. Dazzled by the brilliant May sunshine, I looked up towards the church and, behind its ancient and clean-cut spire, the car park.

A crowd of bleary tourists sat outside Pâtisserie Valerie sipping their lattes, dissecting enormous croissants whose flakes were lifted by the breeze and flung skywards. It was the breeze that gave me hope. The cool breeze that blew low over the waters of the Thames, up Gracechurch Street, along Bishopsgate and then lifted the hairs on my arms and the awnings of the Brushfield Street shops. I ran in a frenzy straight down the road as a white Escort van backed into my path. I swerved, heard yelling behind me, slipped on leather soles, and then was across Commercial Street and into the shadow of the church.

The church rose out of the murk of the surrounding buildings like an arm from a lake. I used to gaze at it while I worked. Standing with phone clasped between shoulder and ear, I would lose track of my thoughts as I stared at the spire. It seemed to represent something pure and hopeful as it battled to break free from its earthly surroundings. I wrenched my mind back to the present. It was heating up. I pushed open the door of the car park and threw myself into its damp air.

Cold railings were slick beneath my palms. I lurched, drunk with speed, from side to side as I climbed. Each turn promised to be the last and wasn't, each door promised to give out onto the lofty and dangerous roof and didn't, every floor was full of dark shadowy cars. Cars that had parked before me that morning, cars that hadn't been held up by a statistically improbable combination of red lights and stalled buses and elderly road-crossers; cars that would have been, if not a safe place to leave a two-year-old boy, then not a fatal place, not out there on the wide roof. As I came out into the impossibly bright daylight, I saw the Polo parked on the other side of the grey tarmac roof. Saw the baby seat over the top of which I could make out his blond head.

He wasn't moving. The window I had left open a crack reflected the sky. No sound of crying. My fingers against the warm metal of the door handle, fumbling with keys, then the door opened and the smell hit me and I clutched at the safety belt, struggled with the buckle and pulled at the black straps to release him.

A torrent of useless images assaults me when I try to reconstruct things now. A thin memory of breath pushed from tiny lungs, small chest rising upwards and quivering for a second and then nothing. His face was set very calm, none of the red rage I had expected. Mouth pinched and disapproving, flecked with yellow-white spume. His pale skin was pulled tight around veined temples brushed with blond hair. I lifted him, his body limp and yielding. I pulled off his socks – I don't know why – and his feet were dark with burst blood vessels. His back was wet against his T-shirt and the sweat dripped circling downwards to the ground as I held him to my chest, poured a week-old bottle of Evian over him that I found scrabbling amongst torn maps on the floor of the car, kissed his hot face and fanned him and then into the car and down.

I cradled him as I drove blindly down the endless ramps and through red lights and up pavements towards Waterloo and when we arrived at the hospital I pressed his chest against my ear, allowing myself the luxury of a moment with him, and there – perhaps – the slow thump of a heartbeat. I ran into A & E shouting *Jesus help me Jesus my baby*. All was motion. Doctors took Luka from my arms, laid him carefully on a trolley, and set off down long corridors measured out by banks of strip lighting. I ran alongside stupidly gripping his little hand. The oxygen mask was too big for him and a male nurse with tattooed forearms held it to his tiny face. Finally a door I couldn't pass. I sat and dialled your number, my fingers fat and clumsy on the Blackberry keys.

You arrived in a storm of contained energy, your hands moving very quickly as you spoke to the doctor. You were seven months pregnant and bore your great belly before you like a weapon. You were not crying. You stood over me and looked down but I couldn't meet your eyes. Your eyes were so dry, so far from tears, so cold. I turned away from you. I leant against the white hospital wall, pressed my forehead against the clammy plaster and closed my eyes.

CHAPTER 1

Edinburgh and London

Throughout university I dreamed about moving to London. Forever looking ahead, rarely pausing to savour bright moments, I raced forward. We all did. When Edinburgh winds pulled the scarf tightly around my throat, sent Vero nestling to the warmth of my arms, bent Henry low, shielding his streaming eyes with bony fingers, we urged ourselves onward, against the wind, towards London. The only friends we encouraged were those with London flats and London lives; we lived for the Easyjet flight on Friday nights, fluttering southward in our evening dress, champagne spilling from plastic cups as we landed.

In the headlong rush towards experience we blasted ourselves away from our youth, towards a future of wrinkled disappointment. But no one stopped to tell us that we should be sucking it all in, searing the images onto our memories, baking the emotions into our hearts. Because soon it would be all that we had.

*

Vero was standing with her back to us, arms spread. Her black shawl shot out behind her in the wind, witchlike. It was early evening and the sun faced us, picking fingers of light through the towers and spires of the old city. Above a great cloud threatened rain. Darkness gathered. We began to run down the hill. Henry soon overtook us, his long legs bounding over tufts of heather, mounds of earth. Vero tripped and I stooped to help her, felt the heaviness of her shawl against my cold fingers, the heat of her body beneath. Looking back up the hill, I saw night assembling in the east, knitting itself in the shadows of the Calton Monument. We sped downwards as rain stung our skin. Down and across the road and laughing into the bar of the Balmoral where Henry was already perched breathless on a barstool with a bottle of wine and three glasses. Memory dyes these days golden.

We existed as glamorously as we could. Henry, whose father ran a fusty broadsheet with plummeting circulation figures, received an allowance that paid the rent of our New Town apartment, enabled him to pick up dinner bills and buy drinks unthinkingly. Vero always seemed to have enough to get by. She had a rich uncle, doting godparents; the thought of Vero poor was somehow distasteful. She gave the impression of great wealth even when I knew she was down to her last ten pounds: money always appeared from somewhere, and she'd leave a pile of notes on my desk when I became desperate, a message from her scrawled across the uppermost Queen's face in eyebrow pencil.

I met Henry in the Teviot Underground bar on my first night at university. I had spent the day wandering in and out of large rooms collecting and returning forms, signing up for societies, enrolling in the options for my English degree. And everywhere I went, striding ahead of me with a cluster of wide-eyed girls in his wake, was a tall, angular boy with a shriek of blond hair and flushed cheeks. That evening I threw myself down into the cramped subterranean bar and the tall boy was sitting at a table in the corner. Whilst all the other seats at the table were occupied, he seemed somehow alone, his head jutting above the others, his eyes moving in shy circles across the room. He lifted his pint to his lips and I saw the girls watching

2

him as he drank, saw their gaze rest upon his throat, the thrust of his Adam's apple. He set his pint down, raised his hand and beckoned me over, smiling.

'You're doing English, aren't you, yes? Would you like to sit down? You'll have to grab a chair. My name's Henry Grey.'

We became friends very swiftly, tripping over ourselves in our conversation that night as we moved from the bar to a club and back to his room, which was cluttered with trinkets and books, hung about with rich throws and bright cushions. Black-and-white photographs lined the walls. The early days of our friendship we hardly slept, talked late into the night, explored the dark city together. He was eccentric and shy and trusting, his quiet voice lisped slightly and his long bony fingers fished for words as he spoke. And still the girls followed him, watched him in clubs as he danced in great spasmodic leaps, lost in the music, freed for a moment from his self-consciousness.

Edinburgh surged past in a parade of black-tie dinner parties and reeling balls and trips to magnificent houses in the Highlands. With Henry's help I lied and sketched out stories that allowed me at least a weekend pass, a short-term ticket into the midst of this high-living crowd. Henry and I stumbled from lectures to the pub, from the pub to meet Vero at Montpellier's, then drunken to dinner and dancing.

When Vero came into my life it was still Freshers' Week, and Henry had gone for dinner with a friend of his father. There was a party for English students at the Voodoo Rooms. I was wearing a rented tuxedo with a clip-on tie; I felt awkward and out of place amongst the boys in their tailored dinner jackets and the girls in their silver gowns. The music was too loud, and I was bored of looking at the beautiful blonde girls stumbling gracefully across the dance floor to speak to boys they had known for simply years, the boys who had been at the local

3

public school, the boys whose fingers had been the first to slip scratching under the waistband of their sensible white panties.

I walked out into the late September night. I remember the crowds heaving around the Café Royal, the glow of Princes Street reaching out before me like an arm heavy with jewelled bracelets. I lit another cigarette, unclipped my tie and dropped it to the pavement. I heard a noise, perhaps a voice, and looked up. On the balcony of a room at the Balmoral a girl was standing, watching me. She upended her glass and sent it spinning down to crash on the stones below. She blew me a kiss and turned back inside. I walked across the road and through the heavy revolving doors into the hotel.

I sat and drank a beer in the low-lit bar, chatting idly to the barman. He was a graduate student and we were talking about his research and the cold of the city in winter when he suddenly fell silent. I turned around and it was the girl from the balcony. She was half-turned away from us, standing in the entrance hall of the hotel. She wore a backless black dress and high heels and stood beneath the great chandelier. Under the intensity of the light it seemed as if she were captured in a black-and-white photograph. The light bore down on her very pale skin, her black hair, her dark brow. But then our eyes were drawn down her face towards red lips moist with champagne. She threw her head back and laughed to herself, then stepped out into the darkness.

The barman looked dazed and then motioned as if to shoo me out.

'You have to go after her. Go! The beer's on me.'

I went out into the cool night. A red coal glowed on the edge of the terrace, over towards the corrugated roof of the railway station. I walked over and found her there, smoking. She smiled as I approached, took me in her arms and kissed me, smoke and booze and a mouth dry from champagne. When

4

she pulled away, I put my jacket around her shoulders, letting it fall gently down onto the bare, goose-bumped skin. With her cigarette gripped between her teeth she grinned at me and crossed her arms over her chest to turn the collar up.

'Hello, I'm Veronique. People call me Vero. What's your name? You're very handsome.'

We walked back into the hotel arm in arm. She scampered over to the front desk and picked up a chocolate wrapped in foil. She unwrapped it, letting the foil fall shimmering to the floor, and placed the dark chocolate in her mouth, chewing thoughtfully as she walked back towards me. She was wearing high heels that would have rendered any other girl of our age hookerish but on Vero they seemed to confirm her sophistication. In the lift she kissed me again and I could taste the bitterness of the chocolate, could feel how it clung to her tongue, left a film on her teeth. I ran my fingers down her back and felt the tautness of her shoulders, the soft cartilage ridges of her spine. She spoke in a voice that was rich and deep and wicked.

'I'm at a party some guy is throwing. He has rented the whole floor and a girl on my law course asked me to come with her. Boring people, but it's free champagne and it's more fun than the place I was at before. Shall we go in?'

The lift doors opened and music and cigarette smoke and laughter filled the air. Vero walked down the corridor first, trying the doors, looking for wine. A boy wearing tartan trousers and an untucked tuxedo shirt staggered towards us.

'Vero. Thank God. I thought you'd left. So good to have you here. Everyone is getting stuck in down the hall. Come and have a dance with me.' He tugged at her arm.

'No thanks.' I stepped forward, lifted the boy's hand from Vero.

'Who are you?' He looked very drunk, his face reddening as he brought me into focus.

5

'Charlie Wales. Friend of Vero's. She asked me along. Hope that's OK. Pleasure to meet you.'

Vero and I walked past him and into a room full of sweating bodies. We dodged through the crowd, picking up a bottle of champagne on our way, and out onto the balcony. We sat and talked and drank and discovered that we were living on the same staircase in halls, that she had been watching me for a few days, had seen me walking past earlier and recognised me more than she thought she should – like an old friend who hadn't happened yet was how she described it. We kissed gently, curled up in the corner with my jacket over our legs. Days dyed golden.

I remember a dawn. October in our final year. Vero and I had broken up, made up, broken up again, started seeing other people. But still she and Henry and I were inseparable. We had flown down to a house in the South of France, excitement fizzing off us as we slouched onto the plane to Nice, feigning ennui but secretly glorying in the glamour of the invitation. We stayed up all night at a club in Cannes and rode back on woozy mopeds through the thickening morning air, beeping horns and accelerating up hills scented with rosemary and lavender and wild fennel. We lay like discarded plimsolls around the pool. The dawn sky was a conch, pink fading out to white in the heavens. Swallows flung themselves down low over the pool to catch insects, the water dyeing their tawny breasts turquoise. Vero trailed her feet in the water and I saw the fingers of the pool's forgotten night-lights dance up her legs, becoming lost in the shadow where her thighs met under a denim mini-skirt.

One of the twins whose parents owned the house had rolled joints and we blew smoke skywards. Henry talked in a slow and lazy voice, describing cloud formations, the migratory patterns of birds. Vero laid her hand on my chest and I leant down and bit into the skin between her thumb and forefinger. She pushed the hand further into my mouth, wincing at the pain and then smiling at me. She rolled away into the pool and dived under the water, her black hair spread out like kelp behind her as she swam. Kicking off her skirt and turning a circle to remove her T-shirt, she lifted herself up on the other side of the pool wearing only her pants. The boys whistled and she turned and looked straight at me as the sun rose behind her.

I longed to live with the light touch that our friends at Edinburgh achieved, longed to move with the same soft padding foot through the world, unconscious and uncaring of the weight of a life lived pressed close against cold necessity. I wanted to offer Vero that existence, hold out to her the future of thoughtless spending and uncaring extravagance that I knew she coveted.

When she first left me, towards the end of our first term at Edinburgh, I burned with envy at the gifts that her flush-faced aristocratic new boyfriends heaped upon her. I liked to think that she was only playing with them until I was rich enough to keep up. I used to sit at the end of her bed as she told me about the break-up of another relationship; I would flick through the fashion magazines and interiors magazines on her desk as we talked, and I was certain that if I could buy her these glamorous dresses, take her to these sun-dappled hotels, furnish a home with these lavish objects, she'd be mine again. And when we moved down to London, I had but one desire – to become swiftly, splendidly rich.

Our entire social circle was going into the City. The stock markets had risen manically all the time we were studying, and the banks and brokers, insurance companies and law firms saw graduates as a source of cheap, hungry labour. The pact was clear – give us your twenties and we will make sure you don't have to work in your forties. There were stories of recent graduates receiving million-pound bonuses. They'd come back to do the Milk Round, shooting their cuffs and talking over-loud in the pub where they'd buy us all drinks. But my friends had an advantage over me. Their fathers all worked in the City, or had close relationships with the banks that supported their property empires, shipping lines and chemical plants. In order to continue to exist alongside them, I too sent off the job applications, turned up at the recruitment fairs, bought books on accountancy and corporate finance. I would earn more in a year than my father had earned in his life, secure Vero and a gilded existence, buy my future with my youth.

*

One Wednesday night in December I came back to the house in Fulham from another failed interview. I held the CEO's card in my hand until it was damp and Tube-grubby, letting it fall between the bars of a basement skylight as I walked up Parsons Green Lane. The card bore a leafless tree in raised silver. Silverbirch Capital was one of the aggressive credit hedge funds that had colonised the West End in recent years. They didn't tell me in so many words that I hadn't got the job, but the receptionist handed me my coat with a particular reserved sympathy that I had learnt to recognise and fear. We both knew that I carried the stink of failure about me. She held out my battered trenchcoat and gave me a gentle pat on the shoulder as I left. I placed a cigarette between chapped lips as I stepped out into the biting wind. Arabesques of unsettled snow blew up around me as I trudged along Berkeley Street and down into the Tube.

A grey-brown surgical glove lay in the road outside the

house in Fulham. I searched for keys in the lining of my jacket, trying not to tear my pockets any further. The gate to the house squeaked its familiar greeting and I opened the door and, for once, Henry and Vero were both there. Vero had cooked cassoulet and the house was warm and fragrant and full of light.

As I walked into the dining room Henry popped the cork on a bottle of champagne he'd stolen from his father's cellar and sipped off the foaming spume that tumbled down the green glass.

I threw my coat on a chair in the corner. 'I didn't get the job.'

'Did they tell you that, Charlie? Bet they didn't. Bet you got it.' Henry leapt up, came over and hugged me, put a glass in my hand and I saw Vero standing in the doorway of the kitchen watching us and smiling.

'Well, they didn't say so exactly, but I know the score by now . . . Although I think the CEO liked me. But I just understand so very little about their world.'

'You'll be fine, darling.' Vero's voice was a purr, soft as the shawl that sat around her shoulders. 'You're so down on your-self. Look at you, eh?' She took my chin in the fingers of her left hand and turned my face to the light. 'We need you to stay happy. It's such a shame to see you with your beautiful face all wrinkled up like that. I count on you, Charlie. Count on you to make things seem bearable. Remember that. Now we eat.'

Vero hummed to herself as she brought the steaming casse-role to the table and served us and we sat around and talked and reminisced self-consciously nostalgic, our voices delight-fully gnarled with cigarettes. It was a kind moment in a god-awful year. I leant over and planted a kiss into the pile of Vero's thick, smoke-sweet hair.

Snow fell and began to settle. Henry opened red wine and we watched the snow build up around the French doors leading to our tiny concrete garden. We remembered scenes from our childhoods. In her husky voice Vero described the Normandy of her youth and her crippled father – a brilliant surgeon who had contracted polio working at a hospital in Sierra Leone.

'. . . And we were so full, just staggering, walking along lanes after lunch. My brother and I would hang back, smoke cigarettes, my father surge ahead in his wheelchair. I remember the sun hitting the grass at such a low angle, just exploding off the dew . . . My papa would wake me sometimes, four in the morning, and drag me to his room to listen to a piece of Bach that had ripped him from his sleep, or to shout at news of American elections . . .'

Henry's world was altogether more difficult. His parents lived between Chelsea and Suffolk, desperately grasping onto an image of old England. His sister, Astrid, had tried to kill herself. His speech, like his eyes, seemed to approach things hesitantly, worried that things might move before he got there.

'. . . My father wrote a piece on, well I suppose it was on difficult teenagers, but it was really just about Astrid. For the weekend section. Astrid was poleaxed by the thing, poor girl. So ashamed to have it all out there, public. I think perhaps it was after that my mother decided to put her in the home. If you . . . Maybe you'd come and visit her some time. It would do her good. I noticed that my parents seemed to give up on each other once Astrid had gone. As if they had been trying for her sake . . .'

My own story was terribly mundane. A childhood of various shades of grey. Some name-lost girls and dabbling in drugs, but this only made it more depressingly similar to every other kid growing up in a seaside town listening to music that spoke of the glitter and thrill of the city. I longed for escape and Edinburgh had provided that – as far away from the dismal south-east as I could get. I had written plays for my tiny school theatre, dreamt of becoming a playwright or a theatre critic, and Edinburgh with its Festival and an English course centred on Shakespeare had seemed perfect for me. Of course when I got there the parties and the coke and the glamour took over and the theatre was something we attended only occasionally, always drunk, and left in the interval.

We were silent for a time as the snow continued to fall and the air above us grew blue with cigarette smoke. I watched Vero fiddling with a strand of hair, wrapping it around a finger. It almost caught in the end of her cigarette and she moved backwards, surprised, saw I was watching her and cast me a swift, shy smile. I cleared the plates as Henry put his feet up on the windowsill and sang softly to himself, his voice coming through the smoke-filled air in whispered bursts. Vero joined him when she knew the words. They both laughed when she got them wrong. They were singing nursery rhymes and Christmas carols and I felt breathless and tired and happy.

Then Vero went off to bed, and Henry and I opened another bottle of wine and he spoke in his gentle voice, all angles as he sprawled in his chair trying to get comfortable. He leant backwards and stretched out his fingers, plucking words from the air as he spoke. His lips were purple from the wine and his cheeks had a high colour, but his eyes were always cool and distant.

Henry was taking photographs for a book about London's homeless for a publishing friend of his father. He took pictures of grey-eyed tramps under grey bridges above the grey-watered Thames. He spread out some of these pictures on the table. I saw a man holding his child up to the camera as if trying to ward off some evil, an old woman wringing her hands above a fire in an oil drum. I felt that Henry somehow felt himself to be safer behind the lens of a camera. It was his way of approaching the world head-on. Henry continued to look down at the pictures as he swirled wine in his glass. His voice came quickly.

'Do you . . . do you still love her, Charlie?'

I looked across at him, sighed out a stream of smoke.

'Of course I do. I think I might always love her.'

Henry put his fingers down on the table so that their tips turned white. His eyes filmed over for a moment, then rose towards me out of the dim light.

'I remember seeing the two of you when we were first at Edinburgh, looking to the two of you as, as I suppose some sort of representation of how things could go right. How things might work out for the people who deserved it.'

I laughed hollowly.

'Christ, Henry, I don't call this worked out. I'm a member of the long-term unemployed, she's doing a job she hates, and all I can think about is how to earn enough money to get back with her. That if I was able to whisk her away to the sun, away from London, it might reignite something. Tragic, isn't it?'

'No. No, I really don't think it is tragic. It's a bit sad for the moment. But things will work out for you two. And at least you have each other.' He lifted his hands from the table and held them out in front of his face, examining his fingernails and the skin of his knuckles in the flickering light. I took a sip of wine.

'I did something very strange last Thursday, Henry. I had been to an interview at an insurance company on the Strand, a middle office job. Not amazing pay, but I'm slowly losing my previously exacting requirements. I just want any job now. Anything that wouldn't be a complete humiliation. I only had £20 to last me the week, and so I decided to walk home. It was five in the evening and I figured it would take me an hour.

'It was raining very gently but insistently – you know the

12

sort – and soon my shoes were slopping and my trouser-legs soaking up the puddles. I was standing outside the Ritz and a cab passed and sent up this great wall of water that drenched me, and I knew I'd have to dry-clean my suit again. At first I was furious and then just crestfallen. I decided – fuck the money – I'd go into the Ritz for a drink. I walked in and it's all so gold, and I stood there dripping, steaming, as fur-lined women waddled past me towing their fat husbands. I must have looked lost because three porters came scurrying over to ask how they could help.'

I leant over and filled Henry's glass, then refilled my own. I moved to sit alongside him. We both faced out of the window into the dark where the occasional flurry of snow was caught by candlelight.

'I was shown through to the bar and, of course, the cheapest beer was seven pounds, and I had been hoping that it would be glamorous and thrilling. I think I went in there to remind myself why I was after these City jobs in the first place. But it wasn't thrilling at all. There was a table of middle-aged women who had been up to London shopping and were drinking ridiculous cocktails with umbrellas and glacé cherries. But otherwise the bar was empty.

'I sat for a long time over my beer, listening to the terrible jazz and the sound of cars tearing through puddles outside. Then a girl I recognised came in. Suzie Applegarth – do you remember her? She was in the year above us.'

'Yes, of course. I think our parents are friends. She's . . . she's very pretty. Rather thick, but lovely to look at.'

'Well, she sat at the bar and ordered herself a drink; she didn't notice me sitting there with a thimbleful of beer left in my bottle. She ordered a glass of champagne and perched there at the bar, very still, and she looked terribly happy. After a while Toby Poole came in, looking slightly older than he did at Edinburgh. He swept Suzie up off the stool, and they hugged for what seemed like ages before he ordered himself a beer and they sat very close together, touching each other as they spoke. I caught some of what he was saying. All about his job, and a fund he had been asked to manage. He loosened his tie, and she insisted that they have another glass of champagne to celebrate.

'When they left, I waited a moment, paid my bill and followed them. I scooted across the road and stood in the shadows. But they weren't going far. Only down to Le Caprice, where they sat at a table in the window, and ordered more champagne. I stood in the rain, watching them from the shadows across the road, envying both of them so much. Wondering why that kind of easy success didn't come my way. I left after an hour or so and walked home feeling terrible.'

Henry was still staring out into the darkness. I could see his ghostly reflection in the dim light. Then he turned towards me and clutched at my hand, his eyes suddenly bright, his voice jagged.

'You shouldn't feel jealous of people like that. They . . . they haven't got a patch on you. Bloody Toby only got his job in the first place because his father is a non-executive director of the bank. As soon as you get a job, I know you'll do better than these oafs. Charlie, you . . . you shouldn't be hiding in the shadows. You weren't made for that. What about giving up on the City? I know the money is crazy, but you won't enjoy it. That work does nothing for the soul. Look at poor Vero. She hates her job, completely miserable. Why do you want to be like that?'

I lit a cigarette and thought for a moment. Henry swirled his wine in his glass.

'It's hard for you to understand, Henry. You've always had money. You've always moved in that world, the world of our friends at Edinburgh. For me, it was something very new, painfully different from what I had known before. I spent my childhood watching my parents worry about money. It wasn't that they were very poor. They were just middle-class, I suppose. But they never had enough cash, and it just ate away at them. They used to tell me how everything they spent on me was such a great sacrifice for them. For me to have piano lessons, a new football kit, whatever toy was a playground necessity. And going shopping with my mother, I'd watch her agonise over every purchase, wringing her hands in the middle of Safeway. So even as a very little child I had this sense of money as something vastly important, crucial to a happy life.'

I felt myself growing angry, stood up and began pacing, conducting my words with my empty wine glass like a baton.

'Then I came to Edinburgh, and suddenly there were all these people who had never worried about money. And they lived these glamorous, spectacular lives. You and Vero both seemed so extraordinary when I first met you. Like something out of a novel. I had always done well – admittedly in the very small pond that was Worthing High School – but I was a success at everything I tried. Schoolwork, the plays I wrote, cross-country . . . So I just presumed that if I tried hard, I could make sure that I never had to worry like my parents did. And as I saw more of the lives that you people lived, I wanted to be one of you.'

I sat down again, lit another cigarette. Henry took one from the packet and held it unlit in his mouth for a moment, then turned towards the black window and I saw the flare of the match die down to flicker against his face.

'You're a strange chap, Charlie, so worried about the future. I try not to think about the future at all. I'm . . . to be honest, Charlie, I'm absolutely terrified of growing old. There's the problem with having a gilded childhood. You never want to leave it. I think it's maybe why I take photographs. They give me the sense that I can pause time. Slow things down and not have to face the ghastly idea of responsibility and getting old and ill. I'm only twenty-three and already so much seems to have passed ...'

I fell asleep with him still talking, my face pressed into the table; I was vaguely aware of him ruffling my hair and then I was alone.

I sat up suddenly and picked crumbs from my cheeks. It was still very dark outside. I heard Vero's alarm going off. It was this that had woken me. Her hand fell down upon the clock heavily. She sighed, padded down the corridor to the bathroom coughing. She was at one of the big law firms, was specialising in corporate debt restructuring. She had wanted to work pro bono at Amnesty or Liberty but got sucked in by the slick machine of the Milk Round, snared by the salary.

So many of our friends had fallen into the same trap. Laura and Mehdi were two of our closest friends from university, a couple who had stuck with us when we stopped calling anyone who didn't have a title and a trust fund, a couple whose solid and unspectacular love had encompassed us even in the foolishness of those starstruck days. Now they lived down the road in Fulham.

They had been persuaded that an accountancy qualification was just what two idealistic anthropologists needed to get under their belts before they went off and explored the world. And they bought into it – the idea that they could work hard for a few years and then leave to research tribes in the Kalahari, early civilisations in Java, fossilised femurs in the foothills of the Andes. But the exams and the drudgery and the grey misery of figures and spreadsheets and inventory levels and accounts receivable were taking their toll. They knew they were eating into their future with every day that they didn't dare to set off into the great uncertainty of the world; they were paid just enough to live in London but not enough to save, and already they looked defeated, already Mehdi had the air of a man at forty-five, hair thinning, friends gone, wondering where the fuck it all went. All of that hope.

That December morning I ran to the window in the front room at six and watched them pass by as they did each morning, walking down the dark street together, hand in hand. I could see that they walked in silence, heads down against the cold, Laura's scarf streaming out behind her like smoke from a chimney. I made my way upstairs. We were all stranded, all of us trapped by London and money. All of us waiting for life to begin. I flung myself through the door of my room and into a grumpy sleep.

The clock read ten minutes to eleven when I crawled out of my duvet. My room was the smallest and sat next to the bathroom at the back of the house, perched above the kitchen like an afterthought. It had been tacitly agreed that I wouldn't pay rent until I found a job. I felt bad about this, but my friends were generous in all things, and I loved them for it. My phone was ringing somewhere in a pocket.

'Hello? Yes? What!'

I had got the job. It was the CEO of Silverbirch, an institution I had heard about even at Edinburgh. Sharp and violent moneymakers who were paid bonuses that read like telephone numbers. The CEO said that he had liked my anarchic approach to the markets. Thought I would be a useful contrary voice on the team of analysts. My maths and accountancy would need some work, but they'd train me up. I would start on £22,000 a year plus benefits. Could I be there on Monday at eight? Yes, yes, of course I could. Of course. I hung up and drew back the curtains to reveal a world new-made by snowfall. The brightness stung my eyes and my tears carried on flowing as I shouted, jumped onto my bed and bounced up and down and laughed. Henry came in, his hair pointing straight upwards, a kimono worn over a pair of striped boxers.

'You got the job? I always knew you would. Let's celebrate.'

He threw his arms around me and wouldn't let go even to descend the narrow staircase. We flopped onto the sofa and Henry opened a bottle of Scotch and poured it in a golden stream into my mouth. It spilled down from my lips onto my chest and Henry took a long swig and passed the bottle back to me. The sharp liquid stung my chapped lips as I felt the warmth hit my belly. We spent the day drunk watching television and it slowly settled in that I had a job. That I would be able to afford the rent. Start paying off my student loans. Answer the phone to anonymous numbers without the worry that they'd be heavies hired by American Express. I called Vero first. Before my parents, before anyone. Her happiness confirmed my own. Her voice was hushed at first – she was in the law library revising. Then I told her and she shrieked and I could feel the stares of her colleagues down the line and pictured her jumping up in delight.

'Oh Charlie . . . That's so wonderful. I'm so proud. God, everyone wants to work at Silverbirch. Trust you to get a job there of all places. I knew we had something to celebrate last night. I love you.'

She told me she loved me a lot. I didn't like it because she had never said it whilst we were a couple. Only when our relationship had become broadly platonic did she start using the words of love. I heard her come tiptoeing, very late, into my room that night. She muttered something under her breath, laid a soft kiss on my forehead, and edged the door quietly closed as she left.

Chapter 2

Silverbirch

I was late for my first day of work. Yellow tie on blue shirt or red tie on white took up more time than I had expected. An old man slipped at the top of the escalator at Earl's Court and I helped him up; his shaky hands pushed down hard on my shoulders as he leant against me to regain his breath. It was twenty past eight when I walked into the grand office on Berkeley Square. The receptionist recognised me and smiled, took my careworn coat and pointed me towards a corridor that opened out into a large room. It was a long open-plan office with desks sat in groups of four separated by filing cabinets. The walls were hung with antique maps showing the evolution of geography. From a flat world defined by the steps of Alexander, Marco Polo and Magellan to the age of empires to the great red mass of the USSR. I walked past these faded attempts to pin down the shape of things and knocked on the CEO's door.

He was a tall, white-haired man with a tan that matched his leather desktop. His name – Aldous Stringer – was engraved upon a single gold bar that sat on the desktop. His eyes were bright and penetrative; there was something of the wolf about him. He lacked sincerity, but wore this lack as a badge. He looked like a successful Midwestern businessman-turned-politician. Or like a bad actor playing that politician in a TV soap. He drank fine wines and kept a mistress and lived exactly as I imagined a high-powered banker would. He always blazed one lap of Berkeley Square in his Porsche before plunging into the underground car park in the mornings. He wore red braces in some double-bluff ironic reference to the eighties; nothing about him was wholly serious, nothing sat on solid ground. Books lined the walls of his office. And not just works on finance. I saw a red leather set of Shakespeare, some Defoe and Swift, some serious philosophy. Khalil Gibran lay face down on his desk, but I didn't hold that against him. Better than the Bible or *The Art of War*.

He smiled at me, nodding to some internal music, and pointed to a chair. A green-shaded lamp sat on his desk and more maps on the walls. A certificate from Harvard hung above his huge chair. Screens jostled for position on a side table – Bloomberg and Reuters – and on every surface photographs of a blonde woman and beautiful blond children and the CEO holding a fish the size of a Shetland pony. His speech had the depth and poise of an acquired accent, clipped and slightly austere. I imagined him as a child, his voice breaking late, trying desperately to thrust aside any traces of his Estuary roots in some second-rate public school.

'Welcome to Silverbirch. That's not a phrase we use with great regularity. A lot of people want to work here. You're an English graduate. You know nothing about finance. We're taking a risk on you. But I like taking risks. It's how I got all of this.'

His gesture encompassed not only the office and the company and the Mayfair address, but also holidays on palm-fringed beaches and shooting parties with titled playboys and beautiful women.

'You will make a fortune here. Let me make that clear. It's not a question of which Porsche but how many, got it? We work hard, we play in moderation, we dress sharp – I see you've made an effort, but please get down to Jermyn Street and buy yourself a proper suit because we bloody impress everyone that works with us and you look like a professor in a provincial polytechnic. Now get settled in, introduce yourself to the team, and make a success of yourself. I like you, Charles. You'll do well here.'

He turned back to the wall of screens and, with a few clicks, graphs started to appear and I backed out of the room into the main office. My desk faced down Curzon Street and I could see policemen outside the Saudi Embassy and Hyde Park at the end; the snow had begun to melt, leaving grey gravy sloshing at the feet of the businessmen who strode purposefully to meetings and dazzling ladies setting out with the nimble, nervous steps of sandpipers for their shampoo and pedicures.

Silverbirch invested in bonds and loans issued by corporations and banks, and also complex financial structures that were somehow quite beautiful on the page. I marvelled at the charts showing a multitude of dancing bright arrows describing the flow of cash from a group of mortgages into a special-purpose vehicle and then into a further structure combining these asset-backed securities, then back to the investor via a series of Caribbean tax havens. My eyes swam at the complexity and exoticism of it.

I was to be an analyst. The analysts dealt in figures, scanned weighty reports and legal documents and sifted through the rumours that flowed onto our Bloomberg screens and then, when we had distilled this down to one of three simple words – buy, sell or hold – we made our recommendations to the portfolio managers.

The PMs sat at the opposite end of the room, the partitions surrounding their desks higher, their chairs of real leather, the silver-framed photographs on their desk a representation of their aspiration – to be like the CEO, to live his life, to earn his money. They were all in their mid-to-late thirties, all violently demonstrative of their superior knowledge, wealth and status, scornful of the miserable analysts whose reports lay unread on their desks for weeks as they practised their golf swings and spoke in loud, knowing voices about their holidays in New Zealand and their racehorses and bonuses. The tone was identical to that of the loudest, most cocksure of our group at Edinburgh, and I looked upon the portfolio managers with the same muddle of envy and admiration. Just as at Edinburgh, I longed to sit alongside these people, ached to count myself one of them, watched and mirrored their gestures, their clothes, the cruel sneer of their lips as they barked into their BlackBerries. They carried about them the inviolability of wealth. They were led by David Webb and Bhavin Sharma – two former government bond traders who were violently competitive and sought at all times to outshine each other in the eyes of the CEO and the market.

My desk was next to the head of the research team, a man with the colossal beard of some ancient Russian sea captain. He coughed into a handkerchief that was spotted with blood. He spoke rarely, occasionally choking whispers down the telephone to his wife and his doctor. His name was Colin but he was called Beardy. In our team of analysts there was a Greek boy, Yannis, who had no volume control and carried out every conversation as if he was on the deck of a busy aircraft carrier. He waved his arms as he spoke; even if one hand held a telephone, it moved in frantic tiny circles, spinning away from his mouth and then back towards it, bestowing a strange Doppler effect on his listener.

Also in the team was a portly older man who played the euphonium. He had to leave early on Wednesdays for band practice. He had a florid face with the burst nose of a winter-drunk tramp. His grey hair was feathery and he smelt of old books and root vegetables. Finally, an American girl with big brown eyes and nasty brown suits called Madison. She drank a lot of coffee and over the day her large teeth would stain to match her suit and eyes. She was bright and thoughtful and reserved. She pulled her hair back tightly with a black Alice band, save a few strands that escaped and danced over her face and in her eyes. The severity of the hairband stretched the skin upwards on her face, giving her the look of a startled lemur peering out through foliage.

Beardy gave me Daniel Yergin's *The Prize* to read on my first day and I learnt about the oil business, began analysing pipeline companies in the Caspian Sea, daydreamed about night flares seen from a hotel window in Baku. The analysis itself was stultifying, poring over financial documents and cashflow statements deep into the night. Looking back over five years of annual reports, I'd run my hands through my hair, unable to make out the meaning of the relentlessly upbeat doublespeak of the Chairman's Message that always opened the publication. How the business was going from strength to strength one year and then, the next, everything had fallen into shit, but the brave and noble oligarch was remaining at the helm to steer the company through the time of turmoil. The operational updates from projects in the Congo and Surinam and Indonesia spoke of unfortunate explosions and collapsed pipelines in terms of their economic impact, didn't consider the hollow-stomached wives waiting, choking back tears, at the gates of the refinery, beaten back by guards as they sought out news of their husbands.

Silverbirch believed very firmly in face time. As evening approached on my first day at the office, I had begun to collect together the papers on my desk, turned off my computer as the clock in the bottom right-hand corner crept towards seven o'clock. Beardy looked over his half-moon glasses at me. He spoke in a quiet voice, wheezing his words towards me.

'Something on tonight, Charles? Do you want some more

reading? We tend to stay at least until the CEO pushes off. If you want to look at Shell's accounts for me, I'd appreciate a note on the latest figures. Seemed that last I looked they were missing out on a substantial amount of growth in the Gulf. Go and grab a coffee if you're flagging.'

I sat at my desk until ten, when Beardy left. I gave him a five-minute head-start and then made my way bleary-eyed to the Tube.

During lunch-breaks and throughout those long evenings when I sat at my desk, enough work done for the day to justify my employment, but too tired to start something new, I'd plan how to spend my bonuses. In those early days my lust for money was limitless, for the trappings of wealth, for the cars and the houses that would show people that I had really made it. I would spend hours logging onto property websites – Knight Frank and Harrods Estates and Hamptons International. I'd set the minimum at a million with no maximum and prowl around the country houses with their squash courts and polo paddocks and follies and walled gardens. Then I'd stroll around Berkeley Square smoking cold-fingered cigarettes and stare into the window of Jack Barclay and picture myself pulling up at parties in my black Bentley Continental, with Vero on my arm, and our friends from Edinburgh forming a tunnel of applause for us as word got around of my latest financial success. Those dreams of material gain were so sweetly addictive, the picture of myself as the lord of those honey-bricked manors so seductive, that it began to seem only right that I should stay at my desk well into the night.

I watched David Webb as he worked, hung around the printer that sat behind his desk and listened to him striking deals and closing out trades, heard the acid in his voice. I wanted to be able to speak like him, command traders with ruthless precision, send investment bank salespeople scuttling with the threat of my wrath. I stood at the printer as he executed a trade that would make the company ten million pounds.

'What? Don't go back on me now. This is a fucking good trade for you. I don't need to remind you about the amount of business we've done this year. The importance of this relation-ship to your fucking career. Now step up to the price you quoted last night, do the trade and we'll celebrate over dinner tonight. My treat and you can bring the wife. We're done. Great. That's fucking great. I was getting embarrassed for you there, Danny, but you've got balls. I always knew you had balls.'

The dream of becoming a portfolio manager, of living like them, building possessions like a carapace around me, drove me on to finish one more write-up, to put together one more spreadsheet, analyse one more deal before going home.

We were all working hard. Even Henry, who seemed to be out every night taking pictures. His eyes had taken on a hollow stare and his cheeks seemed to be emptying of flesh in sym-pathy. Vero was never back before midnight; she always stuck her head in the door of my room when she came in, always smiled with weary eyes and a tiny lip-quiver that betrayed how much she was hating it. She would sit on my bed sometimes, lean back against my raised knees and choke back tears of tiredness and defeat. I'd reach over and hold her, pressing her head against my chest, massaging thin shoulders through her blouse and she'd speak in a tiny voice, a heartbroken voice, the voice of one who can no longer bear to look in the mirror.

'I'm so tired, Charlie. So bored. I just . . . I just bloody hate them. The partners who wait around all day doing fuck-all and then dump a pile of documents on my desk at seven-fifteen just as I'm thinking of sneaking out. And then I have to eat pizza or Chinese – which I hate, it makes my heart race, I can feel it in my veins all fatty – and work until the lights begin to flicker, and I'm so tired and I start crying and the other trainees look at me like I'm crazy, but I just don't care.

'I was working with one of the older associates today. She's a really sweet woman, big eighties hair and everything. Has helped me with the stuff I don't understand. She has two little boys – her desk is covered in photos of them and the wall of her office has their paintings stuck all over it. It's the only bloody office that has any colour in it. I was sitting with her working on this bond deal when her email pings and it's a brief of what we have to deliver for Monday. I read it over her shoulder and it was so much work. We had to prepare a whole offering circular over the weekend and I looked down and suddenly I could see she was crying. She hadn't seen her boys the weekend before and now she was going to miss them again. She told me to leave the office and just sat there with her head in her hands for an hour.'

I opened my window a crack and we smoked out into the dim glow of the night. Vero finished before me and I watched her cigarette butt dance downwards into the darkened garden.

'I'm so lonely, Charlie. Sometimes I wish that we were back together. Just so I had someone to be with. Look at your eyes tonight. They are so beautiful. So shy and beautiful. No wonder so many girls loved you at university. No wonder I did.'

There was a pause; I reached out for her, slid my hand along the fragile curve of her stomach, brushed hair from her face and kissed her, felt the pulse of her lips beneath mine hot and desperate. She laid her head on my shoulder and hugged me tightly. I tried to slip my erection up into the waistband of my boxer shorts so she wouldn't feel it. I held her and poured all of my love into the embrace. Then she pulled away.

'I love you, Charlie. We'll be together one day. I'm sure of it. Sleep tight, darling boy.'

And I drifted off to sleep with her words folded like a note

26

in my mind, at the top of a special drawer where I put those things that I wanted a little too much, things that burnt me if I looked at them directly.

Vero had to go away for a while just before Christmas to work on a deal for a chemical company in the Midlands that wanted to issue a bond in the New Year. She had to cancel her Eurostar ticket home. She'd be spending every day until Christmas Eve working on the deal. She called from a Travelodge in Derby and we laughed together at the ridiculousness of it all, our laughs rising into that realm where tears and screams threaten and the laughs have to be clamped down before they spill into other, darker emotions. She told me that she was pretending that she was in prison, she had to do her time but then she'd be out. She started crying and the phone was dropped against a wall and I called out her name but heard nothing.

In retrospect, it didn't seem like a terrible time. It felt at least that we were working towards something tangible. That in a few years we would be settled and qualified and wouldn't have to work so hard and would maybe have time to have dinner together and laugh and go partying and not worry about money or whether Vero was eating enough or where Henry was at five a.m. on a Tuesday night. Things were about to get so much worse, that looking back on that period of apprenticeship I can get bleary-eyed. At least there was hope back then. At least we had each other.

CHAPTER 3

Friends Fall Apart

Henry had been spending time away from the house. Every two or three nights his door would stay open and the darkness of the interior was like a shadow on my conscience as I walked up the stairs to bed. It was the worst time of the year. Late January and the world felt leaden. Vero was painfully thin and I had to stand over her to make sure she ate. But I couldn't watch her at work, or in the bathroom after meals, and she got increasingly emaciated until she bore her breasts before her like a burden on her chest. Her clothes were still immaculate, her make-up perfectly applied, but she had begun to cough late at night, she smiled rarely, stared off into nothingness over dinner.

Henry walked into my room one night as I sat, knees pulled to my chest, trying to make sense of a series of documents explaining the functioning of the credit derivatives market. Hedge funds were being set up to speculate in these instruments. The PMs discussed the complex structures one could forge from derivative contracts in eager voices, spoke of the revolution in risk-taking that would follow. I had asked Bhavin Sharma for some background reading on this new market and he emailed me the documents that I now sat staring at through tired eyes. I was surprised to see Henry in the house. My bedside light flashed along his cheekbones as he stood over me.

'I was thinking . . . maybe we should have an evening out. The three of us. Spend some time together. I haven't danced for a while, haven't watched you and Vero dance together. I thought it might be fun, might help us all. Christ, I hate January.'

'Sure. I'd love that. What about tomorrow? Shall we go to Boujis? Pretend we're still young and have money? All the Edinburgh crowd will be there.'

'Yes. Let's do that. I'll speak to Vero.'

He stumbled from the room and I turned back to the documents, rubbing my eyes until they stung to keep myself awake.

I was in a good mood as I strolled into the office the next morning, hung my jacket on the back of my chair and wandered to the kitchen to make breakfast. Beardy was taking more sick days. People were worried about him. I was working with Coffee Teeth and Yannis on a trade receivables securitisation; it was complicated and the documents were constantly referencing other documents that we didn't have, or that were only available in Portuguese, which none of us spoke. But my good humour endured. And Coffee Teeth's breath didn't bother me, and Yannis's voice seemed positively melodious as he commented on the rising price of oil and the leaping stock markets and the vast inflation in property prices.

'Oil's getting crazy, baby. Oil's going rocket high. Fuckin' oil, man. Fuckin' OPEC. You're long you're strong, you're short you get caught. Greed is good, baby. Greed is good.'

I walked out under grey skies at lunch to buy a soggy sandwich from Pret A Manger. A Lamborghini was parked outside the office and I could see David Webb gently running his fingers over the steering wheel, caressing the leather and then moving his hands downwards to the gearstick. I stopped at the cashpoint to withdraw money for the evening ahead. My card was returned at the first attempt. I checked my balance and felt sick, leaned forward against the cold metal of the cash machine. My rent, student loan repayments, the travelcard. I had just been paid and already I was deep into my overdraft. I stamped back past the Lamborghini which Webb was now revving loudly, sending pigeons up in a spiral above him as he pulled away with screeching tyres.

In the office I searched through drawers and pockets and gently edged a pound coin from Beardy's otherwise bare desk and I found that I had £12.50 to last thirty days. Poverty made me feel dirty and shameful. I nervously picked at the raised silver numbers on my cash card with a thumbnail, scratching off the paint to reveal blackness beneath. I waited until Coffee Teeth had gone down to Starbucks and Euphonium was lost in a research paper and Yannis was in a particularly intense bout of self-interrogation, then picked up the phone.

'Mum. It's Charles. How are you? How's Dad?' I spoke to my parents so rarely I found her voice surprising, soft and somehow more loving than I remembered it.

'Charles, darling. How's my little banker? How's the job? Oh I wish Dad was here. He'll be sad to miss you.'

'The job's fine, Mum. It's all going really well. It's just . . . I've got a temporary cashflow problem. I know what we agreed, but could I – just this once – borrow a few quid? Just until my next pay? I'm so sorry, Mum. Please don't tell Dad.'

The pause was awful. I could hear her sucking her teeth and pictured her rolling her shoulders back the way she did when anything caught her off guard. Then she spoke.

'Charles, darling. I've . . . I've got about a hundred pounds I can send you. I just haven't got any more at the moment. You do need to be more careful, darling.'

'I know, Mum. I promise I'll try. Can you send it now? Before the post office shuts? I've got to go. Bye, Mum. Thanks.'

At nine-thirty I stood in the rain outside Boujis. I was still in my suit and felt awkward and shop-soiled and old. There was a long snaking line of young people with their collars turned against the wind. Vero and Henry were yet to arrive and I stood

30

self-conscious, half-recognised by the girls who strode from taxis and up to the doorman and were ushered through the crowd in a haze of perfume. Their scent hung in the air long after they had passed. I was soaked through when Henry and Vero appeared from the Tube station and threw their arms around me. Vero was wearing a black dress of tiny sequins that was cut very low in the front and clung to her body. A silver necklace glittered in her cleavage. Henry negotiated with the doorman who finally allowed us down the stairs and into the club.

We sat at a table at the back of the room and Henry ordered a bottle of vodka. I had loosened my tie and removed my jacket and caught the scent of my own hot body every so often. We downed shots, refilled and downed more. We were all very quiet even though the music was, this early in the evening, not much more than a background thump of bass. Vero was wearing very dark nail varnish. In the dim light of the club her fingernails looked black. I watch her tear a credit-card receipt into tiny pieces, and the scuttling black nails looked like beetles on the table. She collected the squares of paper into a small mound and laid her hands down flat. Then she leant forward, her voice tired and harsh from the alcohol.

'Why are we here? I mean look around us. Look at these people, these people who resolutely live their life in the key of C – no invention, no subtlety. Why are we constantly hanging on the coat-tails of these stupid millionaires? Is it your fault, Henry? Because you have money. You move so easily amongst them.

'Or is it you, Charlie? You were so bright and cynical about all of them; I never felt that it was anything more than a joke for you. That it was some kind of cultural tourism trip for you. Not something you'd spend your life chasing after. Because none of them are happy. And none of them love us. And I've lost respect for both of you because of it. I feel so empty.' She turned away, and then she took a deep breath and gathered herself up. She leaned over to me and I felt her hot moist breath on my neck.

'I'm sorry, Charlie. I just started thinking today about how I should be studying for a doctorate or working in Africa for some charity. That I should be anywhere but here. I think of my papa. What he did with his life and how ashamed he'd be of what I am now. I'm trying to blame both of you. But it's my own fault. It's my own bloody fault. I want the Marc Jacobs coat and the Balenciaga bag and the wallet from Mulberry. I want that more than I want to help people, more than I want to stay up all night trying to catch out Nestlé in a complicated legal battle. My papa would be mortified.'

I poured us another drink and put my arms around Vero. I spoke quietly, so that Henry had to move forward to hear.

'I don't know how to answer you, Vero. Because I'm as confused about it as you are. I don't know how we fell in with that bunch. I was thinking about the wonderful people in halls – Laura and Mehdi and all the others. And how we'd left them to spend time with people who were less intelligent, less human.

'I'm sorry if you aren't where you want to be; that it's all so shit and cheerless here. And I'm sorry that I'm not planning a play for the Festival or writing reviews for a highbrow theatrical website, but we all made those choices, and it's trite but true that it was a long chain of little decisions, a series of mistakes and ill-chosen priorities and . . . and we ended up here. We had so many ideals, so many dreams, and we ended up settling for money.'

I still had my arms around Vero, stroked her hair, ran my fingers over the sequins of her dress, watched her necklace move within her cleavage as she breathed. She shuddered and spoke.

'We're twenty-three. We're so young. But time is passing. I want to be having fun. I want to make the most of my youth. Ah, fuck you all.' She smiled. 'I'm sorry for bringing it up. I've been feeling so emotional recently. Missing my parents' house in Normandy, missing the sight of my mother feeding the geese in the garden, my papa wheeling through the gate in the evening with his cigarette and his briefcase. I miss bloody pastis and good croissants. I'm like some parody of a Frenchwoman, eh? *Santé, mes amis*. Bottoms up, eh?' She drained her glass in one gulp, smiling, something mad in her eyes. Arms in the air, she strode onto the dancefloor, shouting along with the music.

I danced with a girl with an expensive-looking smile called something Victorian like Elspeth and we grew increasingly drunk; Henry had a wrap of coke, and we took turns to go into the loos and came out with everything burning brightly around us and the music quickening in our blood.

Vero was kissing a blond boy on the dancefloor and I sat on the sofa and watched her with a knot in my stomach. Elspeth came and sat in my lap and we began to kiss and then it was three a.m. and I couldn't find Vero. Henry had seen her leave with the same boy. He was sweating as we made our way out into the night where drunken young and beautiful people stumbled slowly, like insects on their long legs, through the downpour.

'I want to show you somewhere, Charlie. A place I've been going to. It's . . . it's kind of amazing. I think you'll like it. There's a cab!'

We made our way through the shining streets down to the Embankment and then along to Vauxhall Bridge, over the river which was ruffled with rain, and then down a small one-way street to a long, dark row of railway arches. The taxi slowed, the cabbie muttered something about not wanting to go any further and so Henry paid him and we got out and walked. The rain fell like bicycle spokes in the pools of light from flickering streetlamps. There seemed to be nothing in the world but the grey violence that roared down around us. A skip stood in the road, blocking cars; we made our way around it and saw the reflection of flames burning under one of the arches further along to our right. The faint sound of music and low voices, the rain falling into the sludge collected in the skip. We were soaked through, the white shirt I was wearing lay transparent against my pebbled skin and my jacket was heavy like a pelt around my shoulders. Henry's hair, pushed back from his eyes, fell in waves around his ears and down the back of his neck.

When we reached the arch, I saw fires lit in oil drums either side of the entrance. Another fire was burning in the middle of the arch's cavernous interior, the flames throwing shadows onto the grey and red brick. At first I thought that there was only a handful of people within, but as I learnt to read the movement of the flames, as my eyes became accustomed to interpreting the forms that were grouped on the earthen floor, I realised that there were perhaps thirty people crouched around the fire, huddled in sleeping bags in the corner, sitting around a battered tape machine that was spitting out some old-school trance music. Some were fucking in the back, writhing under blankets, rolling backwards and forwards like landed fish. Someone was perched on a stepladder reaching down into a pot of paint, marking out a pattern of white spots on the ceiling, frequently consulting some sort of a chart. Two girls danced to the music; turning like dervishes they spread out their fingers like the fingers of concert pianists. Two more painters were working along the back wall, moving carefully over snaking bodies. Lamps lit their work and it looked like Guernica, black and white and skulls and gunmetal.

One of the girls sitting around the fire caught sight of us, rose and greeted Henry with a kiss on the lips. Her brown eyes were shadowy and her skin bore the traces of a tan from long ago, now she was just sallow. Her short golden hair was pushed back into a halo above her head and her smile was jagged and knowing, set in a face with small, pointed features. She had a cultivated kookiness; was the kind of girl who'd sit on the floor at parties even if there were plenty of chairs.

'Jo. Thought we'd stop by, if that's ok? This is Charlie. He's a friend of mine.'

She looked at me with quizzical eyes, ancient eyes, then turned to the group sitting around the fire. All of them were white-skinned and hollow-eyed, but at the same time their complexions were clear. Their clothes also gave the impression of bedraggled cast-offs, but were betrayed by the quality of the material and the recherché detail. They wore jewellery in their ears and eyebrows and noses, all glittering silver and diamonds. Jo smiled at the group wickedly, then turned towards me.

'Nice to meet you, Charlie. This is our little world. Henry's our most recent recruit, aren't you, darling?' She reached up to stroke Henry's hair and he danced a little two-step with her up to the fire.

'Something to warm you up? You look like refugees. Conrad, cook these boys something up. Make it snappy, chef.' There was something sharp and aggressive in the way she said people's names.

Henry reached into his pocket, drew out a twenty and handed it to Jo.

'Thanks, love. Here we go. This'll do the trick.'

She handed Henry a half-litre bottle of Imperial vodka. In the light of the fire I could see it was empty. Then Henry bent over the bottle and Jo held a lighter below it. As he inhaled deeply I could see a dirty white rock set in a hole in the bottom of the bottle glow like a tiny sun and white mist rushed up into Henry's mouth. I had never done crack before. I thought about trying to duck out, then saw Henry's eyes suddenly full of violent life and so I leant over the pipe as he lit the bottle from below. I felt the glass warm up beneath my fingers, choked on the first breath, then drew the acrid smoke deep into my lungs.

Instantly, sparks leapt across my brain. Everything was suddenly very clear and I could see that the man on the stepladder was painting out the cosmos on the ceiling and identified Orion's Belt and Ursa Major and then the painting at the end of the room seemed to leap towards me in three dimensions and I felt the pain of the world, felt its divisions and heartache, and when I looked into Jo's eyes they were the black eyes of a witch. I took a deep breath of air, felt faint, took another deep breath. The boy called Conrad, who was taller than Henry, and wore a turquoise shirt open at the neck, grabbed hold of my hand.

My heart felt like it was about to jump from my ribs. A constriction spread from my left shoulder down into my chest. I staggered backwards and desperately sucked in air. Conrad squeezed my hand, looked with his cool green eyes into mine.

'Don't breathe too much, you'll make yourself panic. Just take it easy; it makes you feel like you're not getting enough air but you are. You really are.'

He led me like a child through the tunnels that fed into the main hall like tributaries into a delta. Sudden lights appeared and then passed by like comets. I was panting at the heat one moment and then shivering the next as we moved into caverns of dank air where the ceiling dripped constantly and a green light glowed from the walls and onto our faces. I let my fingers trail along the cool brick of the tunnel walls, feeling the recesses of damp mortar, the beat of the pulse in my fingertips. All the time Conrad was talking, leading me forward, distracting me from the painful hammering in my chest.

Then my heart was beating softly and firmly, and I was back in the main hall, dancing in a pool of light. Jo danced away from me then towards me, and there was something bitter in her beauty. At one point she danced up to me, shaking her shoulders down like she was about to charge, luminous with energy. The reflection of the flames fell across her in bars, separating her moving body into a series of cubes of light, shifting and fluid in the dimness around her. I backed into a corner as she rose up, grasped a handful of my hair and kissed me, slipping her small tongue into my mouth. I pushed past her, stumbled to the front of the hall and found Henry warming his hands over the fire. I sat down next to him and we stared deep into the flames.

'Do you remember the circus in the Meadows? You and Vero and I went in the first year?' I was speaking hesitantly, unable to judge the pace of my words, feeling close to passing out, wanting more of the earlier rush.

'Yes . . . I remember. We were really drunk. We sat in the front row, didn't we? Vero got freaked out by the clowns.' His voice seemed to come from a great distance.

'Do you remember the trapeze artists? And the high-wire act? I was just thinking about them. How we're like that. They weren't any good. They looked like they'd just learnt to do it, they were always almost missing the catch, almost slipping from the high-wire. And it made it terrifying and compelling to watch. If they'd been brilliant, it wouldn't have made us clutch at our seats and hold our breaths. It was because they were novices that it was so amazing.

'I feel that we're like that now. That we're all just managing to hold on, every step is important, and with one slip we could go spinning off into space. I'm proud of us for getting this far, proud that we're living together and looking after each other. But we mustn't forget that we're also novices, stumbling through this world. We need to carry on looking after each other.'

But I was talking to the fire and Henry was lying with his face pressed against the cold stone floor. His lips were thin and grey and there were smudges across his waxy cheeks and his high forehead. He looked like a wounded soldier as he drew his knees up to his chest and shivered. When we came out into the ugly morning it was growing light over the Thames.

Huge yellow cranes reared up like herons over the river inserting silver-blue blocks of apartments that sat smugly behind their vast balconies. Smaller cranes climbed up the sides of these glittering wharf buildings like egrets perched on cattle. Henry and I sat on a bench in the uncertain light as weary taxis pushed southwards, their work over. Dirty leaves rotted on the ground, soaking up the dregs of the night's rainfall. My head was tight and pain glowered behind my eyes, occasionally thrusting forward sharp forays into my temples.

'So who were they, Henry? They seemed . . . seemed more than just druggies. What's going on in that place?'

He lit a cigarette, passed it to me. His cough was raw and scraping. Sharp, painful breaths syncopated with the lapping of the waves against the quayside.

'I'm surprised you didn't recognise some of them. A few were at Edinburgh. Most at Oxford or Cambridge. I suppose you could see them as dropouts. It's not just that they've decided not to work. It's . . . it's more than that. They're glorying in their youth. Idealistic, maybe that's what I'd call it. Conscientious objectors to the miserable wage war. They are all well off, parents are politicians and bankers and lawyers. All of them come from good backgrounds, but they have seen what we're putting up with and they refuse to go through it.

Quite sensible if you ask me. No effort to integrate into this . . . this great tragedy we call our lives. They hang out here most of the time, taking drugs and having sex and talking. Conrad's father is a property developer and he's lent the arches to them until he decides what to do with them. I have just felt so happy here, it's somehow more real than our lives at home.'

We walked along the south side of the river, finding things to throw in – rocks, sticks, cans. We stopped at a small café in Battersea and tried to eat a fry-up but we couldn't force the food down and the world lost its glamour and I stopped marvelling at the colour of the skin of my hands. We walked home in silence, the greyness of the day opening above us like an oyster, stained yellow by the night's last streetlights. I called in sick to Euphonium, who was slightly cold and questioning when I told him I had food poisoning. I fell into my bed and the sheets were soon damp with my sweat and I woke up around lunchtime completely terrified.

Chapter 4

Going Home

I had been at Silverbirch for seven months when the summer came upon me like a fever. It was a July of dog days followed by violent showers, sunshine that was white and withering and remorseless and drilled into the cranium, sudden floods sending rivers rushing down the Fulham Road, soaking clothes instantly.

I had agreed to go and visit my parents in Worthing one weekend. I hadn't seen them for several months, hadn't spoken to my father since moving to London. It's not that we weren't close. It was that they were so desperately bourgeois, and I was a little ashamed of them, couldn't imagine what Henry or Vero would think of the little terrace house one block back from the beach where arthritic women eased their worn-out joints up and down the promenade. They had been excellent parents – loving me delicately and distantly, like some rare and precious orchid that they had raised and now stood back to admire. But I still had enough of the adolescent in me for that to be a half-hidden truth; something that would only show itself when the revelation could be twinned with the knowledge that it was too late to do anything about showing them that I appreciated it.

I blamed my father for the fact that I didn't live in a castle by a spumey loch. I resented his lack of materialism, especially since it caused him and my mother so much discomfort. I remember my mother coming down to breakfast, her hair shock-high on her head, her body caressed by that particularly offensive smell that parents brewed under their bedclothes. I was seventeen. Sulky and glorious in that perfect era of freedom that exists between the end of GCSEs and the start of A Levels.

'Morning, Charles,' her voice was slack with tiredness. 'Your father was up all night. He sat at the end of the bed looking at his old business cards, fretting about money. I'm so worried about him.' She shook her head and realised that I was staring at the bottom of the stairs where my father stood, leaning heavily on the banister. He saw us watching him, flung open the door to the bright morning and stormed out.

Once he told me he would have liked to have more children, would have liked to give me a brother or sister, managing to make me feel both inadequate and strangely lonely at the same time. But one child was all that they could afford, and by the time I was born already one business had gone down – teaching presentation skills to bored local councillors and travelling salesmen. Then another attempt to make it as a publisher of self-help books written by a friend who was constantly broke and often sleeping on our sofa during breaks from his demanding Spanish wife. So my father settled into a kind of frantic unemployment, broken only by learned articles for the *Evening Argus* on jazz and the short stories of Chekhov. My mother taught geography at the local secondary school to allow us to afford the kind of low-octane middle-class life my parents had once rejected but now embraced.

We used to holiday with my aunt who lived in a very English farmhouse perched on a very English-looking hill in central France. My father would sit in a swing chair and read short stories – John Cheever, William Maxwell, Raymond Carver. The day would pass by in the rise and shine and dip of the sun and he would sit quite still, only moving in the chair when the breeze rocked it gently and he would stretch out his legs to stop the swaying. He resented my aunt – his sister – who had married a wealthy and sickly insurance broker who had left her enough money to indulge her passion for creating 1950s rural England in the heart of France. The days passed in a froth of unspoken envy.

My mother would play ping-pong with me and we'd go for long walks over rolling countryside that turned from Dorset to Scotland to Cotswold-cute in successive valleys, but never looked like France. I now think back on those walks as precious, as something wonderful that my mother and I shared. But at the time I couldn't wait to set out on my own, and spent the time I wasn't out walking locked in my room, sprawled on the floor filling notebooks with poetry and song lyrics and plays which I was certain would catapult me onto the world's stages and television screens. When Edinburgh rescued me from those summer holidays, I felt like kissing her streets in gratitude.

*

I was the only one in the house with a car – a battered blue Polo my grandfather had left me in his will. I had agreed to take Vero to a friend's house in Brixton on my way down to the M23. She was wearing a huge floppy pink sunhat. She had gained a little weight, and seemed happier than during the winter.

Henry was visiting his sister in the nursing home. He had left early that morning in the bright sunlight, before thick stormclouds had descended. I hadn't been back to the squat under the arches with him: I think he knew that I had found it sordid and scary. He had given up his project on the homeless, had started taking pictures of his night-time escapades instead, and when I looked through them I recognised the cavern in south London with its fires and its starry ceiling. His face was so thin that his cheeks seemed transparent and his eyes those of one with some profound thyroid problem. I wondered whether they would mistake him for an inmate at his sister's convalescent home, hoped that they might. Somebody needed to help him.

Vero and I talked quietly about him as we drove over the river. We were both worried, but what could we do? Tell his father? Try to speak to him? We put off the confrontation, said we'd deal with it after we all got back. I hadn't told her about the night after Boujis, just as she hadn't spoken about the boy she'd gone home with. It felt as though we were drifting apart, and none of us had the strength to bring us back together. Now Astrid had taken a turn for the worse and Henry spent his time at home in agonising whispered telephone conversations with his parents. I dropped Vero in Brixton and let myself drift into the melancholy flow of the motorway.

The heavy summer skies dropped in around me as I left the protective embrace of the Downs and drove the spluttering Polo into Worthing. The town was full of discarded memories, full of places that should have felt symbolic and significant and redolent of my youth, but I had willed them into the past and they had slipped quietly away. Past the shopping centre next to the station with its boarded-up supermarket and the night-clubs where I had danced with girls who had sweated too much for my taste and let me kiss them and fuck them too soon because they had seen in me a way of escaping. But they all knew I'd never take them with me, and it had made them even more eager to please me; those with boyfriends had left them and those with morals had cast them aside, but I had never cared for any of them. It had seemed like the right way of doing things back then, but as I drove past the Factory and the Kasbar and the Frog Pond I thought about those girls with their delicate little lives and I felt a sense of shame and regret.

As I pulled into my parents' quiet street I thought about the scorn and shame I had poured down upon the normality of the lives that surrounded me. I resolved to make everything better, to be a better son, a better worker, a better friend to Vero and Henry. But still something in me shuddered at the sight of the little house with its little garden and double-glazed windows and camellia bush buxom in the centre of the garden. My mother was standing on the doorstep watering a pot plant as I drew up outside.

I picked up my bag from the back seat and embraced my mother as she scurried towards me. She smelt of lavender and furniture polish. She felt smaller in my arms than I remembered.

'Charles. Oh darling, you look well. So grown-up. I was just popping out to the shops. I've been busy this morning. Working on my project. Did I tell you I had decided to do an art course at the College? I'm creating a collage out of 1950s magazines. Quite a nostalgia trip. Will you drive me to Safeway?'

It felt strange to be driving her after so many years of sitting as she took me to piano lessons and cross-country matches and the doctor. But we fell into a comfortable silence punctuated only by her occasional exclamations on the price of vegetables in the supermarket and the long queue at the checkout. I insisted on paying for the groceries, even though I hadn't returned the hundred she'd loaned me five months earlier. There seemed to be so many parties that summer, so much that needed money.

As we were loading the bags into the car, my mother cleared her throat. She took a breath, exhaled, took another deep breath. I ran the trolley over to a pimply ginger boy in a green

44

jacket who thanked me as I helped him gather several strays back into their pen. When I got back to the car my mother was still standing by the open boot. The clouds had cleared and the sun caught strands of grey in her hair. She looked tired and old. She cleared her throat again.

'Charles,' she began. There's something about parents when you go home after a long absence. They use your name more, touch your wrists and lay their dry hands over yours, pat you on the shoulder and the cheek as if to prove something, to confirm the vital legacy they have left now they are passing into the evening of their lives.

'Charles,' she repeated, 'I need to speak to you about your father.' Cancer rang like a bell in my head. 'He's been having a very difficult time. We have been struggling for money even more than usual. He has been acting very strangely. He feels like such a failure. It started off with him not sleeping and then . . .' With horror I watched large silver drops forming in her eyes; I had never seen her cry before. She turned away but the sun drew wet trails down her face and I saw the tears collect on her chin and drop, reflecting the world as they fell to the tarmac.

I put my arms around her, and it felt less awkward than I thought it would, and I took her soft, fragrant hair in my hand, and pulled her head towards my shoulder. I could see the boy in the green coat watching us.

'It'll be all right, Mum. I promise it will. Dad's tough. You know he is. We'll all be all right. I'm sorry for not coming back more often. I'm so sorry.'

We stood for a while longer as the sun fell around us, and then I drove us slowly back to the house, my mother occasionally shaking with sucked-in sobs. I picked as many bags as would fit wrapped around my wrists and elbows out of the boot and walked into the kitchen.

My father was standing in the garden, looking over the wall towards the sea, above which sat an evening sky streaked through with lilac and rose clouds. His shoulders were slumped and his jacket hung loose. He wore the air of a man defeated. I walked up behind him, knew he heard me. He didn't turn, but looked further up, where the sky was turning slowly into a deeper blue. A soft wind blew at the mint bush at his feet, where it stretched itself out from the small strip of earth onto the pale patio stones. The smell rose up, thick and oily, surrounding us. I put my arms around my father from behind, and felt him lean into my embrace. I continued to hold him, turning him towards me, realising how much smaller than me he was. He looked up at me and smiled.

'Charles. Thanks for coming down. I was so looking forward to seeing you. I'm so sorry about this. About you finding me in this state. It's a disgrace. I know it is.'

'Let's go inside, Dad. I'm so sorry I haven't been back for so long. It's beautiful down here. Look at the sky. It's like something in Malibu or Santa Barbara or one of those golden Californian sea-cities. Let's have a glass of wine, Dad. I bought a bottle of Beaujolais.'

My father walked inside with the nervous, mortified steps of a latecomer to a dark cinema edging past lovers' knees, muttering nervous apologies. I stood on the patio for a moment longer, inhaled the air made fresh by the closeness of the water and the coming of the night, looked down at the hopeless flowers whose colours had faded to grey in the dying light.

As we sat at dinner I made myself talk, spoke joyful lies about the job and my friends and the books I had read, and filled every silence with bland positive jabbering.

'It's wonderful being in London. Just so much energy on the streets. And so many exhibitions to go to, and the theatre, and the authors who speak at Waterstone's on Thursday nights. We have so much fun and it just doesn't matter that none of us have much money. We all muck in together, manage to put on decent dinner parties and afford a few nights out. It's really quite wonderful.'

All the time, I thought how I had never spoken to my father about how I didn't care that he wasn't some big roller. How having him beside me as a child, taking me to school in the mornings, sitting with me as I did my homework, walking me down to the beach to swim on summer evenings: all of this was more than compensation. I had told myself that it was his mild-mannered sensitivity that had prevented him from being in a position to buy me all of the beautiful things that those gilded children at Edinburgh had possessed. I had never realised that if one of his businesses had taken off he would have been snatched away from us, and we wouldn't have had the shy, smiling beauty of his company around us.

After dinner my parents went to bed. I knew that my life as a banker – I couldn't persuade him that what I did was anything more than a glorified bank manager – disgusted my dad. He had been a Communist in the seventies, had lived on a commune in Cornwall with my mother for a year, despised the silver sheen of the big cities. I loved him very much, and watched him walk shakily, arm in arm with my mother, up the stairs and into the darkness. I sat at the table and finished the bottle of wine, swirling it in the glass.

You are never alone when you return to your home town. For with you travels the ghost of your younger self. He instructs what you see, and he makes that place a mirror to you. You reveal and hide elements of each other: maybe you feel the slight shudder of disappointment that lurks in the corners of his young eyes. That you haven't charged into town atop some golden Mercedes chariot, that you aren't walking through the summer night scattering banknotes to the homeless men who slither their existence under the barnacled struts of the pier. And you too look somewhat shamefully back on that hungry adolescent, with his glittering lust for the big city, his unrealistic aspirations, his provinciality and his clothes and his haircut, which tie him to a place and time long left behind.

That evening I walked along the seafront and the last quivering rays of the sun flung themselves over the pier and it really did seem a better place than I had remembered it, with music coming out of pubs and young couples drinking at picnic tables. I tried to take stock, tried to get a measure of what I needed to do to make things better. I needed to earn an awful lot of money. If not, I could have asked Henry's dad for a job on the newspaper. Being a journalist would have been wonderful, but you had to do the time, had to have written for the university newspaper, had to have a portfolio. I was too busy having fun at Edinburgh to turn up at the *Student*; I could have so easily written theatre reviews, could have spent just one day a week working in a romantic smoke-filled room putting together copy. But there was so much I could have done and didn't, so much I should have achieved and hadn't.

Waves sped towards shore, long barred shadows moving in the last horizontal beam of sunlight which swept across them. I stood and watched the waves and saw that they appeared to lose heart as they approached the beach. Some looked as if they wanted to turn back; others slowed down and seemed to consider their options. Just as they were about to break on the pebbles, the waves reared up, not like horses but like mice chewing their paws and sniffing the air. Then, with a sense of anticlimax, the waves unfurled themselves upon the piled pebbles with a loud, dispirited sigh.

By the time I turned back homewards I realised that I had solved nothing, that I had just confused myself further, that I was truly lost. I stopped at the pub at the end of the road that led from the seafront up to my parents' and had a pint, watching the stars quietly appear.

There was a girl singing in the pub. Her voice stumbled on the high notes, rising to a screech during a cover of a Tori Amos song, but the deep notes were mellow and velvety and I walked into the bar to watch her. She was in her early twenties, not much younger than me, but I saw the dreams in her eyes as she addressed herself to the grizzled patrons sitting around the bar in the smoky little room. Her skin was greasy and pockmarked, her hair lank from her day job, but she smiled as she sang, and she caught my eye, and I thought I saw her nod some recognition. But perhaps it was just that she was grateful that there was someone young watching her. I thought about waiting for her to finish, getting her to take me back to her place, thought about what it would be like to fuck her. But I was tired from the long day and wanted to be in my old bed, so I put down my glass and walked the familiar route away from the sea towards the squat pebbledash house where my mother lay, twitching and groaning in her sleep, and my father stared at the ceiling, clenching and releasing his fists.

After a lunch where conversation flickered in short bursts over the table, I left my parents waving at the gate, my father wrapped in my mother's thin arms, thunderclouds rolling in above them from the sea. Shadows passed across the bonnet of the car as I drove, dappling the rolling hills and secret valleys of the Downs. I moved stutteringly through London's southward bleed, through the grey vacuum of Croydon, over the river, and pulled up outside our little house.

*

When I returned from my parents' late Sunday night, the house in Fulham had been silent and empty. I spent the

49

Monday working quietly in the office. Euphonium was on tour with his brass ensemble. Beardy hadn't been in for two weeks. Coffee Teeth and I were putting together cashflow projections on a Swedish mattress company. I thought about all the beautiful blond people who'd fuck on those mattresses, the bonny babies that'd be born in quiet white hospitals as snow tumbled outside, thought about the old people with calm blue eyes who'd die on those mattresses.

Vero was in the middle of the exams that would see her qualify as a solicitor and revised late into the night in her law firm's library. When I got home I cooked myself beans on toast and went to bed unsure of whether I was enjoying the melancholy taste of solitude. There is some deep instinct that tells us that solitude should somehow be improving, a strengthening experience for the psyche. But it is hard – how do we know that it isn't just the inherited Puritan reflex that tells us that things that we work at must be good for us? I missed my friends that night, and they stalked my dreams, all of my friends, tripping across a dancefloor to music played by the girl from the pub in Worthing. I was pulled from these dark and ruminating dreams by the sound of Henry retching violently.

He hadn't been able to pull the bathroom door shut behind him, had missed the bowl of the toilet against whose cold rim his face lay, a face grey and stained with tears and puke and snot and I took that head in my hands and drew it towards my chest.

'Christ, Henry. What're you doing to yourself? You poor bastard. Come on. Let's get you cleaned up.'

I lifted him to his feet, my hands cold under his arms. Suddenly he seemed to grow very heavy; I tried to support us against the shower but the door opened and we both fell in. Henry gurgled apologies, then puked onto my T-shirt. It was a small amount of puke, thick like a cat's and he laid his face

50

down in it. I saw that Vero had come into the room, wearing a Snoopy T-shirt and black pants. Together we leant Henry against the side of the shower as we undressed him. Vero's hands became those of a nurse, brisk and clinical and loving at the same time. She had large dark rings under her eyes and she coughed a hollow little cough every few minutes.

We washed Henry and I looked at his cock all shrivelled and curled up on itself like a snail as Vero soaped the puke from his face, washed his arms and his chest and between his legs and his scrawny buttocks. She then cleaned his bony feet and I saw her smile to herself for a moment at the ridiculous symbolism of the act. We slung him crucified between us and carried him to his room. I hadn't been into his bedroom for a month or so and it had the damp unwholesome air of a teenager's. Vero went to the window and opened it. We sat side by side on the bed looking down at his tired eyes. Vero reached over and stroked his hair, still wet from the shower. She swung her feet like a child and took his hand in hers and it was such a picture of devotion that I had to turn away.

I went to my room and changed my T-shirt and pulled on some tracksuit bottoms. On the way back to Henry's room I splashed water on my face in the bathroom, and there was something cinematic in the instant as I looked up at myself, drips running down my face, my eyes dark under a heavy brow. I opened the window to usher out the stench of Henry's stomach lining and then twirled in the plughole with the end of my toothbrush until the puke had disappeared. I walked back up the corridor to check on Henry.

Vero was spread out on the bed, one arm across Henry's shoulders, a thin smile on her lips. She was fast asleep. I picked her up; she was surprisingly light and burrowed her nose into my chest as I carried her into her room. Her skin was almost as grey and tired as Henry's; her features seemed crumpled, defeated even in sleep. I laid her down very gently and watched her body tense, quiver, then relax. I pulled the duvet over her, kissed her furrowed forehead and turned out the light. She coughed once more as I closed the door and the sound crept slowly over my skin.

Henry's arm had become trapped underneath him. I had read how this causes potassium to build up in the isolated limb which, when released upon the body, finds its way to the heart and kills you. A major cause of death in tramps. I lifted Henry up, tucked him in as I had tucked in Vero, was about to kiss his brow when, seeing him shake and start to retch, I turned and grabbed the bin. His eyes were open wide suddenly. Bold grey eyes that looked with confusion at the world illuminated by the desk lamp in the corner of the room. I took his hand.

'Charlie. Thank God, it's you. What's happened? Where's Jo? I've got to find Jo. She was really sick. She'd done too much.' He sat up and I put an arm around him. He began to struggle, made as if to rise, I pinned him down. He began to shake with tears; huge racks of sobs rent his lean frame and he hugged me very tightly, screwing his fists up at my back. Grabbing handfuls of my T-shirt he cried out Jo's name.

'Shhhh . . . Shhhh . . .' I stroked his hair. 'She'll be fine, Henry. It's you we've got to worry about. Lie down, now. Come on, Henry, calm down.'

'I left her at the party in Notting Hill. In a club under the Westway. I needed some air and she came out to be with me and then we were both in a car park and she was puking and crying and . . . and I think there was blood coming out of her . . . And I said I'd get help. But I just came back here. I didn't know what I was doing. Let's go together. Can we go in your car? Please, Charlie, please?'

He was cadaverous, wasted and desperate. The clock by his bed read four a.m.

'No, Henry. We can't go. You're in a mess. Just lie there.' He struggled hopelessly but I could see that he knew I was stronger, knew I was right and he drifted into a sleep that was disturbed by twitches that caused frowns to cross his face like clouds crossing a mountain. He let out sharp cries every so often, tearing the fabric of the night.

I sat there until dawn, waited for Vero to rise, heard her crashing around pulling on her dressing gown and then a pause as she remembered the events of the night before; she came into Henry's room with her hair falling in deep strands around her eyes. She pushed it back and looked at me. Henry was holding my hand.

'You're still here. Thank you, Charlie. I've got to go. I have my exam. Will you stay with him?'

I realised I'd have to, found that I felt bad about letting Coffee Teeth down, that I had begun to feel an obligation towards my work, towards my colleagues, towards the institution that was Silverbirch.

'Yes. Yes, that's fine. Good luck today, darling.' I gently disentangled Henry's fingers from mine and stood to hug her. I knew my breath stank and that something of the smell of the room and the dampness of the air clung to me, but Vero held me very tight against her and when I looked down she was smiling, but her smile looked hard and forced, worse than tears.

Two weeks later and Henry and I were walking by the side of the Great Ouse, watching the flatness of the East Anglian countryside stretch itself out under the eternal sky. It was damp and cool; summer showers blew in from the North Sea, came upon us as we walked, moved past and on towards London. A bittern called in the reeds by the river. Coots and moorhens scuttled in front of a grebe like the servants of a Persian prince bowing and scraping before his finery. Henry looked better, his skin had taken on some colour, his clothes had the clumsy comfy air of the country – a fleece, brown cords, a pair of brown brogues. His mother had taken a week off work to nurse him. She cooked great meals of ham, roast chicken, spinach and watercress soup, sticky toffee pudding and treacle tart.

The morning after his collapse I had called Henry's father at the office as Henry lay sleeping upstairs. Parents have a way of making you feel very young when they act with resolve. Henry's father came and picked him up two hours later, the navy Jaguar purring in the road as he charged briskly into the house, packed a bag of clothes and a toothbrush and then left. Henry smiled at me, turning his head as he leant against his father; he looked at me and then past me, lost and distant but happy to be in his father's arms, to be going home.

Vero went home too. She called later that same day sounding tired and crazy and far away.

'Charlie, it's me. I couldn't take it. I realised as I sat down for my exams; I just knew that it was such a waste of time. That I didn't want a job where I had to know anything about conveyancing and land law, about commercial property and foreclosure. I got up and walked out and got on the Eurostar to Calais. I'm at home. I called the office from the train and told them I had quit. How's that for decisive, eh?' She laughed manically. She was a little drunk, on the edge of tears.

'Of course they told me I couldn't just quit like that. That I had to bloody sit through HR meetings and submit a written request. I told them I was going into a tunnel and just hung up. So simple. I'll be back to pick my stuff up. I just want to get my head together again. Spend some time with my parents. Work out what the hell I want to do with my life. I'll miss you, Charlie. Listen, don't get used up. Don't let them take away what makes you who you are. I'm so worried that you'll end up like those awful guys with their dead eyes and I couldn't bear that.' She called out, hand across the receiver. '*Oui papa. J'arrive* . . . Charlie, I have to go. We are going to dinner. I will have a cider to toast you, the survivor, the only one left. Take care of yourself.'

I sat silent, staring at the telephone in the darkened hallway. A car alarm which had been screaming at the back of my consciousness thrust its way forward; I felt lonely, and hung my head. My two best friends, the only two I loved, had left me. I was alone with a job that didn't interest me and the people I had thought of as my friends at Edinburgh, the social set I had battled to become part of, now hid themselves in expensive restaurants and exclusive clubs. I worked the next few weeks on autopilot, then left the office early on a Friday evening, made my way through a London buzzing with the sexual vim of a summer's night to Liverpool Street where I took the train up to Ipswich and Henry.

I had telephoned ahead and spoken to him; his voice was flat and sad. Jo had turned up, sick and bloody but alive. Her parents had found her asleep on the doorstep in the crisp brightness of a Notting Hill morning. She had no memory of finding her way home, could not explain the bruises that covered her body or the red tartan blanket that lay over her as she slept. She was thinking of moving to India, thinking of joining a kibbutz. She didn't think that she should see Henry again. They were too intense together.

As we walked beside the river Henry told me about how he and Jo had met at the clinic in the Chilterns one Sunday in February when he'd been visiting his sister. Jo was about to be let out, had been self-harming, addicted to speed, suffering from panic attacks, night sweats and depression. They sat and talked over a cup of tea in the warmth of the clinic's country-house drawing room. He kissed her on the cheek as he left, wrote his number on a pocket handkerchief. She had gone back to the clinic to serve out the remainder of the fortnight that her psychiatrist had insisted upon. But before going she had told him about the commune down in the no-man's-land under the arches. About the group who were turning away from the lives their parents and teachers had planned for them, turning towards a brighter, less materialistic future.

'I miss her,' he said, striding ahead of me along the stone path. 'I bloody miss her and her ideas. I miss hearing her talk about the things that matter to her. The way . . . the way her voice would rise up into the voice of a child when she discussed the weightiest issues. It was as if she was afraid of what she might say. As if she tried to negate the weight of it with the childishness of her voice. But her eyes would get very old as she talked. Like there was some . . . some great and ancient wisdom in her. Did you notice how old her eyes could look? I wanted to bring her up here. Bring her out to these enormous skies and the air which feels like it's cleaning you out, rinsing you with its dampness.'

We walked in silence by the great river as a skein of geese cut through the sky to the south of us. A watery sun limped towards the end of the day, lacking the motivation to define the outline of the branches of trees that hung down over the banks towards the sea in a green cloud of lush foliage. Henry kicked at a stone but otherwise there was no sound. The rains had passed and the wind dropped, stilling the chatter of the treetops. The geese no longer barked in the sky, nor could we hear waves striking the beach along the distant shore.

CHAPTER 5

Alone in the City

I moved into a small flat in a red mansion block further up Munster Road. The apartment was on the ground floor, and my bedroom window opened onto a grey and sombre courtyard. When the rains came they would collect in a puddle in the yard and I liked to listen to the deepening crescendo of the drops as I read by the black desk lamp that sat beside my bed. Animals lived in the courtyard, night creatures whose rustling steps soundtracked my dreams. When the wind spiralled down the sides of the great brick building it howled and blew rain in through the window, tearing on the hairs of my arms. I sat and read throughout the wet and dreary end of that summer; I read on Tube trains, and at my desk at Silverbirch, and on more Tube trains, then back on my bed. Every moment I wasn't working was spent reading. The drawing room of the little flat was bare save for a sad grey armchair, with fluff peeling from the arms and broken springs, which I had moved to the centre of the room. I bought a small coffee table from an antique shop on Lillie Road and piled it with books. Then I sat in the uncomfortable chair, picked at the fraying arms, and lost myself in other people's lives.

It was as if I was making up for the studying I hadn't done at Edinburgh, as if I was trying to teach myself some of the things I would have learned at the lectures I didn't attend, or talking to the bright and serious people whose company I avoided. I looked with avid eyes at the books read by my fellow Tube travellers: a small plover-like woman in a green coat reading

Bullock's *Hitler and Stalin* on the District Line at Gloucester Road; a Rasta with dreads like Cuban cigars and tattoos double-dark on dark skin reading Dr Spock's *Baby and Child Care* on the Piccadilly line with a glorious grin on his face; a florid old duffer in tweeds with brushfire eyebrows deep in *Lolita* on the platform at Earls Court. I hid *Herzog* inside *Trader Magazine* as I sat at my desk and I tried to take myself away from the world I had fallen into.

I went to the theatre on my own in the evenings. I queued up for cheap returns, flung myself out to watch experimental performances of Beckett and Brecht in dark Wapping warehouses, shadowy interpretations of Shakespeare played out in the candle-lit crypts of high Victorian churches. I telephoned Henry after these plays, sat on the top deck of a bus as lights reflected in rain created Jackson Pollock patterns on the windows. He was working for his father at the newspaper, helping on an investigation into tobacco advertising, living at home and commuting up to London in his father's Jaguar every morning. He sounded tired, relieved, healthy. I tried to put off thoughts of my empty flat and the slick sheets which should have been changed weeks ago, and the little tragedy of cheese on toast with the radio on for company when I returned.

There was a tramp who lived outside the new flat. I had been living there for a week before I realised that it was a woman. She wrapped herself into her dirty clothes, melted into the pavement, leaked into the bags she carried around with her. She was chased from shops where she'd half-heartedly shelter from the rain, and most nights ended up under the scrawny tree which stood at the entrance of the mansion block. Her smell was extraordinary. Something dark and dangerous. This was not the odour of a sweating body, not a smell that one associated with life at all. She smelt like rotten pork, like something flies would flock to. Every morning as I passed her on the way to work, trying not to wrinkle my nose as I bent towards her, I left her an apple. It became a habit, something I looked forward to. The simple act of buying a bag of apples at the corner shop, washing one of them in the grimy sink as I left the house, placing it gently on the ground beside her. She never thanked me – perhaps she could not speak. But it established a bond between us, and the days when I walked out into the tremulous light of morning and she wasn't there were poorer for her absence.

Moving out of the old house had been miserable. Although we had not been there quite a year, the newness of the life we lived in the house had stretched out time. As with any place which marks the beginning of a new era, it took on special significance. After two months of living in stasis, keeping Henry and Vero's rooms just as they had been like a mother mourning her truck-hit child, Vero's father and brother arrived to pick up her belongings. Their arrival announced the end of any pretence. Part of me was pleased to be thrust from the scene of my memories. It was a cold, low-skied September day. They came in a silver Mercedes van and offered to drive my few possessions up the road for me.

Vero's brother, Guy, was tall and wore thick spectacles behind which swam limpid green eyes. He worked at a refugee centre in Calais and seemed initially severe, but was merely serious, thoughtful. He pressed my hand with long, cold fingers when he stepped from the van. He smiled distantly at me.

'You are Charlie? I have heard Veronique speak of you. It is good to meet you. I must say we are very pleased to have her back and . . . and I'm sorry for you. That things don't seem so good for you. Here, let me help you.'

Vero's father stayed in the cab of the van whilst we loaded it up. He was small, wiry, his eyes fiercely interrogating the city around him. On the way to the new flat I sat beside him, trying not to look at the withered legs that hung down over the seat and wobbled with every bump in the road. He placed a small hand upon mine, but it was not a kind gesture. He gripped my hand very hard. His English was precise and formal.

'I had very great plans for Veronique. She always made me proud. You should have seen her at nine, ten. Extraordinary! The girl was like a dynamo, always moving, always thinking. And so beautiful, so passionate. She used to come and watch me in surgery when we were in Africa. Never flinching, she would watch me cut open chests with her eyes fixed on the detail of what I was doing. Incredible! She has been ruined here.'

He shot out an arm as we passed a boutique where handbags with gold buckles gleamed.

'I don't know what you boys were thinking. It makes me so angry to see you wasted like this. Young people of promise! But now she is back in France. And she will have to unlearn all of this. She will work with her brother in the refugee camp. This is real work; this is something the Vero I know will grasp with both of her hands. She will become decent again. Not this girl who is so obsessed with appearances. You have noticed, I am sure, that when a girl becomes aware of her own beauty it is instantly diminished? Hers will return. I always tried to be very close to her. We will re-establish that closeness now.'

Guy and I unloaded my books and clothes whilst the old man sat in the cab staring straight ahead. The wind picked up and blew newspapers and plastic bags high into the air like birds. Guy pressed my hand as he stepped into the van, started the engine. Vero's father leant out of his window.

'Good luck, Charlie. You seem like a good person who is

trapped for the moment. I cannot help you as I will help Veronique, but I wish you luck. Goodbye.'

I watched them drive away, the images of trees caught dreamlike on the silver side of the van.

Work had begun to encroach further into my life. Beardy left the office one Friday night and it was announced in the staff meeting on Monday morning that he had died. I was the only one to gasp, and quickly turned it into a cough. Beardy was replaced the next day by a man called Lothar who had wanted to move away from Investment Banking. Euphonium told me that he had been elbowed out after an affair with his boss's wife. Lothar had a high, vein-streaked forehead and narrow white lips. He gave a short speech to our team. I watched his temples throb blue as he spoke.

'I want you all to work very hard. Tiredness is just weakness. Don't slack and we'll be friends. Let me down and we won't. Live and breathe the companies you cover. I want you to know their numbers like you know your own birthdays. Life is not easy. Life is not fun. What we do is serious. Take life seriously.'

Two days after Lothar's arrival there was a brief moment of humour, an occasion to smile in that otherwise dreary autumn. The CEO sent round an email warning that there was to be an anti-capitalist protest in Berkeley Square. It could turn violent – we were all to take great care. The company would not be held liable for employees who confronted the anarchists. We were to dress inconspicuously and attempt to enter the building unnoticed. I went to bed that night rather excited by the image of the rioting crowd. I could imagine myself as one of them: my hair pulled into dramatic spikes I would protest against the repellent inequality of it all, would burn the small amount of money I had earned on the jewelled grass of the Square, would shower eggs and slops down upon the capitalist whores.

When I arrived at work the next morning, dressed in a navy jumper and jeans, there were only three protesters in the Square. Two of them looked rather embarrassed to be seen with the third, a punk with a bright red Mohican who was already drunk and holding onto the railings as if he was on the deck of a violently pitching ship. The other two protesters – a dark-haired boy and a girl with dreadlocks – wore German Army jackets and clapped their shoulders against the early-morning cold. I felt scorn for them both, then analysed this scorn and saw that I envied them their inability to integrate into the world of toil and commerce. I envied their unquestioning commitment to a cause and pictured them returning that night to a meal of lentils accompanied with cheap wine and sincere conversation, before an hour of energetic, humourless sex.

The CEO called us into a meeting at ten to schedule lunch breaks and arrange for a staggered departure at the end of the day. When he entered the room there was a quick giggle that was swallowed immediately. The CEO wore grey suit trousers with a severe crease, a pair of very shiny black shoes and a Bob Marley T-shirt with the words '*Rastaman Vibration*' written upon it in alternate red, green and gold letters. Marley was posed in profile smoking a long joint and I could see the imprint of one of the CEO's nipples against the end of the joint. The T-shirt was clearly quite new, and some of the print was flaking where a maid had ironed it. The CEO shook out his white hair and placed his hands together. I couldn't look at him; I felt a wave of panic as I choked back guffaws.

'Well,' he said jovially, 'looks like the hippies don't get up as early as we bankers.'

The room exploded with laughter. I gripped Euphonium by the shoulder and felt myself shudder as I laughed. The CEO stood slightly bewildered, then smiled at the reception his joke had received. I kept my head lowered and worked hard for the rest of the day, unwilling to risk a roar of laughter at the sight of the CEO.

I had been allocated coverage of some of Beardy's companies and spent hours trying to decipher his spidery dead-man's writing in the margins of annual reports and in the pages of thick yellow legal pads. The markets were still soaring; no company was spared the investment bank analysts' relentless optimism and every graph we printed out for the portfolio managers was a sharp slope inclining upwards. I could see why they thought that they didn't need us: every decision they made was correct because it was impossible to get anything wrong in that world of virtuous circles of capital and falling interest rates with China and India always roaring up on the heels of the western economies. I knew that nothing I said made any difference, so I too subscribed to the sanguinity of the portfolio managers, joined in celebrations when they notched up ridiculous trading gains: twenty million pounds in a week was Bhavin Sharma's record; he ordered pink champagne for everyone in the office and we stood around, watching the delicate silver bubbles rise through rose liquid, until he charged from the room and we stood at the window and watched as he roared around Berkeley Square in the Maserati that had just been delivered for him.

There was something gross about it. Coffee Teeth kept making long and rambling speeches in morning meetings about how the markets moved in cycles. How the prices of bonds were unsustainable. How capital was not inexhaustible and the US consumer was becoming increasingly stretched. What she said made some sense, but then I looked at her furrowed spinster face, the angry eczema that clustered on her knuckles, the spots between her eyebrows. She was so unglamorous, so clearly not meant to exist in this sophisticated world

63

of designer clothes and powerful motor cars and parties made sharp with cocaine and Cristal. Not that I lived in that world either, but it was a world I was working towards. I worked very hard, tried to learn from Beardy's nervous scribblings, began to see numbers and balance sheets and cashflow statements in my dreams. I spent my weekends in the office churning out reports on Ford and GM and Chrysler, wandering up to pizza restaurants on Oxford Street for Sunday lunch where I'd sit and read Pynchon until it was time to go back to the office.

*

That autumn I was more alone than ever before, so hollow that I rattled if I took the steps to the Tube too quickly. Part of the reason I was depressed was because I seemed to run out of money a day earlier each month; even so, I'd buy myself expensive wine at Jeroboam's on Davies Street or Lea and Sandeman on the Fulham Road in an attempt to lift my spirits; or I'd walk past Waterstone's on my way home and pile myself high with books that I'd read until my eyes bled with tiredness; or I'd call up a girl from Edinburgh and take her on a date to some mid-priced restaurant – Chez Gérard or Patara or Strada – and we'd sit with absolutely nothing to say to one another, and she'd walk off into the rain with scorn perched upon her nose like pince-nez.

I spent myself into a new type of debt. Grown-up debt. I took out a staff loan from Silverbirch to pay off my credit cards and my overdraft and yet the money still disappeared too quickly, and I was left with derisory stubs of debt that mounted up each month as I failed to repay them. And the loan from Silverbirch tied me to the job even more. I carried on spending, and even when my bonus came in that cold dark Christmas, it failed to make much more than a modest dent in my debts, and all the time I continued to look at vast country houses on the internet, continued to press my greasy nose against the windows of car dealerships, started betting on stock movements, which never went my way and left me feeling both stupid and poor.

Insecurity crept like a childhood monster behind me, springing up and inspiring real terror whenever I had a moment of respite. It took me years to realise that few people in finance really understand what they are doing. It is a game of abstract bluffing, a bet on the next man being marginally more stupid than you are, or not being brave enough to point out your mistakes. Complex concepts are created by acne-scarred quantitative analysts in the research laboratories of the big investment banks, exported to the broader markets and accepted unquestioningly. Everyone is stalked by the spectre of being uncovered as a fraud, and so when markets go up, everyone rushes to buy, not wishing to be castigated for their inability to spot a bargain. But when markets go down, panic truly sets in, and traders scramble over one another to sell assets that they once held closely about them like dear friends. The weakness of spirit and the flatulence of these people would be laughable if they didn't wield so much power.

Coffee Teeth and I were sitting at our desks. It was dark outside. February was bitterly cold and it could have been any day, any hour, but it was seven o' clock on a Saturday evening. The CEO was giving a presentation on the state of the economy to the Bank of England and Coffee Teeth and I had to write it. I looked over at her as she worked, her head bent low over the textbook she was reading. All of her suits were brown. Her hair was greasy and of a nondescript colour somewhere between brown and grey. There was a whitehead between her eyes, just above the gold bridge of her glasses. She had fur on her face where a man's sideburns might be. It was the white and stroke-

65

able fur of a Persian cat and I was embarrassed to see her looking at me with bashful curiosity as I stared at her facial hair. She was blushing, but then we both smiled and I stood up and stretched as her cheeks faded. She had become quite beautiful in the flash of her smile. She spoke in long-vowelled Bostonian, her voice low and masculine.

'Shall we go for a bite to eat? I'm so tired. I can hardly keep my thoughts together, can hardly move my eyes across the page.'

I helped her into her camelhair coat, stood with my back to her in the lift, stretching up on my toes as we descended, straining against buffered gravity. The plane trees in Berkeley Square were heavy with earlier rain, massive in the light of the buildings around them. Coffee Teeth and I headed up to the north side of the square.

I watched an old man with the swinging jowls of a Great Dane step, protective arm around hesitant wife, into the road. They paused to let a taxi pass, then crossed with jerky, painful steps. I envied them their age. They did not have the vast bleak plain of middle age stretching out ahead of them rutted with mortgage payments and school fees and child support and ISAs and all the other drains on hard-earned money that I foresaw in the vision of my future. They could walk happily into the dark waters of death and leave their children to worry about the taxes and the medical bills and the markets. I stopped for a moment to watch their halting movement up Davies Street, let Coffee Teeth wander ahead, then trotted to catch her.

The restaurant was dark and empty, an Italian that had been popular decades earlier. We left our coats hanging on the back of the door and sat in the window. A solitary old waiter with quivering hands took our order, his notepad hovering perilously close to the flickering minaret of the candle flame.

Coffee Teeth let out a long sigh, slipped off her suit jacket and smiled again.

'It's nice to get to sit with you outside of the office, Charles. It's been a tough few days. It's a difficult market. I find it very hard to get any sense of perspective when all you're focused on is the latest set of figures coming out of a company – and they've only been brilliant recently, the endless wonderful numbers that just seem to stack up and stack up and I start thinking that the world has gone mad, you know? Am I mad or just plain stupid? It feels like everyone else gets the joke and I don't.' She lit a cigarette and chewed at a hangnail.

'It can't go on like this. I spent three years at Brown and two at Wharton learning about the markets and everything I learned there told me that this can't continue. That we're due for a crash. But no one listens to me when I speak in morning meetings. None of the PMs pay any attention to me because they have their eyes and their minds focused on the massive bonus, the huge figure that they have already spent even though it's ten months until bonus time. And they are terrified of anything that could seem to threaten that bonus. I caught Bhavin looking at some huge Chelsea townhouse on the Foxtons website the other day when I was putting some research on his desk. And it sounds like this will be the first year that Catrina gets seven figures. It's funny what you can pick up from the secretaries. They keep their ears open.

'It's horrid to feel that I have such little impact because I really love my job. I love the brightness of it all. Skyscrapers really excite me – you know, the sight of sun on a skyscraper in New York or the red lights that spot the highrises of Tokyo at night – they seem to represent something magnificent. I always loved going to New York as a child, looking up and imagining my father in his suit making a daring presentation to a room of awestruck executives. It's such a fascinating job and yet I feel like no one ever listens to me at all.' She cast her eyes down and back up at me, and I realised that I had never looked deeply into her eyes. And when I did I saw a kind of hopelessness, and I suddenly became scared that the look in her eyes was reflecting back to me my own future. She smiled, and coughed out a crackled laugh.

'But maybe that's just me. I worry too much. Spend too much time on my own. Too much time working and thinking. My mother's always saying it when I go home. I make her watch financial television at Christmas. Talk to her about bond markets and credit derivatives and asset-backed securities. She doesn't understand any of it, of course. But maybe that's the point. Maybe I need to speak to somebody who doesn't understand it, who sees it as something unnecessarily complex and rather boring because it helps me realise that there are people who can live without the markets, can exist without the rush and the buzz of it all. Sorry, Charles. I'm talking too much. Where's our food? I'm starving.'

The waiter brought our steaming plates to the table. Coffee Teeth had ordered garlic bread and spaghetti vongole, perhaps with the express intent of making sure that I didn't get any ideas about seducing her, but more likely because she was the sort of girl who didn't think about her breath, her skin, the bushy eyebrows that broke like waves above her glasses. My ravioli sat in a watery red sauce that held oil in pools that glimmered in the light of the candle. It was warm inside and I looked out on the wide and wintry world and felt a momentary cosiness that was blown away by the sight of Coffee Teeth across from me. This woman was in her early thirties: a time when I hoped to have a baby girl asleep on my chest as I watched sports on television during long sunny weekends in some country retreat, an age when I hoped to have millions squirrelled into a Luxembourg account and no mortgage and a wife with a body left unravaged by time.

But Coffee Teeth did the same job as me. She spent her weekends in the office with trips down to Starbucks as her only diversion, her only joy found in snatched cigarettes on the benches that lined the gravel path up Berkeley Square like mourners waiting for the coffin to pass. I pitied her, but I also feared her, because she whispered terrifying possibilities to me. Like it might not all turn out how I planned it. Like I might be stuck in a job that did not interest me or engage me or ever shine with any kind of joy, and it might not be temporary. This might be life. She lit a cigarette as she nibbled her garlic bread. I sat back and smiled at her, held her sad eyes for a moment.

'I'm glad too, Madison. Glad to be able to get to know you. It has been so strange, coming to work in an office where I really know nothing of the world we're supposed to be experts on. It didn't feel like Silverbirch had taken on many graduates before. I was a novice when I started here, just a kid. I always feel like I know so much less than anyone else, I feel so naked and vulnerable next to you guys with your years of experience and your qualifications and your knowledge of the markets back in the nineties.

'Because you've seen things develop. You have watched things building up from the old simple model of stocks and bonds. I imagine that all these derivatives and these structured products are so much simpler if you have seen them mature, if you have watched their first faltering steps. To tell you the truth, I feel so out of my depth sometimes I just want to wring my hands and throw the papers up in the air and walk out. Go and get a job doing something I know about. Turn up at a theatre on Shaftesbury Avenue and offer to do anything. Sell ice creams, clean out the dressing rooms, hang in the lighting gantry. I think I could feel some real happiness working in a theatre. I think I could be really joyful there.'

I drifted off into my thoughts, conjuring up pictures of myself with a pale-skinned girl on my arm, running my fingers through her hair as the curtains went down, sleeping in late in a dusty Soho attic with sunlight streaming through the slats of an old wooden blind. Then Madison began to cry, her face wrinkling into her snotty nose and her shoulders and glasses leaping, pouncing upon her sobs, red eyes opening wide with each intake of breath.

'I'm sorry, Charles,' she said, rising. She fumbled in her bag for a tissue and pressed it to her face. Then she put a twenty down on the table, laid a strangely dry and masculine hand on mine, and walked from the restaurant, wrapping her coat around her as she left. I sat and finished my meal, watching the young drift past the window on the way to nightclubs. It was half-term and blonde-haired girls trailed eager, floppy-fringed boys in their wake like swans leading their cygnets. I thought of them making their way to the clubs on Dover Street and Old Burlington Street and the drinking and the dancing and the embarrassing erections and then the choosing of the one, and fumbles in the cab and creeping over squeaking floorboards past mummy and daddy's room and then the hot sweet heaven of the dark girlish room.

Back in the office Madison had refashioned her make-up and sat staring at a PowerPoint presentation. She had extinguished some of the lights around us so that we could look out, past our screens into the dismal night. I followed the last traced paths of raindrops down the window, illuminated by the dim lights of the outside world. Then I looked over at Madison again. She brought her hands up to her face, pressed the heels of her hands into the corners of her eyes and coughed quietly. We both worked silently, the tapping of our fingers on keyboards and the hum of the air conditioning filling the empty space of the office. Much time passed. It was two in the morning and the lights of the outside world had extinguished as I put together graphs showing China's disposable income and automobiles bought by Indians and consumer debt in the Midwest. Madison stood up at her desk and stretched. I heard her bones click like an old woman's.

'Charles,' her voice was thin and awkward, rendered fragile and stumbling by such a long silence. 'Come over here, I want to show you something.' She was smiling in the half-light, her bloodshot eyes behind her glasses reflecting back an Excel spreadsheet, her skin revealing its every last imperfection in the cold white light. I stood up and went to stand behind Madison, thought for a moment and then brought my hands up to her shoulders and gently massaged the thick knotted muscle of the thin body that was so frail beneath my touch. I stopped quickly, wanting her to know that it was not meant to imply anything, not an attempt at romance.

'Oh, carry on. Please. I'm so tired and my shoulders hurt so much and . . . And it's nice to be touched by someone. It's nice of you. Thank you, Charles.' She rolled her head a half-turn to the left and I pressed my fingers into the taut skin of her neck, saw goose-flesh tumble down her collarbone as a gentle shudder passed through her. The last person I had massaged had been Vero, late at night when she had come home from working on a case that had bored and infuriated her in equal measure. I thought of her in the arms of her new boyfriend, Marc, whom she had described to me as 'a very interesting boy. You wouldn't like him, Charlie. He is too much like you.' I imagined the provincial contentment of their lives, the long walks and fine wines and the anaesthesia of routine. I tried to pretend to myself that Madison's shoulders were really Vero's, that we were at the house in Fulham, or better in our own home, together somewhere hot and scented with night-jasmine. Madison shook beneath my fingers again and began to speak, facing straight forward, her closed eyes reflected in her computer screen.

'I called you over because I wanted to show you something. Something I haven't shown anyone else at the company. I hope it won't make you think I'm sentimental or anything. Or any more so than you do already after my performance tonight.'

'Don't worry, Madison. I have really enjoyed myself tonight. Or enjoyed it as much as I could enjoy a Saturday night in the office. What was it you wanted to show me?'

She opened her eyes, tapped with her mouse and the spreadsheet on the screen disappeared and was replaced by a picture of Madison sitting on a park bench with a grey London skyline behind her. At her side sat a boy of ten or eleven, his skin very black, his eyes wide and looking sideways at her. She was holding his hand; he was half tugging away but not enough to break from her grasp. She was wearing a Wharton hooded sweatshirt and jeans. He was dressed in a black leather jacket with a yellow stripe down the arm and a blue baseball cap. His shoes were very old Nike trainers. I could see holes in the instep. They looked comfortable together. Madison seemed somehow proud of him; he was protective of her. And both of them shone brightly against the dreary background.

'This is Ray. He's my little secret. He's my sanity. I look after him every Sunday and we go to the park, or to a movie, or bowling. He's amazing. His mother died last year and his father is a bit of a mess. I mean he tries hard, but he's really young to look after a boy like Ray. He gives me so much perspective, helps me look at all of this . . .' She moved an arm sweepingly to indicate the room, ended up pointing at the CEO's office. I felt her tendons contract and release as she moved. I looked again at the boy. I saw his cheekiness, the amused air of indolence that covered up the love he felt for this strange, confused girl whose shoulders I pressed beneath whitening thumbs.

'Where does he live? How did you meet him? I think it's a wonderful thing to do. A rare thing. So many of us are just completely focused on our own lives. It must be good to have something to take you away from that.' I was a little jealous of the life that had come into her when she spoke of him, felt suddenly aware of my own selfish insularity.

'He lives in Dalston. It takes me an hour to get there from Gloucester Road. But it's so worth it. A friend of mine works for one of the investment banks and – I guess mainly for PR reasons – they have to spend one day every year working for a charity. She worked for the charity that finds mentors for inner-city kids. She saw Ray for one day, suggested that I take over from her. I mean she has kids and everything. It wasn't as if she could have done it herself. But I used to spend my weekends working or shopping or sitting at home staring at the television. Now I hang out with Ray instead. It's why I need to go home before it gets any later. I need to be on form for tomorrow. Are you nearly finished with your work? We're going to the Aquarium tomorrow. He loves the sharks and I promised to take him. If I don't leave now there's no way I'm getting up in the morning.'

I looked over at my desk. The screen flickered at me. Madison gently lifted my hands from her shoulders, pressed them for a moment before she let them go.

'I'll stay and finish these slides. You go, Madison. Enjoy tomorrow. I really think it's a fine thing to do. Maybe I could meet Ray one day.'

I listened to Madison packing up her bag, heard her computer shutting down. She said goodnight and then I was alone in the silence of the office. I turned out the remaining lights and stood at the window, watched Madison hail a cab in the square below. I sat back down at my desk, sighed and began to type.

When I awoke the next morning sunlight danced amongst leaves in the tree outside my room, flickering on the orange curtains I had half drawn when I staggered in, drunk with tiredness, at five in the morning. My eyes glowed green from the computer screen when I closed them. My dreams were populated by expanding and contracting Excel cells, graphs whose every spike and trough I felt like a rollercoaster, numbers coming towards and rushing past me; then I woke up sweating to find that I had slept through lunch and well into the afternoon. My one day of freedom had been eaten away.

I felt a wave of misery that swelled bright and febrile, breaking through the fog of my exhausted mind. I waited for the feeling to pass, but a sharp fear began to build in my chest, digging in its heels and pressing against me. With a rush that passed through the flat like a storm, like the aftershock of a bomb, panic hit me. I pressed a hand to my heart and felt it beating fast and hard and – wait, there, a flutter – irregular. I was having a heart attack. I leapt up from the bed and raced to the bathroom, thrust my head under the cold tap in the cracked lilac sink, then staggered backwards out of the room, remembering somewhere that the bathroom was the most common place for heart-attack victims to die. I didn't want to die in that bathroom. And I didn't want to die. I could feel the veins in my neck pulsing blood in juddering starts, like cars surging forward and then stalling. I pulled on my jeans, a T-shirt and shoes without socks and staggered out into the cold winter sunlight. The light that came from the ragged sky dissolved rather than revealed the contours of the shuddering world. Eyes glued to the uneven grey paving slabs, sure it was a matter of minutes before my body shut down all together, I leant into the wind and headed up Munster Road towards Charing Cross Hospital.

Whether it was the cold of the air against my bare arms, or the gradual realisation that death was yet to seize me with its bony old fingers, or merely the passing of time, my heart began to slow. The pressure that had surrounded me, pressing in on my temples, squeezing down on my neck and my eyelids and all the soft parts of my body, started to drop. I began to see the dirty brown houses that surrounded me. I felt the hot breath of a bus and saw three girls descend, their hair scraped from pimpled foreheads. Slowly I turned back towards home, stunned by the violence of the wave that had hit me. I watched the skyline rotate as I let my arms spread wide and up to the sunshine. I continued to turn slowly on my heels.

Fear began to mount again as I made my way home, beginning as a quivering pinprick of darkness somewhere in the back of my mind and then growing to dominate all thoughts, all vision, all sensation. But this time it was not a heart attack, but the thought that I was going mad. I had seen my father plummet towards what looked like a breakdown. Perhaps I was headed there too. I opened the door with shaky fingers and crawled into bed. I stared at the weave of the cotton of my pillow cases, followed cracks across the ceiling, spread my fingers upwards and traced the tiny polygons of skin cells, the blemishes and moles, hair follicles and the gentle coves of cuticles breaking into nails spotted with flecks of white. I fell into a shallow sleep.

When I woke it was late afternoon and the world had about it all of the joylessness of Sunday evening. I switched on the radio and it was a BBC phone-in show hosted by a bitter racist and populated by paranoids and psychopaths. All of them could feel the weight of Sunday evening upon them. With the weekend over, it was time to pack bags, time to arrange pencils on the desk in order of size, time to pick out the tie and shirt, write the email that has been niggling and nagging whilst free time stretched out limitless ahead on Saturday night. All of these people having stored up their rage, called in to the radio show, and held forth on immigrants and students and the government. Perhaps they were just trying to put off facing the full brutal force of the week ahead. I could feel the rage that they suffered coming through the radio waves like a piece of violent and beautiful music.

I made myself a piece of toast and listened to the radio show, stirring spoon after spoon of sugar into my tea, watching the unnatural orange patterns cast by the streetlamp shining through leaves which fluttered in the rising wind out in the dreary night. I sat on the armchair in the dark and let the radio voices mix with the sounds of the night. A burglar alarm, cars passing in the windy darkness, the man upstairs ironing his shirts for the week. I heard him cross the floor and then back to the ironing board; he was listening to the same radio show and as he finished each shirt, the frail wire hangers chattered. Finally, I heard him brushing his teeth and singing quiet lonely songs to himself as he padded to the bedroom. I too moved towards bed, exhaustion and fear pulling the darkness in upon them; and I wrapped the cold, greasy duvet around me and buried my head under the pillow.

The next morning the alarm woke me from a sleep shadowed by vague nightmares, corridors with locked doors, dripping taps and creaking floorboards, a face unrecognisable but very familiar always a few steps too far ahead for me to catch. I pulled on my clothes in the dark and looked red-eyed at myself in the bathroom mirror as I brushed my teeth until I had to turn away, scared of what might be revealed by looking too long into that hopeless young face. The feeling of misery, less sharp but deeper than the night before, sat heavy on my chest as I stepped out into the cold rain, pulled my coat high about my face and set out for the Tube. The old lady tramp was rocking slowly backwards and forwards on her haunches, her legs drawn up to her chest, a thin moan advancing and retreating as she pitched, her bones creaking, her thick layered clothes rustling and squelching in the damp darkness. I placed the usual apple beside her and, for the first time, she turned up towards me, baring yellow-brown teeth and wide black eyes which were surprisingly clear but very distant. She looked through and past me, off into some bleak wild distance.

At work, I sat at my desk and felt the blood move in my veins. My hands grew cool and my breathing quickened at the memory of my blind flight towards the hospital, clutching at my heaving heart. The pattern of my fear was layered, textured, complex. As the markets moved around me, as the portfolio managers yelled for coffee and slammed phones into cradles and threw paper planes at one another, I sat entirely still and felt the fear creeping upon me once again. Madison looked at me, at first with friendship, then concern, then, as I ignored her and stared only ahead of myself, through into the electronic depths of my computer, hostility. Euphonium was on holiday in Devon with a lady-friend from the orchestra. Yannis, weekend-tan from a party in Marrakech, lolled backwards in his chair and spoke to his mother in high plangent Greek, occasionally leaning away from the phone to cough and spit gobs of grey-green mucus in and around his bin. Lothar was in meetings with the CEO and I welcomed his absence as the panic washed over me.

The fear came in waves, each one distinct in tone, each personified by a different terror. Firstly was the fear of the attack to come, the memory of the last attack, the sense that the next would be more brutal than the last. I sat and shook quietly, my breathing quickened and my lungs filled in quick hollow pants. I drew the cold still air of the office into my panting lungs. Then I began to feel my heart, the skittering insistence of the pulse in my throat, the painful press of ribs and racing lungs. My thoughts became circular, feasting upon scraps of information I had picked up scanning leaflets in the doctor's surgery or on casualty-ward soaps. Shooting pains in the left arm followed by a stabbing pain in the centre of the chest. I massaged my left shoulder, felt the muscles contract and then quiver. Often heart-attack victims thought they had indigestion. Immediately I began to burp, felt my stomach churning, sat up straighter in my chair. My mind was directing my symptoms and then I felt true terror beginning to bite.

It came at me with a quivering, almost beautiful violence. I stood up, knocking my coffee onto the floor and sending out a spumey whirl of cappuccino from the spout of the paper cup. Madison raised her eyebrows at me and I tried to smile. She squinted at the rictus of my face, seemed about to say something and then turned back to her screen. I rushed down the corridor, hand once again on heart. Then out of the office, out into the misty dankness of Berkeley Square. The coolness of the air sobered me for a moment and I leant against the cold stone of the building and tried to compose myself. I walked slowly, deliberately, my mind following the same path it had taken the night before. Now the immediate fear of physical collapse had passed, I began to worry again that I was losing my mind, that these were the first symptoms of an inevitable decline which would end in a state-run home surrounded by nurses with stranglers' arms.

There was a chemist on Berkeley Street that sold expensive herbal impotence treatments and boasted a wall of vitamin pills like a periodic table of hypochondria. I staggered into the cool dark interior. A little Indian man with a soft, wise smile made me sit down, poured a cup of steaming tea, and stood over me, pulling at the strap of his watch.

'It's my heart. Or maybe not my heart. Surely it can't be my heart at this age? I'm only twenty-four. But it beats so fast. And I feel this adrenalin rushing through me. And I panic. I mean properly panic. Can you give me an ECG or something? Something to tell me that it's just in my head?'

He smiled, nodded to himself, turned away from me and pulled boxes from the pigeon holes behind the long counter. Finally a rectangular green box, raised Braille inscription layered over the label. He popped out two blue pills, placed them in my sweaty cold palm.

'Take one of these next time you feel an attack coming on. Even half for the first time. Then take another half if it doesn't work. No charge this time. See if that helps. If it doesn't, then come back here immediately and we'll run some tests. But I have a feeling this will work.'

He turned back to his wall of vitamins and I pulled myself through the door and out into the misty morning.

On the way back to the office I bought a Diet Coke and sat in the still silent heart of Berkeley Square, squatting under the dwarf pagoda, my trousers damp where they met moist stone. With the panic still present in the outskirts of my mind, still circling like a desert bird, I took one of the pills. It sat bitter for a moment in the back of my throat, and then I swallowed it down.

Long minutes passed and the world slowly dragged life into itself. Faint sunlight flickered at the top of the pale bare plane trees. A blackbird began to sing high above me. The noise of traffic and the relentless bustling hum of London slowly cut through the mist. And the panic disappeared. I felt my eyelids sagging, rose slowly from my crouch and made my way in a floating dream back to the office. The day passed swiftly and in starts. Only occasionally did anything external intrude upon my honeyed thoughts. I returned to the chemist in the afternoon to purchase a packet of thirty-two of the bitter blue pills.

CHAPTER 6

Success

With dead eyes and dead hands I navigated the world. Walking to work in the mornings I pressed half a blue pill into the furry lining of my cheek and felt it melt, bitter and comforting as I sat on the fusty orange seats of the Tube and watched flares of electricity light up the darkness of tunnels. I had stopped reading. Instead I just watched.

It became difficult to imagine the world without the fuzzy blue glow of the pills. I had gone to the chemist again a week after my first purchase, told him I was going on a long business trip. Several months. Would need a couple more packets to tide me over. The old Indian looked at me sadly as he handed over the pills. I sat in long meetings as economists mouthed dismal words about the coming depreciation of the dollar and the end of the bull market and how cycles must turn and I let their words bleed down the walls, let them stir up anxiety in other chests. In my own, all was serene. The pills helped me to appreciate the monotonous nature of my work. As I filled out cashflow statements and balance sheets and looked at the movement of inventories and accounts receivable, I leant towards and away from my keyboard like a pianist lost in the beauty of his music, turning my head slightly as I rocked.

I spoke to Henry rarely. He was living a life of real interest: he now had his name above the articles he wrote, his style was lucid and mature and very human. His work dealt with the minor catastrophes of British life: a women's refuge in Hull that had lost its funding and was having to close; a group of wide-eyed child prostitutes in Birmingham who were being sent home to Albania and the parents who had sold them into slavery in the first place; a veteran of El Alamein who was living in a squalid tenement flat with no heating or running water in Eastbourne. All of the articles were illustrated with Henry's haunting, intimate photographs, a style he had perfected amongst the homeless and destitute who gravitated to the silver lash of the Thames like iron filings to a magnet. On Sundays I read his articles with a mixture of pride and envy. I always texted a word of congratulations. His replies were friendly but formal. We were like old lovers, overly solicitous in respect of what had passed and was now irretrievable.

I needed more pills with each week that passed, and often woke in a pool of cold dampness, my hair slick with sweat, my feet like ice on the carpet as I stumbled to the bathroom and fumbled in the cabinet until I found the little green packet and popped out a dose of calm and sleep and oblivion. Lothar was noticing how sluggish I had become, that my work was peppered with small, obvious errors, that I no longer joked with Euphonium by the water cooler, no longer engaged the portfolio managers in semi-serious arguments about wine or the markets or politics. I approached life with the jaded anomie of an ancient hooker trying to turn one last trick before enforced retirement. Every morning I sat for twenty or thirty minutes on the cold plastic seat of the toilet, reading text messages from Vero and Henry from a year ago, looking at pictures I had taken of them on my blurred and shaky camera-phone.

It was Madison who spoke to me. One Tuesday morning in early March when Siberian winds blew straight up the Thames, across Green Park and down the collar of my jacket, she asked me to go and grab a coffee with her. We stood silently in the lift as we descended; I watched the still-bare branches of the trees in the square whipped by the wind. She was sad that we hadn't taken our relationship further after the night we had worked late together. Not that she had any romantic interest in me, but I sensed that she had rarely – perhaps never – confided in anyone else the way she confided in me that night. That no one else knew how lonely she was, how frightened she was by the emptiness of her existence, her dependence on the rush of the markets, her time with Ray. She had shown me the pale white belly of her tragedy, and ever since I had been silent and dismissive, a shadowy image flickering across the day.

'Are you OK, Charles? You've been so distant the last few weeks. I thought maybe it was just me, but I know Lothar is worried about you. Worried that you're looking for another job. He wanted me to make sure you know that you're highly regarded. That people think very well of your work. He thinks you've taken your eye off the ball recently. I'm worried about you too. Are you unhappy? Is there anything I can do?' She was nervous, she flicked the ash of her cigarette too often as we stood in the grey morning, our coffee steaming, our breath steaming, and the cigarette smoke whipped swirling away by the wind.

'I'm fine. Seriously, I'm fine. I've just been doing a lot of thinking recently. After we had dinner that night, I just realised that I needed to think about where my life was going. And that is what I have been doing. Just thinking.' I flicked my cigarette in an arc towards the gutter and lit another. 'And I'm scared. Scared that the newspapers might be true. That the economists might be right. That you might be right, Madison. That the financial markets might collapse, that the good times can't last forever, and I have done all this work, lost out the past year and a bit of my life all for nothing. Because that's how they get you into it, isn't it? Pay the people at the top enough and you'll have a ready supply of slave labour willing to work themselves to the bone in the hope of one day earning that money for themselves. But what if everything changes? What if the salad days don't last that long?'

She looked at me, and I could see anger in her bloodshot eyes.

'Just fight through it, Charles. There's something big going on next week. Some big reorganisation of the firm. Lothar thinks the CEO might be moving up to Chairman. The top portfolio manager – I guess either Bhavin or Webb – will move up to CEO, which means one of us might be promoted to portfolio manager. You mustn't tell him I told you. It's dead secret. Lothar only knows because he's on the personnel committee and he has a board meeting in his diary for next week. So be patient. Believe in yourself, Charles. This market is all about confidence and you have every right to be confident in yourself.'

We finished our coffees and made our way back up to the office. Her words had punctured the haze of my addled mind. Portfolio Manager. I longed to see those words on the raised black lettering of my business cards. So much more glamorous than Analyst. So much classier. Lothar would remain head of research. Euphonium had no ambition. Yannis was lazy and constantly hungover and brainless. It left only Madison and me. She had been there longer, but she lacked the easy muscular familiarity that I shared with Bhavin and Webb. She wilted quickly under the intensity of their interrogation, looked weak and deer-like when they pressed her for opinions. I could see that they enjoyed her discomfort, that it confirmed something they held true about women in finance. Even Catrina, the one female portfolio manager, a slick forty-something Australian with severe red hair and deliberately ridiculous power suits, seemed to scorn the mousy American girl with her permanently stained teeth and her low voice and darting eyes.

I walked back into the office taller, more purposeful, sat at my desk and opened spreadsheets, checked for errors, went through a cashflow statement I had designed ensuring that all of the numbers stacked up. Lothar came and stood behind me and put a hand on my shoulder.

'How's it going, Charles? Ah, you're working on the pipeline securitisation. Very good. Think that'll fly. Interesting cashflow profile. Keep up the good work, Charles. We need you here.'

I glowed in the light of his public praise, caught Madison's eyes, smiled shyly at her. Somewhere I hated myself. This was the misery of the blue pills. I had become mistrustful of my own emotions, unwilling to embrace happiness for fear it was merely a chemically inspired synaptic shudder, that there was no truth to the feeling. Similarly, any hint of depression or disappointment or even a contemplative questioning of the order of things was met by a fumbling hand in the inside pocket, the relieving sigh of the cracked pill, the deadening drift into a place where time and pain and enquiring thought disappeared. I knew that it was shallow and hateful and far removed from the ultimate goal of who I wanted to be, but I was happy that Lothar praised me. Excited at the thought that I might be made portfolio manager. I worked hard the rest of the day, hammering my fingers into the keyboard until my arms shook.

When I got home that night I sat in my sagging grey armchair, lit a cigarette and phoned Vero. Her brother answered on the third ring. I stumbled in French, reverted to English.

'Bonjour. C'est . . . Pourrais-je . . . Is Vero there please? It's Charlie.' A pause. Was he looking for her or trying to decide whether I deserved to speak to her? I heard footsteps on a tiled floor, heard the phone lifted into the air, heard her clear her throat.

'Charlie! How are you? Why haven't you called me more? I miss you. How's London? How's work? Oh, I have so much to tell you.' Her voice was cigarette-heavy, eager as a puppy, slightly drunk. I felt her fingers cover the mouthpiece as she shouted – a dead sound. '*Oui, Marc. Je suis au téléphone. Commence sans moi.*' Then her voice came back, warmer still, I could sense her curling up on a sofa or chair, could feel her twisting the telephone cord around a finger. 'Sorry. That's just my boyfriend. We are going to the cinema later. Heh, it's the high point of my week these days.'

'God, I haven't seen a film for years. Last time I went was with you, I think. I miss you, Vero. Things in London are pretty horrid. It's so grey. So grey and depressing. Like the whole city is in mourning or suffering from seasonal affective disorder. And I have been having these panic attacks. I think it's from working too hard. And the pills I'm taking to stop the panic are making me stupid. And I don't want to be fired now I have found somewhere that's slow enough to pay me for my muddy-headed work.' I drew on my cigarette, blew smoke to the ceiling, watched it circle the harsh white lamp in its crepe shade.

'You mustn't push yourself too hard, Charlie. My brother had panic attacks during his bac. He had to take beta blockers in the exam hall.'

'These pills are really deadening my mind. I think that's why I called you. Just to feel something. The panic attacks are horrid. Like heart attacks. They certainly feel that monumental. That world-altering.'

'Oh, you poor thing. Why don't you come down and visit in Normandy? It would be lovely to see you. And I'd like you to meet Marc.' Her voice slowed down. She was nervous and I could hear the edge to her words, the hesitation before she mentioned her boyfriend. I pressed on regardless.

'I was hoping . . . What I was hoping, Vero, was that you might come back to London.' I could picture her as I said the words, heard her form her lips into a tactful withdrawal, I continued, faster now. 'I haven't done much of a selling job. Know you must be thinking that London is the last place you want to be. But I need you here. I haven't heard from Henry in weeks. Think he's off travelling with his father. Doing a piece on India for the paper. So it's just me and I can't last much longer without you . . . Please, Vero. Please.' I was shaking and the words were projected from far away, nothing to do with my mind, which was like a lost child wandering in darkness. I felt my pockets, found a pill, crushed it between chattering teeth. I could tell that Vero was sitting up straight now, her finger no longer twined in the cord, her body no longer serpentine on the cushions.

'Charlie. Darling Charlie. It will be all right. You must remember how wonderful you are. And girls will cross continents to stare into your eyes and hold your face in their hands and kiss you. And I will come and visit. I will. But I can't come over. I have a life here. And . . . And I have something I need to tell you. Charlie . . . Marc has asked me to marry him. And I have said yes. I'm so sorry, Charlie. I love you. Really I do. But Marc is what I need right now. He's older than me. He has seen the world, and he came back to be here. Just like I did. Oh Charlie . . .'

I thought about dropping the telephone, leaving her to listen for a while, let her become worried that she'd hear the sound of a shotgun or the thud of a body kicking a chair away and testing the strength of a silk tie. But I realised, even through my hazy mind, that this would have been theatrical and hurtful, so I bit my lip and choked my way swiftly to the end of the conversation.

'Don't worry. That's great. Really, congratulations, Vero. I'm pleased for you. Really I am. And just forget this conversation. I'm over-tired. Honestly, that's all it is. I'll be fine. And I'd love to meet Marc.'

'You call me whenever you need to. And I'll come over to see you after the wedding in July. We'll have fun, just like the old times. We'll go to Boujis together. Just stay strong, Charlie. Stay strong, *mon amour.*'

I hung up the telephone and made cheese on toast, wandered the room in circles eating the moist and greasy bread, then lay down on the bed fully clothed. The howling of the wind shadowed my sleep and soundtracked dreams of Vero flying naked through the air, her body stretched out huge above me. She plunges through the high air, her skin dark against the blue sky flecked with clouds. Birds fly crazy circles around her head. She looks down at me, smiles, and the dream shatters, leaving nothing but the infernal scream of the wind.

I woke in the morning and had perhaps ten seconds of heavenly befuddlement in the very silent aftermath of the alarm clock before I remembered that Vero was marrying someone else, that I would be forever alone, that my dreams of earning enough to buy a wisteria-wrapped country pile and live with her a life of sybaritic sexual excess were never to come true. I arrived at work in an unironed shirt, my hair unwashed and my nails too long and dirty grey. I had taken three of the blue pills on my way in, so I didn't notice the buzz that filled the long office. More energy than was usual for a Wednesday morning. So many phones ringing, and all of the portfolio managers clustered around the CEO's door like ships blockading a harbour. Lothar moved around the periphery of them, trying to pick up what was being shouted back and forth between the CEO and one of the portfolio managers. Madison passed me a copy of *Metro*, turned to an inside page.

'*Millionaire Hedge Fund Manager Leaves Porsche in Car Park for Six Months – "I was Too Busy to Move it" Claims Silverbirch Founder.*' The piece speculated on the CEO's worth, listed his properties, his charitable donations, recalled a memorable meal he had given at The Square where he had tipped every waiter £100 and given the sommelier a two-grand Rolex. With hysterical excitement the paper detailed the £6,000 parking fine, the pinched and guarded words of the NCP official, the short statement made by the CEO's press officer. Only at the very end, as an afterthought, did it mention that he was stepping down as CEO to concentrate upon his role as Chairman with immediate effect. He could not be reached for comment on this news, but it was thought that his replacement would be an internal promotion.

The shouting grew louder and David Webb stormed out of the office, calling over his shoulder and pushing Lothar out of the way as he strode towards his desk.

'I can't believe you made that wanker . . . Do you not appreciate one fucking iota of what I have done for this business? I mean I'm glad. I'm de-fucking-lighted that you'll have to get by without me now. I'm going to enjoy lying on a beach and reading in the business pages about the monumental fuckery he's going to make of the firm. You owed me, Aldous. You owed me and you let me down.'

He picked up his jacket with one hand, a pile of red files with the other and marched towards the door. The room was very quiet. Madison and I, who were the furthest away, moved to stand beside Lothar, who was rubbing his knee where he had hit it moving out of Webb's way. Then the CEO came out of his office, his arm around Bhavin Sharma. Both of them held lit cigars and the smoke spread horizontally, moved by the secret currents of the air-con that whipped unseen through the room. The CEO coughed as he dragged on the turd-like cigar, beckoned for us to draw nearer.

'Sorry you had to witness that unseemly little incident, ladies and gentlemen. For every winner there has to be . . . the opposite. You may have seen the news this morning. Skilfully hidden by our PR people who fed the press some far more juicy gossip about me. Tell a story that chimes with people's expectations, and it's easy to bury the real news. So, firstly, please join me in welcoming Bhavin Sharma as your new CEO. He was always the obvious choice, will do a fine job, indeed I have been grooming him to succeed me ever since he left the world of government bonds and joined me to do something far more interesting . . . When was it? Seven, eight years ago, Bhav?'

'That's right, Aldous.' Bhavin tried to swallow an enormous grin as he exhaled silver-grey smoke. His face seemed to rush towards the strip of strange pink skin that surrounded his mouth. It was perhaps a childhood burn, or the correction of a hare-lip gone wrong, and was partly covered by a tight-cropped black beard, but I could see the skin shimmer as he smiled, and there was something inhuman, something metallic and sickening about the white-pink slash that crossed his mouth. I looked back to the CEO – now the Chairman.

'So I'll be spending more time on my boat, more time with my family. Dirty job but someone's got to do it. You must think of me as a parent who, having seen you grow into something quite wonderful, gives you the freedom to now truly exploit your potential. And I'll be back on a regular basis to check on Bhavin.' Here he aimed a punch at his replacement. Perhaps it was harder than he had intended, or perhaps exactly as hard. Bhavin winced and choked on his smoke.

'Now I'll leave it for Bhavin to announce his first decision as CEO. Ladies and gentlemen, it has been a very great pleasure working with you.'

There was some clapping, Lothar whistled through his teeth, someone banged on a table. I saw Euphonium make a strange trumpeting gesture. Then Bhavin held up his gently smoking hand for silence.

'Thanks, Aldous. Of course you made the right choice. Sad to see Webby go, but that's business. Right then. So replacing me and Webby as sole head of the portfolio management team is Catrina Meyer.' The red-headed Australian blushed, stepped forward into the shadow of her enormous shoulder-pads, tottered for a moment on the needle-thin stilettos that extended beneath her long crane's legs. 'And two further promotions, who will have the pleasure of reporting to Catrina in her new role, our newest portfolio managers, Yannis Lascarides and Charles Wales. Welcome, boys. I know you'll do a great job.'

I was grinning madly around the office; Yannis hugged me as Lothar was pumping my hand and Euphonium murmured something about how well we'd done. I walked over to Catrina, who embraced me in a cloud of Guerlain and then embraced Yannis and then both of us, our cheeks against her synthetic breasts. Bhavin thrust a cigar into my hand, the Chairman was ruffling Yannis's hair and champagne appeared on a trolley with smudged glasses and Kettle Chips. Only then did I look down the room and see Madison sitting very straight in her seat. She was typing furiously; her glasses jumped on her nose every time she pressed the space bar. She shuddered imperceptibly as Euphonium walked over to her and put a large and gentle hand on her shoulder. I made up my mind to speak to her later that day, but Bhavin insisted we go out to Langan's for lunch. We got hugely drunk, moved on to the pub where Yannis and I downed the shots that Catrina and Bhavin bought us, and I was dancing on the bar with my arms held high, and forgot about Madison altogether.

We went to a club on High Street Ken and Catrina staggered away from us as we walked past the bouncers. I followed her, hailed a cab and watched as she vomited on her shoes. I hailed another taxi. We saw her fall backwards until she was lying down on the back seat of the cab. A lone arm shot up and waved to us, the rest of her out of sight as we turned and re-entered the club.

I didn't think about Madison until I came in the next morning and she was sitting at her computer, still very upright. I made my way through a bleary hungover world to my old seat, picked up my books and papers and strode down the office to my new desk with its high partition and walnut veneer and soft leather seat. There was a Blackberry on the desk and a pen with the Silverbirch logo and a leather file with my name engraved in gold letters. Yannis didn't come in until past eleven, although my presence was purely physical. Catrina had taken the day off in anticipation of her hangover, so I had to man the phones and try desperately to work out what my new job entailed. Bhavin came out of his office as I was choking down the last bite of a bacon and fried egg sandwich, grease dripping down my chin.

'How's the desk, Charles? How're the markets? What're you up to?' His piggy face all but obscured his eyes, which were tiny and black. His goatee was flecked with white streaks that could well have been dyed; his hair bore the same regular pattern of distinguished grey hairs. The pinkness of the skin around his mouth was visceral, like the flesh of organ parts caught under the bright white lights of an operating theatre. He wore beautiful Hermès ties and aftershave that was sweet and citrus and mixed in strange swirling patterns with my breakfast as I inhaled. He spoke with the over-emphasised manner of a drunk trying to persuade a policeman of his sobriety. He had brought his putter in with him and was practising hitting a ball through his office and into a coffee cup placed behind my chair.

'Oh. Yes, Bhavin. I mean . . . Oil's up. Eighty a barrel. And stocks are up too. Good shot. US futures higher. Couple of upgrades in autos. Very quiet.'

'It doesn't surprise me. I've been taking calls all morning from traders. Everyone wants to know whether me or Webby won out in the great power struggle. Nice to be able to calm their fears. Webby was far too emotional to do this job. Good lad, Webby – I was best man at his wedding – got nothing against him personally. But he didn't have the nuts for a job like this. I've got the vision. I've got the ambition. Now where's that Yannis? I know we were necking the sambucas last night, but that doesn't mean he gets a day off. I mean seriously.'

I flicked at my mouse, moving the cursor slowly across the screen, glad that I'd made the effort to struggle, nauseous, unwashed once more, through the grimy dawn to the office. I looked at Bhavin as he clicked at the Bloomberg screen, bringing up graph after graph just as the CEO had my first day in the office.

'Why didn't Madison get the job, Bhavin? I mean she's much more experienced than Yannis or me. And she works these incredibly long hours. And I know she really wanted it. I don't want you to think I'm not delighted, but I thought she'd have been the obvious choice.'

He looked closely at me, his eyes narrowing further to thin slits in his face. I noticed a wart at the corner of his left eye. It quivered slightly as he talked.

'Too much oestrogen there, Charles. Too much emotion. Catrina wouldn't have had her. There's a fragility there. A lack of balls. And not just in the literal sense. Do you get on well with her?'

'Yes. Yes, I guess I do.'

'Well, I would try and distance yourself if I was in your place. It's important that you get yourself some respect. That you show them that you're not the little gimp who spent a year brown-nosing the PMs and filling out meaningless spreadsheets that we never looked at. I'd go for a while without speaking to her. Just look really busy the whole time. Like this . . .' He clicked the screen again, picked up the phone, dialled furiously, lifted up a copy of *Trader* magazine, dropped it loudly and threw his hands up in a gesture of frustration. 'You see what I mean. It's all about the impression you give. All about the façade.'

He leant over me, his voice low and conspiratorial, the skin of his mouth twisting and dancing in the light of the computer screen.

'I know I shouldn't say this, politically incorrect and everything, but I don't like working with women. Don't like having meetings with them, don't like having to rely on them. I'll tell you a trick I have. Every time I'm in a meeting with a woman – whether it's Catrina or Madison or one of those butch female traders – and they start trying to pressure me or wheedle concessions out of me or kick up an emotional fuss about something minor, I remember my wife giving birth. I remember the complete loss of control, the screaming and the tears and the snot. I remember how weak she looked and how, just before the baby came out, she shat herself. Find an image like that to use for yourself. Really helps you keep your focus.'

He walked back into his office. I thought I might vomit. I looked ruefully down the room to my old desk. Madison had moved some of her books there. She was standing with the light behind her, and she caught my eye and raised a shy hand. Her glasses moved up her wrinkled nose as she smiled. I frowned, pretended I hadn't seen her, turned to the Bloomberg screen and clicked the mouse violently several times in imitation of Bhavin. The screen went black immediately and a frantic beeping started somewhere under my desk. I saw Madison laughing as someone from the technology department ran over and reached down to the terminal, fiddled for a moment until the noise stopped.

At the end of the day, my liver throbbing gently, my eyes drooping in front of the blurred screen, I packed up my week-end work, hoping I would be able to avoid coming into the office until Monday morning, knowing that I'd probably find a reason to come in on Saturday. Yannis had been excitedly calling his friends, speaking a mixture of Greek and his Eurotrash drawl.

'Portfolio manager now, baby. Portfolio manager. Who's the daddy? Gotta love it. Gotta love the promotion.' Bhavin threw a biro through his office door at Yannis's head and he spoke more quietly. 'Let's celebrate tonight, dude. My brother's in town. Let's see some chicks. Yeah. See you there. Peace out.'

As I slipped on my jacket and stepped towards the door Yannis reached out and grabbed my tie, pulling the knot tight around my neck.

'Charles. Charlie. Charles. Dude, where you going? We gotta celebrate properly tonight, man. Last night was just the aperitif. The *amuse-gueule* before the real party. The real shit is going down tonight, man. My brother's over from Beirut. He knows how to party, that motherfucker. He's crazy, man. Serious crazy. Let me buy you a beer at least. Let's go to the pub. The guys aren't due to be there for another hour.'

In the lift on the way down we stood together at the glass window, looking in at the offices as we descended. The lift stopped on the second floor to allow a fat, ruddy man stinking of sweat and professional frustration to sigh his way in. I looked across the atrium, through a window and into the office furthest from the lift and saw a blonde girl, young, dressed like a secretary, lean across a man's desk. He had grey hair and his back was turned to me. A blue suit jacket hung on the back of his chair. I could see dust particles dancing furiously in the light of the green-shaded lamp that sat on his desk. He laid his head on her shoulder as she leaned across him, and she placed a hand gently on his thinning hair. He looked up and I saw her – plain and tired-looking – smile down at him maternally. Then the lift began to descend again and they moved out of view.

Yannis and I sat in the smoky darkness of the pub. I realised that I hadn't taken any pills since the previous morning. That I had floated through the days in the glow of my success. The thought itself made me panic for a moment. Then I tapped my pocket and found not the packet of pills, but my Blackberry, my new business cards which were subtly more beautiful than before, the letters raised higher on an ecru background, the words *Portfolio Manager* slightly italicised, the dancing silver of the leafless tree flashed even in the low light.

I looked up at Yannis and smiled. He was smoking a filterless cigarette, flicking ash from its end in jerky, effete taps. His hair was slicked back with gel, his tie removed; he had pulled his collar over the lapel of his jacket. A huge gold signet ring glimmered in the soft light on his little finger.

'So, man. If you had to – for work reasons, I mean – if it came down to it, would you fuck Catrina?'

I spluttered into my Guinness, unsure of how to answer, of where the question had even come from.

'Umm . . . I don't know, Yannis. I can't really see how that would happen. But she's pretty old, isn't she? I mean she keeps herself in great shape, but still . . .'

'Her plastic surgeon and coke keep her in good shape, Chuck. You don't mind if I call you Chuck? I had a friend in Miami called Chuck. He was a crazy motherfucker. Crashed his motorbike – boom! – vegetable now. I get my sister to visit him sometimes when she's over there.'

'No. Chuck's fine. My friends call me Charlie.'

Yannis went to the bar again, bought himself vodka and tonic, another Guinness for me. His hands twitched and his legs jiggled under the table and all was movement, all commotion in his body.

'I'm so glad to get away from those fuckin' analysts, man. That girl – what's her name? Madison? – she needs a man. I never met a girl so damned boring. And the other two? Fucking losers. Can't make it as proper traders so they put down all their ideas on paper like it should mean something. I can't wait to screw up that bullshit in their faces.'

We talked about Bhavin, about how he had supposedly come up from selling coffees on the Citigroup trading floor to head of government bonds, then had defected with Webb to Silverbirch on a seven-figure guaranteed bonus. Yannis kept looking at his watch, only seemed interested in the conversation when he was talking. He tapped his fingers, edged a beer mat close to the edge of the table, nudged it so it fell, picked it up and started again. I saw his eyes scan the pub, watched his pupils dancing across the room behind me whenever I was talking. Then his face lit up.

'Hey, hey shitbag!' He called out to a boy who looked like him but squashed in some pressure chamber. It was Yannis's brother and he was perhaps five foot in his built-up heels. His hair was longer than that of his younger brother and oozed down onto the enormous collar of his shirt. It was propped away from his forehead by a pair of Gucci sunglasses. His fat fingers were thick with rings and he smoked the same cigarettes as Yannis. He waddled over to our table.

'Chuck, this is my brother Christos. Christos, this is Chuck.'

'Good to meet you, Chuck. I had a friend called Chuck. Crazy motherfucker. Now vegetable.' He made the sign of the cross with his fat fingers. His accent was thicker than Yannis's. 'We going to get real drunk tonight? Party like it's going out of fashion?'

'Sounds good, Christos. What are you drinking?' I rose to go to the bar, Christos pointed at his brother's vodka and tonic and lit another cigarette. As I squeezed past Christos, he patted my shoulder and shadow-boxed playfully at my chest. He followed me to the bar and ordered bottles of champagne, laying down two crisp fifty-pound notes on the sticky wooden bartop.

'As a chaser,' he laughed at me. 'I feel nervous if I don't have a bottle of champagne on hand. Even in a dive like this.'

We made our way back to the table and Yannis and Christos started shouting at each other in Greek. I couldn't tell if they were arguing seriously. Then Yannis beamed suddenly, leaned over and cupped his brother's chin in his hand.

'This guy is such a cocksucker, man. You be careful around him. Smooth operator with the ladies. I learnt everything I know from him.'

Christos grinned back at his brother and we clashed our champagne glasses together, sending golden bubbles high into the smoky air.

A tall man with blond highlighted hair and pale green eyes walked into the room, theatrically lit a cigarette as he waited for his eyes to adjust to the dim light, then strode over to us and threw his arms around Christos, who rose only slightly higher than his waist. The man was wearing a very skinny black suit, white shirt and black tie. His shoes were pointed and his belt shiny black crocodile. He spoke to Christos in rapid Italian, peppering his speech with hands swirled in ogees in the air, fingers pinched together and then flung apart in explosions.

The tall man sat beside me and offered his hand. He spoke with a clipped English accent that only betrayed his roots with a certain lengthening of the vowels. He passed me a cigarette from a battered packet of Lucky Strike, sat back in his chair, and looked around the small dark pub.

'My name is Lorenzo. But call me Enzo. I am a friend of Yannis. We were at school together in Switzerland. St Gallen. You know it?'

'I'm afraid not. My name is Charlie. Charlie Wales.'

'Ah, you're the Chuck that Yannis is always talking about. It's good to meet you. You got the promotion also? Congratulations.'

We sat in amiable silence for a while as Yannis and Christos continued to shout in Greek, and the pub began to fill up. Secretaries and estate agents first, and then the hedge fund managers, recent colonists of this part of town. Each group remained distinct, clustered in circles facing inwards. We blew our smoke out towards them.

'So, Enzo. What is it you do? How do you know Yannis? I suppose I don't know much about him at all. Haven't really spoken to him about his family or his background or anything. I know he's rich but what does his father do?'

He smiled, turned towards me with his dark eyebrows pressed close together.

'You wouldn't know it from his sons. They're really like fireworks these two, you know? Yannis and Christos's father runs a firm of loss adjusters for shipping insurance. Terribly dull man. He came out of a village in the mountains on the back of a goat. Literally, a no one dumped on the streets of Athens. And now he's the big man. Worth two or three hundred million euros. Lives on a boat and spends his days lamenting his sons' playboy lifestyles and sending people on mad chases around the Philippines looking for ships that pirates have resprayed in Macau, run up the coast and then down through the Malacca Straits. That's a job I'd like. A pirate, I mean. All that fresh air and excitement. And great hair those guys have.

'Until I realise that particular ambition, I'm features editor at *Arena*. Spend my days trying desperately to get inside the mind of a readership I don't care about, my evenings hanging out with people more famous and successful than I can be bothered to be. I really think that magazine workers are the unhappiest people on earth. I suppose I'm lucky that I don't have to worry about money. My father owns the second biggest mobile-phone network in Italy. But I focus on status instead. If I don't get an exclusive interview with the latest hot Hollywood starlet I die. If I don't get flown all-expenses to the big football game, get backstage for the gig with gold-dust tickets, all of this affects me in the most humiliating way.

'But it's the people who work with me that are most tragic. Because they don't even have the money. At least I can buy myself pleasure, spend my way to bloated fulfilment. But magazine people, they have to spend their time hanging onto the coat-tails of the brilliant. They get to see through the keyholes of a world which is forever materially out of their reach. And this must destroy them. They live in miserable flats in postcodes I'd need a Sherpa to find and they writhe and coil with the gross unjustness of it all. And then they catch the long and lonely Tube ride into town and they flash their eyes and flare their coked-up noses at the vapid R & B singers and moronic soap stars. And it all passes so quickly for them, and before they know it they are in a Toyota Camry driven by a half-blind Nigerian trying to describe how to find the dead-end road in N17.'

Yannis leant over to us. He was sweating at the temples; his eyes were wide and very dark.

'Let's go and see some girls. I can't wait any longer. It's so dead here, man. Let's go.' He slapped me on the back, grabbed the collar of my jacket, hoisted me to my feet. 'Glad you got to know Enzo, man. My best friend. Cool motherfucker. Reminds me of you. All about the long words and the charm. You got any Italian blood, Chuck? You look like you might be a little bit Italian.'

We walked out into the cold shudder of the night, made a few abortive forays down quiet cobbled mews streets before we found our way into Shepherd Market, past the red-light windows of second-floor apartments, and then up a curved starlit staircase into a club where we were frisked by a bear of a man. In the main room music from my childhood played: saccharine eighties hits that I had forgotten and loved and was delighted to rediscover. I remembered my mother listening to the songs in the car as she drove me to cross-country matches, humming along and drumming her fingers on the steering wheel, looking many times, then pulling out hesitantly and flooring the accelerator to overtake, sending the car's engine into a high and painful whine.

We sat down and lit our cigarettes in unison; Christos ordered more champagne. After a few minutes a tall black girl, Amazonian, strode onto the stage and began to remove her clothes. First she stripped down to a wire-thin thong and then this too was ripped off. I had been to a strip club before, had visited Betty Brown's Show Bar on Lothian Road with the boys at Edinburgh, had seen the red-pocked bikini lines, the three-day stubble armpits, the girls' eyes that begged for rescue or euthanasia. This was something altogether more wonderful, something quite glamorous. The girl swirled around the pole like a wraith, wrapping her long legs high above her naked body, she flickered like mist through the foot-lights, the muscles in her legs standing out and disappearing into the beautiful dark nothingness between her legs. Her breasts defied all laws of physics, pouncing upwards as she laughed to herself when a small and very drunk Korean man tried to jump onto the stage with her and was immediately wrestled to the floor by another bear-guard. She had dark green tattoos that were just visible against her skin: aboriginal inscriptions and totems that ran across her body like blood, ancient and otherworldly in the stage light. I looked over at Yannis.

'She's amazing.'

'You like it, huh? Pretty fuckin' fantastic this place. The girls are all students, nurses, actresses. Awesome chicks here. Have another drink man. You look like you need it.'

The room began to fill up: a group of Japanese occupied a table next to the Koreans and good-natured banter flowed between them. Then a gang of City traders who had been out with clients stumbled in, loosening their ties and shouting for champagne. I picked up my glass and walked over to the bar that ran down one side of the room as a new dancer occupied the stage. She was smaller than the girl before. She had skin that shimmered with glitter under the lights, her hair was long and blonde and her eyes were wide and innocent; she stared directly at me, her eyes like the gaping mouths of rattlesnakes, drawing me towards them. I stumbled, she mouthed something at me, turned away.

She looked so young. Her earrings were clip-on, as if her mother hadn't allowed her to get them pierced yet. Her fingers were very long, and she held them up to her shoulders and moved them slowly down her skinny, slightly boyish body. Her pubic hair was very blonde, perhaps dyed, quite thick when she opened her legs, facing away from the stage and bent to touch her toes, revealing the pink slash of her labia and the brown nut of her arsehole. I put my hand out and grabbed the gold rail that ran along the bar; it was slick and sweaty and I felt sick for a moment, saw the velvet walls and the red velvet booth cushions like lung tissue, pulsating in the swirl of my drunkenness. Enzo appeared beside me and bought a beer for us both. We watched the girl finish her routine in silence; he tapped on the bar with his fingers, ground out a half-finished cigarette with his thumb and leant towards me.

'Shall we have a private dance? I saw you looking at that last chick. And I'm pretty sure she said she loved you when she was on stage. Why don't we go and get some girls to take off their clothes for us? My treat.'

He strolled to a padded door at the back of the room and spoke to the bear-man stationed at the door, who looked at him closely and then ushered him through. I followed into a labyrinth of booths, low lighting, dry ice at floor level. A girl appeared, took our beers for us and laid them next to a sofa in one of the booths. I sat beside Enzo, felt the greasy material of the banquette beneath my thighs. Enzo spoke to a waitress, and soon the black girl who had been first on stage and then the blonde who had followed her were sitting next to us. The blonde girl was wearing a camouflage-print singlet and white denim hotpants, cowboy boots that were the colour of her skin so it was difficult to see where her legs ended and the boots began. Enzo raised his glass to them both.

'Ladies. My name is Enzo. This is Chuck. A glass of champagne?'

The black girl nodded and Enzo motioned to the waitress. The blonde perched awkwardly on the bench beside me, even though there wasn't really room for her. I moved closer to Enzo and her skinny buttocks shuffled along towards me. The champagne arrived and I noticed that the girl's eyes were the same yellow-green as the liquid in the glass. She held it up to her lips and the champagne reflected dappled hidden lights across her cheeks.

'I'm Loretta. Nice to meet you. Thanks for the champagne.' Her voice was quiet, whispered of a Scottish childhood forgotten in the rush to become the sophisticated city girl. Her eyes were downturned as she drew one leg up to her chest and picked at the stitching of her cowboy boot, playing out the thread with her long fingers. 'Would you like a dance then? Or we can just talk if you want.' The black girl was sitting on Enzo's lap. Her top was already off and the remarkable breasts were edging slowly towards Enzo's pursed lips.

'Yes. I'd like that. I'd like a dance, I mean.'

She rose, kicking off the cowboy boots and revealing large spindly feet, toes that she curled upwards. Her legs had a thin line of blonde hair that ran down from her thighs, paused at knees white-scarred from childhood accidents, and then resumed down the front of her shins. 'Sunday Bloody Sunday' began to play and she put down her glass with a dainty curtsey. Her hips moved gently and she swayed, a little forced, a little sad. Leaning over me she slowly lifted the camouflage singlet over her head. I could see the faint chalky trace of deodorant clinging to her underarms. She dropped the singlet and fumbled to unclasp her black bra. Then small tits with dark erect nipples. She brushed them across my face, slowly wriggled out of her hotpants; she was wearing just a black G-string and she sat down hard on my lap. She rested for a moment facing out into the room, watching one of the other girls – naked, Hispanic, brooding – who was moving rhythmically up and down atop one of the Japanese businessmen. The little man wore a short-sleeved white shirt, yellow tie pulled loose around his neck; he raised his hand and gave me a thumbs-up, grinning a huge grin.

Loretta nestled back onto me, leant her head back so that it rested on my shoulder and looked up at me with her pale eyes. I could feel the gentle movement of her thigh muscles as she shifted her weight on my lap, the rise and fall of her breath as her bony back pressed into my chest.

'So what do you do then? What's your job?' She asked, her voice soft and breathy. The black girl was naked; her arms on the bench and her head in Enzo's lap, she slowly dragged her body upwards, like a dog with broken hind legs trying to greet its master. Finally she was sitting in his lap, his face buried in the cavity between her breasts.

'I um . . .' I saw three of the City traders being ejected from the room by a security guard, two of the strippers looking disgustedly after them. I didn't want to be associated with these boorish characters, didn't want this beautiful girl to think of me as one of the money-obsessed Neanderthals who pawed her and wouldn't speak to her and drew great hardness into their eyes as they placed coke-slick notes in her G-string.

'He's a professional poker player. Both of us are.' Enzo leaned over to us, shifted the black girl backwards a little so we could see him. 'We just won big at the Palm Beach. Chuck there scooped the big prize. Played all last night. We're still on the razzle. We could take you out after this, hang out until dawn and then buy you diamonds on Bond Street.'

'Oh come on,' Loretta leant over and pulled at his tie, looked at the black girl and laughed. 'Will you look at these two jokers? Are you serious? Do you really make a living out of playing cards?' Enzo looked at me, I shook my head to clear it and slipped my arms around Loretta, careful not to touch her breasts.

'Yeah, we do. I live in Lake Tahoe. Only come over to London for tournaments. Enzo's based in Reno. He's a great player. We always hook up when we're in Vegas.'

'Oh, that's so cool. I'd love to go to Vegas. I saw that film with Nicolas Cage. It's such a glamorous place. I like places that have all that glitz and glamour and still have a really seedy underbelly. An Arab guy flew a bunch of us out to a party in Dubai. It was like that out there. All polished glass and gold and yet, out of sight, hidden from that very harsh light, hookers and drugs and debauchery.' She snuggled closer up to me, squirmed as if remembering it, pulled my arms tighter around her and ground her bony arse against my erection. She was small in my grasp; I suddenly felt very protective of her.

'How long have you been working here, Loretta?'

'Not long.' She looked at me sullenly for a moment, then her eyes softened. 'A year. Almost a year now.'

'I suppose that must feel like a long time.'

'A year's a year, you know?' She looked sulky, defensive again.

'Is it good money? I mean is it really worthwhile?'

'Yes. Yes it can be very good. Some weeks not, but it's enough to make you not want to leave.'

'I think maybe all jobs are like that. They pay you just enough to keep you working, just enough to stop you saying fuck it all and taking off into the sunset. Or maybe that's just something to do with our stage of capitalism. That, no matter how much we earn, the cost of the things that seem essential for a decent existence is enough to keep us running on the wheel. We are programmed to feel dissatisfied with what we have. That we are meant to feel miserable and that the only way out is to achieve some mythical level of wealth that will allow us to escape.'

'I'm fine,' she said. 'I'll be fine. I actually like this job. Things could be a hell of a lot worse for me. I just can't get sucked in. I see some of the girls who, I don't know, they believe it all somehow. Get carried away by the talk of the money and the cars and the holidays. I see that it's just a ridiculous joke. Just mad that this is my job. Mad.'

She sipped her champagne, hiccupped, and a little of the gold liquid dribbled down her chin and over her breasts to collect in the soft hollow of her stomach. She looked around the room, then down at me, something rather pitying in her eyes.

Her voice suddenly became hard, her muscles tense against

me. She put down the champagne glass and stretched out her fingers so that they looked like claws.

'Shit, the boss is looking at me. I've spent a bit long with you. Shall I finish the dance?'

She turned to sit on top of me and then lifted herself onto her knees, slipped the G-string off and then she was naked; her body rippled against mine like the sea lapping against the shore.

'Put your hand in your lap,' she whispered, and sat down on my sweating palm, one of her nipples in my mouth. I felt the rise of her pubic bone, the thick-knit, slightly greasy warmth of her blonde pubic hair. I tried to slip my index finger inside her and I couldn't. She rose up and away from me: her pussy was entirely dry, untouched by feeling or excitement, like Bombay duck between her legs. I drew my hand away as the song finished and she stood, not looking at me and gathered her clothes to her chest like a baby as Enzo passed her three twenty-pound notes. She still wouldn't look at me, scuttled away, folding the notes into quarters as she walked through a door at the back of the room.

We made our way back into the main bar, where City boys now occupied every table. The Japanese and Koreans had gone and everywhere there were pink shirts and braces, money clips of twenties and fifties and a fat man with a violent sweating face who threw an ice cube at the girl dancing and was picked up by one of the bouncers and hurled against a wall. The man's friends clustered round, waving fistfuls of money at the guard. At the table next to us, three Asian commodity traders I recognised from Bear Stearns were complaining to the manager that the girls had drunk too much of their champagne. I sat down next to Yannis, exhausted, and he filled my champagne glass, patted my knee and returned his gaze to the girl on the stage.

When I got home the flat seemed very small, the peeling wallpaper and juddering pipes grated more than usual; I was intensely conscious of the tawdriness of my existence, and it made me lust even more after the glamorous life of Yannis and Enzo. I had stumbled out of the club around two as Christos swung punches at a trader who had commented on his size and we were all thrown out by the bouncers. The champagne had given me a headache and the memory of Loretta's body against mine filled me with heartache as I waited in the cold night for a taxi to take me back to Fulham.

*

I went into the office on Saturday morning, my mouth dry and furred-up, my hands quivering slightly. I patted my pocket several times on the way in to make sure that my packet of blue pills was still there; I wanted to avoid taking them but needed the comfort of their proximity, their availability in the event of a crisis. When I entered the office Madison was already at her desk. She was typing furiously, her head nodding like a bird pecking at a feeder. I sat at my desk, tried to read a paper on Ford's relationship with the unions, worked on a presentation on pension accounting that was entirely cribbed from an internet site run by the American Actuaries' Association, saw Bhavin's golf ball lying on the floor by my desk. I kicked the ball down the room, walked listlessly into Bhavin's office and looked at the pictures of his beautiful wife and grinning baby. Unable to face sitting back at my desk, I made my way outside and bought two coffees from Starbucks, poured sugar in a thick white fountain into my latte and sipped it in the lift on the way back up to the office. Madison was still typing furiously and I heard her talking in a harsh whisper to herself as I walked down the corridor towards her desk.

'Compound interest calculation . . . The current ratio decreasing in recent months . . . Leverage too high for this industry at this point in the cycle . . .'

I placed her coffee beside her mousepad and moved Euphonium's chair so I was sitting next to her. She carried on working, refusing to acknowledge my presence. I read her work over her shoulder. She was writing about a packaging company from Norway. Her analysis of the company's operating position, her vicious attack on the company's management, her recommendations as to how the company could get back on track: all were faultless. I thought again how unfair it was that she hadn't been made portfolio manager. Finally she turned to me, and there was a cold and dignified scorn in her eyes. Her voice was hard when she spoke, her usually soft drawl had become clipped and vicious.

'Of course I'm bitter,' she said. 'I have every right to be bitter. Whatever I might have said, we both know that I deserved that job. I know it's not your fault, but I do blame you, I do. Yannis was promoted because his dad wrote another twenty-million cheque to the business. I think his father is worried that Yannis isn't progressing professionally, so he's oiling the wheels a little. That's fine. I can understand that. It's how business works. But I am better than you. And you don't have a rich father to help you out. It just shows how important your kiss-ass routine with the PMs has been. Apparently, Catrina thinks you're marvellous. A breath of fresh air, she says. She thinks you're a genius waiting to be discovered. I think she wants to sleep with you. I'm just . . . I'm just so angry.'

I swirled the syrupy dregs of my coffee in the paper cup, winced at the sweetness of the liquid as I sucked it down. I threw the cup across the office and into Lothar's bin.

'You're right, it isn't my fault. But that doesn't make me feel better about it. Of course you should have been promoted before me. I mean look at that work you're doing. I couldn't write that in a million years. And I know it means so much to you. I'm really very sorry, Madison. I hope we can still be friends. It would be nice to do something together outside of work. Maybe you could introduce me to Ray?'

I took her hand in mine, felt her flinch for a moment and then press my palm gently.

'Listen, Madison, you know how insecure I felt about my knowledge before this promotion. Imagine how I feel now. I'm supposed to start buying bonds on Monday, start making serious investment decisions. I know that Catrina and Bhavin will help me to start off with, but that won't last forever. They'll see through the sham, see through the bravado and the boasting and the spin very quickly indeed. Then I'll probably be fired and you can have my job. So don't feel too hard done by.'

She smiled, her eyes swimming up from behind her glasses. Something ironic and amused swept over her as she let my hand fall from hers.

'You'll be fine, Charles. You know you're brighter than all of them. You've got a fine mind. And Yannis will make you look good even if you're struggling. If you have trouble, just send me an email. Just because I'm cross that you got the job instead of me, it doesn't mean I won't help you out.

'I have stopped seeing Ray. I took him out for a pizza last night and let him know that I can't see him any more. I worry that he was taking my mind off the job. I mean, people say that it's a good thing to have perspective, and he definitely gave me that, but I think he was making me lose focus. We were both really sad. Both sitting there in Pizza Hut crying. But I needed to do it. I spoke to the girl who runs the mentor programme. She was very understanding. I'll really miss little Ray. He was a star.'

She looked like she was about to cry again. I leant forward in my chair, put my arms around her. She didn't sob but my neck felt damp through my shirt collar. Over her shoulder I could see Bhavin at the door of his office, wearing weekend-casual polo shirt and high-waisted chinos. He sneered disapprovingly at me and turned back into his room. I held her for a little longer, then laid a kiss on her pitted cheek and loped back towards my desk. When I sat down I raised my hand and waved to her in full view of Bhavin. The new CEO lifted his arms in exasperation and threw a biro at me.

CHAPTER 7

A Visitor

The markets continued to rise. Research pieces from the investment banks sat on my desk half-read, screaming their 'buy' recommendations on the debt of Ford and General Motors and Chrysler. The risk premium that we were paid for investing in these companies was falling daily as the equity markets soared and the investment banks and the newspaper columns and the sages of Bloomberg TV and CNN spoke of an endless bull market, a thousand years of economic expansion, a world where recession was a quaint word which conjured up people in old-style coats and frocks queuing in a black-and-white half-light in front of failing banks. So the returns fell, and the only way we could make money was by taking greater risks, by borrowing from the banks who were desperate to lend us money and doubling, trebling our bets on the companies we invested in.

The numbers were ridiculous. I could draw down up to twenty million pounds in one go from a revolving facility available to me at Bear Stearns. I outlined how I intended to spend it in our morning meetings. We all sat around the boardroom table at eight a.m., Yannis dipping an almond croissant in a Starbucks latte, Madison throwing back espressos, Catrina breathing into a cupped hand to see whether last night's gin was still there. Euphonium ate a sandwich that his wife made him for lunch: ham and cheese and pickle at ten past eight in the morning. Lothar drew vast and complex doodles of space stations with orbiting satellites in his Black and Red notebook and Bhavin brought his putter in and spent the meeting sending ball after ball whistling down the room towards a narrow channel fashioned between pot plants. I'd speak of the positive GDP signals coming out of the US, how consumer debt wasn't really as bad as it looked, how real disposable income was far higher than at any point in history, how cheap mortgage debt was making the American Dream a reality. I proselytised with the chastened voice of a reformed sinner, ashamed that I had mistrusted the great machine of the American economy, that I had questioned the market experts who had been promising that everything would be fine. And everyone agreed, happy to have things that they had read confirmed by this fresh-faced preacher, happy to sign off on higher limits and greater risk and more leverage.

Only Madison ever raised any objections. She was perhaps trying to cultivate an image as a contrarian, perhaps trying to persuade Bhavin that he had made the wrong choice in promoting me. I saw her attacks on my reasoning as personal affronts, and treated them as such. A distance grew between us again, and I used the fact that I knew that the room was on my side to shout her down. It was much easier to go along with market sentiment and embrace optimism, much easier to believe that the great powers of the Fed and the Bank of England and the giant investment banks were steering us unwaveringly towards a future of comfortable luxury. She'd raise her hand like she was in school halfway through my discourse. I'd always wait until the end before looking at her and sighing.

'Yes, Madison?'

'I don't think your figures are right, Charles. Have you adjusted the earnings for rental payments? Have you stressed them for a potential downturn? It all just seems too rosy . . .'

'Of course I have stressed them. I have even taken the stresses that the company ran and stressed them further. Sometimes things are as good as they look. And with growth in demand coming out of China and India, I actually think the company is being rather conservative.'

'But they are still so dependent on the US. What if we have a recession? Do you really feel comfortable investing in this bond for ten years? Can you honestly say that you've got visibility out that far?'

'Of course I haven't got a crystal ball, but I believe in globalisation, and I believe in management forecasts, and I believe in the fundamental strength of the American consumer. Frankly, Madison, if this company goes bust, we've got much bigger things to worry about as a business than a five-million investment in a senior bond.'

And then Bhavin would step in, and hit the ball as hard as he could at one of the pot plants, and comment that he too was convinced by capitalism and by the markets, and if you believed in them then you could work for him, and if you didn't you could fuck off and live in Cuba. Madison would stare down at her hands and I'd feel guilty for a moment and then see Catrina and Bhavin looking at me with pride and I'd run back to the desk and trade and then look at properties in the Cotswolds on Strutt and Parker's website.

In the evenings Yannis and Catrina and Bhavin and I would stagger out into the smudge of early spring, with the memory of the day's freshness caught in the gusts that eddied around Berkeley Square. We drank at a members' bar on the north side of the square which Bhavin had joined on becoming CEO. He'd drive the hundred yards up the hill in his Maserati or Porsche and leave it parked outside, emergency lights flashing fast and urgent. Yannis and I would always go on out afterwards, often join up with his brother and Enzo and sit around in the Long Bar at the Sanderson or Mamilanji on the King's Road and look at the girls dancing self-consciously and the boys daring each other to drink. Occasionally, I'd invite some of the Edinburgh crowd to join us, or we'd run into them, and I was proud of Yannis and Enzo, delighted that I was seen out with these wealthy members of the Eurotrash aristocracy. We'd sit at the best table, a bottle of Grey Goose on ice and cigars clouding up the air above us. Sometimes I'd have to pay, but Yannis seemed to understand that money was tight for me, even after the rise that had come with my promotion; he and Enzo fought small battles over who would pick up the tab, but neither made me feel guilty or a freeloader.

Enzo always had cocaine on him and Yannis and I would take turns accompanying him to the soft-lit bathrooms. I remember one Wednesday night sitting in a taxi, my mind a twitching mess, and blood began to run down my chin, my nose exploding in protest at the punishment it had received, and I was too far gone to do anything about it; my white shirt turned red, and the taxi driver's eyes were wide as I paid him and staggered into the grimy dark hallway of the mansion block like something from a Japanese horror film.

On other evenings Yannis and I were taken out by our sales coverage at the investment banks, each of them fawning and plying us with fine wines and wonderful food, complimenting us on our promotion, on the reputation of the firm, on our charm and good looks. We'd dine at J. Sheekey and Quaglino's, and at Zuma and Les Trois Garçons, and Yannis and I would shock each other with our cheek, reaching for the wine list and ordering bottles of fabulous vintage champagne with the main course and then straight to Château d'Yquem. Only at the end of the night, when Yannis and I were very drunk, and ready to hunt out the strip clubs or the casinos, and the salesmen had been drinking water for the past hour without us noticing, would we talk business. Only then would they mention the deal they were structuring with us in mind. We should really invest. It was a once-in-a-lifetime opportunity. Should they come in and pitch to us tomorrow morning? Or the afternoon? Yes, better the afternoon. And we'd stumble off into the night with promises made; often we ended up investing in bonds on the back of these dinners, and yet the deals always seemed to make us money, and we could always say no if our analysis didn't chime with the rosy picture the salesmen had painted. But we rarely looked at the analysts' work, and we felt luck and market sense running deep within us. We were superheroes of the market. We were invincible.

All the time the company's funds under management grew, and we became one of the largest hedge funds in the city; the pension funds and the university endowment funds and the sovereign wealth funds of swiftly growing Asian economies poured money into Silverbirch. It was an endless stream of liquidity, and Bhavin flew from meeting to meeting raising more of it: Qatar in the morning and then dinner in Hong Kong and then back to the office for a lunch with the Chairman. The stock market was hitting record highs every day and the value of our investments rose in frantic leaps like salmon heading upstream to mate.

We were sent an email by the accounts department with our profit-and-loss account at the beginning of every day, and it was always Yannis's first question as we sat down in the morning. As I pulled together graphs and research reports to discuss in the morning meeting, Yannis would lean over the partition that separated our desks and shout.

'How much you up, dude? How's Chuck doing today? You making money, bro? I'm up three million this month.'

'Not too bad, Yannis. Not too bad. Up another eighty

grand. Takes me to almost five hundred grand this month. Slow and steady wins the race. I'll catch you by the end of the year.'

I was instinctively cautious, nervous as an old woman around these large sums of money, always worried that my lack of training in high finance, my ignorance of the arcana of investment theory, would be revealed. I hated those morning emails with the profit figure dwarfed by the risk I was taking. But there was something heady and compulsive about the numbers too. Catrina had told us once that we could hope to be paid around ten per cent of what we made for the firm at the end of the year. I had done the calculations, worked out that at my current pace I could hope to make ten million pounds for the fund, meaning a bonus of a million pounds. A figure so ridiculous that I could not envisage seeing it in my bank account, could not contemplate going to the cashpoint and seeing anything other than a minus sign in front of the balance. It would be enough to buy a flat in Chelsea, a sports car, a huge television with speakers mounted high on the walls. I would live like those I envied, exist in their perfect world.

I traded thoughtfully, called around the salespeople every morning to explore opportunities, working out which move to make next like an old chess player. I made a point of writing copious notes on Madison's pieces, asking questions constantly as once the PMs had questioned me. But it was hard not to feel invincible sometimes, when I saw patterns in the markets, felt things aligning, sensed the strange magic of capital flows with me sitting in the middle with unique vision, able to see the mechanism of the great machine of capitalism. When I pulled off a particularly successful transaction, I would stand up with my phone held above my head and cheer silently as I filed my trade tickets. I was deeply alive in those moments. I felt like I had truly arrived, finally made something of myself.

Yannis had none of my reserve. Whilst I only invested in the safest securities issued by large companies who published comprehensive and vaguely comprehensible quarterly reports, Yannis piled his money into whatever paid him the most. I had steered clear of the complex asset-backed securities, put off by the numerous arrows that flowed in seemingly random directions from one tax haven to another, confusing in their thrusting insistence. Yannis had entered into an agreement with a French bank that was trying to expand its share of hedge fund customers which allowed him to borrow double the amount I took out of my account at Bear Stearns every morning. He spent this money wildly, with the manic concentration of a rich man's wife, no longer entirely youthful, storming through Chanel piling her arms high with dresses. Yannis's arrogance annoyed Catrina sometimes, but there was no doubt that he was successful, charming when he needed to be, able to wheedle favours out of other traders with a mixture of this charm and a darker bullying insistence.

*

Henry came up to visit one bright Friday afternoon. He had a meeting at the newspaper's offices the next day and was going to spend the night at my house. I had spoken about him to Yannis, had warned that I'd need to leave early that evening. We invented a conference in the City and argued loudly over which of us should go, since it was likely to be boring, and both of us had work to do, and it was hosted by a nothing bank – some bit-part player from Central Europe trying to establish themselves in the London market. I succeeded in being more vocal and high-pitched in my attempts to avoid it, and so when

Bhavin stormed out of the office, his eyes immediately focused on me.

'Right, you two: shut up. Charles, you're going and that's final. And Yannis, you can put together an explanation in English of that floorplan deal you traded last week. The write-up is just a bunch of boxes and arrows. That may be enough for our analysts to get comfortable with the deal, but it isn't enough for me. Have it on my desk in the morning. Charles, I want a summary of five key takeaways from the conference. Now get back to work.'

I smiled at Yannis. I had been to enough of these conferences since my elevation to portfolio manager to have a list of bland economic truisms to reel off in the next day's morning meeting. Yannis and I had arranged to meet at Embassy on Old Burlington Street at eleven. Henry and I would go for dinner and catch up beforehand. I had just been paid and I was looking forward to introducing someone from my old life to Yannis. I knew he would be impressed by Henry's cultivation and class. Yannis envied my ability to talk about art and music and literature with the senior bankers who came for meetings with Bhavin every few weeks.

Something peculiar had happened to the most wealthy bankers in the past few years. In the eighties they drove red Ferraris and ate bright red caviar and smoked enormous cigars whose ends glowed brightly in the gloomy City bars they inhabited. These men were mainlining money, they were avatars of that most materialistic age, they consumed conspicuously. Rolex watch the size of a saucer and platinum-perm secretary/girlfriend with tits out to here and a place in Chelsea and a house with a helicopter pad in Hampshire. But there was no pretence of culture. No attempt to imply that it was something other than pure material gain that interested them. They enjoyed thumbing their coke-spangled noses at the aristocracy, loved hearing the complaints that a new and boorish type had joined the golf club, or bought the estate next door, or been seen with darling Honoria in the bar of the Ritz.

Hedonic creep set in. And the upstarts who had been happy to flaunt their difference, the young Turks who had boasted of their humble roots, began to lust after delights more esoteric and elite. So the managing directors of City firms now attended the opera, pushing ticket prices up into the stratosphere. I occasionally queued for returns at the ENO and thought back to the time when Henry and Vero and I had attended together and the beauty of the music that seemed to swim around and above us for the rest of the night.

So the City boys began to attend wine-tasting lessons and poetry readings, began to visit galleries and theatres; and in the realm of the arts they spent as feverishly as they had before. Somehow it was all right to bid ridiculous sums for a William Scott or a Bacon at Sotheby's, and then let it slip quietly to the *Telegraph* that you had been the anonymous purchaser. Consumption had to be conspicuous, but made public in a tasteful manner. The traders flaunted their knowledge and newly-found passion for the arts at charity dinners in grand City ballrooms as their wives discussed their art collections and their children's cello lessons and the latest production of *The Cherry Orchard*.

So my time at Edinburgh had not been entirely wasted. I could speak with bright-eyed sincerity about the theatre or literature or the latest show at the Royal Academy. And the managing directors who came into the office always stopped off at my desk to ask if I had seen the Pinter at the National or whether I had read the Booker shortlist, and which did I think the likely winner? I hated myself for giving them the morsels they sought. I could even see them storing away my comments for use at broad-tabled Notting Hill dinner parties where they would invite a photographer and his struggling-actress wife for the thrill of access to their glamorous artistic penury.

As I walked out to meet Henry at a pub on Albemarle Street, I looked up and a cloud was spread across the wide blue sky like a wing ripped from the side of a bird. Henry was sitting at the window. He was plumper than the last time I had seen him, his hair thinning around the temples, pushed back to reveal the white sweep of his forehead. He looked up and his lips drew back from his gums to sip from his beer, then broke into a smile as he raised a shy hand in greeting. I ordered a Guinness at the bar and sat opposite him. The table was an upturned beer barrel, the ashtray a yellow-white scallop shell; John Lennon sang 'Jealous Guy' over the jukebox and everything was misty and sentimental for a moment as I looked at my old friend. A Berghaus rucksack lay on the floor by his feet, battered and covered in stickers from far-off places.

'How are you, Charlie? You look good. I think you've grown. Christ, it's been awfully strange not seeing you for so long . . . awfully strange. And what about Vero? Ready to be the perfect bourgeois housewife? Settling down and cooking *poule au pot* for darling Marc every night? I'm . . . I'm rather sceptical, if I'm honest with you, Charlie. Too much of the warrior queen in our Vero to hang up her chariot so quickly. I really have got so much to tell you. Now, let's settle into these beers and start from the beginning.'

It was the kind of magical recapturing of past times which is the more wonderful for its surreality. It was as if we had never left the house off Munster Road, or like we had never left Edinburgh, we were so full of quiet laughter, able to talk in a manner that is rare between even very close friends: I asked him questions not only so I could later answer them myself; I was truly interested in his answers. And he deployed the same languid humour when we spoke, teasing me gently. We grew drunk as the sky faded behind the window, and the lights came up in the pub, and our scallop shell overflowed with ash, a little of which was whipped into the air every time the door opened.

'Do you remember how we'd drink all day Sunday? Fall into bed completely hammered at six o'clock? I just couldn't do that now. I don't know how we managed. Were we happy? I think of it as a very happy time, but parts of it were just dreadful. You cut such a tragic figure when you were unemployed. And I was really such a terrible mess. I can't tell you what the state of my mind was.'

We both grew slightly maudlin as nachos were deposited on the table and we pulled out great long strings of cheese and funnelled them into our mouths, and the scallop ashtray was replaced, and the tables around us emptied and refilled, and still we talked.

'You know, Henry, I get terribly upset to think of the poor lost thing I was back then. I used to go out during the day, even when I didn't have any interviews, just to be out of the house. I'd sit in garden squares in Chelsea, vault over railings and look up at the houses with their wrought-iron balconies and I'd just boil with the unfairness of it all. But yes. Yes, I do think we were happy. I was very happy to have the two of you around. I felt that things could never be really terrible as long as you two were in the house when I got home.'

He stood up, stretched and made his way to the back of the bar and the bathrooms, pausing for a moment to watch the game of pool that was taking place, smiling as one of the players delayed his shot to let Henry past. It was dark outside now and I watched a couple arguing in the light thrown by a gallery onto the pavement opposite. The boy was pacing up and down, walking off and then coming back to address her, striding around her and then suddenly breaking off to kick at the bollards that lined the road. The girl was very quiet, her bottom lip shuddering every so often. I thought that she was probably in the wrong. His fury had an air of humiliation, his pacing and spitting and clenched features hinted that he knew he had already lost her. He came up very close to her face, shouted, his hands held high above her, as if about to strike. I moved forward on my chair, ready to charge out and intervene. Then he collapsed. His hands dropped to his sides, his face softened into tears, his shoulders shook with sobs and the girl, her eyes very clear, took him in her arms, held him very close to her. His shaking slowly subsided and they walked off arm in arm into the warm promise of the night.

But something about their argument had left a bitterness in the air, and when Henry returned to the table, I felt a subtle change in pressure, a stiffening of the atmosphere around us. He had bought us both double whiskys at the bar and he settled awkwardly back onto his stool. He began to speak, stopped for a moment, began again.

'Charlie, I wanted to talk to you. It's in the past and nothing can be done and yet I need to talk to you about it. Because . . . because it explains a lot of things. And I think you deserve to know. And maybe it will help us both move on with . . . with everything that's happening now. I was in love with Vero. I think you probably knew that. I mean it was very distant and a lot went unsaid and she was clearly much fonder of you than she was of me. But that doesn't mean that I didn't truly care for her. Christ, I find it difficult to say these sorts of things. Not my style at all this kind of emotional unloading.

'All the time at Edinburgh I was just waiting . . . waiting for you and her to break up, for your relationship or whatever it was to end. And it didn't, even after she left you, there was something so strong between the two of you. It was something which meant that I couldn't approach her, couldn't tell her really what I felt unless we were both drunk and then she'd just treat it like this big joke in the morning. Just a big joke. You gave her something all those other boys couldn't give her; it always seemed that there was this physical bond between the two of you that wouldn't go away. It was awful for me.

'She used to kiss me sometimes. When you were off with other girls and she was at a loose end, she'd come into my room – summer of the second year it was. There was something kind of adolescent about it. Occasionally, she'd let me feel under her shirt, slip a single finger down the front of her trousers, but nothing more than that. We'd just sit in a pool of light and kiss each other. They were the best days ever. Quite honestly the best bloody days I have ever had. Tragic isn't it?

'What worries me – and it has really been worrying me the past few weeks – is that I called her one night, not long before she left. I was out of my head on acid and crying and lying on a bench in a park on the King's Road, and I begged her to leave her job, to move to the country with me, to start a new life away from all the sham and swagger of the city. I think . . . I think she considered it. I think I persuaded her to leave. But just not with me. She said that we could never be together, that I had a girlfriend and should be happy with her. I told her that Jo was just a stand-in, a stop-gap, someone to pass the time with until I could have her. She started crying and hung up on me.'

His voice was wretched, his face drawn and pathetic. I felt the beginnings of anger, a tightening in my stomach and my chest, then pity and a weary humour at the ridiculousness of it all. I looked at Henry and he was biting his lip and tipped back his whisky even though there was nothing left in the glass. Vero was marrying someone else and it didn't matter what history of feelings there was, what had happened and what hadn't. I walked slowly to the bar and bought more whisky, placed a glass in front of him and patted his shoulder.

'Fuck it, Henry. It doesn't matter. It really doesn't matter at all. It's not like I ever really had anything with her. Not anything that would last. We were just amusements for her. I think she was the most fucked-up of any of us. And now Marc or whatever his name is can deal with her. And I hope, I really do hope that this means that we can be friends with her. And that there's nothing underlying it. No dark and urgent yearning that only ends up spoiling things. Because she is a fantastic girl. And we are brilliant together, the three of us.'

'Time gentlemen, please,' called the barman and Henry and I smiled and I ran to the bar and forced my way to the front of the queue to buy a final round. When I got back to the table Henry was rifling through his rucksack and pulled out two pale blue envelopes.

'This came to my house for you. I don't think she had your address.'

I opened the envelope which was addressed in Vero's small, slanting hand. It was an invitation to her wedding in July. On the 24th in Neufchâtel-en-Bray. My name in the top right corner. Charles, not Charlie. She had written on the back: '*Please come, darling. I need you to be there.*' I shrugged at Henry, he smiled, and we made our way out into the night. Past the golden fronts and dark interiors of Bond Street boutiques, past the genteel shuttered tailors of Savile Row, past burly doormen and an effete Frenchman holding a guestlist and then down the winding staircase of Embassy, at the bottom of which Yannis and Enzo were talking to three Greek girls of extraordinary beauty.

Something cruel moved within me that night. I was already very drunk when I arrived, and I shouted at a waiter to find us a table in the VIP room that was accessed up a narrow stairway at the back of the bar. The three Greek girls came with us, sat and watched with large dark eyes, as I called out for champagne, introduced Henry, broke a glass flinging my arms out in emphasis of some important point and then immediately lost my train of thought and slumped backwards.

More girls came in and sat around us, and Enzo and Yannis and I made repeated trips to the bathroom to snort cocaine that was harsh and metallic and made us all very cynical, very scathing of the people around us. Henry sat with the Greek girls in silence and watched us. Watched me. It wasn't scorn in his eyes, it was something sadder, something more regretful. And every time I tried to impress him by ordering yet more expensive champagne, by ordering Romeo y Julieta cigars for everyone until our table sat in fog like a mountain peak, Henry backed away a little further. When I reached over, taking the soft face of one of the Greek girls between forefinger and thumb and placed a long wet kiss on her large and squirming lips, I saw him apologise to her. They rose together and went to sit at the bar downstairs for a while. When they came back, I saw pity in Henry's eyes. I deliberately let my wallet fall open to show a wad of twenty-pound notes that I had withdrawn earlier, merely for effect, for the bulge it lent to my top pocket. Henry pretended he hadn't noticed and I put the wallet back. He and the Greek girl spoke in quiet voices, always watching us, never joining in the shouting and the dancing and the arguments that shuttled between us.

I remember during my first term at Edinburgh I had invited a friend from Worthing up to visit. His name was Colin Harris and he was one of very few people from that dreary seaside town that I counted amongst those dear to me. He played guitar in the school band, used to write songs in the style of Nick Drake and play them to me late into the night until my parents banged on the wall. He and I had set off across France together on our bicycles for three weeks after our A Levels, boarding the ferry at Newhaven and pedalling down as far as Beaune, spending what little money we had on wine, pitching our tents in cow-fields and alongside riverbanks, burning our shoulders and our forearms and waking to violent sunlight reflecting off dancing water where we would bathe and then spread out our map to plan the day's route. He was quiet, thoughtful, a bright and soothing companion.

I remember collecting him from the station at Edinburgh. He had taken the sleeper train up from London and his eyes were tired and confused. His small bag had a broken wheel and dragged behind him as he pulled it along. He wore a grubby T-shirt and jeans that were too tight and too high-waisted and I felt a moment of shame that he would be coming back to my halls to meet Vero and Henry and the other grand friends whose company I had begun to cultivate. We spent the day sitting in a pub playing darts, drinking, but there seemed to be very little to say between games, between drinks. He had gone to Brighton University to study music, dropped out after three weeks because the course was too prescriptive, didn't allow him to give rein to his creativity. He was now touring with his band, playing miserable back-rooms of pubs in nowhere towns.

That evening we had gone out to Rick's Hotel for dinner and Colin seemed quite lost in the crowd of my friends with their designer sunglasses worn indoors and their enormous watches and their talk of skiing trips and safaris in the Kruger and diving in Bali. Even when Henry and Vero tried to speak to Colin he answered in monosyllables, ordered the cheapest wine by the glass and then reared back in alarm when the bill came. I had just received my student loan and paid for him, and this seemed to cheer him a little, but still he was nervous around these people with their sophisticated accents and forthright views. We went on to Yo! Below for sake and beer from the tap on the table, and he kept yawning and stretching, and then Vero and I moved off to the dancefloor, throwing ourselves around madly, sidling off to the loos to take the speed that Henry had bought from a man on Northumberland Road. When I looked around Colin had gone.

I found him sitting on the steps outside my staircase when we came home, sweat glistening on our upper lips, heat rising from us in the cold night. Colin had pulled an old jumper around himself and was shaking quietly. I led him to my room and showed him the bathroom and the little fridge where milk and yoghurt were slowly fermenting into rancidness. I wished him a hasty goodnight, eager to disappear into Vero's room and the damp embrace of her thighs. When I woke and went to look for him he had gone. Just a note left on my desk beside a copy of *Catcher in the Rye* which he had sat up all night reading – I could see the smudges of his thumbs on the cover.

'*Charlie,*' it read, '*You have changed. I suppose we all change. Your accent is different and your clothes are different and it seems as if the way you see the world is different. And perhaps I'm a little envious of you with your beautiful girlfriend and your wealthy friends, but I think that on the whole I'm not. Because I don't think you can change as much as you have without losing something of yourself in the process. I will always think very fondly of the time we had at school, the time we spent in Burgundy. But I don't think we can be friends anymore. Maybe if the band makes it, and I'm a high-living rock star, surrounded by drugs and groupies, I'll go through the same thing. I just hope I handle it with a little more grace than you have. Good luck to you mate. Best, Colin.*'

Henry's visit left me with the same feeling of snatching defeat from a moment that should have been glorious: showing off my new and glamorous friends to him, proving that I had achieved at least some of the things that I had set out to achieve, that I was living the life I thought we had all aspired to, that my London was now close to the London of our youthful university dreams. But it was clear that Henry had moved on. And when we repaired to Yannis's portered apartment on Old Brompton Road, with its marbled bathroom and vast drawing room with huge right-angled white leather sofa, Henry sat thumbing through the coffee-table books whilst we snorted more coke and tried to persuade one of the Greek girls to perform a striptease. She was down to her pants and bending over with a fifty-pound note rolled delicately between her fingers, her large firm breasts hanging down and reflected in the glass table, when Henry stood up.

'I've got to go, Charlie. I have to be in at the office tomorrow. Can I have your keys?' There were great circles under his eyes, and he stumbled on his words a little, and it wasn't because he was drunk, but because he had sobered up. The sadness in his eyes made me turn away from the great breasts with their absence of tan lines telling a story of summers spent on yachts with helipads at the rear and dappled sunlit coves and swimming at the first light of morning still high from the night before. I took Henry by the arm, patted Yannis on the back, tousled Enzo's hair, and took the lift silently down to the quiet three-a.m. streets.

Henry and I sat in the taxi on the way home, watching the dark and secret night-City around us. The streetlights clicked past metronomically, the radio mumbled in the background, and I felt a great sense of shame; I pressed my face against the cool glass and felt my temples throbbing, my heart beginning to race. I popped a blue pill into my mouth, crushed it, and fell into a dark sleep for what seemed like hours. When we pulled up outside the flat on Munster Road, Henry paid the driver,

129

and we staggered together into the dank hall with its flaking wallpaper and piles of envelopes that always sat scattered across the floor, addressed to the dead and the departed.

We undressed and stood side by side in the bathroom in T-shirts and boxer shorts, sharing the toothbrush and facewash and it was somehow better all of a sudden; I tried to apologise, tried to make things right with him, but Henry held up a hand to silence me. We lay down on the double bed. I had given Henry my duvet and pulled a sheet and blanket from a cupboard for myself, and we lay and stared at the ceiling. He spoke first.

'Charlie, you don't need to apologise for anything tonight. It was great fun. It really was. I mean a year ago I would have had the time of my life with those amazing friends of yours, and those . . . those quite stunning girls. It was exactly the sort of evening I used to dream of: all that coke and champagne and the glamour of it all. But . . . somehow I'm just so much older now. I suppose it comes of spending so much time with my parents, so much time looking after Astrid. But I think maybe it's more than that. Hearing about Vero getting married, and having this job where I feel I'm really doing something . . . something really useful and meaningful. All of this has changed me . . . changed me utterly. In some ways I envy you. Because I think that things you aspire to, that kind of instant fix of the drugs and the money and the girls, all of that is achievable. And the things I want . . . I don't even know what I want. I want something profound and lasting and I find it sometimes, fleetingly, in the articles I write.'

I was struggling to follow him, caught between the pounding of the coke that still rushed through me and the blue pill which took the edge off everything and nudged me towards sleep. I tried to speak, tried to make myself understood.

'I kept watching you tonight, Henry. And you did seem like

someone else altogether. And it embarrassed me. And that embarrassment made me vile, made me act in a shameful fashion. I'm so sorry . . . I feel like I've fucked things up. And it doesn't matter about you and Vero. Doesn't matter at all because she never loved me and she never loved you and she was just too cool and too wise for us. Maybe if she saw you now. Maybe if she saw this new you she might love that. But I'm just as childish and stupid as I always was. And I'll end up with some blonde girl marginally more stupid than myself and we'll have lots of money and little sex and children who whine and carp for computer games and plastic dolls. But I don't know what else to look for in life.'

I heard the alarm clock of the man upstairs go off, realised that I would have to get up soon, felt a great hollowness in my gut. Henry was asleep, the duvet curled around his arm and pulled up to his face. I slipped out of bed, stepped into the shower which was scalding and then freezing. I put on my suit, washed an apple for the tramp, and left Henry with a soft smile on his lips as I padded out into the grey dawn.

Chapter 8

The Wedding

Henry and I had agreed that we would drive down to Vero's wedding together. The knowledge that he too would find it a mournful and heart-rending experience would make it somehow easier to bear. The weeks leading up to our departure were leaden and ugly. It was a summer that never arrived, days dawning brightly over the polite terraces of Fulham that I passed on my way to work, the sun fighting through the cloudy remnants of night. But rains blew in from the west, and by the time I got to work a cold wind would be eddying around Berkeley Square, the sun hidden by low dark clouds, a light rain that soaked the skin and clothing surprisingly swiftly.

Stories had begun to come out of the States: consumers defaulting on their mortgages, businesses reining in spending, the bankruptcy of one of the smaller construction companies. Madison had something very fearful in her eyes as the markets flatlined. The profit figure in my daily email no longer rose, and Yannis began to see some of his enormous gains eroded as investment banks sold down their holdings, positioned themselves for a more difficult economic environment. But Bhavin and Catrina remained violently optimistic, pressing us to borrow more from the banks that were still lending to us, demanding that we took greater risks, invested in increasingly arcane structures. Yannis began to sweat at his desk. Perspiration sat on his temples and his cheeks, stained the underarms of his shirts, and he sprayed deodorant and Paco

Rabanne aftershave constantly to dispel the stale and startling odour that rose from his desk.

Madison had produced a long and lucid research report that pointed to an imminent crash to rival the Great Depression, a crisis that would suck the marrow from the markets, lead to untold job losses, huge corporate failures, disastrous repercussions for exactly the kind of debt investments that we made. Bhavin dismissed it with his usual scornful vigour, but I remained late at work one night and spoke to her as she sat trembling at her desk, watching oil prices rocket and the stock markets teeter and the insidiously rising unemployment and inflation figures. Her fingers scratched at her eczema, flakes of skin were visible on the desk around her keyboard and hovered in the air, illuminated by the blue-white light of her computer screen. I massaged her shoulders again as I spoke to her, felt again the tension and scarcity of human contact that caused her skin to quiver beneath my touch.

'What if you're right? What if you've been right all along, Madison? I feel like I just don't know enough about it all. I need you to help me here. I've done what I was told to do. I have invested in companies that looked like they were well run, companies that didn't take too many risks. But if what you're saying is right, then they're all fucked. The whole system will go down.'

She turned to me. She looked suddenly very old, very tired.

'I don't know, Charles. I just don't know. I haven't slept for the past few nights. I have been lying in bed and watching Bloomberg TV, crouching under my duvet and sitting in the flickering shadows of the presenters as they talk about the Chinese economy slowing down, and the inflation in food prices which means that millions could starve, and the banks who have been taking too much risk and now fear each other, won't lend to one another, won't lend to funds like ours.

'And I think that maybe it will all go wrong. Because it has been such a long period of stability. And all of the senior guys, guys like the Chairman, the ones who have seen market cycles turn – they have been promoted up to positions where they don't really follow the minutiae of the markets, they're out of touch with the day-to-day risks that their firms are running. Or they have retired. And people like Bhavin may seem like they know everything, but he's only worked in the City for twelve, thirteen years at the most. That's not enough time to have experienced a real crash. Even ninety-eight, which was bad, didn't extend much outside of the emerging markets for any length of time. And 2001 wasn't really a downturn, more a drawing-in of breath, a gasp after the Twin Towers. So these guys have never known failure. I'm really scared, Charles. Scared that our world is about to end. And no one is listening to me, so no one will do anything about it.'

The next day was a Thursday – my last day at work before Vero's wedding. Yannis turned up looking unwashed and crazy, his shirt unironed and showing great slashes of sweat across the back and pools spreading out from under the arms. Despite this, he stretched his arms high repeatedly as we sat at our desks, as if somehow proud of the signs of stress that darkened his armpits. In the morning meeting he tabled a derivative trade with a Dutch bank that would effectively double his risk, but could potentially make millions if the negative rumours doing the rounds turned out to be mere scaremongering. I saw Madison shudder when he suggested it. Even Catrina seemed shocked by the aggressiveness of the trade. But Bhavin stood up and applauded.

'That's the kind of fucking balls we want to see here. That's how we become heroes. Good work, Yannis. Do it. Let's fucking do it.'

Yannis went to the bathroom straight after the meeting and

came back with coke-bright eyes. I helped him to negotiate the terms of his trade, emailing over termsheets to the bank, placing legal letters in front of Bhavin which he signed without reading. As the day drew to a close I looked at Madison, watched the markets which were struggling into positive territory, talked up by the investment banks who were also convinced that the speculation was the fearful chatter of old ladies unwilling to believe in the robustness of the inviolate models which predicted that the good times would continue into a halcyon future. I looked at my risk position – tiny compared to Yannis's, but still enough to warrant a blue pill rushed down with a can of lukewarm Diet Coke. I closed down my computer, pocketed my Blackberry and set off for my first holiday since joining Silverbirch.

Vero was getting married on the Saturday and I had taken Friday off. Henry and I would drive down to Dover together in the morning. Vero had called several weeks before, full of excitement and a kind of bridely breathlessness that surprised me.

'I'm so pleased you and Henry can come. And you both replied in such good French. My mother was very impressed. It will only be a very small affair. Really just family and a few people from the village. Marc would like it if you could come the night before and celebrate his last night of freedom. He and a few of his friends are going into Honfleur. Hardly Amsterdam, heh? But he doesn't want it to be anything too big. Then the wedding. My dress is so funny. Virginal white. All frilly. My papa laughed when he saw me in it. I can't wait to see you, Charlie. It has been too long, *mon amour*.'

Henry spent the night at Munster Road again. We didn't speak of the night at Embassy, nor did we discuss Vero. Instead we spoke about his work, about the markets and the rumours about a potential crash, which he said were being leapt upon with unashamed glee by the underpaid hacks on the business pages of the newspaper. We went to bed early after eating pizza and sitting in the dreary front room with the lights turned low, looking out on the world, both hoping that it was an easy silence that hung in the air between us.

As we drove down to Dover rain attacked the car, exploding onto the windscreen with the violence of a pressure hose. The motorway was a snaking river; lorries threw up great curtains of oily mist behind them. We arrived at the ferry terminal to find that the boat had been delayed by high seas. The port was a wasteland, the café full of long-distance drivers, the rain lashing down over the tarpaulins under which I imagined small, scared asylum seekers were smuggled. Finally the boat made its chugging, elephantine way into harbour, and I drove nervously aboard.

Walking up the steep narrow stairways to reach the deck, I felt my Blackberry buzzing in my pocket. I checked my messages, saw a thick succession of emails from Bhavin immediately preceded by my profit figure. Henry was racing up ahead of me, turned and smiled down and gestured impatiently.

'Come on, Charlie. I want to watch that miserable country bugger off behind us. Put that thing away.'

I turned the phone off and put it into my jacket pocket. I had worked for months without a holiday, had not even had more than one or two weekends out of the office since joining Silverbirch. I deserved a break, was travelling to the land of good food and great wine, going to see my friend getting married. I was going to forget the markets, forget Bhavin, try to relax.

We sat at the window in the restaurant at the back of the ship watching the grey cliffs rapidly disappear into the blackness of the rain. The boat pitched violently, leaping up and slamming down on the water with a cannonade that boomed throughout the great vessel. Pools of vomit slopped around corners, down stairwells, into the restaurant where Henry and I picked disconsolately at dry croissants, watching our coffee spill to join the swirling muck that seeped along the floor. A woman sat at the table next to us with three small children. The youngest was a mere baby and she was trying to feed it with a large breast that swung out of reach with each pitch and rock of the boat. Opposite her sat a pair of wide-eyed children, a boy and a girl who must have been twins, two or three years old, their once immaculate white smocks covered in jam and hot chocolate. They watched with very serious eyes as the cornflakes that their mother had placed in front of them spilled across the table and into her lap. The baby was crying in frustration as its mother tried to steady the tray that held their breakfast and manoeuvre her saucer-sized nipple into the bawling gaping mouth. Tears of milk that leaked from the dark-brown teat mixed with the baby's snot and tears, then dribbled down the screaming child's red face. The woman choked back a sob and, at once, the twins began to wail, laying their heads down on the devastation of the Formica table.

Henry and I stood up, slightly embarrassed to approach the woman in her position. I cleared my throat nervously, but Henry was all action, gestured to the two prostrate children, whose breakfast milk was soaking into their fine dark hair. I picked up one of the twins under each of my arms and swung them into the air as Henry swept the contents of the table onto the tray, emptied this into a bin and returned with huge fistfuls of blue tissue paper with which he wiped the table clean. The twins had stopped crying when I lifted them up and turned circles across the room, a movement which dampened the pitching of the boat. I was rather proud and surprised with the effect. They were both very heavy, and I shifted them so that they lay propped against my shoulders. The mother looked up at me smiling as Henry queued up to replace the breakfast.

I sat and jiggled the children on my knees, reminding me of the nervous movements that Yannis made when he was trading. Smiling, making aeroplane noises, Henry spooned mouthfuls of Petit Filou into each mouth in turn and then I carried them both to look out of the back window at the flying spume that leapt high over the rails and hit the deck with a slap. The baby was fed and asleep in its mother's arms, Henry was speaking in broken French to her, and I held the twins by their moist grubby hands and taught them to roll their legs with the movement of the ship. Finally, they grew tired and I sat and let them fall asleep on my shoulders, drooling and purring night-sounds. Henry bought us more coffee and poured sips into my mouth until the storm died down and the twins woke up with great stretching and grumbling and freed my dead arms.

When we rolled off the ship France was very still, nursing wounds from the recently-passed storm. Branches lay along the autoroute as we drove southwards; red tiles lay shattered in roads as we passed. Thick-necked men were perched atop ladders lashing down plastic sheets as we made our way through Boulogne and Etaples and Abbeville. We listened to Leonard Cohen as we drove, Henry singing along in a quiet and weary voice: the perfect accompaniment for the motorway sadness that hit us as we drove across the dreary flatness of that place. We stopped at a petrol station and Henry looked out across the bleakness of the surrounding countryside, chewing unhappily on the rock-hard ham baguette I had bought. We finally pulled into Neufchâtel as the day drew to its close, still, as if embarrassed by its earlier ragings.

Neufchâtel is a quiet place somewhere between a large village and a small town, overlooked by a many-windowed hospital, houses sweeping down into the valley where a church sits in a square that could be anywhere in France with the PMU bar and the Crédit Agricole and too many *boulangeries*. Vero's house sat near the top of the town, a typical Norman chalet of black and white wood, set within a garden where a marquee lurched, wind-battered, amidst an orchard of apple trees whose young fruit had been ripped from their branches and now lay aborted on the wet grass. A creeper grew up the western side of the house and a strange flag – a yellow sun on a red background – fluttered lamely in the dying wind from a pole on the roof. We pulled into the driveway and Vero bounded out to the car, her hair tied up in a pony-tail, her eyes gleaming.

'You made it! I was worried because of the weather. But I'm so happy you are here. Come in and meet everyone. Come and meet Marc.'

We walked into the kitchen carrying our suitcases. Vero's mother, a small comely lady with high cheekbones and a smile that sent previously unseen creases across her face, embraced us both. Her English was rapid and unembarrassed by its old-fashioned clumsiness.

'I am Patricia. I have heard many things about you wonder-ful boys. I am so happy to have you here. Be very welcome.'

I handed her a bottle of wine and she hugged me again, burying my head in the perfumed boniness of her collar. Vero's father wheeled in wearing a bow tie and a beret like the one Vero had bought me for the previous Christmas.

'Hello, boys. Ah – Charlie – we have met before. I am pleased you are here. Henry, my name is Armand. Welcome in my home. This is a very happy time for us. Our little girl is a precious thing. We must celebrate greatly.'

Henry slightly awkwardly laid a bottle of champagne in his lap and we both shook him warmly by the hand. He then turned around into the large drawing room whose walls were covered in the propaganda posters and reproductions of the graffiti of the Situationist International. I sat down in an old leather chair beneath '*Vivez Sans Temps Mort*' whilst Henry perched on a piano stool beneath '*Ne Travaillez Jamais*'. With their backs towards us, looking out onto the wreckage of the garden, stood two tall men. One I recognised as her brother, Guy, by the very thick glasses which I could see reflected in the window, the long hands with their thin, womanly fingers. Vero walked shyly over to them, laid her arms around both, standing on her toes to do so, and ushered them across to meet us.

Marc was aggressively handsome, dressed in a tan cardigan and jeans, his left ear pierced, giving him the look of a progressive English teacher rather than the local solicitor. His face was weather-beaten, very tanned and lined deeply around the eyes and across his wide forehead. He was older than I had expected, his thick black hair lined with grey, his stubble dappled black and white. He moved with languorous ease, like a panther or a professional athlete. I could see the muscles in his legs rippling through his tight jeans. There was something dismissive about him, something that told me he knew all about me, feared me not at all, pitied me a little. He had a thin white scar above his left cheek. Next to him Vero's brother looked bumbling, unsure of himself. I stood up to greet them both and shook Marc by the hand whilst looking into his eyes, which were blue and darting, like fish in a rock pool, their colour accentuated by the dark skin that surrounded them. Henry didn't move, sat staring at Marc until I stepped over and helped him up. Stumbling, forgetting any French he ever knew, he muttered something under his breath and shook both of the men by the hand.

'I must insist we speak English,' Vero's father said as he popped the cork of the champagne that Henry had brought, letting the liquid spill over into glasses that his wife had laid out. Vero brought another bottle out and we stood around sipping the lukewarm wine. Henry began to tap out a one-fingered tune on the piano. The light dropped around us and Vero's mother began to look nervous. Marc stood apart, refilling his glass regularly, occasionally addressing a word in French to Guy. Henry was mournfully discussing politics with Vero's father when Vero leapt up, grabbed me by the hand and led me upstairs. Henry, relieved, followed.

Henry and I were sharing the guest room which was small and hot, and had two single beds with pink duvets on them. Vero smiled at us and walked away, back down the stairs. I hung my suit in the tiny cupboard that was otherwise full of lacy dresses and heavy winter coats. Henry and I had both brought morning suits, hoping to amuse with their old-world elegance. I could see from the way that Henry threw his across the bed and rattled a box of studs onto the small dresser, that he was not in the mood to amuse.

A car's horn sounded outside and Guy shouted up the stairs.

'Charlie, Henry, it's the minibus. We must go to the stag's do.' I heard Vero correct him. 'The stag do. Are you ready?'

I raised my eyebrows at Henry who was looking more tired and defeated with every passing moment; we descended the stairs and down the ramp at the front of the house into the driveway. A battered white van with steamed windows and its sliding door open sat in the cool twilight. I stepped in and there was a cheer from Marc and Guy and another young man who sat smoking in the back. Marc was wearing a cowboy hat and a large grin and he swigged from a bottle of red wine before speaking. Some of the liquid trickled through his stubble.

'Fred, this is Charlie and Henry. Vero's former loves come to mourn her passing. We must give them a chance tonight to

141

forget. So we speak English until we are too drunk to remember anything, and then we speak French about the things we have forgotten.'

We lurched off down the hill and towards Honfleur. Marc scrambled to the back with Fred, while I stretched across three seats in the middle of the bus. Henry sat on the front bench beside Guy, who looked almost as uncomfortable as Henry. Guy reached down and drew out three beers from a bag on the floor and opened them with his penknife.

'We may as well get drunk, eh? I believe it is the tradition on this kind of expedition.' He looked disdainfully at the two boys at the back who had lit a joint and were furtively blowing smoke out of the slide-window. Fred was dressed in a black suit with a white T-shirt underneath. He too was very tall and had the high-boned face of a European aristocrat. Marc held a bottle of St Estèphe in one hand which he drank in great gulps, refusing to share even after Fred begged him.

'C'est à moi. Je l'ai acheté et je vais le boire,' he repeated.

He held it forward as Fred clambered over to get hold of it. I pulled it swiftly from Marc's hand and he turned to me with a surprising violence in his eyes.

'Who the fuck said you could have some?'

I tilted the bottle back and drained perhaps a quarter before passing it to Guy, who took a small sip and handed it to Henry, who finished the bottle and sent it spinning out of the open window into a roadside ditch. I turned to Marc.

'Marc, we were behind you in the drinking, now we're even. We'll have some fun tonight. I intend to require medical assistance by the time the sun comes up.'

Fred smiled and cheered, and Marc fell back on the seat in a sulk. Guy whispered something to Henry and they both laughed. I crawled back over the seats and introduced myself properly to Fred, who was a banker at Société Générale in Paris and was impressed to hear that I worked for Silverbirch. He presented me with his card, and I promised I'd email him. We spent the rest of the journey into Honfleur discussing the markets' prospects as Marc rolled his eyes in boredom and finally turned his back on us altogether. Fred told me that there had been a record fall on the Paris Bourse that morning, followed by carnage on Wall Street when the US markets opened. The worst Friday on record. He had slipped out of his office under the cover of the panic that the crash had created. I hadn't dared check my Blackberry that afternoon, had left it blinking in the door of the car, afraid of seeing my profit figure, afraid of reading dark stories about the coming storm. I lit a cigarette – Gauloises bought from the petrol station that morning – and the smoke I exhaled was whipped out of the window.

'How do you know Marc then? Is he from Paris?' I turned back towards Fred. Marc was slouched with his face pressed against the glass, apparently asleep, a cigarette burning down in his mouth.

'No. I know him from New York,' said Fred. 'He was a corporate lawyer. Worked on a bunch of big deals with me. Made a lot of money and then took off for a year. Went round the world screwing women and bungee-jumping, taking drugs and skydiving. Then he ended up back here where he grew up. He's thirty-two. You wouldn't know it. Five years older than me. But he was always the craziest of the French guys out in New York. Always at the most fashionable parties, had the best apartment in Tribeca, rented the coolest house in the Hamptons every summer. Man, the parties there.' Fred shook his hand as if trying to dry it and whistled. His accent was an uneasy mix of New York drawl and the clipped Anglicised tones of high-class French.

'We still can't work out why he's back here. Says he always

had a thing for Veronique. Had fancied her since they were young. A bit sick I guess. He's what – seven years older than she is? I just hope this girl's as fascinating as she seems. I could see him getting pretty bored in the winters here. My family's from Auxerre and I only go back there for funerals and Christmas. And even then I leave as quickly as I can. Luckily, it's not too far from Paris.'

We were driving in slow traffic through the suburbs of Honfleur, past ugly houses and trees bent low by the wind coming in off the sea. Finally, we were at the town's heart, night had fallen, and it was suddenly quiet and beautiful. The town's harbour was perfectly square, surrounded by high shuttered houses, seafood restaurants with awnings jutting out onto the quayside, an arch in warm stone protecting the harbour's entrance. I could see people on their boats, the lights jumping on water whose surface was scuffed by a gentle breeze. The boats were unpretentious sailboats, unlike those that sat basking with their polished gilt rails along the waterfronts of Cannes and St Tropez. On one of the nearer boats I saw a father open a bottle of cider in front of his three blond children, allowing the eldest to sip the silver foam from the neck. Their mother was cooking at a small stove and they seemed at ease, enjoying this private moment in the public forum of the harbour.

We had a reservation at the best restaurant in town, which sat on the far side of the basin from where the van had deposited us. We walked along the ancient stone of the quay, looking in at the bars and antique shops and galleries. An air of respectable wealth suffused the place, old couples strolled in the cool evening, ladies nestling into the crook of their husbands' arms. I walked ahead with Guy and Henry. In the distance I could make out a great bridge that spanned the mouth of the Seine, white lights flashing admonition to aeroplanes from the great towers of concrete.

Marc leapt down and ran along a jetty, jumping high into the air and landing on the deck of a boat; he skipped onto another jetty and then was on the other side of the basin waving and laughing to us. Fred followed him, almost slipping as he made the final jump. We saw the two of them disappear into the bright entrance of the restaurant. I put my arm around Henry's shoulder, patted Guy on the back, and we enjoyed the walk across the top of the harbour, past mime artists who were packing up for the day, a girl removing her black-and-white face paint in a hand-held mirror, revealing soft pale skin beneath.

The restaurant was buzzing and Marc and Fred were already sat at the table in a corner overlooking the boats below. From my seat I could see the huge bridge and imagined driving across it in last night's storm, the sense of being thrown into the heart of the tempest. The loss of visibility and direction and contact with the ground was somehow very attractive at that moment. A waiter came to the table and presented menus with a flourish. Henry insisted on taking the wine list, ordered us all Calvados to start – much to the sommelier's disapproval – and then three bottles of Pouilly-Fumé which sat in a huge ice bucket by the table as we downed oysters and mussels and brandy shots.

Henry had a slightly wild look in his eyes. He spent much of the evening deep in conversation with Guy, holding forth on the recent French elections, on the social security system, on the quality of the seafood that continued to arrive on our table: prawns and langoustines, crabs and lobsters, whelks and winkles with needles to extract them and then skate in caper butter which we cut into slices and ate with our fingers. The finger bowls with their lemon slices had turned brackish and held floating traces of prawns' legs and aioli and slick pools of melted butter.

We drank the three bottles of white and moved on to cider, ordering great metal tankards of the sweet autumnal liquid. I was thirsty and tired, became drunk with unpleasant swiftness. More Calvados arrived and I staggered to the bathroom, which had three-quarter-length swing saloon doors. I laid my head against the tiles above the urinal and as I pissed a hot thick jet into the bowl, I fell asleep for a moment. There was a deep throat-clearing from behind me and I stumbled back from the pissoir, splashed my face with water and out into the restaurant.

Marc and Fred were wrestling on the table, throwing bowls and cutlery to the floor, grunting and swearing at each other. Guy held up a chair as if trying to ward off a mad dog. Only Henry sat sanguine, moving his plate for a moment when the wrestling couple threatened to roll over towards him. Waiters stood, arms raised, shouting. Families and couples who moments earlier had been lost in happy conversation stared on with the guilty pleasure of scandal. In a moment of inspiration, the sommelier seized the huge ice bucket and emptied it over the pair and they stood, gasping at the shock, looking from side to side, disoriented. I had a thick wad of euros in my wallet and strode waving them towards the maître d'. He grabbed them from me and pointed towards the door.

'*Maintenant. Dehors. Ou je vais appeler la police. Vite!*'

Marc looked as if he was ready to attack the sommelier, was brandishing lobster crackers threateningly. Fred grabbed him by the arm and steered him towards the exit. Guy pressed more notes into the quivering hands of the maître d' and left, blushing furiously. Only Henry still sat at the table, completely unflustered, his napkin tucked under his chin.

'Do I have to go?' Henry smiled sweetly at me as he took a long sip of Calvados from the bottle and slipped a large green mussel down his throat. 'I have been immaculately behaved.'

I helped him into his jacket. He placed the fullest bottle of wine into his pocket, bowed at the room and let me lead him out into the night which was sharp with sea-breeze after the warmth of the restaurant. Marc and Fred were dancing along the side of the harbour wall, feigning to push one another in, their laughs sounding loud and raucous across the quiet square of the basin. Guy walked up to us, his face drawn down into a clownish expression of despair.

'I thought they acted quite horribly in there. It was over nothing. They were arguing over who had the last langoustine. I mean, we could have ordered more. And it wasn't as if we hadn't eaten enough. It's so shameful. That's my papa's favourite restaurant and we shall never be able to go back there. Never. I must say you two boys behaved very well, however. Thank you for resolving it so calmly.'

I looked at Vero's strange brother with his bottle-bottom glasses and his worried brow and weak chin and I smiled at him. He was passionate about his work, was very earnest, very kind and completely lost in the company of Marc and Fred with their brash worldliness. I resolved to make sure that he enjoyed himself, was pleased that he had struck up a rapport with Henry.

The night grew colder as we moved from bar to bar, drinking Guinness and Calvados mixed into an ugly grey froth in the small glasses which seemed to be refilled quicker than we could empty them. We were thrown out of the bars around the harbour, barred from entering some as word of our riotous progress spread. Fred had stolen a set of antlers from the wall of an Alsatian restaurant we passed, the owner running after us until Henry pressed more euros into the little man's hands. Marc placed them on his head, holding them with his large, thick fingers. He charged at Henry, who at first pretended to be a matador, then, frowning, tried to trip Marc and they began to

147

scuffle, letting out forced laughs as they lunged at one another. Fred pulled them apart and we fell into another bar and drank crème de menthe and Baileys and advocaat and everything foetid and disgusting they could serve us. The evening dissolved into glimpses of lucidity, separate images to be pieced together only much later or not at all.

I remember Guy standing in the middle of the road, cars honking as they passed, lights flashing either side of him. He looked terrified and then bent double and a great torrent of puke flowed down onto the tarmac where it landed with a heavy sound like a belly flop. Marc and Fred held a race along the decks of moored boats, shaking the sleeping families within as they leapt from ship to ship, always coming close to slipping down into the dark lapping water. Finally Fred's foot went through a glass skylight; the boat's owner stood on deck shouting at the disappearing figures, shining a torch which darted around the basin like a night-insect. Fred limped when he reached the shore. Blood ran black down his leg when he lifted his trouser-leg. He winced when I dabbed at it with my handkerchief and removed a shard of glass from the deep vermilion wound.

The police arrived in a raucous old van, blue lights illuminating the tops of the tall and narrow houses that clustered protectively over the harbour. I saw the thin-lipped gendarmes look around for us, their eyes adjusting to the darkness. We disappeared down alleyways, splitting up and running with a speed and energy that drew on itself, sending us careening off into the small and narrow streets of the town. I was running alongside Marc, and it somehow became a race; our feet pounded on the road's surface, salt spray was flung from the sea wall which ran alongside us.

We had left the town behind and there was a steep cliff to our left, the sea to our right. I looked to the side, saw that Marc moved easily, his arms pumping in clean thrusts, his stride long and confident. He was wearing trainers and I could feel the heel of one of my loafers clapping against the sole, ready to detach itself. I would not let myself lose, however, even though I knew that Marc was in charge, that he would decide how far we were going, where we would end. Because of this I couldn't pace myself, couldn't conserve energy for the final sprint, and so I determined to put as much room between us as I could, thought that if I was out of sight, round the next bend and distant, he might give up and return to the town.

I picked up my pace. The heel came loose and span clattering behind me. I ran on the balls of my feet, feeling my heart filling and pumping, the swell of adrenalin as I pushed myself forward with my chest out and my arms pulling me through the cool air. Marc tried to keep up for the first hundred metres, but soon fell back. He didn't disappear altogether, though, and every time I looked around he was plodding away, his head now down, his legs barely lifting from the road, arms at his sides. As I rounded the bend in the road there was a sudden freshness of breeze, clouds cleared and a flash of moonlight skimmed over the low waves of the bay. The bend was long and easy and I gained a second wind, felt joyous and surged forward with a shout.

As the bend finally eased out into a long straight, I saw that the road ended in a rocky promontory, the cliff to my left falling away to leave the sea on both sides. The wind began to buffet me, eddying as if unsure of its direction. Waves chopped and lapped over the spit of land and I saw that I was much closer to the great bridge, could see its slick underbelly, make out the cables in the moonlight, the occasional lorry that thundered over it. I came to the end of the straight of land and stood atop a rock, staring back at Marc who was barely running at all, his shoulders slumped, his hands occasionally coming up as if to thrust aside the breeze that impeded his painful progress. I looked back across the water and could see the oil refinery at Le Havre, the flare of gas-flames burning off into the night, the patchwork of halogen lighting that illuminated the sky above it, the tankers that sat moored in the bay, rocking in the moonlit silhouette of the bridge, divided by the long thin shadows of the cables.

Marc finally came up beside me, panting heavily. Sweat had made his hair slick, and his shirt stuck to him. He climbed up onto the rock alongside me and put an arm around my shoulders. The wind was cold now and he shuddered, reached to find a cigarette, held me out the packet and I cupped my jacket to shield us as we lit up, some sort of camaraderie establishing itself between us as we crouched over the low and flickering flame. He laughed as he stretched tall, blowing smoke into the night.

'Man. That was so tough. I'm too old for that kind of thing. Can't remember the last time I ran like that. You know, we were running and suddenly I just didn't want to stop. Didn't ever want to stop. Was it the same for you? That feeling that you just wanted to go on forever? You were good to run alongside me for so long. Made me feel like I could keep up with you and then – pow! – just at the end you show me that you were just fucking with me. Man, the way you disappeared at the end there. *Putain*, that was majestic.'

I realised, ashamed, that he hadn't thought of it as a race, that he had been enjoying the run for the sake of it, had even seen it as some sort of strange bonding between us, a chance for us to get to know one another. I clapped him on the shoulder.

'I used to run cross-country for my school. Eight hundred metres in the summer. I like the solitariness of running, and the only way you can be sure of being alone is by being in the lead. What a strange night, Marc. I haven't been to a stag do before, but this was amazing.'

We turned back towards the town, smoking constantly, relighting our cigarettes from each other's spent stubs as they burnt out, the moon now bright above us and the wind gently supporting us from behind. Marc's voice was tired and caught occasionally as we talked, the wind in the trees murmuring a chorus behind our words.

'My first stag do was in Vegas, before my first marriage. That was a cool party. All of us had too much money and we believed that we would carry on making that kind of cash forever. We rented Harley-Davidsons and drove out into the desert during the day. Took strange desert drugs like the Beat guys. Fred was there. Then at night we did crazy things in the casinos, got hookers into our hotel rooms, drove around sidewalks on the motorbikes and lost huge amounts of money. Fucked-up but so cool, man. None of us could work for like a week afterwards. Fred checked into hospital his liver was so badly damaged. I wanted this time to be more quiet. More grown-up, heh?'

I looked over at him. He was staring up into the sky, the cigarette hanging from his lip, his hands in the pockets of his tight jeans.

'You were married before?'

'I got married to an American girl when I first moved to New York. It was a mistake. I can see that now. I was scared to be in a new city, bewildered by how big and serious it all seemed. I needed a guide, someone to give me stability amongst all that glass and money.

'I married Lucy just before 9/11. We were on honeymoon when it happened. Lucy was cool but I was very young, and her family were rich and protective and wanted us to come and visit them in Westchester like every weekend. I was a young

French guy with a cute accent and rolls of cash in a new city. As soon as I had her, I felt more sure of myself, more able to walk into a room and have all the girls look at me, you know? The marriage only lasted a year. I still write to her sometimes. She doesn't reply.'

We walked for a while in silence. I could see the town in the distance, was astonished at how far we had come.

'Why did you leave New York? Why come back here?'

'I lost it. Had everything and I lost it, man. I was doing so much coke, and working so hard, and I just got so tired. Became really bored of it all. So I started fucking up things at work on purpose. Started sending really aggressive emails to my clients, trying to get more money out of them. I had decided that I needed one more year of pulling down big money, one more year of making it big. Then I'd come back to Europe. Live near my parents. Raise chickens, heh? I got fired halfway through that year. Surprised I lasted that long. I didn't know who I was, what I was doing. I pitched up on my parents' doorstep a year ago and I was just fucking gone.'

Marc had picked up a stick and was slashing at the bushes as we passed. He surprised a bird and it cannoned off into the night, shrieking.

'I called Vero when I was sane enough to hold a telephone, have a conversation. She was about to go into her exams, her voice was like nervous, scared. She and I were together years ago. One of those strange relationships, you know? I was twenty-two and worked in the PMU bar in the centre of Neufchâtel during my summer holidays. She used to come in and buy cigarettes, glasses of Pernod, beer. Our parents are friends, so of course I knew she wasn't old enough. She'd come in with her friends and I'd ask them for ID but never her. So I could talk to her alone.'

He slashed at the bushes harder, more rhythmically now.

'Man, those were good times. You know when your words seem to have some extra force and gravity? That was me and Vero, sitting in the shitty fucking bar in the middle of this nothing town. We felt like we were the only real philosophers there. That we'd leave together and change the world. And all the time I was away I held that image of her, swirling a cigarette in her hand, slurring her words in the darkness of the bar, as a symbol of everything I left behind. A symbol of innocence. It grew into a symbol of what I wanted to return to.

'So when I got back having fucked up everything – I mean absolutely everything, I called her. Said I was coming back to Neufchâtel. Turning my back on cities. That I had enough money to look after us for a while – I'd do some work for my parents' legal practice, she could work as a teacher in the little school in the town. Told her that I needed her optimism, her innocence. Man, I hadn't even seen her for five years, we hadn't slept together since I was twenty-five – seven years ago. But when she called and told me she was coming to be with me, and asked me to meet her off the train at Calais, and I saw her in the mistiness of the railway station, it was like we'd never been apart, you know? She was my little Vero.'

We began to pass the first houses, made our way haltingly into the town. An incipient dawn chorus trilled experimentally in the distance, fishing boats with clanking metal on the deck slapped through the waves as they made their way out of the port.

'Vero never spoke about you. I thought I knew her so well, but she never spoke about you.'

'I left her in a pretty bad way. It was just before her bac when I finished my legal exams at Dauphine and applied for the job in New York. She and I were lying in bed at my parents' house. It was an amazing evening, the sun just dipping down behind the hospital and the wind coming through the house, lifting the sheets from off her, and I looked down and thought how young she was, how much I loved her, and I knew it would break her heart, that it might fuck up her exams. But I told her I was leaving and she changed, suddenly looked much older, you know? And she just picked up her clothes, held them in front of her and walked naked down the path, stepping into her pants as she walked down the road.

'She was supposed to be going to the Sorbonne, but she applied for Edinburgh at the last moment, after her exams came through – clearing, I think you call it. I think she wanted to be as far away from me, and any memory of me, as possible. I followed her from a distance through Guy. We sent each other emails; he was always very distant but polite with me, unlike the father, who I think might hate me. When I came back, I got Vero's number from Guy. It was the first thing I did.'

He sent the stick spinning over the sea wall and out of sight, lit another cigarette, and turned towards me.

'I think that Guy and his father are pretty upset that Vero and I are together. I mean clearly they are happy to have her back here. It was both of their worst nightmares, their darling girl becoming this materialist snob, obsessed with her looks and that weird English class system. But to have her come back for me – that must have been hard. The old man is a real patriarch, a *pied-noir* born in Algeria, wants his women around him the whole time. When I left her, he wheeled up to my house and tried to get my father to send me outside to fight him. The man's a lunatic. It's hard for people outside to understand why we're back together. But Vero understands, the two of us, we understand each other.'

He strode up the hill and into the town. I trotted to keep up with him. When we reached the main square he looked up at the silver-blue sky and then back at me, his eyes bright. We stood together in the empty space of the square as slowly the town shuddered into life around us.

Marc and I sat in the taxi, watching the first tourists stagger out of their rented houses in search of coffee and croissants. We left Honfleur behind us and moved off into the country-side where the trees hung heavy with rain. Neither of us spoke until we reached Neufchâtel. I was dropped at the bottom of the hill that led up to Vero's house. Mark was staying with his parents. I stepped wearily out of the car and walked up the hill in the rising light. In the narrow streams that ran alongside the road, full with last night's rain, frogs and newts moved. Their slithering bodies disturbed the water, sending out ripples that a heron snapped at until it rose with lazy wingbeats at my approach.

I gently lifted the latch on the gate and walked up the path. She was sitting on the porch smoking, crouched beneath the climbing white rose that grew up the side of the house. She watched me as I approached, flicked a butt in a slow arc towards me. She wore a thick white jumper pulled over pyja-mas and a pair of her father's slippers. I sat down beside her in silence and she passed me a cigarette, put one in her own mouth, then held up the flame to us. Both of our faces were caught for a moment in the light from the flame. I put my arm around her and she rested her head on my shoulder and exhaled deeply. The heron came and settled under a tree above the small pond in the corner of the garden. It kept one eye on us as it dipped its beak into the brown water. Vero coughed, spoke, and her voice sounded very small against the chatter of birdsong in the trees around us.

'Henry came back at three. Carried Guy from the bus stop. I have never seen Henry so drunk. I have never seen Guy drunk at all. I put them both to bed with Alka-Seltzer. What did you get up to? Guy kept moaning about a police record. He puked in my father's briefcase. No idea why he even had it, but he was wandering around the house picking things up, trying to re-organise furniture in the small hours of the morning. Henry was a star, even that drunk he was still sweet and sat trying to mop papers that stank of oysters with a dishcloth. I looked in on them both an hour ago. Henry was sleeping like a baby, all curled up around the duvet. Guy had thrown his bedclothes off and was sitting bolt upright, fast asleep. You crazy boys, leading my brother astray.'

I took a deep breath.

'Vero, there's something I need to say. I can't hold it back, can't let you go ahead with this without at least making you aware . . .' I wanted to tell her that he was just like me. That he was worse than me. That he wouldn't love her enough, couldn't love her as much as I did.

'Charlie, I know. I know all about Marc's past. Know about his present, too. I know that he's been married before, know that he's made a mess of himself. He's far from perfect, but he's what I need now. He's a challenge, and he's felt so many of the things I have felt, he's lived through the same kind of shit. I remember when he left me, I promised myself that I'd never speak of him again, never mention him to anyone, but I'd always go to him if he called out for me. He dumped me just before my exams at the end of school. I remember just stuffing all the feeling down inside until it stopped hurting and was just – *bof* – you know? And now we're back together and I want you to accept that, and see him as a friend. Because that's the only way that we still work, Charlie. The only way we can still see each other. Now you must get some rest. Look at this weather – some luck, heh? Like Edinburgh has moved to hang over the house just for my wedding. Good night, Charlie. I love you.'

It had begun to rain again. The birdsong became frantic and

then disappeared as the birds found shelter under broad pattering leaves, placed soft heads under wings and went back to sleep. I looked out to the pond and the heron stared back. The raindrops fell noisily into the grey-brown water. I stood up behind Vero and the heron climbed with me, flapping wings unhurriedly as it rose into the sky that was the same colour as its plumage. I noticed that the tree that hung over the pond was not a single plant, but two that had joined over time. A thick alder that was now dead, its branches leafless, its trunk hollow and ravaged by boring insects, was encircled by a thin and fragile rowan tree. The barks of the two trees had become melded over the years, welded together by the force of so long a juxtaposition. And now the rowan seemed to support the much heavier dead alder, seemed to cradle it in the embrace of its paler bark. Wind ruffled the surface of the pond, and the rain began to fall more heavily.

I ground my cigarette into the damp earth, placed a kiss deep into the soft hair that was piled high on Vero's head, and made my way inside. Henry was still curled up on his bed, snores rattling in his throat. I lay down clothed, and fell into a light and troubled sleep. I dreamt I was on a huge ocean liner, and the liner was taking me somewhere dreadful, somewhere dark and terrifying. I was walking as fast as I could down the polished wooden deck, and even as my steps took me away from whatever horrifying destination awaited me, the enormous engines of the boat carried it surging forward through the churning water, and I knew that when I reached the rail at the back of the ship I would have to turn and face what we were moving towards. I woke, calmly reached into my jacket pocket and pressed two blue pills out of silver foil. I let them dissolve as I stared at rain running down the window through the crack in the pink curtains.

'Wake up! Wake up, Charlie! We've been awake for ages. I'm getting married today. People will be arriving soon. Get up!'

Vero threw both of Henry's pillows at me and he stood behind her, laughing. She was wearing only her underwear, small black lace pants and a bra that pushed her breasts high on her chest. She saw me watching her, fell back into Henry's arms, leant her head against his chest. He was dressed in his morning suit and looked fresh and clean and happy. I watched him gently stroking the pale hair that ran down the curve of her spine, saw where it became darker as it raced down her back and into her pants. She grabbed him by the hand and they raced off down the corridor together. I staggered to my feet and pulled off my stinking clothes, my shirt clammy with sweat. In my boxer shorts I limped down the corridor, bowing my head against the light. Guy stood in the door to his room, a look of great pain on his face. He was dressed in an ill-fitting suit, his hair plastered back against his scalp, his glasses slightly misty.

'Charlie, I feel terrible. What did we do last night? What happened?'

I stumbled past him, into the bathroom which was pink and feminine, reminding me that there was no lift for Vero's father to get upstairs, that he must have bathed in some other place, that this was the realm of her small and quiet mother. I stood under the shower and let the needles of water turn circles upon my back, let the fingers of water move with whispered breath through my hair. I wanted to be back in London, couldn't face seeing Marc, couldn't bear seeing Vero married. And I couldn't work out why Henry seemed so happy. I cleaned myself very carefully, stared at myself for a while in the mirror, a look of supreme dissatisfaction on my face.

I stood with Henry at the garden gate and greeted people. Every guest commented on our morning suits, the compliments touching and provincial. My waistcoat was sky-blue, the colour of duck eggs. Henry's was burgundy and looked like it was stained with blood. He had rediscovered some few words of French, beamed '*Enchanté*' as people stepped through the small metal gate and into the garden. The rain had stopped but the sky rushed by very close above our heads, a cold wind blowing low clouds skimming over the countryside. Chairs had been laid out by the pond, buffet tables of food and wine sat in the marquee on the other side of the house. Vero's father wheeled himself about in a scruffy dark suit with a grey woollen rug pulled over his knees. Vero's mother looked beautiful; her small frame seemed magnified by her position perched above her husband. Her dress was turquoise and made her eyes seem very dark. I watched as she greeted friends, her husband's hand never leaving hers. She kept looking up at Vero's window; every so often her daughter would wave down to her.

The mayor of Neufchâtel was to marry the couple. He was a bald socialist, his large hands and rough skin speaking of a life amongst labourers. He played nervously with his purple tie as he stood in front of the expectant crowd. There were perhaps thirty people there, all of them older and local. I saw Vero looking down at us. Henry hadn't seen her, but I met her eyes, and she pressed her face against the glass, squashing her nose and her cheeks in a way that she perhaps meant to be comic. But there was no smile on her lips, and it looked grotesque and tragic to see her beauty suddenly erased. When she pulled back from the window and her features reformed themselves, I could see the smear of make-up on the glass.

Marc and Fred came up the path as the last of the guests took their seats. I shook Marc by the hand and he smiled warmly at me, raised his eyebrows in momentary recognition of last night's events, then turned away and embraced Henry. They sat down at the front of the rows of chairs. I looked up, above them, and I saw the hospital. Its windows revealed the sky opening up before it like a shell, and the sun broke through cloud and the heavens above were visible in the reflective windows. Henry and I took our seats at the back and turned as a door banged and Vero walked out of the house.

She was wearing a white dress of very fine silk, and I could see the outline of her bra, could make out the darkness of her pants. Her face was very still, quite stern, as she walked alone down the aisle, between the suddenly hushed guests, and Marc stood up to greet her. He placed her small hands within his, and I watched her stand straighter, reach up to lay a kiss on his cheek. Henry took pictures, standing on his chair to capture them, then dancing round to the front to frame their faces close up.

When the short service was over, and Marc took Vero's face in his fingers and laid a long kiss on her lips, and the crowd cheered, I slipped off and stood at the gate again, looking out over the roofs of the town. A group of children were shooting down the hill on their bicycles. A boy stood up on his pedals and raised one hand in the air, palm cupped to catch the racing breeze. He let out a whoop and the two girls following him rode furiously to try to catch up. He was moving too swiftly, though, and I watched him as he turned to look back at them, a huge grin on his face. Music had started playing. It was Guy on the guitar picking out perfect classical pieces with his long lady's fingers. I watched the last of the cyclists pedal out of view, down towards the town.

Later, Henry and I stood by the pond in the sunlight. I leant on the dead alder, my hands picking chunks out of the damp wood. Evening was approaching and the guests stood scattered around the garden making quiet conversation. A few old ladies left, happy to have seen the ceremony, picking up their steps delicately as they made their way down the path. The garden was surrounded by hawthorn bushes upon which grew great clumps of honeysuckle that streamed scent into the warm air. White butterflies turned circles above the honeysuckle, arranging themselves into marble columns which shuddered in the evening air, then shattered apart and reformed above another vivid clump. Henry was very drunk, had been sinking full tumblers of Calvados, wine glasses of Armagnac, pitchers of cider. He was smoking his fifth cigar, and I could see that he drew on it as he would a cigarette, sucking the thick dark smoke down into his lungs and blowing it out through his nose. He sat down suddenly, his feet in the shallows of the pond, his shoes filling slowly with water.

'Vero's married.' He turned to look up at me with an abject expression on his long face and let the cigar fall into the pond, where it floated on the water. Slowly flakes began to unravel from the cigar; it unfurled itself in the water, stretching out like a butterfly emerging from a chrysalis.

'I mean . . . I mean I knew she was intending to get married. That's why we came here. But if I'm honest with you Charlie, I didn't really think it would happen. I always thought that Vero's so . . . so dramatic, so full of fire that she would have turned it into some great crisis, come to me and asked me to whisk her away from the whole bloody mess. I thought that all morning. She was being awfully affectionate to me, kissing my hands, hugging me, pawing at me in that rather manic way of hers. I thought maybe she was going to tell me that she couldn't go through with it.

'Because, I don't know about you, but I thought last night Marc was . . . well he was really a bit of a tosser. I mean, very interesting and very lively, but . . . really quite a massive tosser. And I thought she'd have seen that. Bloody unfortunate that we'll have to spend time with him now. Oh. My shoes are getting wet. Give me a hand will you?'

I hauled him up and we wandered back into the marquee where Guy was strumming gently to himself in a dark corner behind a wall of disco lights, the guitar now unamplified but still clear over the drone of bees and quiet voices in the garden. Vero was standing in the middle of the dancefloor, her arms stretched down to her father, who sat in his chair smiling broadly, his head nodding to the soft music. The wheels of his chair squeaked as he rocked slowly on the slippery tiles. I stood smoking for a while as Vero and her father pulsed gently in the flashing lights.

People assembled for dinner at seven, coming hesitantly into the marquee, reluctant to leave the unexpected warmth of the evening. As we sat down, Vero's father struck a knife against his glass, coughed and began to speak in his fast, deep voice.

'Veronique's friends have come all the way from England. They looked after her there, and the least we can do is look after them here. I will therefore ask you to be gentle in your criticism of my English. *Alors* . . . Since I am old, I will be brief. These young people are excited at the life ahead of them, they do not wish to sit listening to an old man when they could be dancing and drinking. But as an old man I also have a right to bore you a little, to tell a few stories.'

He took a long swig of white wine, wiped his mouth with a hairy wrist, and continued.

'So . . . Many years ago, when Veronique was a little girl, we were spending the winter in Sierra Leone. I was working in the hospital there and Guy and Veronique used to come and help me. I remember Veronique as a very small girl, just six or seven, passing me a scalpel for a cataract operation, holding a woman's hand whilst I operated on her child, walking down by the harbour and looking deeply at everyone, asking questions of everyone. Her seriousness was so striking, her compassion so visible. So you understand that this was a very special person from the start.

'Then my daughter disappeared to Scotland, and to London, and when she came back to visit, I found it hard to recognise her. It is difficult for fathers, watching their daughters grow up. With my son, perhaps, change was a good thing, a sign of his move towards manhood. With Veronique, every change was a loss. Now she is back with us. Back in Neufchâtel which is not as glamorous as London or as picturesque as Scotland. But this place is real, and it is the real Vero who has come back. She has returned to be with the boy she always loved. This is typical of the Veronique I knew. Such determination! Her work with her brother – translating for refugees at the centre in Calais – this is the sort of work that Veronique was made for. I feel as if she has taken a long detour, and now she is back in the correct place. So thank you, Marc, for bringing her home to us.'

He leant forward and took another sip of wine, coughed for a moment and turned to look across at his daughter, tears catching in the corners of his eyes. Rain began to fall on the roof of the marquee, a sharp squall that pounded very loudly on the plastic above us. Everyone in the room looked at Vero's father, unsure of whether he had finished. The skies unleashed one last deluge and then it passed. When the rain stopped it was as if the room had been holding its breath: an exhalation. Vero's father smiled and continued.

'So welcome home, Veronique. We have missed you. Now drink, enjoy, celebrate, my wonderful child. This evening is yours.'

Vero laughed and clapped her hands together. There was a round of applause as Vero stood, scooted around the table to her father and placed a kiss on his cheek. As she sat down, Marc stood, his eyes pale in the bright disco lights that were trained upon him.

'Thank you, Monsieur Cavellin. I know I speak for the whole town when I say how honoured I am to know you, how proud I am to come from the same place as a man of your integrity, your achievement. And I must thank you above all for producing Vero. She has always been present in my life, even before I knew her. The first time we were together, we were like greyhounds in traps before a race. We were constantly shifting, edgy, eager to escape. The two of us have wandered the world, have explored across the continents separately, and yet we have returned here, to Neufchâtel, to you friends and family, to be together. And at the end of our journey we have found each other. I will now make sure we never leave this place again. Because here there is honesty, here there is happiness, here there is peace. And nowhere in the great world did either of us find those things. And nowhere are those things so present as when I'm at home, with Vero in my arms, listening to the sounds of the town I know and love so well in the distance. For now we have stilled that need for movement, cured ourselves of that restlessness and ambition.'

He placed a hand firmly down on Vero's shoulder. She shifted, her smile dimming for a moment.

'Thank you all for coming. Continue to enjoy yourselves. Vero and I will be honeymooning at home, working in the garden, enjoying the summer when these English people leave and take their weather with them.' A brief mutter of laughs from those who were following his rapid words. 'Thank you particularly, Charlie and Henry. You have taken great care of my little Vero. You kept her safe when I was away, and she is lucky to have friends as loyal as you. Now please, raise your glasses, to my wife, Veronique.'

We stood, I raised my glass and turned to Henry. He was staring straight at Vero, his mouth an angry line, high brow hanging low over his eyes. I saw her catch his glance and smile, then her smile disappeared and her eyes flicked quickly away. Henry remained standing too long, glowering at the bride and groom, a cigar hanging from his lips. I eased him down to the table, stubbed out the cigar, settled him back into his chair and poured us both a glass of Muscadet as terrines of venison pâté were placed before us. He sat in silence for most of the meal, staring down at his hands, picking at the food, coughing violently every so often.

After dinner Henry and I stood in the corner as Marc and Vero turned circles for the first dance: 'Lovecats'. They were laughing, smiling at each other, lost in one another. A trestle table served as a bar at one end of the tent. I walked over, keeping out of the line of old women with their cameras, and poured us both a glass of cider. Fred came and stood with us, looking very bored; when the old people joined Marc and Vero on the dance floor, all of them moving their ancient joints gamely in time with the music, the three of us made our way outside into the warm night.

Fred had a wrap of coke and we sat on the porch and laid out lines on the battered wooden table. Henry looked nervous at first. I knew he hadn't done drugs since the night I'd found him puking in the loo, knew that they scared him. He looked at me for a very long time, as if it was a test for me, and when he moved his head down and snorted the line noisily I felt I had somehow failed. We sat and talked as the music played and time passed and delicate old couples trundled down the garden path arm in arm, the bright fabrics of the women's dresses disappearing last of all into the darkness. I saw Marc and Vero make their way towards the house, Vero pushing her father up the ramp and into the bright yellow rectangle of light.

Fred had taken a bottle of Calvados from the marquee and we passed it between us and I could feel the coke fighting the alcohol in my body; I was happy and tired and empty at once. Marc came out and sat down beside us, swigged from the bottle. We sat in silence until Henry stood unsteadily, murmured something that none of us caught and staggered off. I watched Henry stumble over to the tent. I waited for a moment, looked up into the craziness of stars unfurled in the sky above, then followed him.

The marquee was silent and dark. Henry was slumped in a chair, gurgling snores coming from his half-open mouth. I jumped as I saw Vero in the centre of the room, watching him. She was in her pyjamas, her hair piled on her head again. Her eyes were very large and shone in the pale light. I saw that her feet were bare and she was shivering slightly. I began to sing 'Lovecats' in a ridiculous high voice. She smiled at me and I moved towards her.

We danced in the dark, her feet laid on top of my shoes, her arms clasped tight around me just under my arms. I could smell the dinner on her breath, could smell the day's nerves on her skin and in her hair. When I stopped singing, unable to remember the words or keep up my clownish babbling, we stopped moving, and the world seemed very still and silent, concentrated for a moment just upon us. I leant down and kissed her cheek, moved my lips across her skin towards her lips. She stepped back off my shoes, her arms dropped to her sides.

'No,' she whispered.

'Vero, I love you.'

'Charlie, no. Please, not tonight. You can't tonight.'

'Just one last time. Please, just one last time.'

I stepped towards her, slipped my arms around her and pressed my lips hard against hers. She shuddered for a moment, and then I felt her thick warm tongue slip inside my mouth, and we were pressed together, and I could feel the pulse of our blood moving, unable to distinguish between my body and hers, and I didn't need to close my eyes because we were hidden and safe in the darkness. I pressed my hands into the small of her back, moved down her body until I held her arse, felt the softness of her skin beneath the flannel pyjamas. She pushed herself back again, turned, ran from the room, knocking over a chair as she left. I sat down beside Henry, and sank my head down onto the table.

I heard Vero and Marc leave in the early hours of the morning. They were arguing, her voice deep and sharp, his fast and yelping. Fred stepped into the tent for a moment, tripped on the fallen chair, stooped to pick it up with gentle, shaking hands. Finally I stood and stretched, reached out to tousle Henry's hair until he awoke. We trudged to our room like unhappy children stirred from the car's motorway-dreams by weary parents. I helped Henry undress, and fell asleep with the taste of Vero still heavy in my mouth.

We woke late in the morning and Vero's mother made us croissants and milky coffee which we drank from yellow bowls. She and Guy stood waving at the gate as I started the Polo's rattling engine and pulled off down the hill. The last I saw of Neufchâtel was reflected in the blind stare of the hospital's great windows. We sat in silence as the country sped past until we reached the industrial drabness of Calais. Henry turned to me, smiled, lit two cigarettes and placed one in my mouth.

'Well,' he said, 'that's that, I suppose, Charlie.'

Chapter 9

Madison

I read the business pages of the *Sunday Times* on the ferry, poring over the stories about mortgage defaults in the Midwest and the potential bankruptcy of one of the major sub-prime lenders, and the huge drop in the value of the bond market, the jitters in equities. Commentators used words like *credit crunch* and *depression* and *stagflation* and I felt helpless as the boat chugged through still waters towards Dover. I scanned through the messages on my Blackberry. My profit figure had fallen £20,000 on Friday morning. Bhavin had called an emergency meeting for Monday morning. The newswires hummed with prophesy and speculation. I had an email from Yannis asking me to call him urgently. Madison had composed a long and flustered email at four a.m. on Saturday morning telling me about the day's events.

Charles

I'm still in the office. Bhavin has just left. It looked like his eyes were bleeding they were so red. Yannis lost £800,000 today. He's still up for the year, but you know how risky his positions are. You know how much he's borrowed, the weird illiquid securities he has invested in. Bhavin sat with him for three hours earlier. I heard shouting. I don't understand why it's suddenly all so bad. The economy still looks OK. I haven't seen anything to justify things falling so sharply. It's an overreaction. I think. I don't know what to think any more. I think we're all trapped by what we have learnt. By the way things have been for so long. What if these are the death-throes of late capitalism? You're a philosopher, you read – tell me. Is it all over? I can't leave the desk, even though I'm alone now. I'm worried that something terrible will happen if I do. Come back soon, Charles. We need you here.

Madison.

I looked up from the Blackberry and saw Henry playing a computer game with a much younger boy. It was a fighting game, and Henry was bent low over the joystick, furiously pounding the buttons with his fingers. The young boy, who was wearing a tracksuit and baseball cap, a diamond earring glittering in one ear, two vertical lines shaved into his eyebrows, seemed very calm next to the frantic, contorted figure. I saw Henry's character – a Chinese girl – fly backwards in a defeated arc and, as she fell, the boy's character – a green monster with a wild frizz of red hair – leapt through the air, perched on the chest of the fallen player and ripped the black and beating heart from her chest. The boy turned with a thin grin on his lips and Henry slumped down onto the arcade machine. I felt sick and exhausted, and moved through heavy doors out onto the deck. I stood looking down into the steely water, a light breeze playing in my hair, seagulls circling above.

I heard the doors bang behind me, and Henry placed a hand on my shoulder. He lit a cigarette, leant and placed it in my mouth, then lit his own.

'I'm not as good at those games as I used to be. Remember in the Union at Edinburgh they had that game? I'd beat all comers – I was invincible. I must have lost the knack somewhere, lost my reflexes and my will to win. Scary, when the younger generation begins to overtake us. Let's go and get a drink, I'm depressed.'

I dropped Henry at Liverpool Street before driving home

169

through quiet streets to the flat. It smelt damp in the hallway, and I saw that water had leaked into my bedroom from the courtyard, where great pools of rain still sat stagnating over the blocked drains. I laid down old T-shirts to soak up the water and turned on the radiators. It was a Sunday night and as planes screamed in the air above the house, I felt the old familiar melancholy, cooked myself a lonely meal and listened to the man upstairs rowing on the telephone with his ex-wife.

I heard him throw the phone to the floor and I lay in bed and listened to him cry. I worried in a useless, circular fashion about work the next day, resisting the pills that sat by my bed for an hour until the misery got too much and I split one in half and swallowed it down with a glass of water that had been in the room for a week and was now misty with bubbles. Rats scuttled through puddles outside. I fell asleep missing Henry, thinking about Vero. The man upstairs was listening to 'The River' by Bruce Springsteen on repeat. I heard his sobbing increase with each chorus, his broken voice mumbling along and then just a vaguely tuneful moaning. I woke up sweating, the heat turned up too high, my sheets wet and the world silent and empty around me.

Madison was standing at the window talking to Lothar when I entered the office the next day. I was the first of the portfolio managers to arrive and I sat at my desk waiting for my computer to warm up, reading and rereading the hopeless headlines on the front of the *FT*. Madison began to shout and I saw Lothar place his hands on her shoulders. He shook her gently until she calmed down. The two of them walked down the room together and stood outside Bhavin's dark office.

'Good day you picked to take a holiday, Charles,' Lothar said.

'It was awful, Charles. Truly awful. Just a mad stampede, everyone rushing for the exit at once. I can't believe that we're going to be at work as normal.' Madison was tugging at the collar of her shirt. She looked like she hadn't slept all weekend.

'Bhavin has called this big meeting at nine. We need action, we need to change direction. We need very firm leadership.' Lothar talked in a staccato voice, marched up and down swinging his arms as he spoke.

Yannis and Bhavin came in together. There was something frayed about both of them, something ragged in the way they lurched into the office. Yannis leant over the desk and embraced me and the stench that came off him was extraordinary and brought to mind immediately the tramp from outside the flat. I pushed his arms from around my shoulders and tried to back away. He walked around, trapping me. I began to edge myself backwards over my desk.

'Chuck! So good to see you, bitch. How was the wedding? You move on from that chick now you've seen her shack up with some guy? Man, you missed some crazy shit in the markets. Oil's jumping up and everything else is just heading due south. It's been fuckin' crazy, dude.'

His hands shook as he logged in to his computer and tapped his credentials into the Bloomberg terminal. Bhavin walked out of his office and stood looking uncertainly over towards us.

'Where's Catrina? Charles, I never want you to leave this fucking building again. Bad market juju on Friday. Seriously bad juju. I want you to mark all of your positions as the runs come in today. Don't wait for the email tomorrow morning. I want everyone to know exactly how much they're down. We're going to get together with the whole company at nine, let everyone know what's going on. Until then I need you to start ringing round: extend your credit lines ready for the bounce. Nothing has changed in the market. This is a short-term correction that's being driven by a few buck-toothed Cletuses who've stopped paying the interest on their mortgages in

Nowhere, Arkansas. This is not a fundamental market correction, and I want us to be buying on the dip. Things will come back hard when the Chinese and the Japanese start buying. We need to get in there before them. Where the fuck's Catrina?'

The clock ticked towards nine and Yannis and I called around all our contacts at the investment banks, repeating Bhavin's lines about the short-term nature of the drop, how we needed to be able to draw down double, triple our daily credit lines in order to take advantage of the momentary fall in the bond market. Madison came and stood behind me as I pleaded with an Italian commercial bank whose business I had previously scorned to open up repo lines to us. By the time people started to move towards the boardroom, Yannis and I had called every name on our Rolodex. He was more of a networker than I was, better connected through his father's friends. He had extended his line at Bear, laid the foundations of new facilities from Merrill Lynch; the market was desperate to give him money. In his action they saw purpose, drive, optimism – a palliative to their own sense of helplessness. Yannis hung up the phone, yelled triumphantly, and we walked together into the meeting room. As we made our way down the corridor, Catrina slunk up behind us, her bleary eyes cracking at the corners as she attempted a smile. I saw little puffs of powder where her make-up shattered. She stood beside us and I was hit simultaneously by Yannis's body odour and Catrina's stale gin and cigarettes and I placed my hand over my nose, breathed through my mouth. The whole company sat around the large table, or stood leaning against the walls of the boardroom.

Bhavin clapped his hands, his pig-eyes suddenly bright. He turned his hands upwards in the manner of a politician welcoming a group of party loyalists and I could see beads of sweat on the palms, the shimmer on his short fingers.

'Thanks for being here. I won't be long and I won't be dramatic, but I need you to listen very carefully to what I say, because your careers and the future of the firm depend on it. There have been some issues in a very small section of the mortgage markets in the US. It has nothing to do with the bonds we invest in. We have deliberately steered clear of sub-prime. I think Yannis even has a short on the sub-prime index, don't you, Yannis? So the message is: don't worry, stay sharp, don't read the financial press too much – they're just envious guys who couldn't hack it at the sharp end of the industry. You know that old saying "If you can't do, teach"? Well if you can't teach, write journalism. This won't last long, it needed to happen and we're glad it has, but we need to be completely focused on making the most of the recovery when it comes. Bond spreads were getting so tight that our business model had begun to look shaky. This minor correction has given us a new lease of life. Any questions?'

He stepped forward, thrust his goatee into the air and rubbed his greasy hands together. Madison cleared her throat, raised her hand. Bhavin made a show of looking around the room, sighed, and called on her.

'What if it isn't short-term, Bhavin? What if this feeds through into the broader markets, starts to impact normal mortgages, the US consumer on a wider scale? Because we have huge exposure to the mortgage market. Yes, we've done well to stay out of sub-prime, but what if this is just the beginning of the crash? Did you read the papers at the weekend? Did you watch CNN? People are really worried. I know you dismiss them as journalists, but these are guys who have watched the market over many years. They're bright guys.'

Bhavin turned his palms up again, smiled and started to speak.

'Madison, Madison, Madison. You're always the pessimist.

Why don't we have a chat after this? I can walk you through the numbers, ease your fears. I just want everyone to know that there is zero chance of this being an issue even this time next month. I guarantee it.'

That evening I stumbled down to the chemist, rapped on the glass as the little Indian man was turning the sign to Closed.

'Hi. Hi, sorry, I just . . . I lost my pills. Need some more. Can you just give me another month's worth? Please?'

He tutted, rummaged behind the desk, looked at me with his owl's eyes.

'You need to stop taking these. Very bad after a long time. Meant to be a short-term thing.'

I nodded, snatched them from the counter, threw down my money and left the shop at a run.

Back up to the office and Yannis was slumped at his desk like a stroke victim, shuddering occasionally. Bhavin's office door was shut and I could hear him shouting in Hindi on the telephone. Catrina was drinking openly from a bottle of Gordon's on her desk. Madison sat in front of her computer, utterly still, hands resting on her keyboard. I sat down, stared at the number on my screen, the amount I had lost that day, the amount I had to send to Bhavin before I left. £300,000. I looked over at Yannis. Sunlight was coming in the window, flickering through the trees which were buffeted by a gentle breeze. The light beaded on the end of his eyelashes. He smiled and gestured to me. I followed him down the corridor to the loos.

He stepped into a cubicle, beckoned for me to follow him, closed the door behind us. He laid out two thick lines of coke on the seat, bent to snort his, handed the note to me. I was fuzzy with the pills I had taken that day, terrified that everything I had worked towards was being destroyed, that my profits were being eroded and I would be left with nothing at the end of the year – no bonus, maybe not even a job. I felt the coke burning at my nostrils, had inhaled so hard that it felt as if it had reached up to my eyes, stabbing sharply at the softness of my optic nerves. We sat back down at our desks and tried to plough through the reading material that was bombarding our inboxes – harrowing research reports out of the US, more upbeat pieces from European banks who seemed to agree with Bhavin's optimistic view of the market, a miserable article by Madison that painted a bleaker picture of the situation than even the most negative of the US banks. But the coke was powerful; I felt my knees jumping beneath my desk, and I let the words swim before me.

It was the worst week in the history of the bond markets. We tried to stand in the way of the storm. We drew down our credit lines and bought everything we could, bought bonds that were trading as if they had already defaulted, paid sums so ridiculously low that they must be bargains. We were sure of it. Sure until we saw the next trader's run, and the bonds we had just bought were marked twenty per cent lower, and by the end of the week I was down over a million pounds, all of the graft and the grind of the year disappeared down the wires that led from my Bloomberg screen. I thought of the furious shouted negotiations in order to win concessions that had earned me an extra twenty or thirty grand, remembered the long nights working on trades, the fierce fire that had burned in me when I thought of myself inviting the Edinburgh crowd to dinner parties at my Chelsea apartment, large windows open to the green and fragrant summer street.

There was one afternoon I remember during this terrible period. I had been arguing with a trader, screaming at him down the line after he reneged on a trade. I was on a constant comedown, jittery from the coke. Madison stood silently behind me wrinkling her nose as I tried to find someone else who would trade with me. She had taken to standing ghostlike over me, always silent, knitting her hands in worry as I worked. Yannis was yelling at another trader who had cut his trading line.

'What the fuck? You smoking shit? Gotta be strong, baby, gotta be strong. Don't cut me now. Another week. Just gimme one more week and all will be fine. You gotta believe in Yannis, baby. Yannis is the man.'

Catrina screamed down the line during a conference call with one of the rating agencies. They had put our credit worthiness on negative outlook, were threatening to downgrade us due to the abysmal market conditions and our lumpy exposures to the auto companies. The noise was constant and punishing.

At around six-thirty the shouting stopped. A sudden and poignant calm fell over the office. I looked up from my desk and saw that everyone had clustered along the western edge of the room. Madison, Euphonium, Yannis and Catrina, members of the settlements and technology departments, a huddle of secretaries; all of them very still, watching, silent. The computers continued to hum; a telephone rang out every so often, quickly silenced. The room held its breath. I walked slowly towards them, trying to see what they were looking at.

Bhavin stormed out of his office.

'Why is it so quiet? We've got a business to run. Make some calls, can't you? What the hell's going on?'

He walked up to Lothar who was standing on his chair looking over the heads of the crowd at the window.

'What's going on, Lothar? Why has everyone downed tools? Is this some kind of a strike?'

'It's the sunset, Bhavin. Everyone is watching the sunset.'

'Sunset . . . Oh . . .' – he had caught sight of it – 'It's . . . That's fucked up.'

Bhavin walked beside me as I found a space where I could see the flood of light that spread out across the western sky. I looked along the line of faces, and saw each one rapt in quiet astonishment. I could see people on their way home stopped in the square below us, hands held to shield their eyes as they stared up at the majesty of the sunset. And then I looked over to the buildings that stood along the east side of Berkeley Square, and I could make out a similar line of people standing against the window, all of them with the same distant, childlike expression in their eyes.

The sky directly above us was dark with approaching night. Stormclouds clustered purple and malevolent, promising skin-lashing rain, shimmering in the holograms of the glass buildings around us. Stretched out along the horizon, interrupted by thick black clumps of rain, were bright swatches of the sunset. Each of these violent expositions of the sun's dying light was subtly different: canary yellow and green in the north above Oxford Street; then orange bleeding into magenta huddled over the Hilton and above Curzon Street; then colours only just discernible from the surrounding rainclouds in the south – mauve and navy crashing together like waves in a turbulent sea.

These blasts of colour extended along the horizon like ripples from a skimmed stone. They were an archipelago of light, islands of hope in the dark and dangerous sky. We leant forward towards the window as one. Bhavin muttered something to himself about Capri. Catrina started singing softly.

Then the lights began to fade. A sigh escaped from the crowd as first the green, then the orange, then finally the indigo above the Albert Monument, all faded into the darkness of the storm and the night. Rain began to fall and the last wistful spectators below us held copies of the *Metro* above their heads as they scurried away to bus stop and Tube and car park. As night swept in bearing cold rain, covering everything with a veil, it was as if the last sign of hope, the last sense of optimism had left us.

I sat at my desk that Friday night and buried my head in my hands. I had been taking pills just to make it through the day. Blue pills on the Tube and during the morning meetings where Bhavin was looking increasingly desperate, his sweat now dripping from his fingers, flung in shimmering arcs across the room when he moved his hands. Yannis's perspiration had also extended its dominion, now spreading from beneath his arms and meeting between his shoulder blades, staining a pair of wings across his back. He spent his time with his hands behind his head, stretching back on his chair revealing those dark damp patches with the reptilian pleasure of an exhibitionist. We sat wringing our hands, sifted through the morning papers and research reports as we drank triple lattes, double espressos. We looked between the words, through the newsprint, under the coffee cups, always trying to find something that told us when this would end. Because the losses were not sustainable. We had already started to eat into reserves, started to spend our way through our investors' money, had already spent all of their profits. The fund's model was not designed for a crash like this. Every corridor smelt of fear. Catrina sat at her desk talking to herself, talking to her Bloomberg screen.

'This isn't right. This isn't fucking right. We must be wrong. I think we're wrong. What if we're wrong? We're fucked if we're wrong.'

She didn't drink at the desk again, but I could always smell the sweet sharpness of alcohol around her, hiding malevolently beneath Guerlain and chewing gum and a shampoo whose scent, distressingly girlish and innocent, hung in the air around her red hair. She kept up her monologue throughout the day, occasionally calling a bank and screaming trading instructions. I couldn't make out what she was doing, couldn't follow the fast barking voice, the nasal harshness of her Australian accent. Yannis and I continued to spend, continued to accumulate huge positions in bonds and loans and asset-backed securities.

Salesmen from the investment banks called us up, searching for hope in our voices, trying through us to find some anchor, some guidance. They talked with glee of the tribulations of others whilst waiting for the inevitable losses to hit their own organisations.

'Hi, Charles. How's trading? Bought anything cheap recently? Did you hear about the Frenchies? Lost a hundred million on their correlation book. Nasty business. Think they're in line for some pretty major lay-offs. Did you get the marks through on your CDO portfolio? I know they were very low. Nothing we can do. I'm sorry. Things'll pick up. You'll see. Buffett will start buying things. The Chinese government are putting a rescue plan together. Who do you think is next for the kitchen-sink job? Who's going to write down their investments to zero next? Christ, can you believe this market? It's brutal. Just fucking brutal.'

I listened to these men and the rapid oscillation between hope and despair, greed and fear in their voices, and I thought to myself how the market is just a reflection of the psychologies of the traders who operate within it. All of these high-achieving, driven characters with their terribly fragile egos. Marketing types reliant on rapid and multiple injections of success to keep their confidence afloat. The market was plummeting so precipitously because there was no one to stand in its way. Everyone conformed to this basic type, and so everyone behaved in the same way when things went wrong. The flight from mindless exuberance to blind panic had swept away any rational middle ground.

Euphonium came to stand by my desk one afternoon, his big nose dribbling and gurgling with hayfever, his hands worrying at the frayed end of his tie.

'Charles. I just wanted to say good luck. If there's anything I can do. Feel bloody useless if I'm honest. Anything I can do at all.'

He placed his large hand with its thick pelt of tangled black hair over mine, and squeezed. I looked up to see strange currents running in those usually lifeless eyes. I rose, stumbled to the bathroom and looked at myself in the mirror. I was grey, my features drooped. My eyes were hooded and sunken into sockets that were surrounded by skeins of crows' feet. I splashed water on myself, swallowing the cold water that entered my mouth, allowing it to spill down my chin and into the loose collar of my shirt where it cooled my body.

In the late afternoons Yannis and I took coke to stay awake. It was the most beautiful time of the day, as the brightness of the summer sky faded into coloured dusk, and the leaves of the plane trees in the square seemed electric, quivering in the caress of the light. We sharpened every evening with white powder. When we returned to our desks we saw everything moving together, understood the hidden paths that linked the markets, could contemplate recovery and profit and success again. The buzz lasted until after dinner, until the pizza boxes that sat beside the desk were sodden with cold grease, bearing slivers of crust and discarded silver onions. Then we'd mark our positions to traders' runs, and Bhavin walked out of his office and we'd tell him how much we'd lost, and he'd turn back without a word.

Yannis was managing to stay ahead of me. He had more profit in the first place, and was calling in favours with traders, calling on friends of his father, bullying our competitors to help us prop up the tumbling prices. I felt a failure as I saw him surging through the markets picking off traders who dared mark their positions down too far. He had an instinct for bargains, an ability to shame the traders he dealt with. Where I was cowed and terrified by the Bloomberg screen, Yannis seemed to embrace the ridiculousness of our position, loved being the sole voice of optimism in the plunging market. Listening to him out of one ear as I scanned the market for any companies that looked viable, sustainable in the face of the macroeconomic disaster we were facing, I heard traces of a complex web of favours called and favours owed, quid pro quos of dubious legality and no morality.

'Marcus, good to speak to you, bro. How's the market treating you? I know, I know. Fuckin' shit's the word. Bet your bottom dollar that the dollar's hit the bottom, baby. That's what I say, that's what I say. Now let's do some fuckin' business. The credit-card deals you're showing out on your run . . . Yeah, the floaters. I'll take them off you. I'll pay fifty. I know, dude, I know. But it's a buyer's market, and I got money to burn. Now listen: I'll pay sixty, but you need to mark them at seventy for the next month. And the Chrysler bonds I bought Monday? Yeah. Mark 'em at seventy-five. OK? You got all that? OK, we're done on twenty million. Asset-swapped to sterling. You got it. Cool. Thanks, bro. I owe you one.'

At the end of the week, as I stared ahead terrified at the great vacuum of the weekend – nothing was worse than working except not working – I told Bhavin that I had lost three million pounds. I walked into his office, pre-empting his visit to the desk.

'Fuck. Fuck, Charles. How did you do that? I thought you were more conservative than Yannis. Thought that was your problem. A bit of a lack of balls. Three million. Fuck. Yannis is only flat. He's managed to lose everything he made, but at least he's not down. A great result given the week we've just had. I don't know about fucking Catrina. I haven't seen her since lunch. Oh well, enjoy your weekend. Next week is recovery week. Wait and see: you'll be up three million by this time next Friday. Take care, Charles. Take care. You're a good lad, Charlie.'

He looked at me hopefully, smiling. I thought how sad it was that he was so rich and powerful, and yet he seemed to need to be my friend. Perhaps he really was trying to make me feel better about things, but I sensed the eager desperation of the school loser, perpetually bullied, trawling the playground looking for someone to give his lunch money to. I thanked him, backed nervously from his office as he began to tap away at his keyboard.

I sat at my desk a while longer, chewed down a blue pill and felt my eyes reddening around ten o'clock. Madison was typing viciously and didn't see me come up behind her. I massaged her shoulders as she finished her work and we walked down to the Tube together, a gentle silence between us as we made our way down into the dim greyness of the Underground. She kissed my cheek half-forgetfully as we parted, a distant smile on her thin hard lips. I fell asleep on the Tube and woke in Wimbledon to find a drunk with a food-stained beard and dark ugly fingers trying to edge my wallet from my jacket pocket without waking me.

The weekend I spent in a blur of blue pills, not even trying to count the number I was taking, paying no attention to the side effects: drowsiness followed by late-night wakefulness, hunger pursued by a violent nausea, fierce headaches that caused me to bore down into the mattress, clamping a pillow down over my head, trying to disappear into the fabric. I called Vero late on Saturday night. Her voice was heavy with sleep, glutinous.

''Allo. Oui, Charlie? God, what is the time? Are you OK? Is that you?'

I was silent for a moment, trying to fish words from my shuddering mind.

'Vero.' I managed a harsh whisper and then nothing, I sat with my face screwed up, battling to speak.

'Oh, Charlie. Charlie.'

I continued to stutter wildly and, after a deep breath, I heard her whisper 'Goodbye.' The line's silence mocked my own. I found a bottle of vodka in a cupboard in the kitchen and took a great burning gulp, spilling the liquid down my chin where it evaporated, leaving my skin cool and dry. I passed out and slept through Sunday, taking another pill or a swig of vodka whenever consciousness threatened to break over me.

Monday morning arrived like a blessing, the necessity of dressing and showering and negotiating the Tube and minor conversations rescuing me from a further plunge. I wondered how many people lived like this, edging desperately from one day to the next, clutching with trembling fingers at the rituals of everyday life. I thought of the man upstairs, imagined him contemplating the aching emptiness of his existence, the deserted social life, the utter lack of hope or love.

When I got into the office it was very quiet. I sat at my desk and heard the air conditioning moaning, the fans that cooled the computers humming, the tidal murmur of traffic outside. Madison and Lothar came in and their voices sussurated comfortingly. I sat reading the *FT* until Catrina arrived, something sharp and vibrant about her. She wore a black suit with shoulders like wings, her nails were painted vivid red, and her eyes were darting like grey minnows, looking down along her cheekbones at me.

'I need all of the numbers. Get me everyone's numbers. I want exactly what was reported on Friday night. Then sit down with Madison and put together three scenarios. Bad, OK and optimistic. She's already working on it. She and Lothar and I have been in all weekend. I was a little surprised not to see you. I know you're not an analyst any more, but we really need your brain on this one. Shit, I have a meeting. I'll speak to you later.'

She scurried off, head bowed, flicking through a notebook and chewing her red, fleshy lip as she walked.

At ten to nine neither Bhavin nor Yannis had arrived. Catrina sat in a meeting room with Lothar closely examining spreadsheets that Madison had printed out for her. I sat at Madison's desk and we mapped out potential developments, analysed the interplay between the equity markets and oil prices, constructed a picture of the future from the mess of the present. At ten we walked down to Starbucks together. She fizzed with nerves, pacing up and down the lift as we descended, ordered two double espressos, one of which she sank like a tequila shot at the counter.

When we came back into the office the Chairman was standing in the centre of the room. He wore a dark grey suit and a white shirt open at the collar which accentuated his tan. I could see creases in the corners of his eyes and his white hair was longer than before, wispy like surf above his ears. He was speaking with Euphonium, leaning backwards and laughing, using his hands a great deal and giving the impression once again of a politician. But this time it was a politician under pressure, a leader who has misread the will of the people and is now forced to exaggerate convivial gestures, to underline his ability to cope under pressure. Catrina walked purposefully towards the boardroom, gathered Lothar along the way, and called for us to follow her. Madison and I led the technology geeks and the girls from settlements and the secretaries into the bright room with its long walnut table. The Chairman followed last, still speaking to Euphonium about fishing.

Only when we were all in the room did he take charge,

stepping into a spotlight that seemed to have been placed there over the weekend, positioned purposefully to shine in the silver breakers of his hair. He looked older than when we last saw him, smaller and less certain of things. His voice was still rich and rolling, measured and modulating like the politician he was.

'Well, here I am. Really rather thought I'd seen the back of you, but the thing they don't tell you about retirement is how awfully dull it is. You see, there are only so many fish one can catch, only so many restaurants that serve decent food in the Bahamas, only so many books that really interest one. I'm back here because I still own thirty per cent of the business, and I'm not seeing what I worked so hard to build knocked down by a few idiots mistiming the market. So I'm here for a while, and I'm afraid you'll have to get used to it. But seriously, I'm happy to be in the office again. Can't tell you the mixture of relief and frustration I felt when Catrina and Lothar called me last week to tell me of the problems you've been having.'

He smiled broadly, nodded at Catrina and Lothar, tried to look most of us in the eyes as his gaze circled the room. I stared wearily back.

'It won't surprise you to know that I've let Bhavin Sharma go. It's important in business to recognise one's mistakes, and then address them aggressively. I thought Bhavin had the makings of a great financier. Thought he was a chip off my not inconsiderable block. I was wrong. This is a long and painful crash we're headed into. Any fool could have seen that. If it wasn't for Catrina and Lothar shorting the market, shoring up our capital position, effectively saving the business, I'd only be here to hand you your P45s. As it is we all have another chance. I need us to concentrate on selling everything that we can. All cash goes into short-term securities. I need you to manage down risk across the board. When I looked at the risk positions this morning, I could have wept.'

He pressed his palms together, his voice dropped.

'The other thing I ask of you is honesty. We also fired Yannis Lascarides this morning. He was mismarking his book, getting traders to misquote positions for him, had a huge holding in sub-prime mortgage deals that he decided not to tell anyone about when their price fell. We're still trying to work out quite how far he's down, but it looks like ten, maybe fifteen million. That's a huge amount for a firm of this size to lose. So if you're losing money, tell us, and we'll help you fix it. From what I can tell Charles did a fine job of keeping his risk to a minimum even whilst following Bhavin's ridiculous instructions. Now on a positive note, Madison Duval will be joining Catrina and Charles on the trading desk, and we'll try and hire in another analyst to support Lothar and Robin. Go out there and save this business, be smart, make money but above all don't lose any more. We'll ride this out because we've got some of the best people in the business. Now good luck to you all. My door is always open.'

So began the process of trying to regain what we had lost, clambering back up the slope we had tumbled down, with our hands bleeding and our legs weary and our breath hacking in our chests as we trudged back up. Catrina was suddenly everywhere, an effervescent presence demanding that we work ever harder, standing over us as we traded, shouting at us through her shining red lips if we didn't make every trade count. She spent hours with the Chairman going over the company's books, sifting through our positions, outlining market moves many steps ahead like a wily chess player trying to predict the play of a talented but irrational opponent. Madison had inherited Yannis's book and I saw her turn white when she saw the scale of the problem that faced her, the size of the sub-prime trades, the illiquidity of the loans to American companies neither of us had heard of, the complexity of the asset-backed securities. She became increasingly silent, increasingly still, began to weave a web of this quietness around her, discouraging intimacy.

Walking out to buy lunch with Madison we would deliberately avoid the bustle of Berkeley Street. And on the way home I zigzagged through Shepherd Market and down to the bus stop on Piccadilly. It was important to avoid the billboards, to navigate away from any street corner where '*City Bloodbath*' or '*Market Carnage – Latest Reports*' might scream at us. And where copies of *Metro* or the *Evening Standard* were left in the kitchen at work, we slipped them into the bin without looking. But the panic was everywhere. I would turn on the radio in the mornings to hear news of overnight stock-market routs in the Far East. Commentators – always the same oily-voiced economists from minor stockbrokers – would speak with a mixture of blithe, unjustified optimism and pure fear as they muddled through explanations of the crisis. On television bullying newsreaders would grill clueless politicians and I was pleased that I hadn't bought myself a set. Taxi drivers would try to ask my views on equity prices as they ferried me to meetings in the City and I'd flick the switch to disable the intercom, speak loudly to no one on my Blackberry.

The first weekend of the Chairman's restoration, I woke up early on the Saturday morning and walked through the close summer air to Madison's flat on Gloucester Road. It was situated in a tall modern building of pale stone, set back slightly from the road. I rang the buzzer and took the stairs up to the corridor which looked something like a hotel: burgundy carpet and long corridors stretching into the distance, newspapers left on the floor outside some of the rooms. I was carrying notes on the companies in Yannis's portfolio, a primer on the more arcane deals he had bought, coffees from the Starbucks over the road. Madison appeared at the door and ushered me in.

She looked shy, was dressed in a brown velour tracksuit twinned with brown loafers and a smart pink shirt. She wasn't wearing her glasses and I smelt her recently showered body and stepped into a cloud of sharp lemony perfume. It was a wonderful smell and I pressed myself into her neck as we embraced, the coffees slopping foam into the air from plastic vents. I watched the foam slowly settle on the carpet.

Her flat was small and very modern, full of expensive electronic equipment: a huge television, a beautiful chrome coffee machine. The furniture was also very modern, but there was something sad about it, as if it came from the house of someone dead too young, or a company that had gone bankrupt. An L-shaped sofa of tawny suede sat strewn with carefully casual cushions, its perfectly brushed material untouched by slumped night-bodies. An armchair stood in front of the television, but I could tell from a worn patch on the carpet that Madison preferred to sit on the floor, her knees pulled up to her chest like a child. I asked to use the loo and saw the bathroom was full of designer make-up, flasks of perfume, enormous bottles of salon shampoo. We sat at a glass table by the window and watched the sun struggle to push out through the dense clouds.

We worked all day, talking only occasionally. I smoked out of the window and watched the passing of tourists below, thought how insubstantial and transitory was this part of London, full of hotels and serviced apartments for foreign workers and the townhouses of country grandees. As the sun finally came out, low in the sky to the west, we stopped our ruthless plodding analysis. She turned her head up to me. Her eyes were red from reading and the rarely-used contact lenses. I smiled, placed a hand on her shoulder. She shrugged it off, then, as if relenting, placed her hand over mine. I spoke quietly, unwilling to disturb the silence that had descended as we worked.

'I'm meeting up with Yannis tonight.' I had called him on the Friday night, whistled as he explained that he had been marched from the building, his possessions in bin bags, a security guard on either arm.

'They're calling me a rogue trader. Worried that the press will get hold of the story. Have promised to give me a reference if I keep quiet,' he had laughed.

Madison looked at me with a curious sideways glance, winced.

'How can you bear to see him? After everything he did. After the mess he made of it all. I couldn't look at him now, especially as I'm the one that has to try to sort out his book.'

'I don't blame him, Madison. He thought he understood the rules. And he did. He just missed the one that says not to get caught. He was hiding things really well. He thought he could get through the whole downturn without ever taking losses. And maybe he would have been right. The sub-prime stuff looks dodgy, looks like it might lose money. All the rest of the bonds are fundamentally pretty sound. Good investments even. He was manipulating prices, but so what? In this market prices are just a canard. Whether you mark something at ninety or seventy or fifty it doesn't recognise the fact that the markets have stopped working. No one is buying and no one is selling and no one is lending. The system has collapsed and we're worrying about what price Yannis was putting on things. It's ridiculous. I'm more of an idiot for carrying on like nothing has changed, using the same rules as before. I'm like Wile E. Coyote, running over the canyon, willing myself not to look down.'

She looked dejected at my answer, stood and stretched at the window, letting out a long sigh.

We were awkward around each other that evening, clumsy in our use of words, our mouths stiff from inactivity. She plucked two beers from a tiny fridge in a kitchen which looked futuristic and unused and we sat watching the light fade outside the window. I left her standing with her beer staring out into the fragile electric evening. As I walked down Gloucester Road I could see her still at the window, the sooty air softening her through the distance. I turned and raised my hand to her, but she didn't see me, and I walked down into the Tube and caught a train back to Fulham.

I thought of her as I sat on the near-empty Tube, waiting between stations in the hot dark tunnel where occasional gusts of leathery wind blew. I thought about how alone she was, the paucity of her existence with no friends and no interests outside of her work. I couldn't decide whether her life deserved greater sympathy than those traders who cultivated hobbies with the same manic drive that they devoted to their work: mountain biking or kite-surfing or motorboats. I liked to pass the desks of the traders as I went to meetings in the big City banks and note how they marked out their personalities, tried to establish their individuality. A picture of a plain girl in a silver frame, a copy of *Extreme Sports* magazine, a pair of crampons or a clay pigeon left in an obvious place. Perhaps Madison had it right – learn to prize work above all else and free time no longer exists; there is no need to jam weekends and holidays with desperate adrenalin-fuelled pursuits all of which only fleetingly fill the great vacuum of life.

I met Yannis and Enzo in a pub on Fulham Broadway. The pub was full of men wearing shirts emblazoned with the cross of St George, women with downturned mouths and screaming children choking down chicken nuggets and fat chips. It looked like one of the pubs that lined the motorway out of Worthing, the entire establishment and its patrons transplanted from a desperate provincial town and stranded in wealthy west London. Enzo looked mildly horrified by my choice of venue. Yannis stared around the room with interest, twitching his nose at the strange scents. We sat and watched with half-attention as a football game went through its dying last minutes, one team battling valiantly to equalise despite the obviously superior skill of their cultured Continental opponents. The landlord of the pub supported the losing team and was leaning over the bar, pint in hand, roaring obscenities at the screen, at the referee, at anyone who came too close. When the final whistle blew he sank back, his head in his hands, and disappeared slowly down behind the bar.

'I'm going to work with Enzo, man. I'm going to write a column about life in the City for *Arena*. Tell it like it fuckin' is, baby. An insider's view of the greed and the slime. I'll be called "The Rogue". Pretty cool, don't you think, Chuck? You'll have to give me some ideas, let me know what the latest shit is.' Yannis was wearing a dark suit like Enzo, a blue Oxford shirt open halfway down his chest revealing a thick pelt of black hair. He was high on coke and clenched and opened his fists frantically as he spoke.

'Of course I'll help you, Yannis. I'm glad you got something so quickly. And I'm jealous of you. Everyone is so interested in finance now that it's all going wrong. Schadenfreude at the arrogant bastards who had it good for a little too long. When do you start?'

'Next month. My father was telling me I'd have to come and work for him in Athens if I didn't get something quickly. And that was never fuckin' happening, man. No way I'm going back to being Daddy's little boy and having him vet the chicks I bring home. My father's a control freak, Chuck. Completely crazy guy. I would have worked as a fuckin' gigolo rather than go back to stay with him.'

Enzo smiled at me, nodded his head.

'If the same thing happens to you I'll take you on like a shot,

Chuck. Yannis says you're the smartest kid he's met. Can you write? If not, you can do picture editing or something. It's about having good people and you're good, Chuck. I like you.'

'Thanks, Enzo. The way the markets are looking I might take you up on that. And, yes, I can write a bit. Haven't done anything for a while, but I used to write plays at school.'

We sat for a while as another football game started. It was some sort of tournament, being played in a country where the fans let off bright orange flares. Smoke hung in drifting banks over the bouncing supporters, the colours brighter in the glare of the floodlights and the heat haze of the distant stadium. An English team was playing and the bartender seemed to hate this side as much as he had loved the earlier team. Every time the pasty team in red got the ball he booed and roared; when they scored he mirrored the silence of the partisan fans in the stadium. Yannis and Enzo were going to a party at Purple and I walked with them down towards Stamford Bridge, waved them off and turned back home through the warm bright night.

I walked home, tiredness making the overspilling bars swim before me, making me wary of people, sending a wave of panic over me. I thought about how easy it was for Yannis. How the money he had behind him meant that he could embrace the change of career, could suddenly become a journalist, achieve the lifestyle I had long lusted after. And it wasn't just that he could get by on whatever pittance Enzo was paying him, that he didn't need to make money because his father had bought his flat and his allowance was enough to fund a truly debauched life. It was that the solidity of the wealth underpinning him allowed him to treat life with flippancy and devil-may-care. Whereas the job at Silverbirch had come to define me, and the success or failure of my life would be decided by how I managed my career, Yannis was able to flit from one world to another, grinning a wry amused smile at the silliness of it all, but never threatened by disaster, never feeling the weight of the future weighing on the present.

The next week saw the markets plunge further. I had sold half of my portfolio by Wednesday, had taken a further million in losses, but was in a position where I was able to see a way through the crisis. As long as it didn't last too long, as long as the banks that lent to us kept their faith, as long as companies retrenched and cut costs and were cautious, I thought I'd make it through. And when prices began to recover I would have cash put aside to take advantage of the rally. On Tuesday night I ate dinner in my empty front room with a smile on my lips, reading a long letter from Henry which recalled our time at Vero's wedding. I slept and dreamt of them both, that they had come to stay with me in Fulham, and the markets were better, and I had bought a house with great high windows for us all to live in.

Madison had spent the whole of Monday morning locked in a room with the Chairman and Catrina and finally emerged with her eyes very red, her skin flared up and rising in dusty puffs from her wrists whenever she moved her arms. She sat down at the desk beside me and began to cry. I scooted my chair over to her, put an arm around her shoulders, ducked down and whispered to her.

'What's up? What's wrong, Madison?'

'I won. I won in the end. But they made it really hard for me. We shouldn't sell Yannis's portfolio in this market. It's crazy. At least the stuff you own is liquid. At least you know that someone will buy it. They don't understand how obscure these structures he bought are. Some of them were made just for him. There's no way I can sell them in a market like this. Not without taking three or four times the loss we've already suffered. It's so ridiculous of them. So typical. It's almost as if they want to punish themselves by selling into a crash. Catrina seems to think that she could do it. That she should do it. But the Chairman gave me the job and I'm going to see it through. They want another meeting at the beginning of September. But we hold off any fire sale until then. We've just got to hope that this is short and sharp. I really believe that this is the right thing to do. The markets will return to some sort of equilibrium. Before things were too bullish, ridiculously overvalued, but now panic has driven the market to the opposite extreme. We need to wait for calm, for moderation. All the sovereign wealth funds, all the private equity money, all the pension funds – they've got to start buying at these prices. And when we find the bottom, then I think we'll see a pretty sharp rally. When everyone's back from their summer holidays at the beginning of September things will be better. And that's only three weeks away.'

I rubbed her shoulder, pushed my half-drunk latte her way. She took it and swigged, smiled at me so her glasses wrinkled on her nose.

'Thanks, Charles.'

'I know it's going to be fine, Madison. The market moves in cycles, you've always told me that. And we're not going back to where we were, but I really think this sell-off has been overdone. I'm sure things will be better in September. You did the right thing. It's the right decision.'

It wasn't the right decision. Every day I watched her losses escalate – since her discussion with Catrina and the Chairman they had become her losses rather than Yannis's – saw the figure pass twenty, then twenty-five million. Madison made me mark her book every evening, unable to look at the prices which continued to fall, prices supplied by traders who were taking huge losses on their own positions and were happy to spread the misery. Madison spent three nights in a row sleeping in the Chairman's office, stretched out in her tights and blouse on his sofa. She made me get in at six-thirty to wake her when she stayed over at the office. She looked like a child as she slept. I bought us both croissants and coffees and watched, touched, as she slowly reached herself out of sleep, rubbing her eyes and stretching like a cat. She'd smile for a moment as I tickled her feet to wake her, then she'd remember where she was and why she was there and misery would flood into her eyes, and she'd cover her face with her hands. It made me want to cry just looking at her.

September arrived, ushered in by showers that came from nowhere out of deep blue skies. I was constantly soaked, my suits steamed in the warm office air. I was always forgetting my umbrella when I went out to smoke or buy lunch, half-pleased to feel the warm rain coursing through my hair and down over my forehead to drip from my nose. Madison didn't leave the office that first miserable week in September. I had managed to turn a profit in the last week of August, had taken advantage of a momentary pause in hostilities when the markets seemed unable to move further down, even tried to move a fraction higher before the wave of sellers who, like Madison, were waiting for the slightest sign of a recovery, dumped their bonds onto the market, sending prices spiralling further downwards. I was doing more and more of Madison's work. She was frazzled, burnt out by the bright glare of failure. She seemed very old suddenly, granite in her silence, utterly removed from life. I thought about calling her mother, thought about speaking to Catrina, trying to get someone to help her.

We were standing outside the front of the office, smoking furiously. It was a Monday morning and the markets had opened down again. Madison was glittering with a fine sheen of rain. It stood in crystalline formations on her brown Burberry raincoat, hung in pearls from her ears. She had a meeting with Catrina and the Chairman at eleven and I tried to speak of light, insubstantial things. I told her about Yannis's first column for *Arena*. It was a sprawling diatribe against badly-dressed traders, a withering attack on the dress-down culture of the investment banks, spewing scorn on the chinos and button-down collars and brown penny loafers of the Americans who had come to colonise London, bringing with them their Brooks Brothers and Hilfiger and Ralph Lauren. But Madison wasn't listening. She turned to me with blank eyes and I saw that the eczema had finally overtaken her. It shattered the edges of her thin lips, roared across her cheeks and into the corners of her moist eyes, spread scales over her forehead. I watched her bring the back of her hand to rest against her cheek where she moved it gently, rubbing skin from both her face and the scaly hand.

'What if the markets don't move in cycles, Charles? Who says they have to? It's just something we have learnt. Something that we are supposed to believe because it has happened that way in the past. Surely if this market has taught us anything it's that the past is no guide to the future. All these losses on sub-prime mortgages – they're entirely new. None of the models predicted this collapse because it had never happened before. Do you remember how we persuaded our-selves that it would all be fine? All because the models said it would? And they were wrong because they could only use what had gone before to predict what would happen after. And history is just history. What if it's only down from here? How do I go into the Chairman's office and tell him that we should continue to hold out for a recovery if part of me thinks that prices might continue to fall?'

She looked at me pleadingly, her hand still pressed against her cheek, cigarette smoke dying quickly in the damp air.

'And what if they do, Madison? What if the markets collapse

and we go to some communist future where we have to barter for goods? Is that such an awful thing? I'd back myself to be good at that. Just because this attempt at civilisation has failed doesn't mean that we have failed. You'd be good at whatever you turned your mind to. Nothing can take away your sharpness, your vitality. You just need to learn to relax. Don't let these things get on top of you. Go in and tell the Chairman that you've changed your mind, talk him through the advantages and disadvantages of selling the portfolio. He's a good man. He'll understand. He'll respect you for it.'

Madison was in with the Chairman and Catrina for an hour. I walked out in the rain to buy us both lunch, spending more time than usual choosing sandwiches; I bought her a chocolate muffin that I knew she allowed herself on special occasions. I had only known it was her birthday a few weeks earlier when I saw the muffin unwrapped on her desk, caught sight of an email from her mother over her shoulder. I went and bought her a bunch of flowers from Moyses Stevens, put them in a cereal bowl and left them on her desk. She had sent me a short and embarrassed thank you and never mentioned it again. I strolled into the atrium of the office with the lunch bag under my arm and saw her striding towards me. I called out to her, but she raised her hand, turned her face away, and rushed past me and out of the building into the rain. I ran after her.

She hurried across the road accompanied by the barks of taxi horns and was standing under the canopy of trees in the square. I crossed the slick dark road and stood beside her, my hand on her very thin shoulder.

'What's happened, Madison? What did they say?'

'She . . . They . . .' She turned to me with eyes that were very distant, very clear. I watched her mouth open and close and then nothing came out. She stepped silently into my embrace, but held her body away from me. She rested the top of her head against my chest and stared down at the ground. I felt as if she were drifting away from me, floating slowly out of my arms. When she spoke her voice was very small, little more than a whisper.

'Catrina sold the whole portfolio this morning. Offered it at a ridiculously low price to one of the investment banks. They snapped her hand off. We lost a hundred million in total. They didn't even give me a chance to make my case. Said that it had been a mistake to give me the portfolio in the first place. I'm so humiliated, Charles. So angry and humiliated. She has always hated me. Told me that she had been against me being made portfolio manager. I feel such a failure. I thought that this was the only thing I was good at. And I've failed here too. I'm not pretty, my skin is falling off me in great sheets and no one knows why. I don't dress well – I'm the female version of those people Yannis wrote so amusingly about. I haven't got a boyfriend and my mother is the only person who I can really say loves me, and now I've messed up the one thing I really thought I did well.'

I should have said I loved her. Because I did. I spent more time with her than anyone, looked forward to seeing her in the mornings, enjoyed buying her coffee and watching it stain her large teeth brown as the day passed. We were a team facing the same terrible battle together and I cared deeply for her. But I didn't say that I loved her. Instead I opened the bag and held out the muffin, which looked small and synthetic in the misty light under the great dripping leaves of the plane trees. She took the muffin and ran. I watched her running up the gravel path between the benches that sat empty under the weeping trees. In her Tod's loafers her stride was long and graceful: she was an excellent runner. She surged up past the Porsche dealership, around the corner and out of sight, accelerating all the time.

Madison didn't return to work that day. As news spread of our huge sale, the markets sank lower. Stories flashed up on Bloomberg calling the company's viability into question. Journalists telephoned from the news services asking for comments on the rumours of our potential insolvency. The Chairman was majestic in the face of the crisis. He answered questions with a cold voice, reeling off statistics about the strength of our liquidity facilities, the credit lines we had at major banks, the significant reserves we had put aside against such an occurrence. Catrina and I sat silently in his office as he charmed and bullied the journalists, responding in French to some worried investors, staying on the phone late into the night to field calls from the *Wall Street Journal* and *Barron's*. I left the office in the small hours. The Chairman was still sat very upright at his desk, his fingers pressed in a tent above a circle of soft light thrown by the green-shaded lamp. I whispered goodnight to him and he smiled up at me. It was a tired, good-natured smile. He raised one hand as I left the room.

Madison wasn't at her desk when I came into the office on Tuesday morning. Catrina arrived breathless and agitated, like a doctor coming late to the bedside of a fading patient. She pounded her Bloomberg in impatient anticipation of the markets' opening. I waited until nine to call Madison. By this point there were already signs of a rally. The Fed was creating a vehicle to rescue failing mortgage lenders. It was thought that the Bank of England would drop rates by half a per cent. The Chairman's bullish statements of the day before had been turned into gushing articles by the press who praised Silverbirch for aggressively repositioning the portfolio into more secure investments. I wanted to tell Madison that she had been right. That the market was rallying. The system hadn't collapsed: things move in cycles. Her mobile went straight to voicemail. I got one of the secretaries to find her home number and it rang and rang until the shrill noise of it began to give me a headache and I hung up.

'Where's Madison? Today of all days I thought she'd want to be here. Got a bit too hot for her, did it?' Catrina's voice hissed at me, her eyes flashing to the empty space where the Bloomberg screen stared blankly back, reflecting the ordered piles of research and carefully positioned pens on Madison's desk.

'She's . . . She's not well. I think she has gone to her mother's. She'll be in tomorrow.'

I worried about her as I made my way home that night, thought about passing by the strange flat on Gloucester Road to check on her. But it was close to midnight and my eyes were aching, my tongue dry and covered in painful ulcers. I tried calling both her numbers again as I walked back from the Tube. As I got into bed I resolved to log into her computer and retrieve her mother's details, call and check that everything was fine. I was sure she just needed a rest. Needed some time away from the markets which had let her down.

Madison Duval was ahead of her time. She had predicted the crash when we were all looking forward to a century of prosperity. She had foreseen the rally which buoyed the market for the next few days. She saw design in things, understood the complex linkages and patterns which moved the world. She even managed to foreshadow the wave of suicides which swept through the City that autumn, borne on the remorseless east wind that emptied the streets and grabbed air from the lungs.

She was found by her mother early on the Wednesday morning. Although she had cut her wrists – and I imagined her pleasure in taking a knife to those scaly symbols of the world that had betrayed her – it was drowning that killed her. She had taken a handful of sleeping pills, washed down with a bottle of vodka, and sunk gently into a hot bath. Its waters ran pink by the next morning when her mother had passed by to check on her, unable to reach her on the telephone. Her head had sunk down low into the water. She had vomited once – I imagined a thin trail of chocolate muffin snaking out from her thin lips. Then she sank below the water and the urge to fight was suppressed by the warm embrace of the drugs and alcohol. I pictured her mother standing above her in the fastidiously clean flat, reaching down into the water and clutching her daughter's mottled face to her chest.

The Chairman called Catrina and me into his office just before lunch. I had been searching through Madison's emails trying to find something from her mother, but only work emails seemed to be saved in any of the folders; her email account was as neat and precise as her apartment. I saw the Chairman's grave face and thought that the fund was going under. I felt panic rising in my chest, all the fear of penury and failure rushed towards me. Then the Chairman spoke, his voice gentle and warm, his eyes cast downwards towards his old man's hands, inspecting liver spots and the silver hairs that dusted his knuckles.

'Madison died last night. She took her own life. I'm so sorry. I really don't know what to say. There was a note. I think . . . I think it all got too much for her. I'm so very sorry.'

I felt my mind empty, felt the heavy silence of the room press upon my eardrums. Catrina gripped the arm of her leather armchair until her fingers turned very white, accentuating the deep red of her nail varnish. She leant forward and began to cry like a child, great heaving sobs coming from her throat. I reached over and took her white hand in mine, felt the blood rush back into it as she squeezed back.

Later, there was an announcement in the boardroom to the entire company. Some gasped, a few of the secretaries began to sob quietly. I saw Euphonium smile grimly to himself. Lothar looked distraught, his eyes filling until he turned his face to the wall. The Chairman spent the day speaking to police, to journalists, to Madison's mother on the telephone. I heard his voice echoing in the silent office as he spoke of her desperate need to succeed, the pressure of a falling market, his great sorrow. Four of us went to the pub together at lunch. Catrina and Lothar sat together, heads down, talking in whispered voices to one another. I sat facing Euphonium. He was sipping slowly, thoughtfully, at his pint of Guinness. His big red nose had dipped in the froth and I reached over and brushed my hand across his face, removing the grey-white patch. He smiled awkwardly at the intimacy of the gesture.

'Bloody sad. I liked the girl. She was so clever. So very clever. Can't imagine what it must be like for her mother. Always seemed to me that they were all each other had. Her mother moved over here to be with her. Used to listen to Madison on the telephone to her. Sounded like a very special relationship. Wish my lad loved me that much.'

I walked to the bar to buy another round and Lothar stepped up beside me to help me carry the drinks. His high forehead was furrowed and his skin seemed grey, as if Madison's letting of her own blood had somehow drained all of us. He stood next to me as the pints were pulled, watched the golden wine poured into a large glass for Catrina. He placed a hand on my shoulder, opened his wallet and pulled out a photograph. A blonde woman with blue eyes and a piercing, intelligent stare was holding a child by the hand. The boy must have been two or three, was still a little unsteady on his legs and had the flattened features and downturned eyes of Down's syndrome. He was smiling at the camera.

'My wife and my boy. His name is Uli. I don't see enough of them. Don't spend enough time with him. He is so wonderful.

Some people might think it a curse, but to me it has been a blessing. Truly a blessing. Something like this, it makes you realise . . . makes you realise so much.'

I didn't know what to say. I picked up my pint and raised it to him. He nodded and sat back at the table. I saw him show the picture to Catrina. She smiled and began to cry again.

Madison's funeral was held a week later in a small church in West Brompton. The entire company took taxis from the office; everything was left for the day. The markets had continued to rise, but there was something hopeless in the recovery. I felt the energy flowing out of the rally almost as soon as it had begun. None of the underlying economic indicators justified the optimism. The Fed and the Bank of England couldn't prop up the markets forever. The market was like a skimmed stone: however many small leaps higher it made, it was always destined to plunge back into the depths. I sold more of my portfolio down, began to take short positions where I could, positioned myself for the coming storm.

The day of Madison's funeral dawned bright. Starlings were roosting in the tree outside my flat and I heard their gossipy chattering as I made my way down Munster Road in the rising light. We sat and talked at our desks all morning, leaving our Bloomberg screens blank, speaking about Madison in low voices. Catrina was gushing in her praise, clearly troubled by memories of the sharp words she had used to the girl, the bullying and the driving and the criticism. The press had leapt on the story of the young woman's death, saw it as an indictment of the industry, of the age. There was a long piece in the *Evening Standard* describing the straight-A student from Boston with the thrusting ambition, the talent for lacrosse and cross-country running, a few short words of praise from the Chairman. The picture they used was taken at Brown and showed Madison surrounded by fellow students sitting on the grass. One girl played a guitar and Madison looked up above the camera, her mouth open in song. The newspaper had dimmed the rest of the photograph, circled Madison in black.

We filled the small church. I stood between the Chairman and Catrina in the second row as an organ made breathy arpeggios out of sight. At the front was a frail, dark-haired lady who introduced herself as Annie Duval, Madison's mother. When I told her my name she pressed my hand between hers, and I felt small fragile bones crackle. I felt ashamed, felt I should have done more to help Madison. I mouthed some soft words and held the old lady's eye. She seemed very strong, seemed to have some vast reserve of fortitude which enabled her to stand here with the people who had contributed to her daughter's death. The organ stopped and then began to play a Bach fugue. I saw the priest enter. As the door closed a girl dressed in a dark grey suit slipped into the church, pulling a boy in his school uniform by the hand. I recognised him as Ray, the boy Madison had looked after on Sundays. The girl looked familiar, was quite beautiful, stared back at me from under a halo of dark golden hair with eyes that seemed very old, very sad. I faced forward.

The coffin stood on a platform in front of the altar. I felt a moment of panic as I thought of the weight of her body in there, the solidity of her flesh, the wasting and putrefaction that had already begun on that young corpse. I imagined worms sliding over her skin, thought of the time at Edinburgh we had left half a chicken in the bin when we went away for a weekend to London, and when we returned it was alive with maggots, swarming and writhing with this ghastly imitation of life. I hoped that they had cleaned her teeth, that her large teeth shone in the darkness of the wooden box.

The priest began to mouth vague familiar prayers. I looked over to the Chairman and saw his face set very hard. The sun streamed through the stained glass of the high window as the priest asked us to take a moment of silence to remember Madison. I pictured the light of her eyes over the table in the Italian restaurant that night in February, felt her thin shoulders with their knotted muscle under my fingers. Then Madison's mother approached the pulpit, leaning on her stick and taking aggressive steps that demonstrated her contempt for the knotted wood in her hand. She tapped on the silver microphone and began to speak.

'Thank you for coming. I'm Madison's mother, Annie. I'd like to read a short poem.'

I stared at the stone floor as the old woman's voice, querulous suddenly as a cloud covered the sun and the church was thrown into darkness, spun out the words of the poem. The first stanza stayed with me, echoed in my mind for weeks afterwards. I heard it half in the old woman's high voice, half in Madison's deep tones.

> *Pour the unhappiness out*
> *From your too bitter heart,*
> *Which grieving will not sweeten.*

The poem seemed to encompass the bleakness of that time, seemed to capture the misery and sadness that drew in upon us as summer was blown away by the freezing winds of autumn.

After the funeral we went to a pub off the Cromwell Road and stood in clusters, our voices small and sombre as the clouds thickened overhead, bringing with them rain and shadows which hung upon our faces, hid our eyes and our mouths in gloom. Madison's mother sat leaning on her walking stick at a long dark table. The Chairman had bought her a glass of sherry and they spoke with their heads close together, their age

205

a common language. I saw Ray and the strangely familiar girl enter the pub and move over to a shadowy corner. I left Euphonium and Catrina standing together: they had nothing to say to one another; he looked above her head, out towards the road and the cars with their windscreen wipers moving frantically to throw off the heavy rain.

I recognised the girl as I moved towards her. It was Jo, the girl from the arches south of the river, Henry's girl. Our eyes met and I saw that she knew who I was. She looked slightly embarrassed, moved her hands down her neat dark suit as if to excuse its formality, the incongruity of her current attire compared with the last time I had seen her.

'Hi. Jo, isn't it? And you must be Ray. Madison told me all about you, Ray. Would you both like a drink?'

'That would be nice. A vodka and tonic, please. And Ray will have a Coke.'

'I'll have a Budweiser.'

'No, you won't, Ray, you'll have a Coke. Your name's Charlie, isn't it?'

'Yep. I remember you. I was with Henry a few weeks ago. He's doing really well.'

'I know, I see his work, read his stuff religiously. Strange to see how we've all grown up, isn't it?'

I walked to the bar, bought their drinks and a beer for myself and sat down beside Ray. Jo was striking, her skin very tanned and her strange eyes dark and wary. Ray looked disappointed with his Coke, pulled at his tie and shrugged out of his black blazer.

'Did you know Madison, Jo? Were you a friend of hers?'

'Not really. I knew her slightly. I work at the children's charity where she met Ray. One of the things I do there is run the volunteer programme. As well as looking after the young ones during the day. I'm a matchmaker, I suppose, finding friends for the kids we look after. Ray was one of the first boys I set up with a mentor when I joined. Madison was fantastic, always gave so much to Ray, spoiled him rotten, didn't she darling? It's so sad, so very sad what has happened to her.'

We sat in silence for a while, watching the Silverbirch employees slowly filing out of the pub, heading back to the office and the markets through the cold dark afternoon. The Chairman was the last to leave, bowing to Madison's mother as he raised his umbrella and stepped out into the rain. He waved at me as he flagged down a cab and disappeared. Madison's mother sat staring into the distance, sipping distractedly at her sherry. She hobbled over to the table, pulled out a chair and sat down painfully. She cleared her throat a few times, coughed into a dark red handkerchief.

'I wanted to speak to you, Charles. Madison often talked about you. Said you were very kind to her, helped her through the most difficult days. I wanted to say thank you. You are a good boy. I can tell that. In her note . . . in her note she wrote a lot of nonsense. A lot of strangeness about cycles and the crash and the problems she had with her skin. What did I do to that poor girl? What is it that I did to make her like that?' The old woman shook her head and sobbed a little into her handkerchief. Then she rose, climbing up with the help of her stick, and shuffled towards the door.

'Mrs Duval, can I get you a taxi? Sit down and let me find one for you.'

I walked out into the rain, felt my hair and my suit growing damp. Two taxis roared past me and then I stepped into the road and a cab squealed to a halt in front of me. I ushered the old lady out into the growling machine. She pressed my hand again as she stepped inside, leant over and placed a kiss on my cheek, leaving a greasy smudge of lipstick and the scent of make-up that was somehow comforting. When I re-entered the pub, Ray was at the table on his own, drinking in long gulps from my pint.

'Jo's gone for a piss,' he said, smiling angelically up at me. His hair was cut very close to his head and a scar ran from one temple down beside his eye. He smelt strongly of cheap deodorant and adolescence. I gently took the beer away from him.

'How old are you now, Ray?'

'I'm twelve on the fifteenth of October. I've just started Year Eight. I'm at Hackney Free. Shit uniform, isn't it? We could wear what we wanted at my old place. Madison killed herself, didn't she? No one will tell me, but she always looked like she was sad, like she'd lost something she loved.'

I didn't know how to respond, looked toward the loos hoping that Jo would appear. I turned towards him, set a grave expression on my face.

'Yes, she did, Ray. She committed suicide. She was very sad, you're right. I knew her quite well and I'm so upset that it came to this. It didn't need to happen. She had a great deal to live for.'

He looked at me quizzically for a moment, moved his fingers together in a tent the way I had seen the Chairman do ten days earlier. His voice became very serious, as if he was trying to grow into the gravity of the situation.

'I thought about killing myself when my mum died. But it's a shit thing to do, isn't it? Because my dad would have had no one then. And he was already well cut up about my mum. So it would have stopped me feeling sad, I'd have been all happy up in heaven with my harp and all the virgins and everything, but it would have made things even worse for my dad. So it would have been a really bad thing for me to do.'

He banged his Coke down on the table, suddenly angry, ending the conversation. Jo emerged from the loos, as I placed a soft hand on Ray's shoulder. He shrugged it off and turned towards her.

'Can we go now, Jo? I'm bored.'

'That's not very polite, Ray. But I do need to get back to the office. Charlie, listen, what are you up to this afternoon? Do you need to be back in the office? Perhaps . . . If it's not an imposition . . . Perhaps you and Ray could do something together?'

I looked at my Blackberry. Thirty new messages. One from Catrina asking when I'd be back in. She needed help. The rally looked like it was coming to an end. I smiled at Ray who was staring at me with his large black eyes.

'That'd be fine. Let's walk down to Fulham Broadway and catch a film, maybe grab something to eat?'

'Can we go to Subway? I fucking love Subway.'

Jo smiled and then suddenly corrected herself, forcing a stern look into her shimmering eyes.

'Language, young man. Listen, Charlie, why don't you give me a call? Here's my card. It's really good to see you again. It's such a cliché to say what a small world it is. I don't think I believe in coincidences any more. Will you put Ray on the train? He can find his own way from there.'

We waved goodbye to her and then Ray and I stepped out into the pounding rain, jumping from puddle to puddle, splashing each other with our soaked shoes. He started to run, laughing wildly, and I ran beside him, drawing in deep breaths of the damp sooty air.

Chapter 10

Ray

I left the office early on Friday night, unable to endure the accusatory emptiness of Madison's desk or the markets which were in freefall once again or the nagging presence of Catrina standing over my shoulder, questioning my decisions, barking orders at me. As I walked down Berkeley Street I pulled out Jo's card. It was small and flimsy compared to my own and bore a picture of a grinning clown. I called her as I leant against the window of Marks & Spencer outside the Tube.

'Jo, it's Charlie. From the funeral.'

She sounded flustered for a moment. I heard a door shut and then her voice, racing, slightly manic.

'Of course. Charlie. Hi. Hold on . . . It was good to see you the other day. I mean, tragic circumstances, really awful, but it was very nice to see you again. How are you? I can't get over Madison killing herself. Poor Ray is just mortified. He thinks it was somehow his fault.'

Her voice slowed down. I heard her settle into a chair, imagined her lifting her feet onto a table. I pictured her thin legs with Adidas trainers at the bottom of tight jeans sticking up high in the air.

'It was good to see you too, Jo.'

'Yeah. Pretty cosmic. Crazy after all this time. Don't you get the feeling that life isn't linear? Things move in bursts. I feel like it's been one of those bursts. Everything has moved so quickly recently. Things are better now. Better than they were.

'Listen, Charlie, if you're not doing anything already . . . I mean you probably are, but just on the off chance, would you like to come to a house party with me on Saturday night? It's an artist friend of mine who has all these very trendy friends and it would be nice to have someone normal there to speak to.'

'Sure. I'd love to. I'm not sure how normal I am, but of course I'll come. I had so much fun with Ray the other day. He's a really sweet boy.'

'He's great, isn't he? Listen, the party is in Spitalfields. One of those old Huguenot houses. Why don't we meet at Liverpool Street at eight and we can grab something to eat beforehand?'

I spent Saturday morning shopping in Chelsea, trying to find clothes suitable for an east London house party. Finally I gave up, rushed home and pulled on a pair of black jeans, a black sweater and a grey corduroy jacket, thinking that I looked somewhat intellectual and mysterious, if a little gloomy. I stopped by the office on the way into town and sat at my desk sipping a Starbucks, a sense of profound melancholy coming over me at the taste of the warm coffee. I sat down in Madison's chair and ran my finger over the desk to collect the few traces of her skin that had been missed by the cleaner's brush. I held my finger to the light and saw the tiny polygons of skin flickering.

The Chairman had sent out an email encouraging us to call a counsellor that he'd hired, for us to inform him immediately if we felt that we were working too hard, if we were suffering stress because of the state of the markets or the pressure of our jobs. I knew no one would call. Madison had ended her life rather than seek help, and we were all a little like Madison, pushing ourselves towards those ever-distant goals, that shining land of Cockaigne that capitalism kept always just out of sight, just around the next bend in the road.

I stood in the middle of Liverpool Street Station watching the busy world pour past me. Families travelling to Stansted Airport hurried by, fathers pulling reluctant sons, mothers picking up toys dropped by mewling children. A football game had just finished, a local derby, and supporters in white and red tops were making their way through the station, yelling good-natured abuse at one another, some of them singing and chanting with their arms around each other's shoulders. It was quarter past eight and I began to think that Jo wouldn't arrive when I saw her descending the escalator. She was wearing a black summer dress that was lifted slightly by the wind, showing tan thighs and scabbed knees beneath. Her hair seemed lighter in the vastness of the station. Blonde highlights played through it. Her dark eyes sparkled warmly as I hugged her. A closeness had grown between us with no warning, so that it felt entirely natural to hold her tightly against me, feeling the softness of her body through the light dress. She wore a cardigan knotted around her shoulders that she pulled down to cover her chest. I saw beneath it the small cleavage, the subtle rise of her breasts which were lifted by her shallow quick breaths.

'Sorry I'm late, Charlie. I got in the most awful muddle on the Tube. Went four stops in the wrong direction, lost in a book. You know how it is.'

'That's fine. I haven't just sat and watched people like that for a while. Let's go and grab something to eat. Do you know somewhere around here? What are you reading?'

She pulled out a dog-eared Sudoku book, smiled and took my hand, pulling me through the throng of the station and out into the chilly night air. I took off my jacket and placed it over her shoulders, slipped my arm around her and we walked down Brushfield Street, past the monstrous modern development that was appended to the old market like some ugly but high-tech prosthetic limb. We crossed Commercial Street and came out onto Brick Lane. I had never been there before and the vibrancy of the lights and the calling of the touts and the smells were overwhelming and wonderful. Jo stepped past several of the gesturing young men, smiling and waving her hand at them. Finally we stopped outside a curry house on the corner. She made her way inside and beckoned for me to follow.

We sat at the window in comfortable silence, watching the bustle of the street outside. She was very beautiful there in the noisy restaurant, her hair dimly shining above her dark skin, her hands worrying at a popadom, shattering it into tiny pieces on the metal plate. I ordered us both a beer.

'So tell me Jo, how did you get here? You seem so . . . so self-possessed, so together. When I saw you under the arches, you were, well, you know . . . Do you remember, in the blur of it all, we kissed? I can hardly believe that you're the same mad girl that I met back then.'

She laughed a little, stopped dissecting the popadom and took a swig from her beer.

'I do remember that kiss. Very naughty of us when I was seeing your friend. So how did I get here? What a question. I didn't go to university. I wasn't really academic at school and my parents thought it would just be a waste of time. So I didn't take A Levels and went straight out to the Caribbean when I left school. Worked on a yacht looking after the children of the super-rich. Amazing thing for a girl of my age. But it was all terribly shallow. I met Conrad who was the son of one of the people that chartered the yacht. He had just left Oxford, was looking for a little fling, but of course I took it terribly seriously. I followed him back to London and started hanging around the arches. Everyone there was on drugs, all of them thinking that they were creating some great existence, some credible alternative to the material world. Just shows how drugs mess your mind up. But I was the youngest one there, and they all rather looked after me, took me under their wing and when Conrad finally managed to convince me that he no longer wanted to sleep with me, I found other boyfriends. It was a really very sad time for me. I spent days just sitting by the fire and getting wasted and falling down into bed with whichever boy came along. I was very young. Still in my teens.'

Our food arrived and I bit down on a fat prawn, spraying red juice across the table. Jo laughed and mopped at me with her napkin.

'So how did you escape it? Why did you leave?'

'In the end I moved back in with my parents and took the job at the charity. I had realised that the only way to be happy, to find real contentment, is by helping other people. Again it sounds very trite, but I feel it so strongly. Every day I give people more of a reason to live. And I'm talking as much about the City people as the kids they mentor. That's why it was so sad that Madison had to give up seeing Ray. It gives a form and structure to both sets of lives, means that there is always something for them both to look forward to. I have been working there for over a year now and I love it, I really love it. Look, this is a card that the kids made me. I always keep it in my bag. It helps remind me of what I'm here for.'

She pulled out a brightly coloured postcard which was covered in ugly pictures of Jo drawn in scratchy felt-tip, six tiny representations each of which mutated her in a different way: one elongated her nose, another gave her huge swollen thighs. It looked like a Christmas card made by the severely handicapped and I watched Jo's bright eyes as she looked at it and I felt awkward and scornful of her simple joy. She tucked the card back inside her book and took a swig from her beer.

'Maybe I should spend more time with people, Jo. I sit every day and look at numbers, wade deeply through abstractions.

Sometimes I barely speak to another human for days. The only person I used to speak to in the office has just killed herself. Doesn't say much for me, does it? I wish . . . Do you think I could start seeing Ray? I'd be happy to take him out on Sundays. I always see it as a day to fill, dead time. Most Sundays I go into the office just for something to do. Would you mind?'

'I'd love it. He called and asked me exactly that after you took him to the cinema. If you could become his mentor. He really liked you, Charlie. And Ray's a good judge of character. Don't be too hard on yourself. You haven't sold out yet. There's still a fire in you. I can tell when people have embraced the City completely. Sometimes people come to me asking to mentor kids. It's always because their friends or partners have pushed them into it, they drag their heels, look reluctant and nervous, can't meet my eye or the eyes of the kids I introduce them to. People disappear into the numbers, lose themselves in the symbols of their success, the relentless drive for more. I never let them become mentors, the ones who have lost their souls. I know they won't stick it out, know they're beyond saving. But it's so wonderful when I meet someone like you, someone who still has feelings, still loves the world. You'll make a great mentor, Charlie. Listen, we ought to go.'

She insisted on splitting the bill and we stepped out into the neon brightness of the street. A light drizzle had begun to fall and it smudged the lights around us, caressed Jo's hair and her face, fell upon my hand as it lay upon Jo's shoulder as we made our way down Hanbury Street and then left onto the row of imposing old houses. The party was being held at the far end. The door was open and we walked together into the musty interior. People were sitting on the wooden stairs, lying draped over the sofa watching a film with the sound down. We walked towards the back of the house and into the kitchen where a group of young people sat around the large oak table smoking.

'Hi, Jo. Welcome. I'm so pleased you came.'

A tall boy with a dark beard stood up and embraced her, lifting her from the ground. I looked out of the French doors at the back of the house and saw that the garden was an enormous greenhouse, stretching back twenty metres into darkness. Dense foliage grew right up to the door and a tropical dampness and heat seemed to waft in from the garden.

'Roland, this is Charlie. Charlie, Roland. Roland is a wonderful artist. My parents own some of his work. Oh my God, the garden is even madder than before. Oh that's brilliant, Roland. Have you had any more trouble with the council? They are always threatening to tear down his greenhouse. The neighbours complain about it. They say diseases breed in the undergrowth. Do you mind if I show Charlie your studio? I really think he'd love your work.'

'No, go on up. But have a drink first. Beer? Here you go.'

We both took a can of Red Stripe from the grinning man and then made our way up the loud wooden stairs, dodging drinking couples. It was dark towards the top of the house. Jo pushed open a door and took my hand as we stepped into the blackness. She flicked on a switch and a soft light shone around the high room. Hundreds of birds hung from the ceiling, beautiful birds of paradise with long gaudy tail-feathers. I saw that they were made of old tin cans, strips of fabric, cigarette packets. Jo flicked another switch and birdsong began to echo around the room. At first it was a low chirping, then single songs broke out, long and liquid in the stillness of the high night. Slowly the birds began to turn in the air. We lay down on the floorboards, still holding hands, and watched as the birds turned above us. The singing slowly stopped, and I suddenly felt Jo's presence very close beside me, felt her hand moist in mine. I turned to my side and looked at her. She was staring up at the birds, who were rotating silently.

'Thanks for bringing me here, Jo. I feel like you have already rescued me a bit, you know.'

She smiled, still didn't look at me, then jumped up and pulled me to my feet.

'Wait until you see the garden. The garden is really wonderful.'

We passed down the stairs. In the kitchen Roland waved at us, grinning. I grabbed two more beers and followed Jo into the garden. It was very hot, and I could see the rain on the dirty glass, could feel the denseness of the air around us. Jo pulled aside a frond of ferns and I followed her down a mossy path. As soon as the fern curtain shut behind me, it was absolutely quiet apart from the gentle lapping of water. A small waterfall fell down a mossy bank into a pool on one side of the greenhouse. Animals made out of the same discarded objects dipped their heads in the pool. Birds hung from the ceiling again and shimmered in the tops of the palm trees. They were orioles and hoopoes and bee-eaters and all so brightly coloured in the soft light that was thrown up from behind the waterfall and under the pool. All of the light moved with the shimmer of the water as Jo leant back against me and sipped at her beer.

'I used to come here when I had decided to leave the commune. Roland is such an amazing man. He and his boyfriend Frank practically adopted me for a while. I used to just sit here all night and watch the animals, watch the waterfall. Have you seen the armadillo? The monkeys – look, up there. There's a baby hippo here somewhere. It's so wonderful. I'm glad I could show you all this, Charlie.'

She turned towards me and I placed a kiss on her warm lips. We were both sweating in the tropical heat of the greenhouse. She let her cardigan fall to the floor and I laid out my jacket. We sank down and I put my arms around her, pulled her towards me and kissed her. Her tongue was small and darting, moving in and out of my mouth. I was aware of the curry I had eaten, a little embarrassed. She pulled away from me, smiled.

'I wish I hadn't had that curry.'

'Don't be silly. Have some more beer. You're really great, Charlie.'

We lay for a while longer, then made our way back inside holding hands. Jo spoke to strangers easily, moved amongst the assorted artists and authors, academics and minor celebrities with grace. I watched her, feeling very proud. Thoughts of Henry nibbled at the edge of my consciousness.

I went home with Jo that night, crept up the stairs of her parents' majestic house on Elgin Crescent, lay in her bed in the attic conversion whose skylight looked across the glittering night towards the Westway. We lay side by side for an hour, talking, holding hands, nestling against each other in the warmth of the duvet. I could see her smiling in the dim light. Finally, something seemed to possess us both and she tore off my boxer shorts, I lifted the pyjama top over her head, slipped the bottoms off her long legs. We ground our bodies together, felt the surge and thrust of the life within us, the violent urges that forced her thin pelvis against mine, desperate, searching.

When it was over we lay panting and sated. I wrapped her tightly in my arms, pressing her head against my chest. She fell asleep quickly. I watched the dawn slowly breaking in the uninterrupted sky above us. She had forgotten to draw the blinds and I watched the light come up on her body, watched the brightening of her breasts and saw her heart beating in her ribs. I kissed her nipples gently, she awoke and we fucked like old friends, happy in one another's company. When she came it was like air escaping from a bottle, a sudden rush that caused her to sit up suddenly, her hand clutching her heaving chest.

I had breakfast with her, enjoying the adolescent awkwardness of meeting her parents. Her father was rather noble and grey-haired, her mother dark and younger, a bustling intelligent woman who hummed along with Radio 3 as it moved from Mahler to Brahms to Schubert. Jo wrote Ray's address down for me and told me she would call him and tell him to expect me at noon. We stood on the doorstep; she wore a Japanese dressing gown over her pyjamas. She leant down from the step and kissed me as I slipped my hand beneath the robe and felt the softness of her skin beneath the silk pyjamas, the slight bulge of her belly. She watched me walk away down the street, only turning to go inside once I was almost out of sight. I caught a cab home in the wonderful emptiness of the early weekend morning.

Ray's father's flat was on the ground floor of an ugly grey block off Kingsland Road. I parked the Polo outside and walked with some nervousness past the other apartments, some of whose windows were boarded up. I heard the sound of loud television, a baby crying, smelt frying bacon and dampness. I paused outside number twelve, pressed the bell, waited. Ray opened the door a crack, then pulled back the chain and stood warily watching me. A dog rushed towards the door. I put my hand down to greet it but it merely stood growling until a large man wearing a white vest and jeans came out into the hallway. He spoke in a kind of muttered yell as he pulled at the dog's studded collar.

'Get back there you fucking thing. Get back there, now. You must be Charlie. Jo told me about you. She's a good girl, Jo. I heard about the last bird, what was her name? Madison? Shit's fucked up, isn't it? Raymond wants to go swimming. Can you take him swimming? Go down Clapton way?'

'Sure. Of course. I'll need to buy a swimming costume, but of course we can go.'

'Don't be crazy. I'll lend you some trunks. Come inside. I'm Tony, by the way, Raymond's dad.'

I stepped into the small, hot flat that smelled of the dog and stale cigarettes. Tony sat me down in the kitchen, poured me out a cup of tea and went to search in his bedroom. I could see through the crack in the door that Ray shared a room with his father. A camp bed stood in one corner of the room, a Batman duvet tucked neatly over it. Ray's school uniform sat folded on the end of the bed. With a shout of triumph Tony located the swimming costume and came into the kitchen brandishing a Tesco carrier bag. The trunks were black Speedos, still damp from the last time they were worn.

'Here you go, mate. Don't bother washing them. Just bring them back when you're done. Tea all right?'

'Yes. It's great. I'll have him back after lunch, if that's all right. We'll go to Subway for lunch, Ray.'

'See you boys later. Got your keys, Raymond? I'm going round Danny's to watch the football.'

Ray turned his nose up at the rusting Polo, edged into the seat cautiously, then tuned the radio to a local drum-and-bass station.

'I thought you earned a load of money. Aren't you a City boy? How come you drive this piece of shit?' He tapped his hands on his knees in time with the music.

'I work for a hedge fund. It's kind of in the City. But I'm still very young. Haven't really had a big pay day yet. Hopefully won't be too long.'

'I thought everything had gone to shit? My dad says you're all going to lose your jobs. I'll have to come and take you out, pay for you to go swimming, if what I hear is right.' He seemed to find this very funny, rocked backwards and forward, laughing to himself.

'I think it'll probably all be fine in the end. I imagine I'll keep my job. I'll just have to work very hard, really dedicate myself to it.' I was aware that I was supposed to be setting some sort of example for him, giving him a positive role model.

'Do you like your job? Do you enjoy this hedge fund thing?'

I pressed my foot harder on the accelerator. I thought for a moment before answering.

'I don't love it, Ray. I'm someone who likes people, likes talking and things you can touch, things you can hold on to. My job doesn't give me much of that.'

'I don't get it. If you're not making loads of money and you don't like it, why do you do it?'

'Because one day I will earn lots of money. And then I'll be able to retire and do something I really enjoy. I'd like to write a play or be a journalist writing about other people's plays. If things go well, I could be out of the City doing something I like by the age of thirty-five.'

'That shit's fucked up, Charlie. If you don't like something, don't do it. Don't hang around just because some day someone might write you a big cheque. Fucking foolish, if you ask me.'

'Thanks, Ray. Thanks for the advice. Very helpful.'

We parked near the swimming pool and walked through the wide wooden doors. I paid for us both and Ray handed me a greasy grey-green towel.

'I got this for you.'

We walked into the changing rooms and there were smells and sights that I hadn't encountered since childhood swimming trips in Worthing. The floor was covered in a sharp blue cross-hatch, the lockers rattled as we walked past and I smelled disinfectant and chlorine and athlete's-foot powder. Ray and I changed together. He stood brazenly naked in front of me, stretching his legs out on the bench. I looked at him quickly, then away, embarrassed.

'Good, you're not a paedo. I didn't think you were, but you can't be too careful these days.' His voice often took on this strange adult inflection, and I heard echoes of Madison's low tones in there, as well as his father's more earthy notes.

The Speedos were far too big for me, and I had to tuck my cock back between my legs to stop it from slipping out of the front. Ray stood curled-up with laughter at the sight of me.

'You look a fucking wanker, Charlie. Seriously. Such a wanker.'

In the showers he turned to me, suddenly serious, his hands on his hips.

'I may as well tell you now that I can't swim, Charlie. No point fucking lying about it, is there? I've got to go swimming with school next week and I need to learn how to swim today so I don't look a twat in front of the girls. Can you do that?'

He battled bravely in the pool, thrashed his arms and legs, swallowed litres of water, sank to the bottom a number of times. I rested my hand on his chest and tried to move his arms and legs correctly. He managed to propel himself forward until I took my hand away, when he would begin to panic, windmill his arms in great circles, sink slowly to the floor of the pool until I reached down to pull him out, spluttering and indignant. After an hour I told him we had to leave. He smacked his hands down on the water.

'I need to learn to fucking swim.'

The lifeguard shot a warning look in his direction. I flipped him on his back, took his feet in my hands and pushed him towards the deep end.

'Now kick. Kick, Ray.' He began to sink, then with a huge effort he shot out his legs and began to power through the water, sending up a great spray behind him. People cleared out of the way as the wall of water surged towards them.

'Use your hands. Move your arms backwards and pull the water.'

He arched his back and flapped his hands in uneven circles,

began to turn to the side, corrected himself and, his mouth set in a determined line, he made his way in stuttering bursts of speed towards the far end of the pool. When he touched the blue tiles he let out a choked sigh of delight, pulled himself out onto the side of the pool, and lay back dramatically against the cold tiles, exhausted.

I continued to see Ray every Sunday for the rest of that cold autumn. We would often go swimming, followed by a luke-warm greasy sandwich in Subway on Mare Street. Otherwise we would sit in close darkness at the cinema, watching 18-rated horror films after I had sneaked him through the ticket check wearing his hoodie pulled up over his face. Best of all were the days we walked over Hackney Marshes, up towards the ice rink and the stables, suddenly chasing each other over the frosty white ground. I looked forward so much to the crisp mornings in east London, and Ray flourished, presenting me with glowing school reports and swimming badges, furnishing me with great detail about his first kiss with a girl called Leanne. I told him a first kiss behind the bike sheds was a cliché. He told me to fuck off. I invited Tony to join us for our lunches in Subway, and found him a clever and gentle man, still reeling from the death of his young wife, bitter at the world but desperate for his son to succeed in life.

I began to spend every weekend at Jo's house. Leaving work on a Friday evening felt like an enormous release. I would walk up to Bond Street and take the Tube to Notting Hill, then march up Portobello Road in the darkness, looking in at the warm lights of the pubs and restaurants I passed. We would go out to E&O or the Electric and eat grand meals together, drinking until we were slurring our words and pawing at each other under the table, then back to her cosy room nesting in the rafters of the tall white house. And it didn't matter that Jo wasn't some great intellect, that she needed to be home early some nights in order to watch some dreadful reality television show, that she lay in bed in the evenings reading *Grazia* and *Heat* whilst I read Henry James. She was so gentle with me, so full of quiet concern and we were never stuck for conversation as we sat in restaurants and talked about small, insignificant things.

Her parents were often away, owned a villa in Salon-de-Provence, but when I came down to breakfast and saw them they were solicitous and affectionate, asking after my work and Ray. Jo's mother always had a new piece of classical music to play me. She would wait for a particular moment of inspiration, holding her hand up, breathless with anticipation. Then when the moment arrived, she would move her head in eccentric time to the music, nodding backwards and forwards in appreciation.

The suicides began in earnest at the beginning of November. There is something hard and harsh even in the name of that cold month. And when the winds blew from the east it was difficult even to raise my head from the pillow in the mornings. I wrapped two scarves around my neck, pulled thick gloves on my hands, wore two pairs of socks under my shoes and still I froze on the way to the Tube, stepping gratefully onto the steaming train as it pulled into the station at Parsons Green. The heating in the block of flats on Munster Road shuddered with the effort of maintaining warmth in the face of such a violent assault from the east. Sometimes I woke at night to find that the radiators had given out altogether. When this happened, I pulled all the clothes I could onto my shivering body, hugged a scalding hot-water bottle against my chest and dreamed wistfully of the room under the eaves of the house in Notting Hill where Jo's warm body was waiting for me. We had discussed moving in together, but I was working very hard and preferred to keep her away from my weekday self, not wanting her to see me tired and grizzled, coming in late reeking of cigarettes and failure. I kept her for the weekends, had her tanned body as a beacon of light that shone through those gloomy Friday afternoons.

Whilst Madison's death had been quiet and contained, the suicides that swept across the City that winter seemed orchestrated, conducted by some heavenly aesthete. The dance of death was a beautiful one, showing a profound understanding of the importance of that final image. The way the press reported the suicides seemed to increase the search for beauty in the final act, causing the young people who were no longer willing to endure the drudgery of existence to aim to outclass each previous death, leave the image burnt longer on the collective retina.

It was the first week in December. The world was very dark, and Christmas seemed just too far off to offer any solace. Although, since bonuses had been slashed or abolished across the whole industry, and wives still wanted Chanel, and the children needed the latest computers, and everyone had to be seen skiing, no one was looking forward much to the holiday season anyway.

One of the Canary Wharf investment banks had just announced huge losses, fired its entire credit-trading team. The CEO had resigned and the whole company gathered in the vast marble atrium to welcome his replacement. As the new CEO stepped onto a podium, breathed deeply and began to address the bank's staff, something swung like a great wild pendulum behind him. The CEO turned around, ducked for a moment fearing some sort of attack. The pendulum swung back, still twitching violently in the air. Finally the figure moved slowly enough for people to make out what it was. There was a gasp. A woman cried out. Paul Stuart, the former head of credit trading, hung from a long steel rope, which he had measured very carefully to carry him directly behind the CEO as he began to speak. He had been allowed into the building the night before to clear his desk, and had hidden in the lifts' engine room overnight. It was an hour before anyone was able to cut him down. His face had turned very blue. There was a picture of him hanging there as the bank's staff hurried past, eyes averted.

Jo called me that night as I turned out the light in the freezing flat, my hands squeezed between my thighs for warmth.

'Charlie, it's me. I saw that awful story on the news. I can't believe it's another one. I need you to know I love you. Please don't ever forget that you can come and live here. You don't need to earn money, you don't need to do anything but be there for me. I don't know what I'd do without you, Charlie.'

'I understand, Jo. It will be fine. I'm tougher than that. Maybe before you and Ray, before I had something to live for. But not now. Not now I have you. Goodnight, darling. Sleep well.'

The markets had effectively closed down. The banks were writing off billions in bad debts, and companies were unable to issue new bonds. I was still in the red for the year, but managed to claw back small gains trading indices and short-selling in anticipation of Friday afternoons, which were invariably days of negative news when traders were terrified of being caught holding positions over the weekend. No one came into work on Saturdays any more. Silverbirch's assets had halved in six months, but it looked like the business would survive. The Chairman even took the whole of December off, leaving Catrina and me to run things. Before he left he called me into his study, an apologetic look on his face.

'I wanted to tell you, before you heard it from the others. We won't be paying a bonus this year. I just can't justify it to the investors. We'll put your salary up to sixty thousand, though. I want you to know that you've been instrumental in keeping this business alive. And when things do rebound, I promise you'll be very well rewarded.'

I hadn't really expected anything, but was hoping for a token, just enough to buy Jo and Ray something special for Christmas. I walked up Oxford Street in the happy buzz of Christmas shoppers, faces lit from shop windows, breath fogging the air, fathers with their children on their shoulders, laughing. I found a cheap DVD player and a selection of mildly educational DVDs for Ray and a bottle of aftershave for Tony. Heading down Bond Street, back to the office, I paused outside an antique jewellery store. An austere-looking woman peered down at me as I stared at a wonderful emerald necklace. I imagined the stone nestling between Jo's small breasts, hanging down into her cleavage, and I was desperate to buy it for her. I stepped into the shop, banging my feet on the mat as I entered.

'Hello.'

The woman looked over her glasses at me, ice in her eyes.

'May I help you, sir?'

'Umm . . . the necklace in the window . . .'

'Yes, which one precisely?' Her voice was arctic.

'The . . . er . . . the emerald.'

'Oh, that is quite beautiful, isn't it? Would sir like to see it?' She leant over and placed it lovingly on the black felt display cloth, turning it to catch the light. 'Quite magnificent, isn't it?'

'Yes. Absolutely. How much is it please?'

'This is, let me see, £24,000 excluding VAT.' She looked rather proud of the figure.

I felt distraught, had already been picturing Jo's face when she opened the box. I saw the woman smile to herself.

'Oh. That's a little out of my price range, I'm afraid.' I turned and began to back out of the shop.

'And what is sir's price range, if I may ask? Present for the wife, is it, sir?'

'I . . . I was wanting to spend more like a thousand.' This was already far more than I could afford, would have to go on my credit card, just when I had begun to get my finances back under control. The woman gave a contemptuous little cough.

'We have some lovely earrings here for one thousand umm . . . three hundred pounds. Quite charming little pieces.'

She drew out a tiny pair of earrings each set with an almost invisible diamond. They glinted on the black cloth like two very distant stars. I said I would take them, waited nervously as the old woman had a sharp conversation with American Express, who finally cleared the transaction. I clutched the bag very close to my chest and locked it in a drawer in my desk at work. I tried not to open the drawer as it made me feel queasy every time I thought of the money, how it could have been better spent, how Jo probably wouldn't appreciate their value, would think I was being a flash City boy.

We made a world for ourselves in the weekend skies above Notting Hill. I used to sit cross-legged on the bed and watch Jo walk around the room, her clothes falling softly to the floor, drifting on the air like leaves. The night crisped at the skylights and occasional stars battled against the city glow and smoke to glitter their light down upon us. There was something very moving about the city viewed from on high in darkness; every light represented something hopeful, a promise of intricate lives. When winds whipped rain across the roof I imagined other lovers lying warm under duvets, listening to the tempest and the precious sounds of the body: heartbeats, breathing, sighs.

Before bed I'd follow Jo's naked body to the bathroom, watching the dark skin of her back suddenly surprise into the whiteness of her small buttocks. Sitting on the end of the bath

I watched her shower, saw her move careful hands over her soapy body, watched the small precise movements of the razor running over legs and under arms, saw her eyes shut tightly as she shampooed her hair, turning the incipient crows' feet into dark furrows. She'd smile at me, stick out a tongue, and I'd step from my clothes and into the shower, hold her tacky clean body against mine under the rush of the water.

I remember one night in December we were lying in bed reading like a long-married couple. Jo's parents were at their villa in France and I felt the weight of the empty house beneath us, breathed the luxury of the space we had to ourselves. Some noise, or some sudden silence, caused us to put down our books at the same time. I was naked and Jo wore a pair of my pyjama bottoms. I looked over at her, saw the light fall down the pale white skin inside her wrist, watched the patterns that cut across the skin as my eyes moved down towards her elbow. The scars looked like ski tracks crossing the path of her arms. I saw her watching me, trying to gauge my response, and I sensed the nervousness behind her quiet eyes. Without taking my eyes from hers, I took the hand with firm fingers, pulled the disfigured skin to my lips and kissed it. Then I let the arm drop to the bed and turned back to my book.

We were silent for a while, then Jo leant over and whispered in my ear.

'Thank you.'

She nestled against me and we continued to read late into the night. Jo understood that the scars meant as little to me as the kisses of her former lovers, the tears cried before me, any of the adolescent nights when she held her knees to her chest and stared, rocking vacantly, into darkness. What we had was new-made, perfect, and could not be harmed by the past.

*

On a Friday night just before Christmas, Jo's parents threw a dinner party for Ray, Tony and me. I finished work early, pulled the earrings from their bag and placed the box in my inside pocket. Then I rushed back to Fulham to collect the car. I crossed London to pick up Ray and Tony, driving along the Embankment where office parties were stumbling onto the floating pubs, their faces caught in the lights of the riverboats which chuntered slowly up past the Houses of Parliament. Tony came to the door in a flared brown suit, his tie hanging loose around his neck. He whispered to me in a sharp voice.

'Quick. Before Raymond comes out. Tie my fucking tie for me, will you? I can never do it and I don't want the boy to know his father is such an uneducated twat.'

I stood behind him, felt the quick rise of his breathing under my arms as I reached over and tied a half-Windsor. The muscles of his neck and shoulders were firm and high, only his stomach had lost definition and pushed at the buttons of his shirt. I turned him around to face me, adjusted the knot and smiled at the effect. Ray came into the hallway wearing his school uniform.

'Am I allowed one glass of champagne, Dad? Just one glass? I can't believe I've got to wear my school clothes. It's supposed to be a party. I'm supposed to have fun. At least let me have champagne, Dad. Can I have a glass?'

'No, you can't. Not even one. You're lucky to be invited to a grown-ups' party. I want you to be on your best fucking behaviour, young man. And those are the only smart clothes you've got so just pipe down, Raymond. Have you been to their house, Charlie? Is it pimp?'

'It's pretty nice. Must be worth a couple of million.'

'Fuck me. Don't break anything, Raymond. Otherwise, it's no Christmas presents.'

Tony sat beside me in the car. He made sure Ray was strapped in, then fiddled with the radio. We listened to drum and bass on the way over. Both Tony and Ray made beatbox noises with their mouths, getting faster and faster until one of them lost the beat and they would both fall backwards laughing. We pulled up outside the large white house and stepped into the pool of bright light thrown down from the dining-room window.

I had bought two bottles of champagne and pressed one of them into Tony's hand as we walked up the garden path.

'Nice one, Charlie. I'd forgotten to pick something up. I would have looked a right cock turning up with nothing to show.'

'What about me? I need to give 'em something. Otherwise, I'll look a cock.'

I handed Ray the other bottle of champagne and rang the doorbell. Jo's mother answered and smiled down at us. She giggled like a girl when Ray and Tony presented her with the bottles of Veuve Clicquot. Ray was charming, bowing to the small dark woman.

'What a lovely house you have. It certainly seems like a delightful area.'

Tony ruffled his hair.

'Don't be cheeky, Raymond.'

'I was only saying what Charlie told me to say.'

I laughed nervously and we made our way into the bright dining room. Jo stepped towards me in a long black dress, her hair pulled up in a silver Alice band that made her look very young even as it accentuated her peculiar old eyes. She took both of my hands in hers, stepped on her toes and kissed me very hard on the lips. Jo's father was already a little drunk. He passed very cold champagne around in wide-necked goblets. I saw Tony cast Ray a warning glance as the boy took his glass.

'Don't mind if I do,' he said in a purring imitation of my voice.

'Just the one, Raymond.' Tony placed a warning hand on his son's shoulder.

After a dinner of roast pork we sat in the drawing room and I brought out Ray and Tony's Christmas presents. Jo's mother had bought Ray a set of Arthur Ransome books. He unwrapped them and smiled broadly.

'How delightful. I do love a good book.'

Whilst his father opened his present – a Harrods tie – Ray leant over to me and whispered conspiratorially.

'Who's Arthur Ransome? Can I take them back? Will you get me the receipt, Charlie? Steal it from her bag?'

Ray looked genuinely pleased with the DVD player. I was worried for a moment that Tony would think it was over-extravagant, liable to eclipse anything he could afford to buy.

'Nice one, Charlie. That's something we've been wanting for ages. We can chuck out the old video now. Thanks, mate.'

He insisted on splashing copious amounts of the aftershave I bought him over his neck and on his wrists. I saw Jo's mother's nose wrinkle at the heavy sandalwood scent. I led Jo into the hallway. She was a little tipsy from the champagne, tripped as we walked back into the empty dining room. I drew out the little box and saw the look of excited horror on her face. It took me a moment to see what she was thinking.

'No, Jo. I mean . . . Christ, not yet. I mean . . . No.'

I opened the box and saw a shadow of disappointment cross her face, but then she turned the earrings in the light and the diamonds performed splendidly, catching the flickering of the candles. They looked larger and more impressive than they had in the shop, and I saw Jo hold them up to her ears in the mirror.

'They're beautiful, Charlie. You gave me such a shock then. But thank you. Thank you so much. It's the best present I've ever had.'

She hugged me hard, running her hand up through my hair, then put the earrings into her ears and walked bouncing into the drawing room where her mother gave a little sigh of delight at the dancing light of the diamonds and her father clapped loudly.

I drove Ray and Tony home, and the boy slept in the back, his face pressed against the cold glass of the window.

'Raymond tells me you're not enjoying your job. Why d'you bother? No point in doing something you don't like.' Tony was drunk and had tuned in to a radio station playing late-night love songs. He punctuated his words with yelps of appreciation as Marvin Gaye or Otis Redding murmured sweet nothings through the blackness of the night.

'I need the money, Tony. I won't do it for much longer. I just need to buy a house and get settled and then I'll give it all up, find a job doing something I really enjoy.'

'You probably don't want advice from someone like me. I'm not exactly an advert for success, am I? But I think that life is too fucking short. What the death of Raymond's mum told me is that we never know how long we've got. Same as your woman Madison. Shit like that makes you want to spend time with the people you love, do the things you enjoy, not waste your time doing foolish shit just because it might earn you a bit more cash.'

We sat in silence for the rest of the journey. Ray was crotchety when we woke him, slightly hungover from the one glass of champagne. I sat and watched them walk along the row of flats to their front door. Tony raised a hand and I pulled away into the night.

Jo was waiting for me in bed, wearing only the earrings. I

slipped off my clothes, which were cold from the night, and slid in beside her. She took my face in her hands, kissed me for a long time, then climbed to sit above me. The earrings swung hypnotically in the dim light as we fucked and she threw her head from side to side, sending the diamonds dancing in crazy circles around her head. We hugged for a long time afterwards and I could feel her heart beating hard against my chest. I thought she was sleeping and whispered her name.

'Jo.'

'Hmmm? What? Yes?'

'I think I'm going to quit my job. I think I want to leave the City. I'm going to ask Henry for a place on the paper. I need to speak to him anyway. About us. But I really think it's time for things to change. For me to take my life in hand. To do something I'll enjoy.'

She sat up, turned and kissed me, her eyes as bright as the diamonds that shone in her ears.

'I've been waiting for you to say that.'

Chapter 11

Leaving the City

I planned my departure as I drove down to Worthing on Christmas Eve. I composed a text to Henry in my head, decided I would invite him for a drink and then throw myself on his mercy, asking for his forgiveness for my betrayal, for sleeping with the girl he had loved. The traffic slowed down around Billingshurst and I sat in a queue for ten minutes, the heating turned up high, the windscreen steaming as I revved the engine to keep it running. Finally we began to move and trawled haltingly past a car that had crashed into an oak tree taking the roundabout too quickly. I saw a girl being lifted gently into an ambulance, her neck wrapped in a thick white collar, her legs twitching. Everyone drove more carefully after this, edging nervously around corners, the image of the young girl's parents expecting her home for Christmas, the untouched presents sitting under the tree.

When I opened the door at home it was like stepping back in time. The Christmas tree filled the house with its scent, at once evocative and sad. My father sat on the sofa in the drawing room reading. My mother was in the kitchen preparing smoked salmon and scrambled eggs, our traditional Christmas Eve meal.

'Hello, darling, come in and put your stuff down. Let's have a look at you. Oh, you look well. Is it a girl? It looks as if someone is taking care of you.'

'Well, there is someone . . .'

My father was standing behind me, placed his hand down on my shoulder.

'That's my boy. You must tell us all about her. But firstly come and listen to this record I picked up the other day.'

The evening passed in happy recreation of times past, my mother pottering contentedly around the house, my father and I talking and playing chess and drinking a bottle of burgundy. I lay in bed that night and saw dimly shining on the ceiling the fluorescent stars that I had stuck there as a child. They reminded me of Jo's earrings and, seeing it was past midnight, I texted her 'Happy Christmas'. I thought about telling her I loved her, compromised by adding kisses at the end of the message.

In the morning I opened presents from my parents, ate a bacon sandwich as I unwrapped the books and socks. I had bought my mother a Hermès scarf and my father a framed print of a William Scott painting of a fruit bowl. We walked out along the seafront after lunch and I told them about Jo, about how we had met.

'She sounds like a fine girl, just the sort of girl you need. I'm so pleased for you, Charles. Your face lights up when you speak about her. I can really see you glowing.' My father linked his arm through mine and we raced down to the sea, threw stones into the churning water. I was glad to see him so much better. My mother told me that he was thinking of setting up a literary magazine, had grand plans for the future, was suddenly much younger and more excited about life.

I wrote the text to Henry after lunch on Boxing Day, sitting in my father's armchair in the small and comfortable living room. It read as follows.

Hope all's well. Happy Christmas. Are you in London this week? Would be great to see you.

I drove up from Worthing that evening, optimism pulling

the car forward into thick traffic. I found a new radio station that played soul music, and made my way through darkened south London with James Carr and Ann Peebles soothing the bitterness of the world outside. I watched a family walking alongside the car as I drove through Croydon. They were going out to the pub for dinner and the children scooted ahead on shoes that were fitted with hidden wheels, giving their progress the look of magic.

My phone rang as soon as I got into the flat. I recognised Vero's number, sat back in the tatty armchair and kicked off my shoes before answering. Her voice came at me very quickly. I could tell she was a little drunk.

'Hello, Charlie. Happy Christmas. Why didn't you call me yesterday? I thought we always spoke to each other on Christmas Day.' She sounded a little hurt and it struck me that I hadn't even thought of her the day before, my mind had been only on Jo. It seemed at that moment quite wonderful that I hadn't thought of Vero with sadness on Christmas Day. That perhaps we could be friends without the constantly seething undercurrent of my feelings for her.

'I'm sorry, darling. There was so much going on. I was down in Worthing and my father was on splendid form and really wanted to make the most of his time with me. How's married life?'

'It's . . . It's fine. Marc is fine. I'm spending a lot of time at the refugee camp with Guy. You know, to be close to my brother, this is the best thing to come out of my return to France. What he is doing in Calais, it is really wonderful. I work all day helping mothers fill in the correct forms for their children, making sure that families are kept together, doing work that really means something, and it doesn't matter that I'm not earning a fortune. It doesn't matter that my clothes are grubby and I have stopped wearing make-up. I hear about these suicides in the City and I'm so happy to have left that world. So worried that you're still there.'

'Don't worry about me, darling. I have decided to leave the City anyway. It just all seems so meaningless now. I'm going to ask Henry for a job on the newspaper. It's what I have always wanted to do, what I feel I have been waiting for.'

'Oh, Charlie, that's great news. I'm so pleased for you.' She paused for a moment. 'Can I . . . can I come over and see you soon? You and Henry? I miss you both. It was so good to see you at the wedding, we're such good friends and . . . and I need to see you again.' Her voice suddenly sounded very serious, as if she was about to cry.

'Of course, of course you can. It would be great to see you.'

Later that night I had a text back from Henry proposing that we meet the next evening at the pub on Albemarle Street where we drank the night before setting off for Vero's wedding. I went to bed with a mixture of excitement and trepidation pushing away sleep.

Henry was sitting in a dark corner of the pub with a pint of Guinness. He was hunched over the upturned barrel, his long frame fitting with difficulty under the curl of stairs which rose up behind him. I waved shyly, my heart beating very swiftly, dryness overtaking my voice, momentarily depriving me of my speech. I bought two pints, placed his next to the half-drunk Guinness and forced myself to smile.

'Christ, you're looking well, Charlie. I thought . . . well, to be honest, I thought you seemed rather a mess at Vero's. I mean, nothing compared to the state I was in, but still you didn't seem quite stable. I'm glad you look so chipper now. How's the life of ghastly commerce? I heard about your friend . . . Madison her name was, wasn't it? Terrible, must really bring it home to you.'

I nodded, swirling my drink.

'I have become rather fascinated by these suicides. And not just because one of them was a good friend. There's something darkly compelling about the crescendo they seem to be building towards. I almost expect some great communal statement – the whole of an investment bank self-immolating on the trading floor, or several CEOs getting together and blowing themselves up in front of the Stock Exchange. Although it's never the CEOs that do it, is it? It's the peripheral figures, the people still trying to make it.'

'We're doing a long piece on the reasons behind the suicides. Thought it would catch the hungover early-January mood rather well. I . . . I was going to ask if you wanted to help out? Unless work is too manic?'

He leant back and twisted his body up against the coil of the stairs above him, extending his arms out and stretching himself against the wood. I moved forward on my stool, put my elbows on the table and held his eye.

'No. I'd love to. In fact . . . in fact I was going to tell you something, Henry. A couple of things actually. I'm going to leave Silverbirch. I have decided that it's just not worth it. The pressure and the drudgery. I really don't enjoy the work. It has taken me a while to realise it, because it's such blasphemy to state something so brazenly, but the work is just very tedious. So, I wonder, do you think you might be able to find me something at the newspaper?'

'Umm . . . I mean gosh, Charlie. That's great news. Of course I'll speak to my father. I'm sure he'll have something. The paper's not doing brilliantly, but we're so small that we manage to survive even when other guys are going to the wall. I presume you want something theatrical? Are you sure you could work alongside Gervais Verity? He's such a terribly predatory homosexual . . .'

'I want this so badly, Henry. I really think I'd quite happily suck Mr Verity off, if it meant getting the job. I know how much you love what you do, Henry. I want to enjoy what I do just as much.'

'I'll see what I can do, Charlie. It would be fun to work together, wouldn't it? I always rather dreamed we would.'

'There's something else I need to tell you, Henry. I'm seeing someone. Someone you know and I don't think it will make you happy . . .' He sat back and I could see his mind cycling wildly.

'Not Vero? Astrid? Christ, Charlie . . .'

'No, fuck, no, Henry. It's Jo. I'm seeing Jo. I met her at Madison's funeral. I'm so sorry, Henry. I really didn't mean for this to happen.'

'Jo . . . You're seeing my Jo . . .'

He was silent for a while. He swirled the beer in his glass, tapped his fingers on the barrel. A cynical grin slowly unfurled along his lips.

'It's bloody funny. How well you pretend to be this . . . to be this warm-hearted chap who has been swept away by forces outside your control, how you never meant to work in the City, never intended to be caught up in that world. I think if you look deep inside you'll see that you're just as cold and calculating as all of the other me-types you pretend so convincingly to despise. And I imagine you believe that this . . . this thing between you and Jo was an enormous coincidence, don't you? You are a snake, Charlie Wales. You're perfectly suited for that world you inhabit. I'm going out for a fag.'

I watched Henry push through the other drinkers, watched him step out into the dark blustery night where I had seen the couple arguing six months earlier. Henry paced out of sight and I sat staring down into my beer, wondering if what he said was true. Surely we are all calculating in some measure? Otherwise, we would go through life blindly, unable to influence events, at the mercy of chance and circumstance. I caught myself in a mirror, saw a certain cruelty in my mouth, in the deep-set cast of my eyes. Henry still hadn't returned. I walked out onto the street, looked up and down. He had left. I caught the Tube home, feeling intensely lonely, and sat in my dark and desolate front room listening to the wind howl outside.

In the morning I trudged into work, feeling empty and hopeless on the empty Tube, thinking of families at home, warm, basking in the island of time between Christmas and New Year. I considered calling Enzo, asking him for a job at *Arena*. But I wanted to write about the theatre, wanted to work for a serious paper. It seemed incredible that something as pure and positive as my love for Jo had deprived me of my way out of the grinding boredom of Silverbirch. Catrina didn't even bother to come into the office that day. I trawled the internet, flicked swiftly through some mildly artistic pornography, wondering if the technology department kept any record of the sites we visited, until Euphonium came over to my desk and suggested we go to the pub. I sat, rather glum, staring down at the table as he told me about the Christmas concert he had performed in at St Paul's Cathedral. It grew dark outside and I stood, excused myself and made my way back to the desk, leaving Euphonium slightly drunk and emotional in the bright pub. In the empty office I checked that nothing dramatic was taking place in the markets and decided to leave early.

My mobile rang in the lift where there was very little reception. It was Henry. I answered nervously, heard his voice faintly, the line crackling and indistinct.

' . . . Outside . . . Meet . . . Sorry . . .'

Then nothing. I walked out into the atrium, past the

slightly shabby Christmas tree which had begun to drop its needles. I could hear them fall downwards as I walked by, the motion of my footsteps dislodging the dead needles. They made a noise like shattering glass heard from a great distance. As I stepped through the revolving doors and out into the sharpness of the night, I saw Henry standing in front of the building, a cigarette glowing in his lips. He smiled shyly at me, half-raised his hand in greeting.

'Charlie, look, can we go for another drink? I was an arse yesterday. A complete arse. Same place as before? Pretend . . . pretend yesterday didn't happen?'

We walked in silence down Dover Street and over to the pub. Henry bought us both pints and sat us deliberately at the same table as before, although this time I was nestled below the curving stairway.

'I can't think why you don't seem more cross with me, Charlie. I had no right to say the things I did. Especially after that nonsense between Vero and me. And you're not cold and calculating. You're just a damned good friend. I spoke to Jo last night. She's so happy. I quite honestly have never heard anyone so happy. She says you're the kindest person she has ever met, and that you look after her so well. Of course I still . . . I still care about her, but she was always just a half-replacement for Vero. I knew it at the time, and I was too high to care, or maybe I thought I'd be able to build her into a new Vero. But, deep down, no matter how out of it I was, I used to look at her when we were huddling up in a sleeping bag in the arches, and I used to welcome the darkness, welcome the dying of the fire so I could paste Vero's face onto hers. Sad, isn't it?

'So I'm very sorry . . . sorry that I reacted as I did. Because I think you'll be good for Jo. And she'll be good to you. And in penance I spoke to my father this morning. He's very keen to

242

get you on board. He can't offer you anything firm, but if you'd like to come in and meet Verity, come some time early in the New Year, see if the two of you get on well, my father will do everything he can to squeeze you in. He's very keen on bringing some youth into the paper. Of course I have been a breath of fresh air for the old rag. But seriously, I'd love to work with you, Charlie.'

I felt tears spring to my eyes, placed my hand on Henry's.

'Thanks, mate. I appreciate it. Not just the meeting with Verity. Everything. Thanks.'

'And listen, Charlie, I'd really like it . . . I mean you may think it's rather too strange, and if so I'd understand, I really would . . . But would you and Jo like to come up to spend New Year with us in Suffolk? It's not many of us, just a small gathering of locals, really. But we'd love you to be there. My father has always thought you a great character. And I'd like my parents to get to know you better. Do say yes.'

'That's so kind. Really good of you, Henry. I'll speak to Jo. But I'm sure we'd love to. Yes.'

He lifted my hand carefully from his, drained his pint, and walked from the pub. I watched his tall form through the mistiness of the glass pass out of view.

*

On New Year's Eve I had the day off. Jo was working a half-day at the drop-in centre in Hackney where the children from homes that were grubby with drugs spent their school holidays playing football in the playground, had meals cooked for them, watched films and argued over Playstation games. Jo spoke about the drop-in centre with an earnestness that made me feel uncomfortable, and then guilty for my unease at her sincerity.

'It's structure. It gives their lives a solid structure during the holidays. None of our kids are in gangs. Very few carry knives. We set them up to achieve something with their lives. To become something more than their parents ever were. I love those kids. The way they manage to keep hopeful, manage to joke and play and hug me even when everything in their world is just ghastly.'

It felt like a great luxury lying in bed watching her rush across the darkened room, pulling a brush through her thick hair. Tying a shoelace, her arse thrust up in the air, she came close to toppling. She saw me looking at her and smiled over at me. She kissed me and left and I watched the sky gradually brighten outside, stretching out diagonally across the bed with my hands behind my head. It was a time of great hope. The world seemed to shine with a happy optimism, and I watched the clouds clear and the sky was brilliant blue by ten o'clock as I wandered down onto Portobello Road to buy coffee and a croissant. I sat in the café reading the paper and watching two young children in matching blue duffel coats who were moving up and down the pavement on their scooters as their mother talked to a friend. Their breath stood out very clear in the air and their cheeks were flushed red from the cold. I saw the boy look up at me with very serious blue eyes. I nodded at him and he smiled in strange delight, held his hand in the air for a moment and then pushed himself off down the pavement on his silver steed.

I drove the Polo over to Hackney through streets which were wide and empty and lined with leafless trees. I was early and pulled up outside the large building on Queensbridge Road where the charity was based. It had been a boys' school, was tall and Victorian and imposing in its ugly solidity. It had lost all of the grandeur it must once have possessed, was pulled at by thick ivy and the red brick walls were covered at ground level with graffiti. I walked into the playground, which bore faint traces of chalk from long-finished football games. Weeds grew high in the corners, buddleia with the darkened husks of flowers withered in memory of the summer, willowherb lower down along the cracked bricks of the wall.

In the musty building children's voices were everywhere, like the memory of the schoolboys who had once rushed up and down the corridors. I took the stairs two at a time and stepped into the dining room. The walls were bright with drawings, the air heavy with the smell of lasagne and hot bodies. Jo was standing at the head of the table, one arm around the shoulders of a very small girl who had her head buried in Jo's side. I saw the girl's body rise and fall quickly with tears that were soaking into Jo's grey jumper. Jo leant down and kissed the girl on her soft curls. With the other hand, she was cutting into a bubbling lasagne. Two other volunteers – a bald man with large hands and a fat, smiling woman – were standing in the corner with a pair of older boys who looked ready to fight each other.

I saw that Jo was having trouble keeping control of the table of hungry children, watched as the small crying girl slid from under Jo's arm and ran towards the back of the room, her shoulders jumping with sobs. Jo saw me standing in the doorway and smiled wearily as I walked over to help her. I served paper plates of the watery pasta to the ten children sitting around the table, fielding their questions with a wary politeness.

'Are you Jo's bloke? Are you married? Do you live with her? You look like a gayer. Are you a gayer?'

'Yes, I am Jo's boyfriend and no, we aren't married. We sort of live together and the answers to these alone should be enough to answer your final question. Now who wants some orange squash?'

Jo was crouched speaking to the little girl, who had her head down and was pulling her shoe slowly across the floor making a high squealing sound. The boy at the other end of the table, who reminded me of Ray, suddenly threw a tennis ball at me. I caught it and returned it, slightly harder. His reflexes were excellent. He threw it back and we sent the ball fizzing through the air until Jo laid a firm hand on my shoulder.

'No ball games at the dinner table. I can't leave you naughty boys for a minute.'

The table found this very funny. As we were about to leave, the little girl who had been crying ran over to hug Jo. She wrapped her arms around Jo's waist and spoke in a small, lisping voice.

'Happy New Year, Jo.'

The sky was too bright in Suffolk. There was none of the fuzzy yellow smog, no protective grey buildings to block out the glare. We pulled up the drive of Henry's parents' house with the sky enormous above us, the sun already very low but still searingly bright. Henry was waiting in the hall, had heard the car pull up. I watched him hug Jo and it reminded me of the shy affection of the little girl at the charity. He showed us to our room, which was down an echoing corridor, away from the rest of the house, cold and old-fashioned in its furnishing.

'People will start arriving around seven. You really mustn't expect too much. Just a few family friends. I'll let you chaps get settled and then I thought we might go and hang out in the barn. My father's had a new home cinema thingummy installed and there's a pool table and drinks and everything. I think Pa used my coming back home as an excuse to turn this place into a small gentlemen's club. Come down when you're ready. I really am so pleased you're here.'

We spent the afternoon lazing on sofas in the barn, watched a Hitchcock film with our breath held, our drinks forgotten. Jo beat us both at pool and then we stood in the main dining room as guests slowly drifted in from the bitter night. The women were all very thin and had the cautious geniality of the once-beautiful, aware that they were no longer able to survive on their looks and that they were neophytes in the world of small talk and social grace. The men were ruddy and bearded and I recognised journalists and writers and a former England cricket captain enter and greet Henry's tall, clear-eyed father with much guffawing and backslaps. Jo and I sat on the window seat and spoke gently to each other and the guests came and introduced themselves and they were all so cultivated, so charming and generous. It made me wonder why I had always insisted so violently that I had to live in the dirty seethe of London. Life out here seemed calmer, more thoughtful.

Astrid appeared for a short while before dinner. She was going to a party at a neighbour's house and was wearing a sparkling gold dress. She threw her arms around me when she came into the kitchen. We were drinking champagne, slouched against the butcher's block and the granite breakfast bar. Henry's dad was telling a dry and confusing story about playing golf with the Foreign Secretary. Astrid yawned, leant over and took a sip from my glass. She nodded to Jo, twirled for her brother and then skipped out into the night full of childish excitement.

At dinner I sat next to Henry's mother. She was drinking brandy, was already quite drunk by the main course, but she was a pleasant drunk; giggling like a schoolgirl she whispered slander conspiratorially through her cupped hand.

'He's a dreadful queer. Married her because an unmarried politician was rather frowned upon back then. And since the stroke she simply dotes on him. Look at her feeding him. And it mortifies him, it really does. I feel it is her revenge for his years of sodomy.'

When dinner was over, and we were about to disappear to the barn to watch the countdown to New Year on the television, Henry's mother seized my hand, looked me very deeply in the eyes until I had to turn away.

'You have been a very dear friend to our son. It means so much to us. Henry has told us about your wanting to move into journalism and I want you to know that we'll do . . . Oliver will do everything he can to make it happen. You are a dear, dear boy.'

Jo and I slept very soundly in the cold room as winds rushed across the vast and empty world around us. In the middle of the night I got up to fetch an eiderdown from the cupboard. Jo watched me with misty sleep-eyes as I shook it high in the air and it floated gently down over her, sighing as it landed. I held her body close to me and whispered to her.

'Happy New Year, darling.'

'You too. It is going to be a good one. I can feel it.'

In the morning we drove back to London, our heads foggy as the world outside, which was lost in a thick sea mist. Henry and his parents waved the car off down the road, disappearing quickly into the grey silence that we left in our wake. We listened to the radio as we drove in an attempt to create a solid world in the cocoon of the car, but the signal faded in and out as we drove through sightless Essex. Jo placed her hand on my thigh and then fell into a light sleep as we hit traffic coming into London. Her hand never left my leg, as if the feel of me offered her some sort of protection in her dreamworld.

*

I had to plan my meeting with Verity with great care. I started my coughing early in January, pitched it to jar on hungover, winter-weary heads. It was a high, shrill, persistent cough, which built up into a terrible scream before retreating with a final grim wheeze into silence. Catrina would put her hands over her ears while I coughed; the Chairman shut his door. Euphonium placed a small box of vile lozenges on my desk one lunch. I arranged my meeting with Verity late on a Friday afternoon, and let out barks and hacks all morning, clearing my throat and then noisily swallowing mucous, grabbing my desk and shuddering in silent agony as the fits subsided, dabbing at my eyes with a courageous handkerchief. Finally Catrina snapped.

'Oh go to the fucking doctor, Charles. I can't think with you dying there. Christ, what a noise.' The Chairman clapped in his office.

Smiling bravely, I nodded thanks, handkerchief now held to my face, packed up my belongings and left the office. My throat ached with the effort of drawing out the counterfeit bout of emphysema, but I danced down the road once I was outside, excited at the prospect of leaving that dry and ugly world. I took a taxi over to Clerkenwell Green and met the theatre critic in a dark pub behind a tall row of eighteenth-century houses. Verity was extended along a green crushed-velvet banquette, the table in front of him already glimmering with empty Martini glasses. I stepped nervously towards him, saw the famous drooping moustache, the orange cravat that sat beneath the collar of his slightly grubby white shirt. He was thumbing through a book, kept reaching out blindly for his glass to find it already empty. He looked very old and his long fingers quivered as they flitted like spiders across the table looking for a drink. I went to the bar, sure he'd seen me already and chosen to ignore me. I bought two Martinis and stood above him.

'You're Charlie? My dear fellow, do sit down. Ah . . . a Martini man. Grand. Cheers. What's your view of Ibsen? Have always found him rather too Scandinavian. So bleak, so terribly hopeless. I remember once I saw a performance of *Hedda* where . . .'

I sat and listened to him talk for an hour, occasionally helping to catch a lost train of thought, but otherwise I went quietly to the bar and bought drinks, nodded sagely, poured my Martinis beneath the table and watched him grow brilliantly drunk. I fluttered my eyelashes at him, stared broodingly from beneath my lowered brow. As I helped him to a taxi, he held my hand very tightly.

'I shall very much look forward to working with you, Charlie.'

'A pleasure to meet you, Mr Verity.'

'Oh, do call me Gervais, dear boy. Now give me a bell tomorrow morning and we can discuss the details of your employment. Good night, my dear fellow. Sleep so very sweetly.'

I telephoned him from a meeting room at work, my hands nervously worrying at the cord of the phone. I was to start at the beginning of March, after working my notice at Silverbirch. The salary would be £18,000 plus expenses. Verity spoke about money in a weary, rather distracted voice, as if he was both embarrassed and bored at the necessity of financial gain. I frowned a little at the figure, knew it was good for a journalist, realised that I would just have to make some serious changes in my life. I would cut up my credit card, give up smoking and Starbucks, move in with Jo. The last made all the difference. My lease ran out at the end of May. If I could last until then, perhaps write something for *Arena* in my spare time, it would be fine. I would actually have more disposable income each month without the egregious rental payments coming from my account. I knew Jo wanted me to move in with her, that as her parents spent more and more time in France we would increasingly have the run of the beautiful white house. I felt life in my grasp, could see a brightness around the edge of things.

I handed in my notice to the Chairman at the end of January. The markets remained in their depressed state, with prices falling slowly. Trades had become very rare, and people only sold when they had to liquidate funds to pay off unhappy investors, or when good news moved a particular company higher for a short while. I came into work early the day I had marked out to speak with the Chairman. It was a bleak and frozen morning and the Tube was full of lifeless men with red scabs under their running noses, large red eyes that wept gently at the corners. I sat at my desk and typed my letter of resignation. I felt buoyed by a kind of manic fatalism. The decision had been made and life was rocketing towards new vistas, bright new experiences. I wrote a polite letter thanking the Chairman for his support, telling him how interesting I had found the work, how much I would miss the people and the vigour and thrust of the place. Some of this was true. I worried a little that I would never again experience the heady excitement of those early days, back when I was making money and the markets were soaring and it seemed that all my decisions were right and I felt quite invincible. I remembered the breathless joy of those days with a strange, sour nostalgia.

I walked into the Chairman's office at ten past nine. I was more nervous than I had expected, could feel my heart beating very quickly, sensed the blood rushing through me. I was being carried on a fast tide and could do nothing to change direction, felt it carry me up from my desk and into the dim silence of the Chairman's office where he sat straight-backed reading an article in the *FT*. It was Friday, and the Chairman made a token gesture to dress-down culture by wearing a vaguely humorous tie. It was yellow and showed repeated images of a golf ball landing in a fish bowl, scaring the single inhabitant. I stared at it, wondered how the fishbowl had found its way onto the golf course, or whether, in fact, the unseen golfer was practising inside. I thought about the subversive designers in their atelier in Florence, laughing at the surreal non sequitur of the golf ball in the goldfish bowl. The Chairman cleared his throat and I drew the folded letter from my jacket pocket, laid it on the desk in front of him.

'Oh Christ, Charles.' He read the letter a couple of times and then let it drop gently to his desk.

'You know you're being really foolish, don't you? You've had a rough time. I can understand that. Madison died and you didn't get a bonus and the markets have been really ghastly, but this is all excellent experience for you. You'll make a great portfolio manager one day because of all the pain you have gone through in the last six months. I would always rather hire a guy who'd been blooded in a bear market. That was Bhavin's problem, I think. He learnt the market in the eighties and had that relentless yuppie optimism that typified the era. Couldn't drill it out of him even in the crash in the early nineties.

'Anyway,' he tapped a long finger on the letter, 'you want to be a journalist. Not an easy business. Bad pay, and print journalism is surely something of an anachronism. I'm a little surprised. Clearly you don't come from the same background as some of your colleagues, but that was always what I found interesting about you. I think you'll probably come back, but I'm not going to stop you going. I see a great deal of myself in you, Charles. I left the industry for a while, tried to run my own vineyard ten years ago. But I returned because nothing could match the simplicity of the success in this business. The good thing about money is that it is easily quantifiable. I am an objective success. Difficult to achieve as a journalist. I suppose we should get Catrina in here. Does she know anything about this?'

'No. I haven't told her yet.'

'She'll be mortified. She thinks very highly of you. Listen, Charles. There's still time for us to pretend that this was a momentary lapse of judgement. I'll cobble some money together from somewhere to give you a bonus, and we'll even take your salary up to seventy-five grand. I really want to keep you here.'

I didn't want him to see that I was considering it, so I turned and looked out into the main office, saw my desk and the naked shrine of Madison's desk and I thought of all the dry abstract days spent worrying about the markets and the companies and the constant fear of my own inadequacy and I turned back to the Chairman with a keen clear stare.

'I'm sure I want to go. I have always wanted to try writing. And I have found it just miserable, just so relentless, the negativity of the market. You can't help but be affected by it. I'm really sorry to do this to you, and I don't like leaving things unfinished, but I need to follow this one to the end. I hope that you can understand.'

I called out to Catrina and she came into the Chairman's office, worry creasing her forehead.

'What is it? I have a conference call with Japan in ten minutes, I can't be long.' She sat down on the sofa, kicked her heels off under the coffee table, then fished for them as she saw the Chairman looking at her bare feet shimmering through sheer tights.

'Charles has decided to leave us. Come on now, say your piece, Charles.'

'I'm sorry, Catrina. I have really loved being here . . .'

Her lips closed into a thin white line as a flush of violent red spread high on her cheekbones, seemed to be leaking down from her eyes.

'Where are you going? Are you going to a competitor? Because if you are I swear I will fucking kill you. We gave you a lot here, Charles. Not many were keen to take a chance on some English grad with an attitude problem. And I have turned you into a bloody good trader. I'm not having someone else see the fruits of that. What have we offered him to stay, Aldous?'

'I don't think that money is really the issue, is it Charles?'

'I'm sorry, Catrina. I'm going to be a journalist. Writing is something I have wanted to do for a very long time. I am really terribly sorry to let you down. Of course I wouldn't be so disloyal as to join a competitor. I really am aware of how much you have done for me. I appreciate it, really I do.'

'A journalist? Oh for fuck's sake, you don't want to be a journalist. Earn bugger-all. Seriously, Charles, don't be foolish. Stay here and we'll make it worth your while. As soon as trading picks up again we'll be off to the races. It's ridiculous to have worked as hard as you have and not to see anything from it. I'm sure we can scrape together a bonus, can't we, Aldous?'

'Charles wants to go, and we shouldn't stand in his way. I can't promise there'll be a job for you if you want to come back, you know that, don't you? But we all think very highly of you here. We're sorry to see you go. Usually we'd march people out the door with their belongings in plastic bags, but since you aren't going to a competitor I suppose you should work your month's notice. Thanks for everything you've done here, Charles. You'll be missed.'

He stood up, gripped me by the hand, and I was worried because my palm was sweating and I didn't shake back as firmly as I would have liked. Catrina, downcast, put her very thin arms around my neck and buried her head in my collar-bone. I felt her inhale deeply once, and then she turned and walked out of the office. I made my way out to the lifts, walked out into the sudden light of Berkeley Square. The world seemed changed, altered unrecognisably in those few minutes.

I felt relieved and yet still nervous, aware that I had cast myself into a new and frightening existence. I called Jo on my mobile.

'I've done it. I just did it.'

She shrieked and I could hear a sudden silence around her as the children turned to stare. Her happiness prompted my own, and I ran up path that led between the trees of the square, leaping high into the air with every few steps. Life was moving my way. The world was falling into place.

Chapter 12

Friends Return

There was to be a party at the flat in Fulham. Jo insisted that we celebrate my change of career, had wanted to invite people to the house in Elgin Crescent, but I resisted. The dark flat with its clanking plumbing, dampness and air of desperate melancholy seemed a more fitting venue to remember the life I was leaving behind. The empty drawing room with its piles of books and single tatty chair had come to represent the miserable existence I had led, a symbol of the occasions when I had come close to breaking during those dark few months after the crash. We would have dinner in the cheap Thai restaurant a few doors down from the flat, then we'd come back and drink and talk and bid farewell to that dry old life.

I typed up invitations at work and had a secretary print them out. *Charlie's Retirement Party* in gold letters on a pale blue background. I called Mehdi, recognising his number in my telephone with a sad twist in the chest. I hadn't seen or spoken to him for over a year. But when I heard his voice it was as if nothing had changed; he and Laura still lived in Fulham. They were still accountants, and still wanted to leave. They had moved further down towards Putney but they were within walking distance. Of course they would love to come. Then Henry, who told me how his mother had raved about *that wonderful boy* after New Year. He asked if he could bring Astrid to the party. They were trying to help her socialise more. It would be good for her to be amongst old friends.

Vero took a long time answering the telephone. It was only because I was doodling the answers to a crossword as I listened to the monotonous bleating of the dial tone that I let it ring so long. She sounded sleepy, cross and a little drunk.

'*Oui. 'Allo?*'

'Vero. It's Charlie. How are you, darling?'

'Charlie? Oh Charlie, it's you.' She gave a little squeal of pleasure. 'Did you give up your job? I know you did. I know you're calling me to tell me that you gave up your job.'

I left a pause. 'I gave up my job.'

'Oh Charlie. That's so wonderful. I'm very proud of you, *amour*.'

'I handed in my resignation last week and I'm going to work for the newspaper with Henry. I'll be penning theatre reviews, and I'll have a blog on the website to talk about new writing, fringe shows.'

'Oh Charlie, oh I'm so pleased . . . just so very pleased.' Her voice cracked, I heard her take a deep breath in. 'Now we have all escaped. You and Henry and I have all escaped. It's good. This is really very good.'

'Look, Vero, I wanted to ask if you'd come over. I'm having a party next Saturday and I know it's a long way to come, and I know that you and Marc are really only just getting started on your life together, but it would mean so much for me to have you there.'

She answered very quickly, her tone suddenly sharp.

'Of course I'll come. Of course I will.'

The Friday night before the party Jo spent the night in Fulham for the first time. I had ceased even to pretend to make an effort at work, had left just after three and Jo and I passed the afternoon sitting in a pub on the North End Road. There was a quiz machine and we leant our pints on a small wooden ledge, took turns to go to the bar for refills and crisps. We stood at the flashing machine, reinvested our winnings until they had disappeared, and then strolled in the cold February night through the quiet backstreets to Munster Road.

Jo laughed when I pushed open the door and we walked into the bare little flat. The place did look rather desperate. I noticed brown stains on the carpet spreading from the bottom of a radiator, saw my grey sheets, heard the scurry of rats in the courtyard outside very clearly. Jo wandered between the rooms and then came back out into the front room and took my face in her hands, her laugh now very tender.

'Oh Charlie, why didn't you say something? I mean you described it as being charmless and austere, but this is really just too funny. I wish I had realised, wish I'd known it was this tragic. You've got to live here for a few more months and there's no way it's staying like this. You don't have a television. You don't have any pictures up. Not even a picture of me.'

We ate at a restaurant on the New King's Road and then lay in bed together as a cold rain fell into the echoing courtyard outside. The heating gave out in the middle of the night and Jo wrapped her warm body around me, nestled against me and murmured softly. We woke to sunlight and I went out to buy breakfast from a new deli that had opened down the road and everything seemed very bright under a vivid sky.

Jo left me a list of jobs to do around the flat whilst she went out shopping. I was to move the coffee table to the centre of the room, pile the books neatly in a corner, pin back the curtains and open up the front window, try to get some air moving through the dampness. Finally, I was to take a pair of nail scissors and trim the fraying material from the tatty armchair. When I had done this I showered, pulled on a pair of jeans and sat in the room watching the world outside. I was excited at the thought of my friends being together, delighted that Vero would be there. A cat was jumping nervously along the roofs of the terraced houses opposite. I watched it pause and lick its fine grey fur which then sparkled in the brightness.

I was still sitting in my armchair when Jo's taxi pulled up outside. She was laden with many yellow bags and I stepped out barefoot onto the cold winter pavement to help her in. There is something refreshing and wonderful about bare feet on cold stone, something that feels young and liberating. I picked up as many bags as I could and staggered into the flat. Jo followed, clanking bottles together as she collapsed down into the armchair.

'Let's eat first. I'm starving.'

She had bought us little boxes of salad and savoury Lebanese pastries from Selfridges' Food Hall. It felt very luxurious to sit there eating tabbouleh out of a metal dish surrounded by the bright yellow bags. Jo smiled broadly when I looked over at her, leant towards me and placed a kiss on my cheek.

'I got a bit carried away. I'm so sorry. I just couldn't resist, having seen this place . . . It's just so forlorn. Your friends will think I haven't been looking after you when they see it. I got some booze for tonight, but I also bought a few things to brighten it up.'

She started to unload the yellow bags, and I saw two framed pictures of Penguin book covers – *The Great Gatsby* and *Brave New World* – then a small reproduction of a William Scott like the one I had bought my father for Christmas. The thought that she had put into the presents touched me greatly. I went out into the hall, took the stairs two at a time and knocked on my upstairs neighbour's door. He opened it slowly, a slice of cold pizza in his hand. I had only ever seen him from a distance before, was surprised at how old he looked. He was wearing a pair of high-waisted jeans and a white polo shirt with the cross of St George on it.

259

'Hi, hi there. I'm Charlie. From downstairs. Listen, I hate to bother you, but I wonder if I could borrow a hammer and some nails. My girlfriend has bought me a couple of pictures to put up.'

He looked blearily at me and I wondered if he was drunk.

'Charlie . . . Yes, I have seen your name on the post. Of course, wait here a second.'

He disappeared and I looked through the crack in the door to a front room that was only marginally more homely than my own. It was dominated by a large widescreen television and speaker system, but otherwise the place was very bare: an uncomfortable sofa sat against one wall, a dangerous-looking gas fire glowered beneath the chipped mantelpiece. He returned with an old rusted hammer and several nails. I took them, thanked him and saw that he wanted to say something. I turned back to him.

'Charlie . . . If you're ever at a loose end, why don't you come up and have a drink? We could go to the pub or something.'

His voice sounded very tired, and I could see his belly pushing out against the waist of his jeans, saw the white streaks in his hair which were illuminated by the sun behind him.

'I'm sorry, I don't know your name.'

'Gavin. My name is Gavin.'

'I'd love to hook up some time, Gavin. I'm . . . I'm actually having a few people over this evening. We're going to the little Thai place before. Why don't you stop by? It would be great to have you there. Unless you have other plans?'

His eyes lit up and a grin broke across his podgy face.

'No, I mean I was thinking of going out with some friends, but I'd much rather go to a party. You're sure you don't mind me coming along?'

I walked down the dark stairway and when I came back into the flat it had already changed beyond recognition. A turquoise bowl stood in the centre of the coffee table filled with water and three floating green candles which streamed out a heavenly scent like honeysuckle. A dark blue throw with a white border sat over the armchair which had been pushed to one corner and there was a fine rug of pale gold under the coffee table. My battered old radio had disappeared and a new shining digital contraption sat beside the pile of books, playing soft sweet music. Jo was standing on a plastic chair fitting a lampshade to the bare bulb. She tottered for a moment and I put my arms around her strong thighs. The new shade cast a much kinder glow around the small room. Then Jo unwrapped silver photo frames, peeling off white tissue paper. She reached into her bag and drew out a picture of herself and then one of Ray and me from her parents' Christmas party.

'I stopped off at home to get these. I think pictures are crucial. They speak of a world outside the flat, make it look as if your life isn't all just this one sad room.'

She placed the frames on the mantelpiece and then stood back to admire her work. I walked over and slipped my arms around her, pulled her against me. The wind came in through the open window and it smelt fresh and clean.

'Thanks, Jo. I'm really very touched. It's a wonderful thing you have done. A truly wonderful thing.'

'I'm just sorry we couldn't fit more in the cab. But we'd only have to find somewhere for it all when you move in with me. I think it looks much better now, don't you?'

We spent the afternoon inflating and tying balloons, sitting on the new golden rug that was the same colour as Jo's hair. She had bought a case of beer and ten bottles of champagne that took up the entire fridge. She made me throw away the huge lump of cheddar and the off milk which were the only other occupants of the tiny wheezing machine. When darkness fell, Jo lit some more candles and turned off the top light. I watched the soft, gentle movements of her fingers tying balloons in the candlelight and the light from the streetlamp outside. As night drew in I saw the old tramp trot past outside, cursing to herself, and I felt a great deal of love for the wretched old lady, wanted to rush out and embrace her. Instead, I took Jo's hands in mine and kissed them, and we lay back on the rug and stared up at the ceiling in silence.

We arrived early at the little Thai restaurant. It was very cheap and served good, hearty food and allowed you to bring your own booze. The walls were decorated with faded pictures of golden beaches and swaying palm trees and I thought how good it would be to take a holiday somewhere warm and dry, somewhere that Jo and I could walk around in our bathing suits, eat in T-shirts under whispering trees. I knew that many of my dreams were predicated upon her wealth, the fact that she would always pick up the tab at restaurants, that we could live in her house without paying rent, and this made me feel guilty, a little emasculated. But she was so gracious about it, so generous and yet unselfconscious about her generosity. She understood that money had caused me to set off down the wrong path in life, and she took great pleasure in showing me that it was not something I'd have to worry about again.

Gavin was the first to arrive. He had changed into a gaudy striped shirt which was very precisely ironed and he carried a bottle of wine in one fat hand, a bunch of slightly sad-looking flowers in the other. I introduced him to Jo and he looked rather stunned by her. He sat down with us and began to thank us for inviting him in long, rambling sentences. I got the pretty young waitress to set the flowers in a vase. Then Henry arrived. I saw his taxi pull up outside the restaurant and his long bony arm reached out a cupped hand to receive his change. He walked in with a huge smile on his face, placed a bottle of champagne on the table and hugged us both, shook hands warmly with Gavin. I called out for glasses and, when the pale bubbling liquid had been poured out, I raised mine to Henry.

'I wanted to thank you. For everything. Before the others get here I want you to know how grateful I am, how much this means to me. Not only the job, but everything. Your friendship and everything you've done to help me through what have been a rotten few years. Gavin, this man is the best friend ever.'

Henry cast his eyes down, embarrassed, then swirled the champagne in his glass and then looked up at me.

'That's very kind, but Charlie did it all himself. Verity loved you, Charlie. I think he's got a crush on you. And I honestly don't think he'll be around that much longer, d'you know? You'll get to make contacts through him, you'll meet all the actors and directors and then when he dies or retires you'll be able to run the whole thing. I know you're going to be such a success. And as for my friendship, well really we've . . . we've seen each other through this ghastly time. I remember when I was quite desperate, and you were there for me. And I have tried to be there for you. Look, here's Astrid.'

His sister had walked from the Tube. Her hair was cut short and she had some sort of glitter in her make-up. Her cheeks were fuller than they had been at New Year and they shimmered in the warm light of the restaurant as she entered. She seemed very pleased to see me, screeched out my name and threw her arms around me.

The rest of the guests arrived in quick succession. Laura and Mehdi, looking older and tired but very happy together. Laura and Jo seemed to strike up an instant rapport, and I heard Jo telling her about the charity and Laura listened rapt. Mehdi sat down next to Gavin and they began to discuss football. They both supported the same team and commiserated over a recent run of poor results.

Tony and Ray arrived next, Ray in his school uniform, Tony wearing the suit he had worn to the Christmas party. Tony had bought a bottle of Veuve Clicquot and presented it to me with a flourish. Ray had made me a card with '*Congratulations*' in large red letters on the front and a picture of the two of us drawn in meticulous pencil lines inside. I hugged him and he feigned self-consciousness.

'Get off me, homo. Serious man, what will the ladies think?'

Yannis and Enzo stepped inside and they were buzzing with coke, but I didn't find it gross or insulting that they had sharpened the evening with drugs. They were charming and full of eager questions about my new job and they both stood politely when Jo got up to go to the loo. Yannis had bought me a beautiful Faber-Castell fountain pen and Enzo a pile of Moleskine notebooks to write in. I hugged them both, poured out more champagne and we were all talking at great volume, shouting over each other and making jokes and laughing riotously. Then a sudden silence.

Vero walked into the restaurant pulling a small black suitcase. She wore a dress of electric blue and, as she stepped through the door, a car passed behind her, catching her in its lights, illuminating her deep dark eyes and the fine soft hair that was piled on her head. I felt my heart shudder at the beauty of her as she moved towards me, holding my gaze with her eyes. Then the spell was broken and she fell heavy into my arms.

'Charlie, oh God, I have missed you, Charlie. And Henry . . . Astrid . . . oh my God, Laura and Mehdi. It's so good to see you all. Where can I put my bag? I fell asleep on the Eurostar. My hair must be all over the place. Is this Jo? Jo, it's like I know you already. I can feel the change you have made to Charlie. He's happy now, aren't you, darling?'

She took her place between Henry and me and I felt every eye in the room watching her. We began to talk again, I asked after Marc and she replied in short, guarded sentences, tried to guide me on to talk about myself. Yannis reached over and introduced himself, taking her hand and pressing his large soft lips to it, bowing theatrically. I was aware that I had turned my back on Jo, but she was deep in conversation with Laura and laid her hand softly on mine when I leant over and kissed her neck.

Ray was sat opposite Vero, and I saw him look at her very shyly through wide round eyes.

'Are you French? *Bonjour, mon ami. Comment allez-vous?*' He looked at me for approval and I smiled back at him. Vero reached over and touched his cheek gently.

'*Bonjour,*' she replied in a soft voice. '*Comment t'appelles tu?*'

'*Je m'appelle Ray,* baby.' He laughed at his daring and Vero leant across and laid a kiss on Ray's cheek, then poured him out a glass of champagne. I saw the young boy fall desperately in love the instant her full lips touched his cheek.

After dinner Henry stood up, tapped a knife on his glass and coughed bashfully.

'Umm . . . It falls upon me to say a few words. It is . . . it is such a wonderful thing to see you all here. I rather feel that we have survived some gruesome challenge, some great disaster. And I know that some of you still work at jobs you dislike, and I would urge you strongly to follow the lead of my dear friend Charlie, and darling Vero, and Yannis, and escape before it is too late. I wanted to thank you all for making the trip over here, to a place that holds such mixed memories for many of us. I have to admit I was rather scared coming back here. I tend to associate Fulham with feeling rather desperate and depressed, but I found I felt only a . . . a warm nostalgia coming back here, remembering drunken times with my friends. So please all raise your glasses to Charlie, to dear Charlie's retirement. To his new career, to a new life of fulfilment.'

There was a great cheer and Jo scurried from the room to prepare the flat for our return. We talked for a little longer and then Enzo insisted on picking up the bill for dinner and we carried any half-drunk bottles of champagne back to the mansion block. Yannis and Enzo had to go on to another party.

'You're doing the right thing, Charlie,' Enzo said, clasping my hand.

'We'll do a book together, bro,' said Yannis. 'We'll write an exposé of Silverbirch when the fuckers go bust. It will be sweet. I'm sorry we gotta head off. Too many parties at the moment. The death of capitalism is being celebrated in a pretty profound way.'

Enzo raised his hand in the air as they strolled off together into the night. I saw Yannis swing once around a lamppost like an actor from a black-and-white film. The rest of us made our way into the still-damp flat.

Music was playing on the new radio and we sat in small clusters on the floor, each group perched above an ashtray in the dim light of the candles. Jo had filled bowls with crisps but none of us were hungry and we sat and smoked and drank champagne, and it was rather bohemian and very lovely. I saw that Gavin and Tony had become great friends, saw their faces move animatedly in the soft light as they opened cans of beer and spoke with great intensity about football. Vero and Ray were talking in a corner. He was speaking earnestly, and I saw her lay a hand on his shoulder as he turned his face to the wall. He was crying and I wondered if they were talking about his mother. Vero invited that kind of intimacy, often found strangers opening up to her, confessing great secrets. I caught her eye and smiled. Henry and Astrid were fingering through the great pile of books, occasionally pulling one out and flicking through it, laughing, reminding each other of the plot and the characters. Jo stood with Laura in the small kitchen drinking champagne from the bottle.

I sat on the floor with Mehdi. His hair, which had once been long and bushy, had thinned dramatically, and was now only thick around the ears. I could see the whiteness of his scalp on the top of his head. He sipped from his glass, flicked his cigarette into the ashtray.

'I'm so impressed that you've managed it, Charlie. Laura and I have wanted to leave for so long. I think now we might really do it. That girl of yours – Jo – she's amazing. She's been telling Laura all about the charity she works for. Laura has always wanted to do something like that. She'd like to set something like that up in South Africa. It's such a great thing to do. And I have decided to do a PhD. I have always dreamed about continuing my studies, going back into that world of science and thought. I have really hated our time in London. I don't know why we came here. It seems so stupid now, but everyone else was coming down here and we wanted to be with you. But now it is time to go. It seems dreamlike, us being down here, us being qualified accountants. Or a nightmare. Yes, it's much more like a nightmare.'

We carried on drinking, talking over the small smoking pyres of ashtrays. Then it was quarter to midnight and Tony and Ray had to leave to catch the last Tube home, and Astrid went with them. She and Henry were staying at their parents' place in Chelsea, and she was tired and overwhelmed at being out again after so long hidden from the world. I saw Henry take her hands in his as she left, press them and kiss her on the cheek, and I thought again what a huge amount of kindness there was in him. Ray shook me hard by the hand, smiling, the streaks of recently-shed tears shimmering on his face.

'I had a wicked time, Charlie. Vero's just fuckin' amazing. Will you ask her if she'll go out with me?'

Tony put an arm around his son. Ray took Astrid by the hand, and I watched the three of them walk down Munster Road together, Astrid and Ray already deep in conversation, their breath streaming silver out behind them in the cold air.

Mehdi and Laura were the next to go and we all hugged in the pool of light under the streetlamp outside. Jo and Laura arranged to meet up the next weekend, and I felt a sincere hope that by breaking my own chains I would help others break theirs. When they had passed out of sight we turned back into the mansion block, and Gavin made his way up to his flat, very drunk, his heavy body loud on the stairs. I heard him sink with a crash onto his bed.

The candles had all burnt out when we walked back into the front room. Jo had opened the window again and the balloons shifted forlornly across the floor, lost souls. Ash had fallen onto the new carpet and I could see patterns in the dark smudges. They looked like thunderclouds spread across a violent sunset. I was drunk and pulled Jo roughly towards me, kissed her neck hard. She squirmed, giggled, and went back into the kitchen. I followed her and we washed glasses together, my arms reaching around her to the tiny sink. Henry and Vero sat close, each perched on a pile of books, deep in conversation.

When Jo and I came back into the front room, something had changed in the atmosphere. I felt a heaviness in the air, as if the natural misery of the apartment had reasserted itself now there were fewer of us to fight it off. Henry stood at the window, his palms pressed flat against the glass. Jo walked over to him and laid a hand on his shoulder, then bent and closed the window. The balloons stopped moving. Vero was staring at Henry and I could see that her eyes were moist. She leapt up, suddenly agitated and clumsy. The pile of books toppled over with a soft thump.

'I forgot. I have a present from my papa. A bottle of Calvados. He said that he had never seen anyone drink Calvados like you English boys. This was brewed by a friend of his. Ten years old. It is so strong. Like firewater.'

She rifled through her little suitcase. I could see that she had packed her clothes in a great hurry. I saw shirts and vests crumpled into balls, caught sight of a pair of her pants which were black lace and looked slightly dirty. Vero drew out an unlabelled bottle and took a long swig. When she dropped the bottle down, some of the golden liquid spilled down her chin and her eyes were aflame.

'Who wants some?'

I took a pull, felt the fast-evaporating alcohol burning down my throat. I choked a little, swallowed more and I felt alive and powerful. Jo and Henry both took smaller gulps. Henry coughed wildly and sat down heavily in the armchair. He looked old and tired and I realised that we were all nearer thirty than twenty, that our youth was disappearing, that we would soon be grown-up and miserable and I felt we needed to mark the time, seize the chances that our youth offered us. I took another long gulp of the Calvados, felt it evaporating in my mouth, shook my head at the strength of it.

We sat talking. Vero was chattering manically, her fingers working the ash stains further into the carpet. Jo sat at Henry's feet, her head against the arm of the chair, and I watched him stroke her hair, saw that she had fallen asleep, heard the gentle sigh of her breathing. Henry was very quiet. I noticed that he didn't look at Vero. We continued to pass the Calvados between us and I grew very drunk. The room began to blur at the edges, the light thrown by the new lampshade suddenly made me feel queasy and I stood up and staggered over to the window. Vero rose to join me and knocked the Calvados bottle off the coffee table. It landed with a crash and began to glug its contents onto the rug. I saw Jo wake with a start. She smiled and stretched, looked up at Henry and laughed at his drunk red face, his tired eyes.

'You look knackered, Henry. Listen, I've got to be over in Hackney tomorrow. We're giving a birthday party for a kid whose father has just died. Can I take the balloons, Charlie? Is that OK? And listen, do you mind dreadfully if I go back home tonight? I'm so tired and I did find it cold last night. Why doesn't everyone come back up to Notting Hill? There's plenty of room.'

I was still standing at the window. Vero had her hand resting on the small of my back. I felt the softness of her little hand. I turned to look at Jo, then stared back out of the window, saw the ghostly reflection of Vero's eyes in the glass, could make out the jut of her cheekbones and the dim wisps of her hair against the blackness.

'You go on, Jo. Vero's staying with Henry and Astrid, and I'd rather like to spend the night here alone. Remind myself of what I'm leaving behind.'

I shrugged away from Vero's hand, walked over to Jo and helped her up. I phoned for a cab as we gathered the sad-looking balloons into plastic bags. Jo bent down and hugged Henry, who was slumped in the chair, smiling wanly, occasionally reaching out for the remnants of the Calvados. We walked together out into the night and she leant against me, her head heavy on my shoulder. I kissed a soft cheek, ran my hand down her back.

'Thanks for everything, Jo. You're astonishing. You do crazy things to my heart.'

I stood and waved as the cab pulled off into the cold darkness and then walked back into the flat. I staggered again slightly as I stepped into the smoky room with the reek of Calvados and the new gold rug already almost ruined with spilt ash. Henry was snoring in the chair, his head slumped down on his chest. Vero stood at the window still, looking out onto Munster Road. She turned around slowly and I could see she was crying, her back moving like a pump handle.

'Charlie. Oh, Charlie.'

She stepped towards me and I put my arms around her, pulled her head to my chest.

'It's not working with Marc, Charlie. It's not working at all. He doesn't want to settle down. He certainly doesn't want to settle down with me. He snaps at me all the time . . .' She started to sob and pushed herself away from me, went to sit on another pile of books, put her head in her hands. I stood over her, looked over to Henry who stirred for a moment and then settled back to sleep.

'Henry says I have made my bed. That is the expression he used. That I made my choice, that I fucked you and him around for long enough. That maybe I deserve this. But I'm so sad. I'm so lonely. *Bof* . . . maybe Henry is right. Maybe I have to stick it out. I can't tell you what it's like to sit there waiting for him to come back from a meeting in Paris, but he never comes back, and I have watched the sun come up in the windows of that fucking hospital so many times. I'm so sorry, Charlie. I finally found something to do with my life that has meaning, finally I feel my life has some purpose, and Marc has fucked it all up. I have fucked it all up.'

I knelt down and pulled her towards me; I knew the shape of her body so well, and her hair was dirty and smelt strongly. I pressed my lips into the soft folds of her neck. We stayed locked together like that for some time as solitary cars passed outside and a church bell tolled two. Finally she stood up unsteadily, leant over to the table and picked up the bottle of Calvados. I watched her take gulp after gulp until the bottle was nearly empty. Then she let it fall slowly from her small fingers, stared up at me angrily and coughed.

'I shouldn't have come, Charlie. I have ruined your party. I'm . . . I'm so sorry. I'm so drunk.' She raised a hand to her face and ran to the loo. I listened to her wailing as she vomited, heard the wailing slowly subside into sobs.

I found a cloth in the kitchen and began to scrub at the stains on the rug. The black faded to grey, but I only managed to cover more of the golden rug in a haze of ash. Finally I gave up, found a blanket to throw over Henry, and turned out the light in the front room. Vero hadn't locked the door to the bathroom and I found her perched on the loo, her tights around her ankles, dress hitched up around her waist. Her shoes had slipped from her feet and stood at strange angles at the bottom of her legs, making it look as if she had broken her ankles. She was slumped forward, and sobbed softly to herself every so often. I whispered her name and she looked up blearily.

'Charlie. Oh shit, I'm sorry. Help.' She stumbled forward onto me and I propped her up as she tore off a piece of tissue, folded it neatly and wiped herself. I helped her to stand, caught a glimpse of her dark bush as I rolled up her tights. She smiled awkwardly at me.

'Thanks, Charlie. You're such a star.'

I put her arm around my neck and led her to my bedroom. She fell heavily down onto the bed in the darkness. I turned on the lamp and undressed her to her underwear. I saw the soft pale skin of her thighs, the skinny shoulders which tapered to arms that looked too thin, childish and fragile. I found an old Smashing Pumpkins T-shirt which I pulled down over her head and then undid her bra beneath it, slipping it out under one arm. The T-shirt was too large for her and I could see one of her tits through the sleeve. She saw me watching her and hunched her shoulders forward so I could see the whole of her body, her breasts hanging down to dark nipples above a hard stomach. I pulled her towards me, saw her look up with fierce eyes. I twisted my hand in her hair, brought her head towards me and kissed her. I could feel her smiling under the kiss. Her mouth was hot and sour with vomit and alcohol. I stepped back, let her fall to the bed, and left the room.

I sat on a pile of books in front of the window looking out onto the empty street. It had begun to rain and the window caught the fine silver patterns of the droplets that were blown against it by the wind. Henry moaned in his sleep. I had found some white wine in the fridge and drank it straight from the bottle. It was cold and good and I felt drunk enough to stay up all night, watching over my friends, telling myself that the kiss with Vero was something historical, just an echo of a love that was now dead. I watched as a young couple walked past in the rain. He held a copy of the *NME* above her head, she crouched beneath it. He was wearing a long trenchcoat and a trilby and she had heavy make-up that had started to run. Vero's hand fell gently onto my shoulder.

'I couldn't sleep.' She was whispering and her voice was slurred and tearful.

She took my hand and led me into the bedroom. I saw her black pants on the floor, knew that she was naked beneath the T-shirt. She was breathing quickly and I could see her chest rise, her breasts held high. We kissed again. The small desk light that sat by the bed cast giant shadows against the walls of the room. I shut the door with my heel as she pulled my lower lip into her mouth, clawing at me with her little hands. She drew her face away from mine and pushed herself against me, then stepped back and sat on the bed.

'Undress,' she said.

I took off my clothes and stood in front of her, slightly bashful after so long. I reached out my hands behind me and steadied myself on the cold wall as she sank her head down onto my cock. I leant forward over her, twirled her soft hair around my fingers, felt the gentle rhythm of her, the gasps of her breaths. Her mouth was very hot and she made little grunting noises that came from the back of her throat. She suddenly moved back, reached over and flicked out the light, and I fell forward onto the bed in the darkness. I lay naked beside her. It was very quiet. I could hear a moth skittering against the window. The rain fell harder now, began to drum in the puddles of the courtyard. Vero was asleep. I sat for several minutes watching her, then slipped my arm around her hot dark body and fell into a troubled doze.

When I awoke it was still black outside. Rats' paws splashed through puddles but the rain had stopped. Vero was moving herself against me. She was still asleep, moaned gently to herself, her breaths jagged and panting. The T-shirt had ridden up above her waist and her naked skin was pressed against mine. As if in a dream myself, I slipped inside her. It was wet and warm and she seemed to envelop me, taking everything of me into her. I moved against her and she let out a little cry. It was the sound of a night-creature, and I saw her hands push the T-shirt further up her body, then pull back on the skin of her chest, flattening her breasts against her, her ribs outlined by the few lights that shone down into the courtyard from higher flats. I placed my hands over hers and both of us pushed down on her breasts, felt the soft flesh yielding. I stayed inside her, moving in tiny circular motions, feeling her dampness overflowing and seeping down her legs onto her soft thighs. Finally we both drifted into a drunken sleep.

Henry was standing over us. It was morning and bright winter light came down into the courtyard. I had forgotten to pull the curtains and felt the light falling harsh and judgemental upon us. Vero had wrapped the duvet tightly around herself and was sleeping, her face still and calm against the pillow. Henry met my sleepy, defensive gaze, shook his head and stepped from the room. I heard the front door slam. Vero woke, stretched and smiled up at me.

'You're such a crazy boy, Charlie. I do love you.'

She turned over, rolled out of the duvet and wrapped her arms around me, kissed me with wet lips, chewing on my neck and my earlobes. I lay motionless as she ran one small hand down my cold body. As she passed over my stomach, I reached up, took her hand and held it in mine. I rose from the bed and wrapped a towel around my waist as Vero watched me with hungry eyes.

We dressed in silence and walked down to the Starbucks on Dawes Road. Couples sat around reading the *Sunday Times* and they were each a rebuke in their lazy weekend contentment. I wanted to feel huge guilt weighing down on me. But when I looked over at Vero's wide dark eyes, saw her laugh childlike as she poured a long fountain of sugar into her coffee, I knew that part of me was glad for what had happened. I felt that she had tormented me for too long and that last night was something close to revenge. She laid a hand down on mine and sipped at her coffee.

'I'm sorry about last night, Charlie. I hope . . . I hope it doesn't cause you any trouble. *Bof* . . . we're like children the two of us. Can't keep our hands off each other.'

My phone rang. It was Jo. I switched it to silent and let it flash away on the table, sniping at my conscience.

'My Eurostar is at twelve. Will you walk me to the Tube?'

We trudged down to Parsons Green under the withering winter sun, and I stood behind the barriers as she pulled her suitcase bouncing up the stairs behind her. She looked round at me just before passing out of sight, raised a hand to me, her face very drawn and grave.

That afternoon I drove over to Hackney and picked Jo up

from the charity. I sat in the car as a long stream of children flowed out of the building carrying party bags. Finally Jo appeared. I had thought that I would hug her very close to me, had imagined that I would bury my guilt under many small acts of kindness, but when I saw her I felt nothing. Jo seemed so weak as she struggled towards the car with leftover party bags hanging from her arms. I thought of Vero's fire, of the shimmer of passion that danced in her eyes, and I couldn't speak to Jo on the way home. It was as if Jo had somehow pushed me into my infidelity, as if she should be punished for forcing me into a bond that made my night with Vero something to be regretted. We arrived back in Notting Hill and ate dinner in silence on our laps in front of banal television. I went to bed early and pretended not to hear her when Jo came into the room.

Chapter 13

A New Life

I thought about Vero in darkened theatres. I spent long evenings watching worthy productions of political plays at the Hackney Empire and the Kilburn Tricycle, and I thought of Vero. Even when I managed to cast thoughts of the night with her out of my mind, even when I was able to fully concentrate on the stage, a character's turn of phrase, or the dark fire in an actor's eyes, would bring her back. She was an infection, and my stomach jumped and heaved, my groin danced under tight jeans, and my nights were white with the image of her hitching the T-shirt up over her ribs, rich with the scent of her dirty hair.

My last week at Silverbirch was also spent watching others. The markets came to life again as those who had been holding out for a swift recovery crumpled and died. Funds that had been living close to the edge and praying that the New Year would usher in renewed optimism, a rally in prices, were disappointed by a bleak and hopeless February. Many of the money managers had prevented investors from withdrawing their cash in the chaos of October and November. They were no longer able to stop the withdrawals, and money flowed in a swift and painful tide away from the hedge funds. One by one, Silverbirch's smaller competitors were closed down as the banks cut their liquidity lines and their investors queued to recover what they could. Rumours again began to circle about Silverbirch's continued viability.

A small band of renegade trading desks, new funds set up by

those who had made their fortunes betting against the US housing market, turned their attention to the investment banks. I watched the banks' share prices tumble as the funds used false rumour and short-selling to inject panic into the market. These same investors were sending the price of oil rocketing to record levels through speculation on derivatives contracts. I watched their actions with a respectful horror. They were making a fortune, but they were destroying the system in which their success would have a frame of reference. I pictured the aggressive fund managers dancing through the streets of a dreary, smoking New York, brandishing their fist-fuls of dollars which had become devalued through inflation, flashing the platinum credit cards of banks that they had helped to drive under.

The Chairman spent all of his time in meetings with expressionless Koreans, thick-necked Russians, vast Saudis in their pristine dishdashes who chain-smoked, misting up the windows of the Chairman's office. He spoke daily to the *FT*, to the *Wall Street Journal*, to his wife who was threatening to leave him, bored of his empty promises of retirement. I listened to him pleading with her, negotiating with quick aggressive forays followed by broad concessions. I heard him use exactly the same tactics that he employed to win over the sceptical journalists. I wondered if it was a possible for a man like the Chairman to have a private life, whether he was so steeped in the markets, so tied to his job that everything became a trade to be executed, everything could be tallied on the profit and loss, and all tactics were acceptable if the correct outcome was achieved.

Catrina was trying to shore up the business, worked long hours with Lothar, selling or shorting anything they could. She crackled with nervous energy, began to wear less make-up and had started smoking. I realised how old she was when we stood outside one lunchtime and she tripped on her high heels, and it looked so much like an old lady falling. I placed a hand on her elbow and helped her to lean against a wall as I lit her cigarette. Lothar had moved to Madison's desk, had taken up the role of portfolio manager whilst Euphonium tried to run the whole analytics department alone. There was no point hiring anyone else until the company got through the crash. Only the desperate would join Silverbirch anyway, given the stories in the press about the company's imminent demise.

I realised that Lothar and Catrina were having an affair on my last evening at Silverbirch. The Chairman had cancelled his meetings with investors, Catrina hung up the phone just before six and the entire firm gathered around our desks. The company was so much smaller than when I had joined. With the deaths and the firings and those who had left for greater job security, the business had halved in size. A secretary pushed out a trolley with three bottles of champagne and a stack of plastic glasses. The Chairman opened one of the bottles with his large, tanned hands and looked disdainfully down at the label.

'Ah . . . NV. Pity. Still, there can't be many drinking champagne in the City this month. It's always sad to see someone leave the company, and we have had quite a few departures recently, but I have always said that there are good leavers and bad leavers, and Charles Wales is certainly a good leaver. After solid service both as an analyst and, latterly, as a portfolio manager, Charles has decided to head off to become a journalist. Now after the time I've been having with journalists recently . . .'

He reached over to me, placed his thick hands around my neck and pressed on my windpipe with his thumbs. The pressure surprised me and I pushed my chin down against his wrists. He loosened his grip and chuckled.

'Charles worked tirelessly through the most difficult times that this company has endured, put the good of the firm before anything else. I get a weekly printout of when people swipe in and out of this office, and I can tell you that Charles worked almost every weekend, worked very late nights. We wanted to give him something really special to remember us by, and, knowing a little about the life of a journalist, we decided to forgo sentiment, and give him money. So here you go, Charles.'

He handed me an envelope. I opened it, saw the cheque inside, made myself read the banal salutations before looking at the amount. Trite expressions of friendship from people that didn't know me, a long and flowery goodbye from Catrina, a small picture of me looking thoughtful drawn by Euphonium. Lothar had written too much, had run out of space until the final few words were hardly legible, squeezed into a corner. I looked at the cheque. It was for £10,000. I sat down heavily. The Chairman lifted his glass into the air.

'Please will you all join me in wishing Charles all the best in his new life. To Charles.'

I sat staring at the cheque, dazed, as the crowd dissipated. Some of the secretaries carried the remnants of a bottle of champagne out to the reception desk with them. I stepped into the Chairman's office, pulling the door shut behind me.

'This is so generous. I . . . I really can't thank you enough.'

He was facing away from me, bent over his desk and flicking through emails, viciously deleting messages.

'I wanted you to have something to show for it, Charles. Otherwise, it just wasn't fair. Catrina and Lothar contributed a grand each. I did the rest. Seemed like the decent thing to do. Now listen, I have to be on a conference call, but really the very best of luck, Charles. I'm sure you'll do fine. And, between you and me, if we make it through, I'm sure there will always be a place for you here. Now bugger off.'

I walked over to him, shook his large hand, and strode out of his office. Catrina and Lothar were drinking champagne together, and I saw something pass between them, a moment's electricity when their fingers touched, and I knew at once that they were together. It was moving to see the flush rise to her cheeks, speed up to her tired eyes, and he suddenly looked more human, deeply happy beneath the vast dome of his forehead.

The next afternoon Jo and I drove down into Mayfair. She waited in the Polo whilst I packed my belongings into a battered sports bag. I raised a hand to Lothar. He was on the phone, but he smiled and waved at me. Catrina ran over, hugged me close to her. The Chairman was at a meeting in the City. I walked along the corridor, running my finger down the mahogany panelling, pressed my hands against the glass wall of the boardroom, gave one last look through the Chairman's empty office to my desk. The same secretary who had taken my coat the day of my interview laid a kiss on my cheek. She was plumper now, happily married to a trader at Lehman Brothers. I walked through the doors of the office and inhaled deeply, trying to keep the scent of the place in my nose. I walked out of the building and threw my bag in the back of the Polo.

I stood next to the car and looked up at the great office tower for one last time. It rose huge above me, looked like it had been designed to cast its shadow over the whole square. The bricks seemed to glow red in the light of the afternoon. In the shadow of the dimly luminous building, I could see Madison standing with a Starbucks in one hand, a cigarette in the other. She waved to me, wrinkled her glasses on her nose and turned away. The wind blew behind me and I heard the familiar rustle of the plane trees. Jo was pressed against the window of the car, watching me. I held my hand up against her face, felt the warmth of her through the glass. We drove back up through the commotion of Oxford Street in silence.

I didn't tell Jo about the cheque. It was sitting in my jacket pocket, felt hot and raw against my skin, but I couldn't say anything about it. It seemed to counteract something that I had felt about the City, seemed to disprove my theory that everyone was selfish and money-obsessed and the richer they got, the tighter they were with their cash. Of course it was a pittance for the Chairman and Catrina and Lothar, it was what they spent taking their friends out to dinner on a Saturday night, the cost of heating their swimming pools for a month. But it meant a huge amount to me. It would enable me to live alongside Jo without shame, and it would have somehow been shameful to tell her the charitable way I had come by the money.

We sat at the bar in E&O that evening waiting for our table. I had booked the restaurant without telling Jo, wanted to watch her eyes light up when I told her about it. She was full of childish excitement, happier than I was at the end of my job. She leant against me at the bar, sipped from my whisky sour with the straw sideways in her mouth.

'But really, tell me how it feels. Is it amazing? Do you feel completely liberated?'

A mist rolled down Ladbroke Grove, a yellow mist caught in streetlamps and the lights of cars. I saw it gather outside the restaurant, rub its back against the long window.

'I'm very happy, Jo . . . It's just . . . It's just, I don't know. I somehow expected more. I was so obsessed by the idea that it was the wrong place for me to be, I was so caught up in that left-wing, snobbish, slightly adolescent disdain for the City, I'm now worried that I left because I didn't think it was cool to work in the City.'

'But that's ridiculous. You hated it. You were so stressed out, you were taking those awful pills, you were completely miserable.'

She pulled back from me, suddenly angry, her voice loud and harsh against the soft music and quiet conversation of the restaurant. I took her hand and tried to pull her towards me.

'You won't understand, because you're one of the few exceptions to this rule, but sometimes I think that nearly everyone hates their job. That all jobs have to have elements of drudgery about them. And why not do a job that at least allows you to earn serious money, enables you to live like a king when you're not at work? Is it something about our generation that working so you can enjoy your free time is somehow not quite enough? That the job has to be eternally fascinating rather than just an acceptable way of putting cash in your pocket?'

'But why do you need so much cash? Why not do a job that you love, that enables you to watch fabulous plays and discuss them in the company of bright people, and not worry about money? Why not just fucking shut up about money, because it's so boring to hear you witter on about it?'

She was on the verge of tears, and I saw other guests at the bar turning towards us with amused eyes. The waitress came and showed us to our table, and Jo made bright, happy conversation, trying to cast the memory of her anger away. I took her hand under the table as we sat and watched the room empty around us much later, and she squeezed very hard, and the force of her grip made me think of Vero.

I took the Tube over to Chancery Lane early on Monday morning and walked up Farringdon Road to the newspaper's offices. I tried to sign in and the security guard told me to wait – there was no record of me starting, no pass had been prepared for me. I sat and fidgeted nervously until the first journalists began to walk through the door. I saw Henry's father pull up outside. Henry pushed his long legs out of the car door, extracted the rest of his long thin body and looked up the steps at me. We hadn't spoken since he'd seen me in bed with Vero, and I expected him to be distant, scathing in silent reproach. But he was excited at the thought of working in the same office as me, and he ran up the steps as I watched his father step out onto the pavement. Henry shook me hard by the hand, we both waved to his father who rushed by, patting my back as he passed. Henry ushered me past the guard and up to the fourth floor. Verity's office was squeezed into a dark corner, piled high with books and scripts. I saw, touched, that he had found a small desk, like a desk from school, and placed it in a corner with a tiny stool. There was a copy of the week's listings magazine and a note for me.

Won't be in on Monday. Why don't you select a few things for us to see this week? Meet for lunch at the Bleeding Heart on Tuesday at one. Book something for Wednesday and Thursday nights. Enjoy!

Henry chuckled drily.

'I'm afraid that's rather typical of old Verity. I'm bloody sorry. Listen, come and bother me if you get bored. Now I must dash. It will get better, believe me.'

I read the guide, called up the Barbican and the Gate for tickets, and sat back on the stool. It was ten past ten and I had nothing to do. The room outside his small office was almost empty. A homely girl with mousy hair was typing furiously the other side of a row of empty desks. I tried to catch her eye, but she was transported, lost in the manic thumping of her computer keys. I stretched, read through a couple of short plays which had been left on the desk, looked surreptitiously through Verity's drawers. There was a small flask of gin which

I sipped at nervously. It was old and tasted of metal. A few letters from furious directors threatening Verity with professional ruin and physical harm. I logged onto his computer and played a game of online chess. Henry couldn't meet me for lunch so I walked over to Pret A Manger and had the same tired damp sandwich I had eaten every day at Silverbirch. I spent the afternoon looking at Vero's number in my phone, forcing myself not to call her.

It was hard to disguise my sense of disappointment when I got back to Jo. We watched television in silence together, picking at pizzas she had ordered, both of us glum and listless. I went to bed at nine-thirty, left Jo watching some asinine reality show. I was irritable and snapped at her when she complained about me going to bed early. But the voice of the gormless narrator on the television was drilling into my head and I watched Jo's glazed eyes, saw her mouth hanging loosely open, and I wanted to smash the television and thrust a book into her hands, wanted to storm from the room and out into the night. I shouted at her as I trudged upstairs with a copy of the *New Yorker*.

'I'm working now. And work was shit. I mean it wasn't even work. It was sitting in a dark room doing fuck all. If it's a problem, I'll sleep in Fulham. I'm going to the theatre on Wednesday and Thursday, so I'll sleep in Fulham then. I've got the flat, I might as well use it.'

I trudged noisily up the stairs and flung myself into a troubled sleep. When she came in I felt her take my head and lay it gently in her lap. She had undressed and I felt the soft skin of her thighs, the tickle of her pubic hair. She stroked my hair with her nails, scratching gently at my scalp until I thought about kissing the soft thighs. But I was tired and I rolled away from her, pulled my pillow over my head. She sat up for a long time. I listened to her slow breathing as I drifted off to sleep.

I had to wait for Henry to let me in again the next morning. Only Verity could request a security pass for me, and he wasn't due to be in the office until Wednesday. I filled the morning doing the crosswords on old newspapers that lay scattered around the little office and set off early for lunch. I made my way down Farringdon Road, into the small courtyard and down the stairs into the dark restaurant. A waiter greeted me in French and showed me to Verity's table. He was sat in a corner, a Martini half-drunk in front of him. He stood as I walked towards him, took my hand in both of his and grinned broadly.

'Ah my dear boy, I'm so dreadfully sorry about yesterday. Most impolite. Sit down, do sit down. Martini? Yes, why not indeed? You look tired. Have some red meat, something to perk you up. On the dear old paper, so don't hold back. Steak? Yes, steak'll do the job nicely. I was in Wiltshire for the week-end. Have a ghastly boring aunt. Old as Methuselah and rich as Croesus. My brother has been wooing her, trying to ensure a greater slice of the estate. I spent the weekend remedying that. My bastard brother has been playing the children card against me. He has three boss-eyed little twerps. Says he needs the money for their school fees. I tried to make her see that I was a much finer investment, much more aesthetically pleasing. So did you get us some tickets? Have we before us two glittering evenings of entertainment?'

'I booked us in for *The Tempest* at the Barbican. Some African reworking of the play with drums. Thought that looked fun. Then *Antigone* at the Gate. Hope you haven't seen them?'

'Oh gosh, no. I try to go to the theatre as little as possible. Only when I really have to phone in a review I totter along and even then I usually leave at the interval. I tend to go by what my friends say. I find in life that if you surround yourself with really stellar friends, you hardly need to do anything other than buy an occasional round of drinks, a bottle of champagne or two. I'm hoping very much that you'll think of me as one of your friends. You see, a great pal of mine has just come into rather a lot of money and has built himself a simply splendid place in Mallorca. I intend to be out there most weekends. Terrible for old bones this London winter. But you'll always be able to reach me on the telephone. And I'm quite happy for you to park yourself at my desk when I'm not in the office. I'll sit beside you whilst you write about *The Tempest* and *Antigone* and then it's over to you. I'm sure you'll do a grand job.'

We sat and drank until late in the day. I was apprehensive at the thought of Verity not being around, not being there to guide me through my initial faltering steps as a journalist. He told me that I had to write under his name to start off with. That it would be good training for me, trying to emulate his prose. He took my hand in his cold, damp fist.

'When you write, make sure you're never nice. Nothing bores so much as niceness. The last thing I need is for people to think I'm developing charity in my old age. Until I say other-wise, I want only negative reviews. And, given the tripe that has been playing in the past few years, you shouldn't have any trouble.'

Verity stumbled as he rose from the table. He walked out without his jacket and I found it lying in a heap on the floor under his chair. Verity was standing shivering out in the little courtyard.

'Ah, the jacket. You are a good lad. I'm sure you'll do a smashing job.'

So I sat in dark theatres in those grey damp days as March bled into April and I thought of Vero. Just as I had never been satisfied with the money I was earning at Silverbirch, just as I was disappointed by the job at the paper, so I could not find happiness with Jo. Her gentleness, her sweet small moments of thoughtfulness, all were nothing to me next to the memory of Vero's body. I went to the theatre more than I needed to, made excuses to spend the night in the bed in Fulham where I would lie in the darkness thinking of what had passed there that dank night in February. Finally, I called Vero, sat on the tatty chair with the blue cover wrapped around me, my bare feet on the grey-gold rug.

'Charlie. I was afraid you'd never ring.'

She paused for a moment, I could hear her worrying at the cord of the telephone, sucking on her lip. Her voice was high and complaining.

'Why has it taken you so long? You should have called sooner. I'm so sorry about everything. I didn't mean for it to happen as it did, I miss you, darling.'

I was very cold, felt draughts blowing through the flat, skimming along the floor with their wintry fingers snapping at my ankles.

'Don't worry. It's over. It's in the past, Vero. How're you? Have you told Marc?'

'What? No. Of course not. I suppose . . . I suppose that this is something that is just between us. And Jo and Marc will have to live with it. Or rather they won't because they will never know, eh?'

'Are things better between you? I have been telling myself that what happened was just because you and he were going through a bad patch.'

She sighed and I heard the hiss of a cigarette lighter.

'*Bof* . . . I think it was naïve of me. Naïve of me to expect that it would be like when we were young again. That Marc would change himself for me. He is in Paris a great deal. I get back from the camp and the house is dark. I shower in the dark, try not to think about him. He is like all French boys. Always wants to be young. Doesn't realise that he should be living like an adult now. He doesn't like my cooking, Charlie. This is the worst thing of all. He insists that we go to eat with his parents every Sunday. Because his mother is a better cook than I am.'

'That's awful, darling. You're the best chef I know.'

'Thank you. You are sweet. I . . . I think of you often.'

'Me too.'

'It is difficult.'

'Yes.'

She whispered now.

'Goodbye, Charlie . . .'

'Vero . . .'

She hung up.

I took Ray to many of the plays. His company was calming, his disdain for the writing and acting fuelled the caustic reviews that I had to write. I was managing to capture Verity's acerbic style. Even when I loved a play, I had to tear it apart. Ray and I would step out of the darkened theatres into the fresh spring air and I'd hear him chuckling. He'd throw his head back and roar, tears streaming down his face and he'd lean against me and howl.

'It would never happen like that. And people pay to see that shit. I mean, serious. Fuckin' stupid woman would have left him years ago. I love this shit, Charlie. It's like the opposite of real life. Like someone had deliberately sat down to write what wouldn't happen. Jeez that's funny.'

Jo came to *King Lear* at the Donmar. I had secured us seats at the front and looked forward to the evening with happy anticipation. I felt her fidgeting throughout the first act, had to reach over and stop her grubbing for crumbs at the bottom of her packet of Kettle Chips. I found it difficult to concentrate on the play when I could see her out of the corner of my eye bending backwards to look at the other members of the audience, surreptitiously checking text messages with her face illuminated by the light of her mobile phone. At the interval I bought us ice cream and turned to look at her.

'You're not enjoying it, are you?'

'What? Yes. Yes, of course I'm enjoying it. It's Shakespeare.'

'But you have been restless all the way through. You look like you want to leave. Seriously, if you want to, just go.'

'Listen, Charlie, I don't go to the theatre much and I always hated studying Shakespeare at school. It just seems to go *blah blah blah forsooth* and I can't make any sense of what anyone is saying or who is supposed to be angry with who or why. I want to love it. I want to love it because you love it and I love you. I'll try harder in the second half. I'll really try and like it.'

People were coming back to their seats and I turned away from her, gave my attention to the stage and tried to ignore her worrying fingers which picked apart the ice-cream carton.

Jo and I tried to rekindle our love. She was so excited by my reviews, clipped them from the paper and pinned them to the fridge, even though they were under Verity's name and were bitter and spiteful and cold. We went to the restaurants we had visited when we were first together. She dressed with great care, applying too much make-up and laughing at everything. I tried to match her enthusiasm, but I was tired and always drank too much over dinner, fell asleep in the cab home. We used to stagger in the door together, up the wide stairs and into bed where I'd make functional love to her until we both drew apart, aware that nothing would happen. She'd hug her knees up to her chest, and it always made me think of Vero when I saw Jo's ribs sticking out in the shadow of my bedside light.

My phone rang late in the night. It was the beginning of May and Jo and I lay in the darkened bedroom. My arm was wrapped tightly around her and she quivered in her sleep at the sound of the ringing phone, grumbled and rubbed herself against me. Earlier that evening we had eaten at E&O and Jo seemed distant from me. I was telling her about a revival of *Private Lives* at the National when she held up her hand, cut me off and her eyes narrowed like a cat.

'I'm tired of this, Charlie. Tired of trying to piece this back together. I have tried to make things like they were, and you have been a complete bastard about it. I'm sorry if I'm not challenging enough for you. I just can't take your criticism. I can't bear the way you make me feel like I've done something wrong. I may not have had your education, may not have the great cultural mind that you want. But I really cared about you. I really wanted to look after you, to make it all better for you. You don't realise it, but you need someone like me. Someone to save you from yourself. But now you have become like one of those dead-eyed City boys. I can't believe that I thought I had rescued you from that. I . . . I've got to go, Charlie.'

She rose to leave and I reached out and took her hand. She looked suddenly alive, her golden hair radiating out from her small face. I could see the force of her feelings, and I remembered kissing her on the floor of the tangled greenhouse in Spitalfields, remembered fucking her with the diamonds dropping from her ears, remembered her hands tying balloons on the rug she had bought me, and I was full of remorse. I stood up and pulled her towards me, she struggled for a moment.

'No. Not this time, Charlie.'

'I'm sorry. I'm so sorry. I have been awful. Please give me another chance. I have no excuse. But please forgive me.'

I kissed her in the middle of the restaurant, folded notes on the table without waiting for change, swept her along the pavement kissing her still with my tongue deep in her mouth as we walked. I fumbled in her bag for the keys, picked her up and carried her to the bed. We fucked like teenagers, our bodies slick with sweat and both of us panting and grasping at each other's hot skin. When we had finished she rolled over to lie on her back and I could feel the blood slap against her ribs.

'That can't happen again, Charlie. You need to pull yourself together. What we have is good. Don't fuck it up.'

'I won't, Jo. I won't fuck it up. I'm so sorry.'

Around one o'clock I heard the phone bleeping, saw its display reflected on the skylight. I sighed, pushed myself up off the bed and answered.

'Hello.'

'Charlie. It's Vero.' Her voice was very quiet, she sniffed and I could tell that she was outside and had been crying. The wind whispered in trees above her. I stepped out into the hallway, walked over to the bathroom and switched on the light. My eyes squinted at the sudden brightness and I sat down on the bath which was cold against my thighs.

'Vero. Are you all right? What's up? What's wrong, darling?'

There was a long pause. Someone walked below whistling. I heard the high trilling whistle approach and pass by, caught echoes of it long afterwards, jumping down alleyways and across rooftops. Vero breathed in and I could hear her voice catch, heard mucus bubble in the back of her throat.

'I'm . . . Charlie, there's something I need to tell you . . .' Her words now just a whisper. 'I'm pregnant.'

I looked around at the bathroom, my eyes picking out small details: Jo's razor next to the taps, the slight flutter of the curtains, a dark patch on the carpet below the sink. I tried to order my thoughts, form the right sentences in my muddied mind. I walked over to the door and shut it gently, sat back down and let myself slide gently into the bath, lying stretched out against the cold porcelain.

'That's great, Vero. I'm pleased for you. I'm really happy for you and Marc.'

I heard her laugh under her breath.

'It's not his, Charlie. It can't be his. He has been in Paris. I'm sorry, Charlie, I have done the calculations, I have pissed on so many white tubes I can't piss any more.'

My heart began to beat very fast.

'My God, Vero. I mean we didn't . . . I thought I didn't . . .'

'I'm sorry.'

There was a long silence.

'What are you going to do?'

'I don't know. I don't fucking know what I can do. I told Marc. Told him I was pregnant, not that it was yours. He just looked at me like I was shit.' She began to sob, her wails long and loud. 'He left this evening for his parents' house. He just packed a bag and left.'

I put my head into my hands, wedged the phone between my ear and my shoulder, kicked at one of the taps, which bent sideways, sending out a wisp of dust that hung in the air.

'I can't . . . I can't do this, Vero. You know I can't. I'm so young. I can't be a father. Would you . . . I mean I'd come and be there while it happened. You wouldn't have to do it alone.'

'I don't know. I don't know, Charlie. I'll call you tomorrow. I'll call you when I have made up my mind.'

'Wait, Vero . . .'

She had hung up. I sat for hours trying her number but it went straight to voicemail. I heard her voice so many times – in English then French – ask me to leave a message that the words began to lose their meaning, became divorced from what they tried to signify. Finally I slipped my cold body back in beside Jo. I woke at dawn and knew that something was wrong, searched my mind for a moment, remembered and whispered *fuck* to myself over and over.

I went to work very early and sat in the small office tearing up pieces of paper, throwing a tennis ball against the glass wall until the mousy girl, who was called Rebecca and wrote on ballet, came in and asked me to stop. Vero called again just before lunch. Her voice was quick and manic. I could tell that she was drunk.

'I need to see you, Charlie. I think we need to talk about this. Face to face.'

'OK. OK, Vero. I'll come over. I'll come this weekend. I'll come and see you.'

'No. No, I'll come to you. Marc wants me to move out of the house and I don't want my parents to know yet. Not until I have decided. Can you believe it, he sent his mother to throw me out? She came this morning and told me to pack my bags. Told me she never wanted to speak to me or my family again. Bitch.'

'When are you coming? I'm working. I mean of course you can come, you can stay with me in Fulham. Have you told Henry?'

She was silent for a moment and I watched the mousy girl walk towards the door and suddenly turn a beautiful pirouette, her body a flash of movement.

'Yes. I called him last night after I spoke to you. He said I could stay with him, but it's you I need to see, Charlie. We need to talk this through, make it clear because at the moment it is far from clear, eh?'

'Fine. That's fine. When will you arrive?'

'Can you pick me up tomorrow? It's Friday – can you leave early? I'll get in to St Pancras at three.'

I was about to hang up when I heard her voice drop down.

'Charlie. We'll get through this. It will all be fine. I promise.'

I stayed in Fulham that night. I knew that Jo was hoping to see me, certain that we had turned a corner together. Her voice crackled disappointment when I called to tell her that I was going to be late at the theatre in Richmond. She offered to come and pick me up in a cab, but I rang off, distant and discouraging. I tidied the flat when I got home, thought of Vero edging heavily around the little apartment, was terrified by the image. I took a blue pill to sleep, and feeling the warm low buzz was like meeting an old friend.

The next afternoon I stood in the sunlit modern station and sipped at a coffee. I hadn't eaten lunch and I was twenty minutes early; I stood between the chauffeurs with their signs bearing improbable names and kept my eyes focused on the sliding doors, waiting for Vero. She was one of the last to come through, I saw her brisk walk as the doors slid shut and then opened again to reveal her. She stood for a moment in a ray of light and I remembered how I had seen her in the hall of the Balmoral, standing like she was standing now, every feature perfect under the violent interrogation of the light. She scanned the crowd with bright, hopeful eyes, saw me and skipped towards me, pulling her bag bouncing behind her.

'Vero.'

She looked, perhaps, a little fuller around the face, her eyes were rimmed with dark hoods. She looked like a crow, dressed in black she swept towards me, threw her arms up like wings, her black shawl held up into the sunlight. She pushed herself against me and I could feel the heaviness of her breasts. I hugged her head to my shoulder. I smelt wine on her breath and she turned her face up to me.

'Thanks for coming, Charlie. I feel such an idiot. Such an ugly, fat idiot.'

As the taxi made its way through hot halting traffic down to Fulham, I saw pregnant women walking beside the car wherever we stopped, waddling along bearing their great bowling-ball bellies. They seemed to have materialised to taunt me. I took Vero's small hand in mine and pressed it.

'You have noticed too, eh? Pregnant women – they appear. I saw them everywhere in Neufchâtel.'

We sat drinking tea. I was perched on a pile of books and Vero was in the chair. She had taken off her shoes and her legs were splayed wide.

'I'm ten weeks along, Charlie. Ten weeks only. We have plenty of time.'

'I know. I know we do.'

'I like looking down at my stomach. Because you really can't tell yet, can you? You'll be able to tell soon, but at the moment it is only as if I have been eating too much foie gras, too many croissants for breakfast. And so I pretend that it isn't in there. And then I remember, and it is like putting my tongue on a small packet of salt. I wince and suck in my teeth like this. Because it is a sob. This baby is like a great sob sitting deep in my belly, and I'm afraid to breathe out in case the sob rises up and comes out. This baby is just so very important. It's crazy that something this small can already be so important. But it is. Have you told Jo?'

'No. I won't tell her. Not until we know, not until we have made our minds up.'

We sat quietly, watching the afternoon turn into evening. My phone rang and I rejected Jo's call.

I called out for pizza and we sat in the middle of the dreary room, and Vero told me how Marc had become distant after the wedding, how she had tried so hard to keep him interested, thrown herself at him, begged him to stay home. She had offered to give up her job at the refugee camp if only he'd stay with her. But he had a flat in Paris and he and Fred lived like bachelors there. He had taken a job at one of the French investment banks, was specialising in bankruptcy law. He came home rarely.

Darkness fell and we lay together in bed. The window was open and I could hear Gavin singing Bruce Springsteen to himself in the shower, could hear the distant hum of traffic and the roar of planes queuing to land at Heathrow. Vero was wearing a pair of tartan pyjamas, and seemed very young as I looked over to her. She began to speak, thought better of it, and stared back up to the ceiling. I laid my hand on her stomach, felt the thickening of the flesh, the heaviness there. I leant over to her and kissed her neck. She moaned softly, placed her hand on top of mine on her stomach, edged her face round so that we were kissing. Then we were naked, and our bodies heaved against each other, grinding desperately together. When I awoke she was sleeping peacefully and I had made up my mind.

I brought Vero breakfast in bed. The coffee slopped a little as I lowered down the tray and she dipped her croissant greedily. It felt like we were an old married couple as I sat beside her, the silence only broken by our slurping and the grumbling of her stomach. She sat up straight when she had finished, turned to look closely at me.

'Charlie, I . . .'

'Vero . . .'

'You first . . .'

'I think I want to keep it, Vero. I really want to keep it. Do you think we can? I mean I don't know how we'd afford it, and I don't know if you want to, but I do. I do want to.'

She smiled, leant towards me, reached out her hand to take mine.

'I don't know. I want to, too. But . . . Please let's. Please?'

She buried her head in my neck and we sat on the bed in silence. I was thinking about Jo.

I called her the next morning. I had left the car in Notting Hill and so I took the Tube up through a world that seemed changed utterly. Notting Hill was hot and alive with the market stalls spread out along Portobello Road. I walked past them unseeing. Jo's voice had been nervous on the telephone, I could feel the questions queuing up behind her words. She answered the door and we went to sit in the rather formal drawing room. She wore the same defiant look as in E&O when she had tried to end it beween us, her eyes narrowed like a cat when she is about to pounce. I could see she was preparing for a fight. We sat side by side on the sofa.

Doom hung in the air. I stood, paced to the door, turned back to look at Jo sitting rigid and blank on the sofa. I reached down to take her hands but she pulled them away. I held her chin in my palm, saw how clear her skin was, how soft and childish her dimpled chin looked in my heavy hand. She turned towards the window and I could see the reflection of the panes of glass sitting in her pale eyes.

'Vero's pregnant. I got her pregnant. I'm . . . Christ, Jo, I'm sorry.'

Her face crumpled. I saw her shiver, her head fell down onto her chest and she drew in one deep breath. I put my arm around her and she shrugged her shoulders, fought suddenly, wild to get away from me. She stood and walked over to the mantelpiece. She picked up a candle, an invitation, a jade paperweight, turned them in her fingers, looking for something in the banal solidity of the objects. Then she sat back down and pulled a pillow into her lap, held it in front of her stomach and rocked slowly forward. She looked up at me with still-narrow eyes.

'When? No. No, don't tell me. I know. Fuck, Charlie, I knew it. Get your stuff. Get your stuff and leave. Just leave, Charlie.'

'Jo, I . . .'

She sat upright, head bowed, quivering like a butterfly with its wings plucked off, her breaths coming quick and shallow.

'Leave. Now.'

I left her crying on the sofa. She was looking down at the scars on her arms and crying. I saw her large tears spiral down onto the white bellies of her arms, and the tears followed the scar-lines as they sped across the furrowed skin.

I walked down Portobello Road. The sun was out. Tourists picked at the overloaded tables of antiques. The first drinkers stood outside pubs tasting their pints, swirling the liquid in the sunlight. I felt the physical presence of Jo as I walked those white streets. I wanted to rush back and take her small body in my arms, press those ruined wrists to my lips once again. I knew that I was walking away from the promise of a soft and golden future, knew that she was a better person, a kinder soul than Vero. And I knew I had ripped the heart from her, left her beached and gasping. I really had loved her. Even though I never told her, I did love her. But I was being pulled towards Fulham. Pulled towards Vero and the ridiculous splatter of cells that was growing in her stomach.

CHAPTER 14

Luka

We lived in the tiny apartment in Fulham as passengers live on boats or soldiers live in the war: knowing that this was temporary, we embraced the transitory nature of our existence. Vero didn't unpack her suitcase, we ate from boxes and tins, sat on the bed naked and spooned great mouthfuls of ice cream towards each other. Life seemed to take a breath for those three weeks; Vero would lie stretched out on the bed with my head cradled in her lap, and I'd press my ear against her belly. When I look back on that warm May I remember Vero standing in the little bath, her buttocks red and glistening, her breasts hanging heavy down as she bent to soap her legs. Holding the shower faucet in one hand, she would look up at me and smile and I felt something warm and homely spreading out into that once-desolate place.

Vero came to the theatre with me in the evenings, and she'd shift in her seat, uncomfortable. Her stomach rumbled loudly during moments of high tension; she had begun to sweat and gave off a rich smoky odour. But she loved the plays. She encouraged me to ignore Verity's advice, to start inserting words of praise in my reviews. But in the dark I sat and worried about where we would live for the next year. The lease on Munster Road would run out in a few weeks and the idea of renewing it filled me with horror. The flat was barely large enough for the two of us; I couldn't endure the thought of a Moses basket at the end of the bed in that tiny room with the gloomy courtyard outside and the misery pouring down with the rain from the apartments higher up, the rats scuttling across the damp ground.

Henry's dad stepped into my office one afternoon. It was bright and the sunlight raked through the empty office. Henry's father was very tall, his shoulders stooped beneath a mop of white hair. He leant against the doorframe of the little office and rapped on the glass to attract my attention.

'How are you, Charlie? I'm sorry I haven't come to see you earlier. I had been meaning to stop by.'

'Fine. I'm fine. I'm enjoying it a great deal.'

'I can tell. There has been a distinct change of tone in your reviews. You're finding your voice. I really think you have a future here.' His voice sank low, conspiratorial. 'Verity will probably retire before long. I think people are rather tired of his bitching. People need optimism, energy in these difficult times. I'm so glad to have both you and Henry here. Wish I'd had you earlier. Might have stopped things getting this bad.' He gestured to the empty office outside. I watched Henry's father walk away towards the lift and thought of my future as a journalist with a warm glow in my stomach.

One night, a week before we were due to move out – we had already started packing books into boxes, folding my clothes into suitcases – Vero and I went to see *Twelfth Night* in Regent's Park. I had packed a picnic for us, a half-bottle of champagne and smoked-salmon sandwiches. We arrived early and sat on the soft warm grass, feeling the memory of the day's heat radiating up through the turf. Then, perched on the warm wooden benches, we watched the play and were transported. I looked over at Vero and she was laughing, her eyes dancing in the dusk. We allowed ourselves to be carried to the Tube by the contentedly murmuring crowd afterwards and rode in companionable silence back to Fulham.

We walked up from the station and took a small diversion

that carried us past the old house. We always tried to go this way, liked to dare each other to press up against the window, to get a look inside that place where we had been so happy and so desperate. It was as if we thought we might catch sight of the younger versions of ourselves, as if we could shout through the window: 'The world is spread out before you! You are young!'

But that evening there was something different about the street. We each saw the blurred sign through the darkness, but couldn't speak its name, couldn't be sure that it was outside the right house, that it wasn't a trick of the light or perspective or the faded buzz of the champagne. And then we were outside the old house, and there was a To Let board nailed to a wooden post against the creaking gate. I looked at Vero and her eyes shone.

'Shall we?'

'Can we afford it? Do you want to go back there? It was miserable, sometimes, but it would feel like coming home. I really feel that this house is home.'

'We'll afford it. And it will be home. A home for the three of us.'

We kissed out there on the street, kissed as we never had when we lived in that place, to the exclusion of all others. We held hands as our lips met.

I transferred money out of savings for the deposit. I calculated that I would be able to cover three months' rent through the remainder of the £10,000 from Silverbirch and my salary. I knew I would have to change jobs. I needed to earn more. Needed to build up a buffer against the world. I flicked through the classified pages of the paper, trying to look for some sort of a compromise, a career that would interest me whilst also paying enough to support us. On the Tube I sat thumbing through *Metro* and I looked at the City pages, and I saw a face I recognised, and the unhealthy slash of skin seemed to draw me towards it. I sat and listened to the clattering of the carriage, which was much louder now, and looked at that very pink skin.

*

I sat in Bhavin's office at Thames Credit Bank watching the sun move across the room. He was staring at me. He had grown his hair out during his time off work, the white streaks had almost disappeared and his hair rose in waves, quiet homage to the Chairman. His beard was fuller and I could see where he had pulled tufts across to hide the pink scar. He pressed his fingers together and his face broke into a smile.

'I'm always pleased to see people spend some time away from the market. Guys work their arses off with the aim of doing something fulfilling and noble when they retire – they talk of retiring at forty-five like it's some fucking great dream. And then when they retire they realise that they have become the market. That the blood of the market is their blood. Because what is the market but a bunch of people trying to stamp on the fingers of the guy climbing up below them? I got my fingers stamped on, I fell, and now I'm climbing back up. And I'll climb quickly above those blinkered fuckers at Silverbirch. They have maybe a month left before they go under. You've heard that? No? Investors have lost faith in the Chairman. He's just got divorced and he's living in the office, but there's something crazy and hopeless about him now. Can't say I'm sorry.'

Buses moved down Bishopsgate outside. I looked down onto the corner of Brushfield Street where Jo and I had walked on the way to Roland's party. Bhavin stood up quickly and thumped his hands down on the table.

'This is where it's all happening. Webby was hired as soon as he left Silverbirch. He runs the whole of the trading business at TCB. Managed to avoid sub-prime, managed to stay short credit at the right time. Now he's shorting equities. Buying up the debt of companies on the verge of bankruptcy and taking a seat on the board. He's making a fortune. He's asked me to come in and run the investment book buying up bank bonds. This is just an amazing opportunity. I'm lucky that Webby's wife and mine are friends. Go to the same gym and see each other when they pick the kids up from nursery. I think he's forgiven me.

'So listen, Charlie, we're not supposed to be hiring, but I want to bring you into my team as a trader. As much to fuck off Silverbirch as anything else. I can't offer you huge amounts of money to start off with, but Webby's got a big allocation of shares. You get given a bunch when you start, earn more as you go along, then they vest and you can do what the fuck you like. But if you want my advice you'll carry on working here. It's a good place. We've got the run of the shop and one day the markets will bounce back. When they do, we'll be ready.'

'When can I start, Bhavin? I really want this. I'll work all hours for you, I promise that. I'll kill myself working for you.'

'What's your notice?'

'No idea. I haven't signed a contract.'

'Then start on Monday. Start today if you want.'

I called Vero, who was delighted. I half-imagined her in the library revising for law exams, remembered her excitement when I told her that I had got the job at Silverbirch. Then Henry, who was distant and cold. I heard him muttering to Astrid with his hand muffling the receiver. They were spending more and more time together, were like a married couple as they moved through London. She was helping him research his articles, was growing stronger and finally moving away from the glum shadow of her adolescence. Finally I called Verity, who suggested in a weary voice that we meet for lunch the next day.

We were in the Bleeding Heart again. Verity was slumped on his chair. I explained my situation, told him that I was sorry, offered to try to continue writing some reviews during the weekends. He hardly seemed to hear me. He finished his Martini in one gulp.

'Aunt Hilda died. Left me nothing. Absolutely nothing, dear boy. I'm bereft, I can't seem to get up the energy for anything now. You're having a baby? What a ghastly business. Too late to erm . . . Yes, I suppose it must be. Well, I have to say I think you did an acceptable job. Recent reviews have been a little on the fawning side. Sorry to lose you, but there are always boys like you. Always you boys with your funny little grins and dark eyes. Henry will find me someone else. He's a dear boy. So very fond of dear Henry.'

Henry came to help me pack up my few possessions at the newspaper. It was a Saturday and the offices seemed even more empty staffed by the skeleton weekend workforce. Our voices were made smaller by the spaces around us: there were no echoes. Henry leant against the window as I packed, his fingers fiddling with first a pencil, then tearing strips from a magazine cover, shredding them and letting them fall to the floor. He was very quiet, observant; watching me closely as I packed books into a box. He cleared his throat, sniffed, and spoke.

'I . . . Charlie, I saw Jo. I called her right after you told me.'

I looked up at him, raised my eyebrows. Sunlight slanted in through half-closed blinds and fell across Henry's face, blurring his features in light and shadows.

'Don't look at me like that, Charlie, there's nothing in the least disloyal. She . . . she has been my friend for a long time. I introduced the two of you, remember? I went to meet her at the charity. It was the end of the day and she was washing up in the kitchen. I walked in and she was there with her yellow gloves on, her hair tied up and all those bright paintings around her and I thought . . . I thought at least she has this. At least she's able to lose herself in these children. Because otherwise I . . . I really think she'd be destroyed. She looked at me with a real bravery in her eyes. It made me kind of ashamed. Because I knew if it was me . . . She really seems OK. Despite what you've done to her, despite the way you've steamrollered over her feelings.'

He turned away from me and stared into the long horizontal bars of light.

'You don't understand that, do you? How someone might feel clearly another's pain, treat them with kindness, step softly around their love. You held out the promise of something to her and then you snatched it away and I won't forgive you for that. I hate you at the moment, Charlie. You need to know that. Goodbye.'

I sat and watched the light fade in the empty office. The bars of light slowly moved across the office and then, just as they were about to reach the wall, they turned from white to gold to grey and then disappeared. When I got back to the apartment, Vero had dinner on the table and we ate in silence, went to bed in silence; something of Jo's condition, her quietness hung over me, and the week passed with that quietness still sharp in the air.

We moved into the house the next weekend. It was the first Saturday of June; warmth brought bugs drifting towards us on heavy air. I carried Vero through the creaking gate, lifted her with one arm as I fumbled for the keys, and as we lay down together on the sofa in the drawing room, all the memories of the nine eternal months that we had spent there rushed over us. I reached out my fingers to her and we kissed and rolled from the sofa onto the dusty floor. The house felt warm and familiar and I peered into my old bedroom, perched above the kitchen looking out onto the tiny stone garden and I imagined the baby there, pictured his bobbing head appearing over the edge of a cot.

I started work on Monday. Vero had cut my hair in the sink on Sunday night and her eyes were sad as her fingers moved quickly, the scissors dancing across my head. She had an appointment at the hospital the next day. I wouldn't be able to be there for the scan, wouldn't see the moment when the heartbeat was first thrust out into the world. But Vero and I understood each other, we knew that I needed to make a life for us. Monday was to be the first day of that life. We would need money, of course, but it was to be a deeper life than the one we had imagined before. No longer the sparkle of diamonds and champagne. The money this time round would be for school fees and bulky Swedish cars with steel-reinforced doors.

I discovered that I had laid out the plans for our future back when Vero and I were together at Edinburgh, and they were very modest despite the ambition of those years. Because rather than the great house and the holidays, I had seen a child suckling from her dark nipple, and the struggle and the joy of raising our family. I woke very early on Monday morning, laid a gentle kiss on Vero's brow and drove through empty streets towards the City.

Those who had survived the crash were hardened, suspicious and angry. Traders no longer made any pretence at interest in my life, didn't suggest drinks or dinner, asked aggressive questions when I called to let them know of my new position. Very few of the salesmen and traders I had worked with whilst at Silverbirch had made it through the cull that had swept the City when the banks realised that the downturn was

going to last for years. The trading floors of the great investment banks were empty. Whole rows vacated by traders who
now met for coffee at Starbucks in Canary Wharf and
discussed who might be hiring, who was next to be fired,
talking about the markets in sad wistful voices.

A feral spirit hung over the trading desks that were still
populated. They were islands of activity in the emptiness of
those huge halls. I walked through those abandoned churches
of finance and saw discarded empty silver photo frames, abandoned clay pigeons and crampons. Traders accentuated their
distinguishing characteristics: they grew long hair, shaved their
heads, wore wide, wacky ties and pierced their ears. Their
desks became shrines to themselves as they clamoured to
assert their own existence. Photos were blown up into posters
and pinned on the walls behind them, voices were always
raised and heavily modulated, ringtones on Blackberries were
personalised and grating. Nobody trusted anyone, and the
misery that I had felt when the crash first hit was everywhere
now, and anyone who dared to predict a recovery was shouted
down, treated as a fool and an impostor.

My desk was in the middle of the trading floor, and there
was no one within twenty metres of me. It was somehow comforting to hear my voice ringing out in the silence of that
massive room. I had to stand on my desk to attract Bhavin's
attention. I felt wild and brave in the great reach of space. I
approached every trade from oblique angles, found myself
saying prayers for their success, cultivated a wilfully eccentric
persona. I covered my desk with postcards that I bought on
eBay, pictures of seaside resorts in Italy with banal salutations
written in spidery spinsters' hands, shots of great sweeping
beaches in Brazil, paintings of dukes and rakes by obscure
Jacobean artists.

Silverbirch went into administration at the beginning of

July. The Middle Eastern investors that had supported them finally pulled out, unwilling to sustain the losses that the company was suffering. Bhavin and I knew Silverbirch's portfolio intimately and we met with Catrina and the Chairman, who were cool and buoyed along by fatalism. We bought the entire book of bank bonds at a ridiculously low price. The Chairman looked very old. His cheeks were sunken and his skin was grey and he shook a little as he spoke. As we left the room he laid a hand on my shoulder. Bhavin and I looked back to him, but he spoke only to me.

'I'm sorry to see you back. It's not a good place. Not a good place for you now. You'll lose whatever it was that made you special. You'll become just like Bhavin and the rest of them.'

Bhavin and I went for a drink in the pub where I had sat with so many of them, and we celebrated, and he mocked the Chairman's weakness, and I laughed with a dull rattle in my throat.

Vero's belly was now growing into roundness, but I was working such long hours that it was as if I was seeing her from a great distance. I would come in the door late at night and find her stretched diagonally across the bed. She'd stir a little and grumble as I undressed and I would stand and wait for her to settle before climbing over her and curling into a corner. She had filled the fridge with vegetables, the dining-room table groaned with fruit; she walked everywhere. Sometimes I woke in the middle of the night and laid a hot hand on her bare belly, waited for a kick which would send me to sleep in a fog of happiness. We had decided not to find out the sex, but, as Vero slept, I felt sure it was a boy, and I spoke to him in the depth of the muggy night, describing the world I would build for him, all the fun we would have.

Months passed in miserable toil. The summer lost steam as July and August disappeared into a smudge of showers. I fought with other traders. There was an attempted coup by another trading desk at TCB which tried to oust Bhavin, amalgamate his portfolio into their own. He repelled it with a vicious tenacity that caused him to start sweating again. I tried to avoid entering his office those days, sat at my desk and looked out over Spitalfields towards the spire of the Hawksmoor church that lay towards Brick Lane. Bhavin was making terrific amounts of money. He insisted on meeting the management of the banks whose debt he was buying and had an extraordinary instinct for those who were merely floating dead and those who were still swimming. He was often in the US and I ran the business when he was away, fending off our competitors and the traders who tried to take advantage of his absence. I remember one evening I had been screaming at a dealer who was trying to buy back some bonds that he'd sold me at a lower price. Needed it as a favour. He'd made a mistake, sold too many of the bonds, needed to deliver to his other client. I stood on my chair, kicking out at the postcards, slapping the phone down on my knee between my yells.

'You are a fucking loser. Look in the mirror. I want you to go and look in the fucking mirror after this. Go and look in the mirror in the bathroom and realise what a loser you are. I'll never do that trade. Not in a million years. I'm fucking insulted you called me. More than that, I'm embarrassed for you.'

I threw the phone down and stood breathing heavily, and I saw David Webb was behind me. He looked rather nervous as I climbed down from my chair.

'How's it going, Charles? You holding things together when Bhavin's away? Sounds like he doesn't have to worry about anyone fucking you over. You guys are doing a great job. Says something for the poor old duffer at Silverbirch. He knew how to pick good traders. Keep it up, Charles.'

I was making a success of myself, although my heart wasn't in it. I felt constantly haunted by the threat of another crash, the suggestion that it might all be over, that I was one of the last rats working away on a ship that had long since sunk. But the shares I had been allocated began slowly to rise in value, and I counted the days until I could cash them in.

I wish I had enjoyed Vero's pregnancy more, wished I had shared the precious moments of pain and triumph, massaged her knotted lower back, sat beside her when the amniocentesis results came through, gripping her small sweating hand. But Bhavin was giving me more and more responsibility, and the business was flourishing, and slowly, as Vero's bump grew bowling-ball round beneath the long black tunics she wore, the markets showed signs of recovery. The US government set up a new entity to drive liquidity in the mortgage markets, the big banks bought the small, companies restructured their balance sheets and consumers slowly started spending again.

The City was overrun with little grey men. Small, worried bureaucrats with beetling eyebrows began to populate the empty trading floors. I walked into the office one Monday morning to find the room swarming with regulators, men with thinning hair, grey suits, rubber-soled shoes, who wore their new-found power with a kind of nervous hysteria. Suddenly there were forms piled high on my desk and every move had to be justified, every decision supported by applications made in triplicate to be approved by the Financial Services Authority. The little grey men crowded together at lunch, taking a full hour and sitting down to eat in the pubs on Bishopsgate where their high voices cut through the air. I used to watch them leave the building at five sharp and they hurried, faces downwards, swinging their briefcases as they made their way back to the suburbs.

Vero accumulated beautiful things for the house. As Jo had decorated the little flat on Munster Road, so Vero decked the house with small luxuries. She walked up to the antique shops on Dawes Road and picked out ancient pretty things – tiny statues and threadbare green cushions and a bedspread. The house began to acquire character. It was cosy and bohemian and eccentric. The house began to look like Vero. She had a tall pile of books about childbirth and we'd sit together when I got home early enough and she'd read bits out to me, and we'd screw up our faces and pretend to vomit up our dinner as she held up pictures of the placenta. I read those books alone at the table when I got home late. I would sit and pick at the cold dinner that Vero had left out for me and I'd read the gory descriptions of childbirth, the brisk, scornful advice for fathers and the passages detailing what could go wrong, the breeches and the haemorrhaging and the stillbirths. When I crept upstairs those nights I would tuck the duvet very tightly around Vero's great body, lay a cold hand on her brow and mutter small, soothing things to her as she slept.

The last few months of Vero's pregnancy come through now as a succession of clear, quick images. Everything was rushing towards that day, circled in black felt-tip on the calendar on the kitchen wall, the fifth of December, when our child would break into the world. I refused to work weekends and Vero and I drove out of London, explored the country listening to the radio in calm silence during that dreary autumn. The passing of streetlights, the clacking of cat's eyes under our wheels, the hiss of the wind against the trees which rushed past, all of these seemed to mark out like metronomes the beating of time, the approach of the day.

We drove down to Worthing and my father was very gentle, his hands resting on Vero's shoulders, his eyes full of a strange dark love for the girl who would continue his line. We walked along the seafront and the October waves were grey and violent, falling down on the pebbles and then sucking back out, churning and spewing around the struts of the pier. Vero stood holding her belly and felt the full force of the wind upon her, and tears came to her eyes, and my father strode up behind her and put his arms around her, and they faced out to sea at the end of the pier and shouted into the wind.

We drove into the hills. Sought out the rounded embrace of hills in which to walk. Vero had begun to move her legs in circular strides like one recently descended from a long horse ride. She gritted her teeth and loped up the hills, and we walked above Devil's Dyke and up Cissbury Ring and down into the valleys around and we bought wellington boots and rain jackets and we trudged through all weathers, our footsteps leading us up and down those hills, dragging us forward towards the day. She spoke everything that came into her mind, talked to me through panting breaths as we climbed, took my hand and squeezed hard as our boots churned up the soft mud.

'If it's a boy, I want him to have a tree house. We need to live in a place where there are trees. And if it's a girl she must have a pony. A palomino pony with huge dark eyes and long lashes. And we must be close to the sea. I want to be able to hear the sea where we live, hear the sound of gulls in the morning. And there must be hills behind us so that we can walk up hills like these ones and see the sea from a distance, watch ships on the sea dancing in the sunlight. Ouch. Help me. Okay. Should we have an Aga? Is it too bourgeois? I love you, Charlie.'

A flock of starlings wheeled above us as I kissed her, and they moved as one object, their feathers glittering purple in the bright light. We drove back to London through the gathering dusk, stopped for hot chocolate in motorway service stations. Vero laid her hand over mine on the gearstick and sighed as night fell.

I painted the little back room a soft yellow that seemed to hold the sunlight at the end of the day. Vero stood and laughed as I tried to erect the flat-packed cot. We made the bed up, laid sheets down and then placed the little Moses basket on top of the sheets. I hung a mobile on the ceiling with birds that reminded me of Roland's sculptures hanging in the wild greenhouse. They were toucans and quetzals and I spun the mobile with my finger and the birds flapped their wings in the breeze. Vero drew herself up behind me, laid her head on my shoulder and I could feel her bump press into the small of my back.

'Do you think he'll be happy?'

'It might not be a he . . .'

'I think it's a he.'

'Yes, I do. I do think he'll be happy.'

Time tapers towards a point. Like the sand in an hourglass, time sheds the non-essential, refining itself into the single pure stream of tiny crystals. We wait, and watch the sands fall between the thighs of the hourglass.

I was sitting at my desk on a cold day at the end of November. Bhavin was in New York and I was alone on the great echoing trading floor, as I stared at a postcard of Rapallo and dreamt about warmth and wine and good food. The phone rang and I jumped, picked it up, spilled the receiver onto the desk, then it was against my ear, and I heard Vero's breath sharp and shallow, and my heart shuddered.

'It's time.'

'Really. Really now? Not a false one.'

'I don't think so. I think. Yes. Yes, this is it.'

I drove madly through the dark streets. The car seat was already strapped into the back of the Polo and I ran red lights and saw the flash of speed cameras in my wake as I rushed back to Vero. She was waiting by the door, very quiet, her bag packed and a tired, serene expression on her face. We drove calmly to the hospital, talking of how we had spent our day. I could tell that she was terrified.

I waited. I sat by her bed in the labour ward and waited. I helped Vero to Lucozade and grapes, ran out to buy magazines and read to her, rubbed her feet and let her squeeze my hands until my fingers were white and sore. And all the time the heartbeat on the monitor screamed at us. Rather than something associated with the birth of life, it sounded like the wheezing thump of a ventilator trying desperately to inflate failing lungs. I watched the heart monitor. Watched the baby's heart speeding up and slowing down. With each contraction the beats rose to 150, 160, and I felt my own heart race in sympathy. Midwives came and went. I sat by Vero as she drew on the gas and air, clutched my hand, cried, shook and drew her knees up and groaned, told me she couldn't go on, drew on more gas and air. At one point I slept.

It was at 5 a.m. that a powerful contraction hit her. Vero sat very tall, panting into the gas mask, feeling at her back to ensure the epidural was still in place. She was silent, her face twisted into a grimace, and I watched the baby's heart speed up. The midwife came in, looked at the monitor and then at her watch. Her face became grave as the heart sped above 200. I felt a rising panic flood through me. Vero choked through her gritted teeth.

'What's going on? Why is it making that noise? Make it stop that noise.'

'It's fine. It's just the contraction. Don't worry. You're doing fine.'

The midwife left the room as the contraction ended. Vero lay back, her arms twitching and her upturned palms spotted with blood where she had dug her nails into them. I watched the heartbeat. It slowed to normal, dipped further, then suddenly nothing. An alarm went off and a doctor came in followed by the midwife. I heard her mutter 'Deceleration,' and then she thrust a sheaf of forms at me. I felt helpless, turned to Vero who was watching me with wide, scared eyes.

'Why is there no noise? There's no noise now. Help, Charlie. Help me.'

I had hated the noise, but the silence, punctuated by the occasional buzz of the alarm, was far worse. I signed the forms and Vero was wheeled out of the room. The midwife handed me a set of green paper scrubs and I tied them around me as we raced through the halogen glare of the empty corridors. I felt like I was drowning. Vero kept asking me what was going on, and I held her hand very tightly as we thudded through swing doors and into the operating theatre.

When Luka was born Vero turned to me and said 'We'll call him Luka, like the song.'

When Luka was born the surgeon had great metal claws strapped to his hands like some Marvel superhero, and I saw them glint and fizzle under the harsh light.

When Luka was born I dressed him under the resuscitaire, pulled blue limbs into a white babygro. He opened his eyes which were lapis blue and sightless and terrifying.

I sat as Vero held him to her skin. He was whimpering, making inhuman gurgling noises in the back of his throat. The surgeon was still moving out of sight and I watched the blue limbs slowly growing pink and I felt only relief that Vero had survived. I only cared about Vero. She was yellow and her hands shook. When I reached to take him back, pressed him to my paper shirt, Vero turned to the side and vomited. I watched the stream of bright orange fluid splatter to the floor and she held her stomach with both hands and retched again.

I sat with them both as they slept and cried. He was having trouble feeding; Vero's breasts looked shrivelled and the yellowness had spread to her eyes. She stared at me with her yellow eyes and tears sped down her face. He screamed a high-pitched angry scream and she thrust her tear-stained nipple into his mouth and he sucked and bit with his very red gums and nothing came out. The midwives passed by with clucking noises and finally Vero took a bottle from them, placed it in his mouth and he emptied it and fell asleep in the cot by her side. She turned her back to him, faced away and held her stomach, sobbing.

'It hurts. My stomach hurts. It hurts so much.'

The midwives made me leave at eight that evening. The baby was screaming again and wouldn't take a bottle. Vero lay turned away from him, curled up in a ball, her shoulders shaking and her breaths coming in raking sobs. I should have demanded to see a doctor, should have insisted that I stay. But the midwives swept me along in their thick arms, made me feel like a neurotic father unable to deal with that warm womanly world. So I staggered down the halls, all the time hearing his terrified screams which seemed to follow me out to the car and home. I sat in the pub until closing time and looked through my Blackberry messages. Bhavin had emailed me pages of instructions, trade recommendations and increasingly frustrated appeals for me to call him. I sent a few one-word responses. I didn't want to tell him about the birth, didn't want anyone to know about it until I was sure that everything was fine.

The guard on the door wouldn't let me in until seven the next morning and I paced the empty pavements, watched the traffic in the darkened streets and smoked cigarette after cigarette. When I finally entered the ward the bed was empty. I grabbed at the arm of a midwife, felt her stiffen under my grip. She guided me down a corridor, into a lift, wouldn't tell me what was wrong. They had been moved into a different ward.

She hadn't been on duty when they left. I stood in the clattering lift and felt my heart beating behind my eyes. When I saw Vero she was hooked up to a vast number of tubes. The baby was in a cot on the other side of a screen. Vero was sat watching him sleep. He looked smaller than any human should be. Smaller than I had remembered him from the night before. I watched his tiny chest rise and fall as he slept. Vero gave a wan smile as I entered.

'I'm ill,' she said. 'I have caught something in the hospital. I will be better. The baby, he has it also. We are both sick. They probably shouldn't have let you in. He screamed all night. His screaming, it is something terrible. Oh Charlie, this is not what I hoped it would be.'

She cried and I reached carefully over the tubes and squeezed her hand.

Vero and Luka came home a week later. She was still yellow and he screamed constantly. I had gone back to work while they were in hospital. I texted her every hour, kept a photo of his tiny body in its clear sterile crib on my desk which I looked at as I traded. Before I drove to pick them up, I emailed Bhavin to tell him that I was taking my paternity leave. I strapped the tiny boy into his car seat and drove very slowly home.

The next few weeks were hell. He cried all night and Vero was too sick to deal with him. She slept for twenty hours at a time, lifted her head to sip broth which dribbled down her chin and stained the sheets. I held her with one arm as I balanced the baby on my shoulder. I could only stop him crying by walking up and down the stairs with his body held very tightly against me. I sat up watching DVDs and holding him. I danced around the kitchen with the screaming baby in my arms. I pressed the bottles against his gums, fed him too much and too little, held the books open as I tried to follow their conflicting instructions. I couldn't face washing the bottles, just walked down to the pharmacy and bought more every morning, the screaming baby's face turning red in the cold.

When he cried too much I placed him in the car seat and drove around the dark winter streets, the radio turned up very loudly to drown the screams. I listened to the angry Sunday-night talk shows, the late-night shows which welcomed in the bitter and disappointed, and I pressed the accelerator down and rode the tide of their anger out to the motorways where Luka would finally sleep. I wore the same clothes for days on end, put off the threatened visits of my parents, cried exhausted tears over the phone to Henry, who didn't mention the bitterness of our last meeting, was kind and gentle with me. I held Luka above Vero as she slept, looked down on her tired yellow face and held his soft cheek against mine. We'd pace the room as he cried and bent double in my arms with the pain in his stomach. I rested my hands against the little tummy and moved them clockwise, massaging, trying to help until Vero reached up to take Luka and her arms shook, and tears streamed down her face and down mine. And then it was Christmas.

Vero's mother arrived unannounced with Guy on Christmas Eve. She took the crying baby from me with her soft pale arms and he looked up at her as she placed the bottle gently between his thick lips. Guy led me up to bed, kissed his sleeping sister, undressed me and laid me down beside her. They were like angels. Suddenly I was able to sleep and Christmas day dawned bright with a clear, crisp sky outside the window. Vero's mother served us Christmas lunch in bed and we sat and watched as she held the baby to her chest and he gurgled and slept. Guy had tidied the house, piled up the empty pizza boxes and washed the dirty muslins and the hundreds of bottles with their dregs of rancid milk.

Things got better. I returned to work and Bhavin was very gentle with me, came to my desk and insisted that I leave when the markets closed at five. Vero's father arrived and pushed himself around the house in his chair, slept on the sofa and cooked delicious omelettes for dinner. My parents came up one weekend and my father held his grandson and the boy smiled for the first time. Luka grew fatter; his legs developed rolls of fat that wobbled when he lay in his cot kicking and staring in wonder at the mobile of bright birds.

Henry and Astrid dropped by often during those fragile early months. Henry would bring pizza and, as the evenings lengthened, he and Astrid insisted on taking Luka out in his pushchair, wheeling him down to Parsons Green so that Vero and I could lie back on the sofa for an hour, watch television and talk. Then Astrid would load and unload the dishwasher, chatting to Vero in her clear young voice as Henry and I sat and talked above Luka's head. The baby stretched out giggling on his sheepskin as Henry tickled his feet.

'I'm proud of you, Charlie. It's extraordinary to see how far you have come. How much the two of you have grown. And just amazing to look at this little boy and to think of his future, the weight of the future falling upon him. And that's something that you two have made. I was wrong about you in so many ways, Charlie. I'm sorry. Sorry I said I hated you.'

'You weren't wrong. You were right about the person I was back then. But people change. You have changed, too. You seem older, more together.'

Henry stopped tickling Luka and turned to look at me with serious eyes.

'I realise now that you and Vero were meant to be together. That . . . that what you have here is very special. And I'm happy for you. But you have hurt so many people getting there. You need to know that Jo . . . that I don't think Jo will ever get over this. You and Vero both move through life without stopping to think of . . . of the collateral damage, of the wreckage that you leave around you.'

'I know, Henry. I feel very bad about it all. I know Vero is very sorry. It's just that when life moves this fast, when we change so quickly, it's hard to apologise for the actions of someone who doesn't really exist any more. I look back on the boy I was, and he really doesn't exist any more. I find it hard to know what his motives were, what drove him to do the things he did.'

The baby rolled onto his front and looked up at me with puzzled eyes. Henry reached down and began to tickle his feet again and the sound of giggles filled the room.

One evening in summer Vero and I sat in the small concrete courtyard behind the house. Vero had hung baskets of flowers around what we optimistically dubbed the garden. A heavy-scented jasmine overflowed above me, spilling down its white flowers, intertwining with the smoke from my cigarette. I was not allowed to smoke indoors, had given up cigarette breaks at work. But, if I got home early enough, and Luka was in bed, Vero and I would sit in the garden and listen to the night settle down around us. A bottle of white wine on the wrought-iron table, a cigarette each as the last aeroplanes bellowed overhead. The baby monitor sat next to the wine and I watched the roar of the engines slowly fade to silence. I took Vero's hand.

'I don't think that the City is ever coming back.'

She looked at me sideways and blew the cigarette smoke away from her face.

'What do you mean? I thought you said that it had to exist. That it'd never go away entirely. I mean, you still have a job, eh?'

'No, I mean I think there'll be something there, some financial system, but I think I'm wasting my time waiting around for the big money to come back. I think it's possible . . . very likely that the days of big bonuses and fast cars are over. There's just too much government involvement, too much public outrage. The scrutiny is going to be unbearable.'

'But I thought you were doing well? I thought you said things were heading in the right direction?'

'I did . . . they are. But not to get us where we need to be. You know, Vero, I always used to dream about buying you the most amazing things. When we were first together, and then when we'd broken up, I used to picture myself buying you beautiful dresses and handbags and all the gifts that your other boyfriends gave you. Or rather like them, but better. Then when I started working I pictured myself buying us a holiday house somewhere outside of Cannes, flying you down there. That's what the old City did to you. Your dreams always grew quicker than your salary. The money could never keep up with the size of the aspirations, the number of things you coveted.

'Now I've been thinking. Thinking that we could leave. We could leave all this. I suppose I have begun to accept that we'll never be fantastically rich. We'll never be the high rollers I wanted us to be. But a good chunk of my shares vest in June and then the rest a year later, as long as I hit my targets. It would be enough for us to live comfortably. I just don't know that I want Luka growing up here in London where so many awful things have happened. This city has been ruined for me, and I think I need to leave.'

Vero pulled her hand from mine, sat forward in her chair, her brow knitting into a frown. I watched her fingers twine around the stem of her wine glass as she lifted it to her lips. I leant to kiss her, whispered into her ear.

'You know, Vero, I always had a clear picture of our life together. I have spent the past few years dreaming up the life we'd live, and since Luka came along I have realised that the dream was a false one. It will be enough for me to have you two. We could get a little place in the country. I could be a teacher; you could work for a local solicitor. I want to be with you two more. I want to be around to see my kids grow up. I won't be one of those fathers who spends all week at the office and the weekend on the golf course. I want to be there for you.'

We were quiet for a moment, and when Vero spoke, her voice was very soft and rustling, like a paintbrush on paper.

'But you have worked so hard. I thought you wanted to run the business when Bhavin left, I thought you had all these dreams about rebuilding the City. And whatever you say, you could make a lot of money still. Running Barclays or whatever you want to do. And part of me now loves it here. Part of me would like to stay. Because surely we deserve it, we deserve to live well, live on the fruits of your success. It was what you always wanted.' She was sitting up very straight, moving her now-empty wine glass in the air like a baton, her eyes bright.

'I know. I did. But Luka has changed things. I mean everyone says that a child does that, a baby makes you look at things differently, but I didn't think it would be like this. And when he was ill, and you were ill, it made me see things with a clarity I didn't think I possessed. I realised that I need to take you both away from here. We need to escape now; otherwise I'm scared we never will. I need you to trust me on this, Vero. When we get enough money together – I should get a bonus this year, and hopefully next year I will make a bit more – let's go back to the hills, back to the places we walked before he was born. We'll find a place there and we'll live in sight of the sea. I'll build him a tree house.'

She turned away from me, pouting.

'I have only just started to feel settled here. I feel as if everything is always moving, that life is always pushing me somewhere new. I'm happy here. Listen, Charlie, the country, the

323

whole idea of escaping the city . . . It would remind me of Marc. I can't go through that again. It scares me. I feel safe here in the city with you.'

'But I'm not Marc. I'm never going to walk away from you. I'm going to spend every day I can with you and with our children. That's what I want from life, what the good part of me wants anyway. I feel myself being leached of all that was good in me by this job. I barely see you, barely see Luka. At the weekends I'm so tired and so grumpy, snapping at you for no reason. There was a moment the other night – do you remember? – when he started crying just after I got back from work. I went in to settle him and he grabbed hold of my tie and started pulling on it, strangling me. It felt like a message.'

She smiled hesitantly, half-leant towards me.

'I just don't know. I suppose it would be good for me to work . . .'

'And he'd go to school in the village . . .'

'Listen, whatever happens, you know I will always follow you, Charlie . . .'

She stood up and laid her arms around my neck, sat down hard in my lap and kissed me. We sat there until it was time for Luka's night feed. I watched Vero holding his sleeping body close to her, and I felt that luck was with us, momentum was with us; a bright future lay ahead.

*

I worked late nights, worked in order to earn enough to live without the night-worry my parents suffered. I had a series of targets to hit in order to receive my full allocation of shares and I needed to make significant profits over the next few quarters in order to earn enough to leave. I worked with a controlled fury, drove myself harder than I ever had before. I pounded the keys of my computer, my Bloomberg, the buttons on my telephone; the staccato clatter sometimes came back to me in my dreams, sending me bolt upright and sweating. But I didn't crumble, didn't reach for the blue pills that I knew were somewhere at the back of the bathroom cabinet. I was certain that everything was coming together, and I brought Vero's face to my mind when I grew tired, I looked only forward. Soon there would be a house with a garden where there were trees, a view of the sea, the embrace of hills around us. We would grow our own food; we would have more children. Vero spoke to me with her voice high and excited, as she pointed out houses on the internet, and I imagined Luka swinging his satchel, walking with slow steps to school through knee-high grass.

It seemed I was wrong about the death of the City. Quicker than I would have thought possible, the desks around me began to fill, and the markets started rocketing again. The empty trading floors were once more full of activity; it was as if the crash had never happened. The banks had fired too many people and the traders who had sat for long months staring at empty paper coffee cups in the Starbucks in Canary Wharf were in demand now. The ability of these people to regain their hubris astonished me. Expensive restaurants were once more packed with flushed, braying traders. Strip clubs reopened; City wine shops ordered case after case of fine wine; bright sports cars roared around Mayfair, reclaiming their territory.

Bhavin and Webb were both promoted. I got Bhavin's job but not his office. I hired traders to work for me and the bonuses began to swell my bank account, and most mornings I walked into the quiet room at the back of the house, and Luka beamed up at me and it was enough to get me through the days, the crazy delight of his gummy smile. My heart caught for a moment whenever I left him; tendrils of feeling hung between us when we were together and every time I broke them it was a wrench, a dull pain.

There were many days when I didn't see him at all, leaving before he woke and returning long after his bath and bedtime story. When I got back from work, shattered, I'd creep in and watch him sleep, his plump arm gripping a teddy bear, standing with the light behind me until Vero gently took my hand and led me to bed. And despite my tiredness, I used to hope that he'd wake in the night. I'd leap out of bed at the merest whimper and hold him closely in my arms, singing quietly until he began to snore and then, regretfully, I'd lie him back down in his cot.

Every day it became more difficult to face the market. Because I still felt it. I sensed the crash every time I traded; heard the trading hall's empty echo even now that the grads were working two to a desk and all was loud chaos; saw Madison's admonitory stare when I bought something without doing enough research, buoyed along by the market's rise. I would never be a successful trader again. The crash had sucked something out of me, something brash and ballsy and heroic. I only wanted to be with my family, away from London, in a quiet place.

A year went by. Vero was pregnant again, and we spent the weekends looking for houses. Luka sang to himself in his car seat as we drove along the crest of the Downs, perched above the coastal plain like raiders ready to swoop. Vero fumbled with maps and printouts from estate agents' websites, carrot sticks for Luka and the packets of the sour sweets she craved. We found a house near Brighton and paid for it in cash. It was a cottage, thatched with flint walls, and sat under the brow of Ditchling Beacon. On clear days the sea was like a backlit mirror on the horizon, and we'd stride down the hill, the sprawl of Brighton below us. The house seemed blessed, protected by the looming Downs.

At Christmas both of our parents came to visit, and we sat around a lopsided Christmas tree in front of the wood stove and the day outside was white with frost and scorched the eyes with its brightness. Gulls rose above the house, calling to each other in the crisp air and reminding me of my seaside child-hood. Luka played with his grandparents, screaming with delight as Vero's father raced backwards and forwards across the kitchen with Luka in his lap. Vero sat deep in an armchair, drinking endless cups of tea and watching us move around her.

We spent every weekend down at the cottage, walked through Vero's pregnancy as we had walked through the last. The weekdays in London were like a penance. We struggled through those grim winter days when I'd get up in the dark and return in the dark, in the endless rain. Time seemed not to exist as I worked and slept and fought off cold after stinking cold, my eyes red, my nose running. But a picture of our house sat on my desk next to a framed photograph of Vero and Luka, and everything was focused upon that shining moment when we would leave the city.

Time, again, tapers to a point. April becomes May. I book the removal men, speaking low into my telephone at the office. I apply to start a teacher-training course at Brighton University. Henry promises me freelance work for the paper until I qualify. Vero's belly grows as the time to leave approach-es and she starts to groan at night, shifting from side to side, unable to settle. Summer looms on the horizon. Bhavin knows that something is up: I'm skittish, unfocused. But I'm making money, and the rise of the markets lifts me in its tide. Then there are only days to go, and I have almost reached the profit target, and soon we will be free.

The day before it happened I sat at my desk watching the sky over Spitalfields change as the sun set, the sharpness of the church spire slowly fuzzing against the evening light. Vero called with Luka to say goodnight, and I gabbled away at him, unaware of the listening ears around me.

'Did you have a lovely bath? And were you a good boy for Mummy today? Oh you are such a good boy aren't you? Dada loves you, yes he does. Sleep well, my prince.'

The continued market rally and the warmth of the weather meant that people began to leave their desks earlier than usual. Several traders stopped to ask if I would join them at the pub. When I declined, they moved off in happy groups, talking about football and their plans for summer holidays and where they'd go drinking. Something hopeful was in the air and, when it finally grew dark, and I piled research notes on one side of the desk, trade tickets on the other, I caught the eyes of the grads who were still at their desks and smiled warmly at them. I knew I had only one trade to go, and I wished I could share some of my joy with them, show them what I had learnt. I took a deep breath, holding the scent of the trading floor in my head, knowing I'd want to remember it.

Some of the research team were still drinking at the Gun and I had a quick pint with them before getting in the car, happy to sit quietly and listen to their banter and watch the night come alive around us. I drove slowly home, the lights of the City sharp in my mirrors, music and laughter and dust coming in through the open windows, and something about the night had the sense of a conclusion, of an ending finally reached.

*

Vero had a scan at nine that morning, so I agreed to drive Luka to his crèche. It was still early and I decided to swing by the office first to pick up papers relating to my final trade: purchasing a portfolio of Central Asian bank bonds which I had already agreed to sell on to a pension fund at a significant profit. Then it would all be over: my shares would vest and I intended to leave London and not come back for years.

My hands were damp on the Polo's steering wheel as I manoeuvred us through the early-morning traffic. Luka, who wasn't used to such early starts, fell asleep as we crawled along the Embankment. He murmured to himself in his sleep, slumped forward in his car seat with a thin silver line of drool hanging down to his lap. I drove carefully up the car-park ramps, looking for a space. Finally we were out on the roof and the air was cool and morning-moist. Lowering the window a crack, I leant Luka gently back in his seat, laid a kiss on his cool forehead, and ran down the stairs towards the office, which seemed very close from my lofty position.

There was already a long line of traders leading up to the coffee stand at the entrance to the bank. One of the analysts who worked for me held out a paper cup as I passed; I nodded thanks and sipped at the steaming liquid as I stood waiting for the lifts to arrive. As I stepped onto the trading floor I was hit by a blast of sound. Traders were waving their arms and shouting, a graduate trainee rushed towards me with a printout from his Bloomberg screen, Bhavin gestured at me from his office in the corner.

'All right, Charlie.' He raised an arm as I walked over and leant against the door of his office, still blowing on the coffee, sipping it and squinting as it burnt my tongue. 'Did you see the open? Things are moving. If you want to get that trade done you better get on it. You don't want to lose that trade, not after the work you've put into it.'

I looked at the printout and saw that the market was moving against me. I could see the car park through the window behind Bhavin's desk. My watch read twenty past eight.

'Right, I'll do it now. Shit. See you later, Bhavin.' I strode out onto the trading floor. 'Someone round up the grads. I want all of the traders working on this. We're going to do this now. Get the screens up, I want to see all of the numbers, let's send the confirms over before they get spooked.' I clenched my fists and sucked on the coffee and stamped along the line of young traders, eager to get the purchase over and leave.

Equities leapt again. News was filtering out of a large takeover in Germany, better-than-expected retail sales in the US, positive Chinese inflation figures. The Russian investor selling the bond portfolio began to ask for concessions, asked if I'd pay all of the transaction fees, then wanted me to raise the price I was paying. I marshalled my troops aggressively, shouted down the line at the investor, persuaded Bhavin to call his boss and shout at him. And I forgot about Luka. I worked for four hours as the day smouldered outside and the tourists emerged squinting into the sunlight and the markets contin-ued to rise, and only at that moment, when the sunlight glittered on the silver frame Vero had given me for Christmas that year. Only then did I remember that I'd left him in the car and fear raced up my arms and into my chest.

EPILOGUE

Back in the City

I sit at my desk and watch the sun move across the wooden surface. The sun heats up the wood under my fingers and, when I have finished approving trades, when I have bought and sold and counted the profit, I lay my hands down flat and feel the stored heat of the desk. My office door is closed but still the shouts of traders are dimly audible over the hum of the air conditioning. I have a meeting at eight, dinner with Bhavin and a banker from China at nine. I shoot my cuffs and pull my tie tight.

I watch a bus unload its passengers in the street below. They stare up for a moment at the great buildings that surround them, crane their necks and shield their eyes from the lowering sun. They are still. I watch a boy take his girlfriend by the hand and they move off down Brushfield Street. They lose themselves in the crowd.

On my desk there are no pictures. Nothing in the room identifies me. I have risen beyond the need to mark out my personality, express my individuality. It is the simplicity of the markets that appeals to me now. The clarity of the balance sheet, the logic of the profit and loss. And I try to lead a life that is equally straightforward. I have narrowed my range of interests. I live near the office in a serviced apartment above Moorgate. Through the long window of my drawing room I can see Canary Wharf. I like to watch the lights go out on the huge towers at night. I sit on my exercise bike and I watch the lights extinguish and I think of the hope and the ambition that drives the people whose fingers gently, slightly regretfully, turn off the lights.

Vero and I maintained something approaching a relationship until Luka pulled through. We immediately decamped to separate beds, although one of us was always at the hospital, so this was not an obvious mark of the end of our love. We spoke only of his progress, his condition, the monitoring of his kidney function and heartbeat and salt levels. But after two weeks, when Luka was well enough to come home, Vero asked me in a very quiet voice to drive them to the Eurostar. She had already packed, and gripped a suitcase in the shadow of her huge belly. Guy would meet them at Calais. She was to give birth in the hospital that overlooked Neufchâtel.

I kissed Luka very hard as Vero held him clutched to her shoulder in the queue at St Pancras. Slowly the line stuttered forward, and I wrapped my fingers around his leg, pressed his face against mine, inhaled the scent of him and tried to hold it in my mind. They passed through the automatic doors and I stood and watched, seeing them inch further away each time the doors swung open. They were moving through passport control. Vero did not turn around, but Luka waved once. He lifted his small hand high in the air, and he smiled and I leapt high, waved back furiously as the doors closed. When they opened again, Luka and Vero had gone.

I like to visit other cities. I spend much of my time on aeroplanes. I fly to meetings in far-off cities and I walk through their parks at dusk and watch the couples who match their strides in the haze of the evening, their fingers intertwined, faces turned to catch the sun's last rays. In Sydney I stroll in my suit through the Botanical Gardens and I see the white cockatoos circling, the enormous bats whose wings seem to rip the air from above me as they sweep overhead. I walk towards the hunched cowls of the Opera House and step aside to let joggers past. In Tokyo there are crows that fly between the skyscrapers. I watch them as I sit in meetings, staring past the business card which I have accepted in my hands as etiquette dictates. In autumn in New York I have a massage on a chair in Central Park from an old Vietnamese man who coughs as he kneads my knotted shoulders.

Henry brings the children up to London to meet me. I take the day off work and stand at the barriers at Victoria, arriving very early at the station in order to allow time for the expectation to build. The three of them laugh as they step off the train to find me waving and beaming. Luka runs ahead and rises on tiptoes to pass his ticket through the machine and then jumps into my arms. I hug Henry and kiss the head of the smaller boy who sits in a sling on Henry's chest. I try not to love them too much.

Henry travelled over to Neufchâtel soon after the baby was born. He was my point of contact in the household. He would hold the receiver up to the cot and I listened hard to catch the soft whisper of breath that came down the line. He looked after Vero and Luka during those difficult days; I was grateful to him. It was his idea that they move into the cottage. It is good for me to be able to picture them there, with the Downs rearing up behind them. But we meet only in London, only in the neutral territories of galleries and cafes and toyshops. Always Henry smiles bashfully, trying not to show how much the boys mean to him, how much he loves the fat arms of the child hanging down from the sling on his chest. Vero never comes with us on these trips, but we speak only of her.

She works for a microfinance organisation in London, making loans to coffee growers in Brazil and clothing manufacturers in Bangladesh. She wears sharp-shouldered suits that remind me of Catrina. Once I saw her at a conference in the Guildhall. She was speaking on a panel about the emerging markets and I stood in a corner and watched her, retreating back into darkness as her keen eyes swept the room. She was passionate, driven, terrifying in her composure. Henry tells me that often she stays up in London, working late on projects or dining with ambassadors and members of government.

Henry and I sat one late summer afternoon in the café at Tate Modern, the baby in the sling asleep and burbling gently, Luka with his face pressed to the glass looking across the Millennium Bridge to St Paul's. We had finished our coffees, and Henry was about to take the boys home. The sun was dropping in a sky that had begun to smudge around the edges, greens and yellows appearing in the corners of our vision. The café was nearly empty and the silence closed around us, thickening the air. Henry's face sat above the head of the sleeping child, serious and pensive.

'Do you still love her?' he asked, his voice very quiet.

I paused, smiled. 'I think I will always love her.'

'I'm sorry for all this. I didn't mean for this to happen. I was just trying to help. Careful, Luka. Don't climb up there.' Luka was perched on a stool trying to get a better view of the Gherkin.

'We got what we deserved, Henry. I'm sure you realise that. I think, perhaps, I always knew it would end up something like this. I was always trying to move, trying to leave, trying to create a new existence. Only now do I feel truly settled, close to content with my lot.'

'Don't think . . . don't get the idea that this is perfect for me, Charlie. Vero doesn't love me. If anything, she still loves you. But I can offer her stability. You two are too much alike. It's . . . I suppose it's dissatisfaction. That's the problem with both of you. Always reaching for the next thing, never happy with what you have. But I'm happy. Even when Vero doesn't call and is away for days and the children are ill. I put them to bed. I rub their backs when they cough. I sit downstairs with the television on low and I listen out for them. And this is enough to make me happy. To raise another guy's kids in a house I don't own, with a girl I love who doesn't let me share her bed. It sounds hellish, but . . . but it isn't. It's something wonderful for me. Listen, we've got to go. I'm sorry; we'll miss our train otherwise. Luka!'

He stood, walked over and took Luka's small hand in his, and strode across the café. At the door, he turned and raised his hand. Luka waved and the baby woke, stretched, and yawned, blinking against the light.

Now I am in my office looking out as the night assembles in the shadows between buildings. I watch it cluster in the eastern sky, watch the great darkness ready to be unleashed, to sweep itself across the City whose dim lights are mocked by the void above them. The night creeps in through keyholes, through the blackness which sits between the bars of drains, steals around curtains and through blinds. The sun sets quickly, without drama, and I light the bright lamp on my desk. Shadows flicker outside the window and I watch the nostalgic glow of buses pass by. A tramp lights a cigarette on the pavement opposite and the flame disappears into the deep crevices of his face.

There is a mark on the wall of my office. I imagine it is the hole left by the nail that once held a photograph of a man and his family, a previous inhabitant. I approach the mark and for a moment it looks like a fly. I expect it to move as I come close. I pick up my trenchcoat, feel the heaviness of it as I lay it over my arm. I move closer and the mark seems to grow larger as I step towards it. Finally I am pressed against the wall, my face hard on the cool white plaster, and I realise that the mark is a full stop.